AMERICA'S GEEKHEART

PIPPA GRANT

ONE

Beckett Ryder, aka a man completely oblivious that he's just mistweeted his way to being public enemy number one

LIFE IS PRETTY FUCKING PERFECT.

Weather's a glorious seventy-five degrees and sunny on this brilliant June morning. My new jogging shoes fit like I'm running on a cloud. The green leafy canopy over Reynolds Park is hitting that perfect level of shade, and I've got my tunes dialed up and nowhere to be until my sister's engagement party tonight.

Ten solid hours of doing whatever the hell I want.

I'm grinning to myself as I run the familiar pathway through the city park, so glad to be back in Copper Valley. Love my job, but there is no place in the world like home.

I nod to a woman pushing a jogging stroller going the other way, and she scowls and flips me off.

Odd.

Crazies are normal when I'm in LA, or sometimes in Europe, but here?

My hometown *loves* me.

I dial down the volume on my tunes and double-check my shirt.

Nope, nothing offensive about a Fireballs T-shirt. They might be the biggest losers in baseball, but they're lovable losers.

I glance lower, and—yep, remembered to put pants on today. Shorts, really. My brand, naturally, but not because they're *my* brand.

More because I picked them to be in my RYDE fashion line because they're really comfortable.

I might've been singing along to Levi's latest hit, but I'm not *that* bad. Sure, I was the eye candy in the boy band Bro Code back in the day, but I can still carry a tune.

She must've mistaken me for someone else. Or her fingers are stuck that way. Resting bitch face knows no boundaries and can happen to even the most innocent victims. Probably not her fault.

I keep on truckin', and an elderly woman on a bench shakes her cane at me and says something I don't catch while her dog yaps along. I pop out one earbud.

"You're a disgrace to good men everywhere," she crows.

I slow and face her, jogging in place. "Ma'am?"

"Your poor momma must be ashamed."

Ah. The underwear police. Not so unusual. While Levi went on to be a pop sensation when we called it quits as Bro Code, Cash took off for Hollywood, Tripp hung up his fame and settled down, and Davis went into hiding, I took my own route.

My post-boy-band career choices have been known to raise a few eyebrows.

"Yes, ma'am. She's horrified. Y'all have a nice day now." I salute her and head back down the path toward the fountain at the center of the park.

In the years since I modeled my first pair of briefs for Giovanni & Valentino, before I branched out into creating a fashion empire of my own, I've had my share of haters. Goes with the business.

But my *momma* isn't ashamed of me.

No more than she was during my boy band days.

If anything, she's amused. Resigned sometimes, but amused.

Ellie—my sister—gives me trouble. So do all the guys we grew up with.

That's why I love them.

They keep me grounded.

Hell, half of them needed the grounding themselves.

The path curves, and there she is.

My fountain.

Okay, fine, she's not *mine*. But she's on the city's crest, and she says *home* to me.

I love home, but running the Beck Ryder fashion empire—yeah, go ahead and snort, it's funny—keeps me away a lot.

I burst out into the sunshine and make the loop around the

curved sidewalk, feet pounding the concrete, mist brushing my face, the five stone dolphins around the fountain joyfully spitting water into the stone mermaids' buckets on the second tier while a circle of seahorses blows water horns.

The early summer breeze rustles the birch and sugar maple leaves shimmering in the sunlight. The air's clear. The sky's my favorite blue. Flowers explode in reds and yellows and purples in the carefully cultivated landscaping that masks the downtown skyscrapers and mutes the noise of the city.

It's my own private welcome home party from nature.

Can't wait to be here more often.

Soon. *So* soon.

I circle the fountain and head back toward the path that leads to Schuler Tower and my penthouse at the edge of the park. Tomorrow, I have to get back to work—there's always work when you're running an empire and launching a new foundation —but today, my staff has the day off, my phone's still on airplane mode, and the whole Copper Valley metro area is my oyster.

No phone, no work, no responsibilities.

Maybe I'll leave the city behind and head up into the Blue Ridge Mountains for a hike. Nap up there in the fresh air. Eat. Eat some more. Get back in time for Ellie and Wyatt's surprise engagement party.

Rumor has it they're serving barbecue.

I haven't had good barbecue in months.

I'm so busy drooling over the thought of real Southern pulled pork that I almost miss the yoga class.

By itself, a yoga class on the lawn by the fountain isn't unusual. But this yoga class seems less into the Namaste and more into hurling their yoga bricks.

Specifically, at me.

They charge me as a group, a yoga-pants-clad mob racing over the hilly green grass, shouting obscenities and shaking fists. One lady has her mat rolled into a cylinder and is leading the pack *Braveheart* style.

"*Creep!*"

"*Jerk!*"

"*You* go home and get your own damn apron!"

My pulse amps into sprint territory.

"Hey, hey." I hold my hands up in surrender while I jog backwards, because seriously, *what the fuck*? "Y'all know I love you. What's—"

A shoe hurtles at my face. Another yoga brick clips my shoulder.

"Get him, ladies," the *Braveheart* lady yells.

Oh, *shit*.

They want blood.

I don't have a fucking clue what I did, but these ladies want blood. *My* blood.

My run morphs into a sprint, but for once, my brain's spinning faster than my legs.

The mother and her stroller and her middle finger. The grand-mother and her cane. And now a yoga class.

I'm outnumbered.

Probably outsmarted and outmaneuvered too.

Another yoga brick.

And I'm still too far from safety.

"Shut up and let your underwear do the talking!" A clump of—oh, man, that's disgusting. Flying horse poop. Awesome.

I pump my legs harder. Knees higher. Like I'm gonna beat Usain Bolt. Running. *Sprinting*. Away from a mob of angry women.

This is new.

As is having a mob of angry women gaining on me.

The ladies usually love me. Or if not, at least they tolerate me with patient smiles.

Maybe a run wasn't the best cure for jetlag.

But how was I supposed to know today's *International Beck Ryder Is The Enemy Day*?

"I'll show you where *you* belong," one of the women screeches.

I don't have a clue where she thinks I belong, or why she thinks I belong there, but I know one thing.

I am totally fucked.

TWO

Sarah Dempsey, aka a geek with no intention of having Beck Ryder's babies

THE LAST TIME I wore sunglasses, a ball cap pulled low over my eyes, and a sweatshirt to go to the store—in June—I was in LA, seventeen, and all I wanted was a pack of Pokémon cards.

Today, I'm low on toilet paper, which is literally the only thing in the world that would make me leave my house. It's not until I'm in the checkout lane with my four-pack of Charmin clutched to my chest that it occurs to me that people aren't staring because Beck Ryder tweeted me last night to *shut up and go make some babies, but not with me, of course*, but because there's no legitimate reason for me to be acting like a celebrity in hiding since no one here knows I'm @must_love_bees on Twitter, and honestly, @must_love_bees isn't a celebrity by any measure anyway.

Damn underwear model.

He's screwing with my head. And my life.

My regular cashier gives me a once-over. "You goin' to a party?" she asks, her gaze drifting between my sunglasses, hat, and the toilet paper on the belt.

"Social experiment," I reply. "Are you more or less likely to talk to people when they come into the store in sunglasses?"

"More," she says the same time the guy at the other register says, "Less. Gotta respect the privacy."

"People only dress like that when they want attention," the grandma behind me informs us all. She taps the cover of one of the tabloids. "Like this guy claiming to be Genghis Khan reincarnated with a penis shaped like a dragon. He wears sunglasses everywhere."

So long as no one asks to see my peen-dragon, I think I'll be okay.

I escape all of them and hustle my toilet paper back to my car, which I now feel foolish for driving, because the temperature is in the high seventies, the sunshine is broken up by drifting fluffy white clouds, and it's only a ten-minute walk from my house to the store.

When I reach my neighborhood three minutes later, none of my neighbors are snooping in my windows.

Not even *Ellie Ryder* next door, who's undoubtedly related to the underwear ape, though we've never talked about family, because *reasons*, but who's also out of town this week.

Or so she said when her boyfriend showed up with his kid last weekend. Something about a pirate festival in the mountains. I didn't ask any more.

I don't get close to people.

Most people, I should specify. There are exceptions. But not my neighbors.

My cat, Andromeda—Meda for short—is sleeping in the front window of my little Craftsman bungalow. And there aren't any unusual cars parked on the street under the oaks and hemlocks.

It's not that I'm paranoid.

It's—okay. Fine.

I'm paranoid.

You would be too if you had my parents and my childhood.

I should probably call them.

I pull into the garage and hit the button to drop the door behind me before I get out of the car with my toilet paper. I drop my haul in the bathroom and bypass my little computer hidey-hole because *ugh*.

It will be *weeks* before my social media feeds quit blowing up over that stupid underwear model and his asinine suggestion that I'm nothing more than an ugly baby factory.

Might as well reinvent myself.

Again.

Especially if the neighbor *is* related to him. And if she remembers my Twitter handle.

She's an environmental engineer.

I'm an environmental engineer.

She likes animals.

I like animals.

It *made sense* to tell her about my science and conservation website.

Whatever.

There are probably thousands of Ryders in Copper Valley.

"You know what pisses me off the most, Meda?" I say to my cat.

She meows back from her perch in the windowsill, giving me a piece of her mind while I nod along. She's half-Siamese, half tabby—I think—and all sass and attitude to make up for not fitting squarely into a box, and we get along very well.

"Exactly. I *finally* had a following of people who *love* science and geeking out over planetary discoveries and new recycling technologies, and there he goes, turning my entire existence into a circus about my uterus instead of about saving the planet."

I don't have to log on to my social media accounts—or my website stats—to know what it looks like. It's the same as every digital public lynching.

Everyone assumes they know the whole story. They post their opinions about it on the internet, then start with the name-calling—on both sides—and post things they'd never say to your face, and eventually someone will find my address and I'll have to go into hiding.

Again.

Dammit dammit dammit.

Not that I didn't enjoy my gap year, but I *like* my life now.

I throw my sunglasses onto the upcycled coffee table in my eclectic living room and follow it with my hat, which lands squarely inside the massive box of *Avengers* bobbleheads that Mom sent last week and that I haven't yet dragged to the basement.

No time like today, because when I have to leave, those can stay behind. Not because I don't appreciate them—I think the Golden Thor is in that box, and *hello*, golden hottie, but please don't tell anyone I said that—but because I anticipate needing to make a fast escape with just the essentials.

I *like* my house.

And it's a big damn pain to change your name on the down-low. Maybe I should skip that step and move to Fiji this time.

"I know, I know, I'm being melodramatic," I say to Meda, even though I'm pretty sure I'm not. It's hard to tell when you know you don't always have a firm grasp on *normal*. "But I promise I won't leave you behind."

She meows at me again, staring at me with one blue eye and one amber eye, hops off her cat bed perch in the front window, and sashays into the kitchen, where she's undoubtedly expecting dinner.

Four hours early.

I trail behind her, because she was five pounds of fur and bone when I brought her home from the shelter, and she can eat anytime she wants.

But as soon as I step into the kitchen, the hairs on the back of my arms stand up.

Someone's in my backyard.

Inside my privacy fence.

Next to my wooden beehives.

He's slinking toward the house in sunglasses, a ball cap pulled low, and a sweatshirt.

In *June*.

And if he thinks he's going to get *anything* out of me, he can think again.

I slip my taser out of my grandma's cookie jar and drop to my hands and knees to crawl over the plain beige linoleum to the back door, then lift my head just high enough to peer through the pane glass window above the doorknob.

He's coming this way.

Shit. Shit shit *shit*.

Meda meows again.

The stranger's head swings my way—the creep is making sure he's not being watched—and I duck down.

But only until there's a knock on the door.

And then it's all action.

I leap up, twist the doorknob, and I yell, "Think again, asshole!"

My heart's pounding so hard it's shaking my nipples. My voice is thick and high because *holy fuck I'm staring down an intruder*, and I don't think, I just point and squeeze.

I can't see his eyes, but I see his lips part under the dark scruff around his mouth and over his jawline. His body jerks once, twice, and then he's down.

Sack of potatoes *down*.

"Oh my god, Beck, I'm going to kill you," a woman shrieks as she dashes through my back gate.

I point the taser at her. "Back!" I yell a split second before recognition kicks in.

I know her.

I know her really well, but my brain is operating on *oh my god, the paparazzi found me* and I *cannot* place this woman, and if she has one of those spy cameras in one of her buttonholes, my picture will be on every gossip tabloid in six hours and my mother will be horrified that I didn't comb my hair today.

She stumbles to a stop and lifts her hands, wincing as she seems to favor one leg over the other. "Sarah. I'm so sorry. I tried to stop him. He thought you'd appreciate the apology in person more than over Twitter."

She winces again, and I know this woman.

I do.

"Who are you?"

She blinks once, then relaxes. "I'm Ellie. Your neighbor?"

My neighbor.

Shit shit *shit*.

I look down at the sack of potatoes with ridiculously long arms and ridiculously long legs splayed out on my small patio.

Then back up at her.

"You let the underwear ape in my yard," I say.

Her lips part, and a slow grin starts across her pretty features. My mother would adore her, because without makeup, she's pretty, but with makeup—and the haircut, and the clothes that fit right, and the style sense—she's really effing gorgeous.

"The underwear ape," she says, nodding slowly. "Yes. I like that. Beck's my brother. Also known as *the idiot who doesn't know how to use a direct message*. He's very sorry. He thought he was congratulating me on getting engaged. In his own, special, brotherly way."

He groans on the ground. "Fuck, Ellie, I told you no titty twisters."

She's smiling wider. "I told him I'd call you first, to make sure you weren't going to...well, I said *call the cops*, but I think this might be better."

"You have an evil side," I say.

"I grew up with *him*," she replies, as though that explains it.

I look down at him again.

He's long. Broad shoulders. Looks lankier in person than on that billboard over I-56 that I pass a few times a week, but that could be the baggy sweatshirt. His hat's askew—Fireballs, nice—and a dark shock of hair is poking out from under the brim. His blue eyes are slightly crossed over his crooked sunglasses, but seem to be coming back into focus as he blinks lazily at me. "You shocked me," he says.

"Didn't recognize you with your clothes on."

And that's really all I have to say about that, so I turn around and walk back into my house.

As far as I'm concerned, we're done here.

THREE

Beck

FIRST RULE OF APOLOGIZING: Make sure she knows you're coming.

Holy fuck, that was a ride.

And those eyes.

All four of them.

Whoa.

You believe in love at first sight? I always have.

Except I don't know if this is love, or if it's just the side effect of a jillion volts to the chest.

"You piss yourself?" Wyatt asks with a grin as soon as Tucker, his kid, dashes to his room to get a toy to show me. My childhood best friend is lounging in the wide doorway between the living room and dining room, listening to Ellie tell the watered-down version of events next door while I hold an ice pack to the pain that's quickly leaving my head, my legs propped over the armrest of the couch.

"Came fucking close," I admit, and fine, I'm still shaking a little.

My sister and my best friend share one of those couple looks, and they both bust a gut laughing.

I'd be pissed, but let's be honest. One, it was probably inevitable that I'd get tasered for something eventually, and B, at least now I know what it feels like. And bullet point four, I ruined the surprise part of Ellie's surprise engagement party since she didn't know I was coming home until Wyatt told her so they could rush to my aid over my tweet-tastrophe, so I owe them a few laughs at my expense.

Even if it's by getting myself tasered.

Not something I'd planned to add to my bucket list, but this'll be a story for the ages once my chest quits twitching.

Though if it really is love, my life is about to get fucking complicated.

Probably not love, I decide.

Probably just the volts to the ol' ticker. Wonder if getting tasered in the butt would have the same effect.

Unlikely, I decide. I should definitely get tasered in the ass next time if there has to be a next time. Which there hopefully won't be.

"I *told* you to let me call her first." Ellie plops onto the couch next to my head and ruffles my hair. "Sarah's…jumpy."

"Rare breed," Wyatt agrees wryly. Dude's a military guy, one of my best friends growing up. Could've joined us in Bro Code, but he was all *fuck that, I'mma go save the world.* "And probably not susceptible to your unique charms."

Sarah—aka @must_love_bees, aka the woman I accidentally epically insulted online when I thought I was sending Ellie a funny private message in response to her posting her engagement rings, aka the woman who tweeted back *This desperate attempt to steal my 51 fans won't work, @BeckettRyder. 49 are scientists & not fooled by your six-pack,* which was honestly hilarious, especially since she has over ten thousand followers—has four eyes in my memory. Four big, dark brown eyes, with big irises that seem to dominate her features and swallow her pupils. Straight nose—both of them. Pillowy lips. And all that wild, curly brown hair.

She's like Medusa crossed with a Peter Pan mermaid. Half scary as hell, half adorable.

"Uncle Beck! Check it out! I have an underwear doll!"

"Levi is so dead to me for giving him that," Ellie announces as Tucker shoves a Ken doll in my face.

Except it's not a Ken doll.

It's a Beck Ryder doll.

"That's the studliest underwear doll I've ever seen," I tell him. "You're one lucky little dude."

"His lips are funny," Tucker says. He's Wyatt's son from his first marriage and near total clone of my buddy, except the kid got his mom's brown eyes instead of Wyatt's blue-gray-whatever they are eyes. Tucker tries to screw his lips up in a smoldery duck-lip configuration, and he gets damn close, which is wrong on an eight-year-old.

Ellie chokes on a laugh, but I hold out a fist for a bump. "You keep making that face, all the ladies are gonna fall all over you before you're ten."

Wyatt gives me the *don't tempt me to give you a wedgie* glare, but I shoot him back a *you're welcome* smirk.

Because Tucker's recoiling in horror. "Eww! I don't want *the ladies*! They're *old*."

"It's what some of us are stuck with, man," I tell him solemnly, though it's been months—or longer—since I've actually had a *lady*.

Or any other form of companionship beyond my hand.

It's what happens when you want sex to mean something after dating one too many women who want to say they slept with a superstar, bagged an underwear model, or got knocked up by a billionaire.

That last one's the one that really did me in.

Twice.

And they were both lying.

"I am *never* growing up." Tucker snatches his doll back and races to Wyatt. "Can I have a cookie?"

"You can have a carrot, because Grandma Michelle is going to feed you cookies out the yin-yang at the party tonight."

Grandma Michelle.

My mother's in heaven.

She's finally getting one of us married off, and getting an instant grandson in the process. Not that she hadn't already adopted Tucker as one of her own—we grew up in a village in our neighborhood, and with Wyatt's small family gone now, we're all he has left—but she's pretty much constantly leaking joy out her eyeballs over Ellie and Wyatt finally realizing the reason they fought so much over the years was because they were soulmates.

They're disgusting. And adorable.

And all those relationship goals that a famous world-traveling empire owner like me will never have. On top of never knowing what a woman actually wants me for—my body, my money, or my fame—when you've been *everywhere* around the globe and still haven't found *the one*, she doesn't exist.

Probably.

But I have family, and a couple foundations that benefit kids, and adopted nieces and nephews between Wyatt and Tripp, so I'm cool.

Most of the time.

Better to spread the love out among the people you know you can count on than hold it back for someone who might never materialize, right?

Someone knocks on the door, and I flinch.

Ellie sucks in a smile. "Relax. I can guarantee you it's not Sarah coming back with her taser. She's not usually that aggressive."

Sarah.

Pretty name.

Still making my lungs twitch too. Probably a good thing she's not coming back.

Wyatt glances through the small windowpane on the door, then pulls it open. "Reinforcements," he tells me.

I start to get excited, thinking Tripp or Davis or one of the Rivers brothers are swinging by, but it's not any of them.

"It was inevitable, wasn't it?" Charlie, my assistant, says with a cheeky grin. "Don't ever keep your phone on airplane mode overnight again, or I'll quit."

Assistant isn't quite the right word.

She's more like my life handler.

"You're officially grounded, and don't even start on *we have to be at blah blah blah event*, because you're uninvited from all of them. Even that farm park in Nebraska that we never replied to about their Goat Days festival has rescinded your invitation to participate in the Goat Race, and they were the most polite of the bunch."

I stare at her, because I hear the words she's saying, and they're starting to penetrate.

The flying yoga bricks and getting tasered were just the beginning.

I didn't just piss off the Twittersphere and half the women in the universe.

I fucked up my entire life.

"The foundation?" I croak.

Shit shit *shit*. She has to tell me I haven't fucked up the new foundation.

She doesn't.

"You have WiFi?" she asks Ellie and Wyatt, and within minutes, she's set up in the recliner next to the couch, laptop open, phone on one armrest, tablet on the other, with no answer to my question. She's been with me for six years, might be twenty-five or might be thirty-five—I've never actually asked—and if she ever notices how many people check her out while we're traveling the world for fashion shows and product launches and photo shoots, she doesn't let on.

"Video conference with your PR and management teams in thirty, and I'm working on getting you set up with a call with Vaughn," she reports, then does a double-take. "Is your hair smoking?"

"He tried to run away and got himself tasered by the neighbor," Ellie offers helpfully.

"Told you to keep security with you here," Charlie replies before going back to her laptop.

"It's home," I scoff.

"And you just pissed off the entire internet. Don't mind the two black cars down the street. I took care of arranging extra security for you. And you should be able to go back to your penthouse within a few hours. I asked the cops to let the picketing go on unless it got violent."

"You can control picketers?" Ellie asks.

Charlie shrugs. "Not really, but it looks good that we're cooperating instead of throwing a diva fit. Once we get Beck on camera with Ellen or Dr. Phil, apologizing profusely, they'll go away. He's disgustingly charming."

"I should really send you better Christmas presents," Ellie says in awe.

"Your parents take good care of me."

"Hey. I bought you *a car* last Christmas," I point out, even though an entire armada of cars wouldn't make up for her having to deal with me some days.

Like today.

"That I'm home to drive maybe two months out of the year. Your parents sent a subscription to the peanut butter of the month club, *and* it magically gets forwarded wherever we are *every month*."

Shit.

I'm bad at giving presents.

And here I thought I rocked.

Also, I like peanut butter.

"Today sucks," I mutter.

"Serves you right for being an ass." Ellie claps a hand to her mouth and looks around, but Tucker's gone.

"That tweet was supposed to go to you, and it was a joke," I tell her. "I would *never* seriously tell *anyone* to shut up and go have some babies. But you're stealing my best friend, you know. Wyatt was mine first."

"I'm already researching the best women's equality foundations for a sizable donation," Charlie says. "It won't solve everything, but it's a start in damage control."

"The foundation?" I say again. "That'll help, right?

She pins me with a look, and I realize I haven't just fucked up. I've FUCKED UP. All caps. This isn't like the time I wrongly congratulated that news anchor on being pregnant on air—I know, *I know*, but I was nineteen and an idiot—and almost got us banned from ever going back to Detroit.

This is way worse.

Because in about ten days, I'm supposed to announce a joint foundation with Vaughn Crawford, the hottest center in basketball, to sponsor athletic organizations for kids all over the nation.

And now I've put the stain of my reputation on the whole thing.

Sent the entire plan through the floor like a flaming meteorite made of cow shit.

Something tells me a video conference with my entire team isn't going to solve this. And there won't be a scandal hot enough in Hollywood to take precedence over me sticking my entire leg in my mouth, Twitter-style, *ever*.

"I shouldn't go to your party," I tell Ellie with a wince, because I'll only be a distraction.

"They'll be talking about you whether you're there or not," she points out.

"All friendlies," Wyatt adds. "But if you can't handle taking the crap…"

I don't deserve to be around *friendlies* today.

And I need to get off my ass, stop feeling sorry for myself, and help my team fix this instead of once again letting Charlie set everything up for me.

It's what she does, and what I pay her well to do, but this is my mistake.

"I need to call Vaughn," I tell her.

She nods. "Oh, yeah, you do. And tread lightly and grovel, because *no one* wants your reputation bringing them down. The *only* thing you have going for you right now is that it'll be hella hard for him to find another co-sponsor who can donate gear as easily as you can."

Yeah.

She's right.

The FLY HYGH foundation isn't just money to fund sports complexes and equipment and administrative fees. It's also getting donations from Vaughn's shoe line and my athletic gear line.

All might not be lost, but Vaughn's one of the good dudes, and he deserves a better partner in this than a dumbass who insults all of womankind on Twitter.

It's time to start groveling.

I push myself to sitting to grab my phone, and my gaze falls on the house next door.

Probably need to go apologize to Sarah the right way too.

When Ellie met me at my building in a getaway car just as I was running up, she filled me in on what happened while I was unplugged. So I took my phone off airplane mode and checked social media.

It's ugly.

Not only am I getting eviscerated, but in the midst of all the support for @must_love_bees, she's also being mocked and called names by people who think her handle is stupid, that there's no honeybee crisis, that giraffes aren't going extinct, that the earth is flat, that atomic particles are a myth, and suggesting she go kill herself for having an ugly profile picture, which is an artistic drawing of Saturn with the rings bent into shapes of wings and a honeybee tail on the end.

She didn't ask to be famous.

And she didn't ask for the crazies to come out.

I did that.

And I need to make it stop.

The question, though, is *how*.

FOUR

Sarah

THERE'S nothing better for stress relief than complete and utter denial with a side dish of crazy.

And I have crazy in spades right now.

The Fireballs are playing tonight, which means my very best friend in the entire universe has invaded my house to watch the game.

And when I say *invaded*, I truly mean *invaded*.

Mackenzie's set up pumpkin spice candles—even though it's *June* —to inspire thoughts of fall baseball. Her Fireballs banner is hanging from my living room curtain rod. She made me change into a Fire-balls jersey—which wasn't *really* a hardship—because they win more often when we both wear Cooper Rock jerseys. Unless we're at the stadium, in which case they win more often if I'm wearing a geeky science T-shirt.

She's also playing music on her phone that's supposed to relax us both.

It's some sort of new age techno with a beat that our pulses are supposed to sync to, so we can be the most excited Zen people in the world watching our home team lose a game.

Statistically speaking, we're in for a bloodbath tonight, because we won last night, but I don't point this out to Mackenzie, because she showed up approximately seven minutes after I tasered Beck

Ryder and has been running my afternoon and distracting me from the internet ever since.

Now, I'm camped on the couch next to her with my laptop pulled up, ignoring the mailbox warnings that it's about to overflow because of all the Twitter notifications, and I turn on the live cam feed of Persephone the Giraffe's journey toward giving birth at the Copper Valley zoo.

I've been tweeting the feed since the zookeepers announced she was showing early signs of labor a week ago, and it's fun to see that almost half a million people worldwide are watching with me.

"Our girl's still pregnant?" Mackenzie asks as she settles next to me with her popcorn.

"She could theoretically go another month."

"I wonder if her being pregnant is good or bad luck for the Fireballs?"

"Maybe she'll give birth to next season's good luck charm."

Mackenzie's my polar opposite. She's blond-haired, blue-eyed, long-limbed, perky-boobed, well-dressed—even her jersey looks stylish, probably because her shorts fit right and aren't stained, and she's wearing it with jewelry—and she's a trash engineer.

Which isn't as different as it sounds from an environmental engineer, but on the surface, we're night and day.

Especially since she's only a trash engineer since she can't get paid to be a professional Fireballs fan.

By the third inning, the Fireballs are down two to nothing, and it's getting painful. Not as painful as thinking about how long it'll be before I'm doxed and someone figures out who my parents are, but still painful. I tell Mackenzie I need to go tuck the bees in for the night, which is a total lie since they're mostly self-sufficient this time of the year, but she doesn't call me on it, so I slip out the back door to make sure nothing's disturbed my hives.

It's part hobby, part me trying to save the world.

All's been quiet at my neighbor's house since the taser incident.

Which I feel mildly bad about, because I didn't really want to have to taser anyone, but who comes through a back gate to talk?

Ax murderers, rapists, and paparazzi. That's who.

After I make sure the gate latch is closed and the bees have water, I head back inside. At first, I think Mackenzie's listening to a commercial, but then I realize, no, she's talking.

To a person.

Who's also in my living room.

"*Ow!*" a male voice says.

"That's for being a dick to my best friend," Mackenzie announces. "Also, can I have your autograph? Ohmygod, I still have that first poster you did back when you modeled for Giovanni & Valentino before they split, and sometimes I—never mind. But seriously. Autograph. You owe me. And if you don't owe me, you owe Sarah."

"I know, that's why—"

"And you better not be bad luck for the Fireballs."

I step into the living room, and *whoa*.

Beck Ryder looks taller standing up.

I mean, duh, right? Naturally he's *taller standing up*.

Also, when his eyeballs aren't rolling in his head, they're really striking. *So* blue. Like maybe all those billboards aren't touched up.

He shifts his attention to me, starts to smile—eyes first, which is *whoa*—and then shrinks a little beside the gorgeous woman with him.

"I swear your sister let me in," he says to me with a gesture toward Mackenzie. "I just want to apologize."

She and I share a look.

Sister?

She doubles over laughing.

The ape's girlfriend humors him with an exasperated smile.

"Do Mackenzie and I look like sisters?" I ask him.

His shoulders relax, and *dude*. The guy's hands are in his jeans pockets—undoubtedly RYDE jeans, which are really freaking comfortable, which I won't be mentioning to him—but his arms are *long*. I wasn't really off in calling him an underwear ape with arms like that.

"No, but that doesn't mean anything," he says. "My sister and I don't look alike at all."

Is he for real? They could be twins—same eyes, same smile, same dark hair. "Only because she got the pretty genes."

"*Sarah*," Mackenzie hisses.

But the underwear ape barks out a laugh and winks at me. "You got that right."

Mackenzie is swooning, but when I say I know Beck Ryder's type —and how much I should *never* trust the charm—I don't mean I read *People* and watch *Secret Lives of the Stars* on late night TV.

I mean even my best friend doesn't know where I grew up.

"Apology accepted," I tell him, because it's the fastest way to get rid of him and that sexy smile, and also because I'm having this weird tingle in my breasts that suggests I shouldn't call him by his real name or encourage him to stay any longer than necessary. Especially with the way his girlfriend is sizing me up.

I want to point out to her that if he's dating her, *really* dating her and not just in some Hollywood stunt that his PR people told him would make him look good, then she has nothing to worry about.

And not just because *why would I ever be interested in a random guy who insulted me on Twitter*? I need to get a grip on my breasts.

Not literally, of course.

I look at Mackenzie. "Game's back on."

"*Oh!*" Her eyes dart wildly between the game and the underwear ape. "Um, are you good luck for the Fireballs?"

"I'm rarely bad luck," he replies with that schmootzy charm. Yes, *schmootzy*, and you know exactly what I'm talking about. Schmootzy can't be trusted. He's a schmaltzy schmoozer with the swoon factor on his side.

Officially outside the circle of trust, no matter what promises are lingering in that summer sky in his irises as he studies me entirely too closely.

He's not here to apologize because he feels bad. He's here to apologize because he's getting bad press.

I hate that I can't trust people to just have good intentions. Maybe he does have good intentions. Maybe he was raised with the Southern manners everyone in Copper Valley seems to have, and maybe he's honestly sorry, and maybe this has nothing to do with people burning RYDE underwear in the streets and him trying to save face.

I *want* to believe he is.

But I have too much experience with Hollywood to believe it.

My best friend is looking between all of us now. She's mostly ignored the ape's girlfriend, but Fireballs baseball is not something to be trifled with, and I know she's sizing them both up to decide if they're good or bad luck.

"How often do you watch?" she demands.

"Few times a summer," Beck says while his girlfriend gives the subtle *not often* head shake.

"*Gah!* Ack. Okay. Okay. We can try this, because it's not like we have a lot to lose. You. Sit. Right there. You. Stand by the plant, but don't look at the cat. Looking at the cat is bad luck. Every time Sarah pets the cat while the Fireballs are playing, they lose."

Meda rolls her mismatched eyes from her perch atop the flowery upholstered rocking chair.

Beck Ryder takes my normal seat.

His girlfriend dutifully stands by the overgrown ficus where Mackenzie insists she go.

And my possibly traitorous but mostly superstitious best friend pushes me to the couch next to the man I tasered a few hours ago.

"Stop freaking out," she tells him when he goes tense and eyeballs me again. "Sarah put her taser away hours ago, and we're only allowed happy thoughts when we're watching the Fireballs."

"I really am sorry," he says out of the corner of his mouth to me while he glues his eyes to the TV, like he's afraid Mackenzie's going to yell at him if he disrupts the game, but they keep darting to me like he's equally afraid to be this close to a psycho.

Legit fear.

Maybe he's smarter than his billboards and Twitter feed make him look.

"It's fine," I murmur back, because I don't want to talk about it, and my mouth is getting a little dry, and he has really long fingers that are fascinating me, and also, Mackenzie will probably say it's bad luck to talk.

Some days I can't remember how she so thoroughly insinuated herself into my life, but she accepts me for the weirdo I am, and I've never had to break up with her because she wanted to meet my parents—and yes, I *have* been through *that* heartbreak—so the least I can do is return the favor and humor her scientific luck experiment.

Yes, I realize science and luck are not related, but there would be this huge gaping hole in my life if she ever quit coming over to watch baseball with me.

"I know you don't have a lot of experience with this kind of publicity," he says, "and if it's overwhelming, my team's happy to help you sort through the mess. Since it's my fault."

I snort. *Don't have a lot of experience.* He has no idea.

"I'm not just blowing smoke," he insists. "I fucked up. You shouldn't have to pay for it."

He smells like Earl Grey tea in a snowy cabin. Bergamot and a thick wool blanket. It should be suffocating in June, but it's making me crave a trip to the mountains.

"Some other celebrity will get caught stuffing the sausage in a pig next week and this will be completely forgotten," I reply. "It's *fine*."

"Quit being an idiot and take advantage of him," Mackenzie

hisses. "Oh, oh, *oh*, run! RUN!" She leaps to her feet and pumps a fist in the air as Jose Ramirez gets a single for the Fireballs.

Meda yowls and darts for the stairs to my converted attic bedroom.

Ryder's girlfriend stifles a smile and scrolls on her phone.

They're a publicity stunt, I decide. Because he's all up in my chili, and she's not even batting an eyelash.

"The Nature Center could really use some funds for updated playground equipment," Mackenzie muses as she sits back down and grabs a handful of popcorn as if she isn't ratting out my favorite weekend project.

"Done," Beck says. "Which nature center?"

"Sshh," she replies, waving a hand at him.

Darren Greene's up. Left-fielder. Her not-so-secret crush who strikes out more often than he gets on base these days.

"Which nature center?" Beck whispers to me.

I shush him too, because I don't believe in blackmail, even when the blackmailee is volunteering for it, but especially when he smells this good and are his long thighs really all muscle, or is it another trick of the soft denim wrapped tight around them?

His girlfriend is frowning at me again, but I ignore her, because Greene hits a single that advances Ramirez to third.

"Sarah!" Mackenzie shrieks as the camera pans to Cooper Rock stepping up to bat. "BATHROOM!"

"Thanks for stopping by," I say to the underwear ape. "Seriously. We're cool. Go away."

I've never been so grateful for Mackenzie's undying belief that me going to the bathroom is good luck for the Fireballs.

Because by the time Cooper Rock is done at bat, Beck Ryder and his sexy body and bright blue eyes and delicious smell will be gone, and my life will be on its way back to being normal.

FIVE

Beck

AS SOON AS Sarah disappears around the corner, I glance at Charlie next to the weird leafy plant thing. She's being uncharacteristically silent through all of this, which means she's either decided there's no use in trying to stop me, or she's getting an idea.

She's half the brains behind most of my operations—okay, probably like seven eighths, really, which is why I pay her so much—and we've worked together so long that I can usually read her, but today, I'm clueless.

Obviously.

It's been a long time since I've reached out to a person in the hopes of just apologizing only to be told to go away.

Most people want my money.

Or a shot at some residual fame.

Or there was that one time I was asked if I could baptize a rabbit, but I try not to think about that.

But Sarah just wants me to go away.

It's odd.

Charlie wanted to dial in the PR team before coming over, but for once, I overruled her, because this isn't supposed to be a PR stunt.

I just wanted to apologize. The right way.

I look at the blonde—Mackenzie, I think Sarah said her name was. "Ah, thanks for the hospi—"

"Bathroom," she hisses at me. "Go on. You too. And she really really really wants to save the giraffes, so go grab this last chance by the balls."

I knew about the giraffes. Charlie did a breakdown of @must_love_bees's tweets and blogs after my groveling phone call to Vaughn, and it's pretty obvious that I'm lucky I didn't get my ass stung off too after she tasered me, and also that I probably should've shown up with a giraffe named in Sarah's honor if I wanted her to accept my apology.

Not that she has to accept it.

It's just weird how quickly she's dismissing me.

Not because I'm as awesome as I let my family think I am, but because I'm rich and famous.

Kidding, I swear. Fuck.

No wonder I got myself in trouble on Twitter.

"*Go on,*" Mackenzie shrieks.

I leap up and head around the corner that Sarah disappeared to, planning to just hang in the hallway out of sight and leave her alone, except the bathroom door is right there on the other side of the wall, and it's open and Sarah's inside lounging with her hip propped against the sink, head down over her phone, and there's no way to avoid the fact that her entire body tenses while her eyes slowly lift to watch me.

Her eyes are so *dark*. Like I can't tell where her pupils are in the middle of all that dark chocolate, and it makes me want to look closer. Or just fall in. Swim there for a while. Work on my backstroke. Or any stroke.

Fuck, I'm getting tight in the jeans.

Her jersey is so baggy, it's hiding her body almost all the way down to her knees, and there's something oddly familiar about her.

Or possibly that's a lingering side effect from the taser.

"Mackenzie sent me," I say, holding my hands up like I'm harmless, just in case she has another weapon. "For luck."

I think.

She heaves a sigh that makes her breasts lift, and I get a familiar stirring down in the family jewels.

Convenient.

Not.

She's not wearing makeup, and I know at least a hundred women who would kill to have her eyelashes.

Or at least wrestle in Jell-O for them.

Most of my acquaintances aren't actually lethal. Learned a long time ago how to avoid *those* types out in Hollywood.

"I thought I was sending my sister a private message," I say into the silence, because it's getting awkward, and I don't like silence.

I like to talk.

Or be talked at.

I'm not really picky. So long as it's not silence.

"I'm sure she appreciated your concern for her loins," Sarah replies dryly.

"She just got engaged to my best friend. I'd tell him the same."

"Lucky guy."

"Yeah, Wyatt hit the lottery when he moved in next to—wait. You don't mean he's lucky because he's my best friend, do you?" I give her the *kidding* smile.

She doesn't smile back, but she doesn't roll her eyes either. Just watches me like I'm a science experiment she stumbled onto without knowing what she's supposed to be testing.

"OH MY GOD HE HIT A HOME RUN!"

I jump at Mackenzie's shriek. Sarah hits a button on her phone, and the sound of a toilet flushing fills the air. "It worked?" she calls.

"SARAH! HE HIT A HOME RUN!"

"You have an app that plays flushing toilets?" I ask her.

"Do *not* ruin this for me," she hisses.

I hold my hands up in surrender again. "Of course. I know not to make Taser Lady mad. Your friend likes Cooper Rock? He's a good buddy. Could get you a signed ball for her."

Now she rolls her eyes so hard her lashes flutter, and there's more stirring in my cock.

"I don't want your money or your fame or your connections," she says. "We're fine, okay? Go away."

"I just…wanted to make it up to you. People are shits, and you were trying to do something good, and I fucked it all to hell because I'm a dumbass who doesn't know how to send a private message on Twitter." I trail her back to the living room, realizing belatedly what's weird about the room.

There aren't any pictures.

Every house I own is filled with pictures of my family.

Okay, yeah, and of me, but it's just funny to watch people jump when they come face-to-face with one of those cardboard cutouts of me in my underwear or the five of us from back in the Bro Code days.

Huh.

I should get Wyatt a cardboard cutout of himself. Ellie would love that.

But the point is, everybody I know has pictures of family somewhere.

Sarah doesn't.

Not in her living room. Not in the hallway. Not in the kitchen—yeah, I'm peeking.

Whoa.

Is she all alone in the world? An orphan? Abandoned? Abused?

Shit shit *shit*.

I fucked up hardcore, and I suddenly want to grab her in a hug and promise her she doesn't have to ever be alone again.

Mackenzie's slumped happily on the stiff upholstered couch, a goofy grin on her face. Charlie looks at me, and I shake my head, because I have this feeling hugging Sarah would only result in one of my nuts finding a new home somewhere between my intestines.

Time to leave the poor woman alone.

At least for now. Maybe in another six months or so, I can casually drop by, we'll have a good laugh, I'll offer to make her some sweet tea—oh, yeah, sweet tea, and cornbread, and bread pudding, and cinnamon rolls, and—and I need to stop thinking before I start drooling.

But she's my sister's neighbor. It'll be hard on Ellie if I don't make this right.

"If you change your mind—" I start.

"I won't."

"Beck will donate a million dollars to the conservation charity of your choice if you let us interview him apologizing to you on camera," Charlie announces.

I start to shake my head at her again—I've tormented Sarah enough, and I'm not interested in pissing her off more—when I realize both of the other women have frozen.

Mackenzie's jaw hits her collarbones.

And Sarah just went a shade of white that resembles bleached summer clouds. But she doesn't let being pale stop her. She spins on her heel and narrows those dark eyes at me. Feels like I'm watching a demon being summoned, and it's fucking hot as hell.

Or maybe I need to cool it with the *Buffy* reruns.

"Does your girlfriend always spend your money for you?" she asks.

"*Girlfriend*? Oh, he wishes," Charlie says with a chuckle.

"Charlie's my executive assistant," I tell Sarah. "And yeah, she pretty much does. Usually very smartly."

"Except today."

"No, today too. Happy to donate to any and all of your favorite causes. Make it two million. I can say sorry bigger."

"How often does he have to buy himself out of trouble?" Mackenzie asks Charlie.

"Couple times a year," she replies cheerfully. "This job is *not* boring."

"You're welcome," I tell her.

"Here's the situation," she says to Sarah. "We have a charity deal that's hanging in the balance. With all the negative press—yes, yes, *rightfully deserved*—we're worried that it's going to fall through, because his partner isn't too happy with being associated with us right now. You're not obligated to accept his apology. You're not obligated to forgive him. But it would be doing a great service to kids all over the nation who would stand to benefit from our new foundation. All we're asking is if you'd work with us to smooth over his lapse in judgment and poor social media skills."

"Hello, guilt trip," Sarah says.

"It's a *million fucking dollars*," Mackenzie squeaks at her.

"Two," I correct.

Swear on the underwear that made me richer than god, Sarah goes so pale she could star in a vampire show.

Mackenzie's not watching the game. She's just sitting there doing a mouse impersonation. Nose twitching, little squeaky noises slipping out of her lips when she's not forming real words.

Sarah's eyes bore into mine. "Contract?"

Smart lady. I like it. "Twenty-four hours. Or overnight. I can get a rush job."

"Probably sooner," Charlie offers.

She licks her lips. Swallows so hard I can see her throat working. Her eyes are getting shiny, her chin is wobbling, and *whoa*.

She's afraid of cameras.

Maybe she's not an orphan. Maybe she's part of a government experiment gone wrong. Or in witness protection.

I open my mouth to call it off, to tell her I'll send five million wherever the hell she wants, she doesn't have to get on camera with me, when she cuts me off before I can utter a syllable.

"You'll talk about the giraffes."

Didn't see that coming, but at least it wasn't a taser this time. "If you're sure you want to do this."

"Not just tonight, but in every interview for the next two weeks and anytime a reporter mentions my name."

Whoa. She's not fucking around. "You know I'm just a stupid underwear model, right? Lot for a guy like me to remember."

"I want it in writing."

"We need the apology video ASAP," Charlie says quietly. She's got that hint of *sorry* laced in with the *you're running out of negotiating room* tone down solid. "The sooner, the better for all of us."

"So the video before the contract."

"I'll make a phone call and get our legal team on it right now. But if you want your lawyer to look over it—"

"Not necessary. I speak Hollywood."

Unease crawls over my skin, and I see it reflected in the flinch in Charlie's mouth.

Not witness protection or a government program gone wrong, then.

Not that I really thought those things were a possibility. Mostly.

Sarah blinks away the shine in her eyes and crosses her arms. "You can use my first name only, and we do the video tonight. Right now. Mackenzie will record it. When I have the contract, you can have the video."

Not exactly unreasonable. I shoot another look at Charlie, who gives a small nod.

"It might take a few hours for hair and makeup—" she starts.

"No hair. No makeup." Sarah slides a look at me. "For *either* of us."

"Sarah," Mackenzie hisses. "At least let them do your makeup."

She shakes her head and leans over to pull out a drawer in the carved bureau along the wall between the kitchen and living room. "Phones, tablets, and computers all in here, and we can get started. Except mine. We'll use my phone."

"Beck," Charlie says, a warning coloring her tone, and yeah, she's right.

This might be a really bad idea, and we might get taken for a ride.

There's no telling how she'll come off on camera. Especially a cell phone camera, with no lights, no makeup, and no crew.

An apology video is supposed to make *both* of us look good.

And it's not that Sarah looks *bad*. She's cute under all the messy hair and suspicion.

But when you've been a celebrity as long as I have, you know the difference a single hair out of place can make in the court of public opinion.

"We've got a guy who can do makeup so it looks like you're not wearing any," I offer her. "The camera's sometimes—"

"No." She points to the open drawer again. "You have two minutes before I change my mind."

"I'm sending an email to our legal team," Charlie tells her. "Let's make sure I've got your conditions right first."

Sarah squints at her, then at me, and I'm suddenly one hundred percent certain we're not just talking to a woman whose Twitter profile proclaims her *Environmental Avenger, Science Geek, and Animal Lover with a fear of needles.*

This is a woman with secrets.

And I want to know every last one.

SIX

Sarah

I DON'T NEED Beck Ryder's money. I don't want anything to do with fame. If I could undo the last twenty-four hours, I would in a heartbeat.

But I *can't.*

All of my secrets will probably be exposed one way or another. The question is how soon, and how much good can I do before then.

This isn't about me.

It's about getting the word out about the giraffes. And the honey-bees. And the endless list of other endangered animals.

My parents could give me money for donations for the giraffes and playground equipment.

I changed my name to get away from their fame.

But they can't provide a platform.

Next to my parents, I'm *that chick who owl bombed her high school prom.* Next to Beck, I'm a frumpy cranky science geek that no one will look too closely at.

And even if they do, they might not connect the dots.

He can give me a bigger platform that won't be overshadowed by my past.

He can help me save the world.

I just have to call my parents and ask them to please ignore any videos of me going around the internet, and deny to their friends that it's me.

So, less than twenty-four hours after my respectable social media presence blew up thanks to his idiocy, I'm pointing him to a spindle chair at my second-hand kitchen table while my best friend misses a baseball game to use my phone to record us.

I really need to come clean with Mackenzie.

Soon.

I swear.

Soon.

"You have to sit on my right," I tell him.

"Ah. So we get your good side?" he asks with a flirty grin.

My right side is my *good* side. My eyes crinkle unevenly when I smile, and I've always thought the right side looks less weird with it, but I point to a heart-shaped mole high on my right cheek, which is probably my most distinctive feature. "Sure."

"Huh. Didn't even notice," he says, and then he pulls his shirt off.

"What are you doing?" I gasp.

"Look." He twists and points to his left shoulder blade, where there's a liver-colored birthmark about the size of a quarter. "I have one too. Mine looks like a Teenage Mutant Ninja Turtle."

"Put your shirt back on." Gah, he's not all that airbrushed in those billboards. Good *lord*, the man is ripped. I try to tell myself it means he spends a quarter of his day in the gym, or that he has a really good plastic surgeon, and also that it's ridiculously stupid that his easy grin is charming my nipples.

Crap.

Am I wearing a bra? The last thing I need is for the message to get lost behind people noticing that my nipples are straining to watch the underwear model in my kitchen.

Good gravy, I just thought that.

And it's not even the weirdest thought I've ever had, but it's been over a decade since I left home and changed my name, so it's been a while since I've had weird thoughts.

I'd really hoped I'd left that all behind.

Also, if I *had* to have my body come back to life after the disaster that was Trent Fornicus last year—and yes, he was just as good at it as his name suggests—does it *have* to happen *now*?

For an underwear model?

"Wait," I say.

Beck lifts a brow.

Dammit, even his *brows* are Hollywood perfection.

He probably manscapes too.

Although, he does have a reasonable amount of chest hair. Not like he's furry, but if he's manscaping, he's not straight-up waxing.

"Wait…for…?" he says.

I shake my head. *Get it together, Sarah.* "I never show my face, so why is anyone going to believe that I'm @must_love_bees and that you didn't just hire someone to stand here and pretend to be me?"

He glances at Charlie, who gives him a *you're on your own, buddy* look.

"You can post the video on your account," he says.

"How will people know you didn't hack me?"

"You already tasered me once. Much fun as it was the first time, I'm not going to do *anything* to prompt that again."

Despite his easy grin about the whole thing, I'm going red. I can feel it.

And I don't do *pretty* red. It's one of the things my mother always lamented. *Oh, Serendipity, I so wish you'd gotten my lovely blush instead of your father's brutish blotches. People will judge you horribly.*

"I didn't know it was *you*," I start, but Beck waves me off, still grinning.

"Eh. I deserved it. For a lot of reasons."

"You're awful happy for a guy who *deserved* it."

His grin goes sheepish. "Bad habit. Terrible habit. Being happy, I mean. I'm trying to quit."

Is he—is he *flirting* with me? "The camera's on, isn't it?" I say.

"Yep, I'm rolling," Mackenzie announces. "Go on. You two are adorable."

I shoot her a *what the hell?* look.

She grins and gives me a thumbs-up.

I sigh. We can edit this out. "Okay. Let's do this." Before I puke.

Or change my mind and bolt for the Himalayas.

Save the giraffes, Sarah. Be the difference you want to see in the world. Best chance, right here.

"You sure?" Beck asks.

I don't like how he's watching me.

Because there's a lot of concern in those pretty blue eyes of his, and he's doing a damn good job of making me feel like his concern is for *me*, and not this foundation that I know he's trying to salvage.

I nod anyway, because the world really does need to know that the giraffes are endangered.

Charlie is standing by my kitchen sink, watching. She's given up her phone, but she's taking notes on a pad of paper.

Beck looks at Mackenzie, and his smile actually fades. "Hey, people of the world. Beck Ryder here with a huge apology to pretty much all of you, but mostly to this lovely lady right here. Sarah, also known as @must_love_bees on Twitter."

I force a smile, though now that we're actually recording, I'm definitely going to vomit. "Hi."

Beck angles closer, and the weirdest sensation of warmth floods my chest when he drapes his ape arm over the back of my chair. Like this is going to be okay, even though I know it's completely illogical for his arm to be comforting.

I guess it's like bungee jumping while attached to a bungee jumping instructor.

You know he knows what he's doing, so you're going to survive, even though you also know that there's still a possibility that this will be the time the cord snaps.

"Tell you a story?" Beck asks me.

I lick my lips, because *dammit*, it's hot in here. "Is it about you?"

His gaze dips to my lips, then back to my eyes, and he grins at me. "My sister would like you. You know she got engaged this week?"

"And you wish her a lifetime of popping out babies and mopping floors and greeting her big strong provider with a baked chicken and a smile every night for the rest of her life?" Oh my god, I sound like a nagging asshole.

"That tweet was in really poor taste, wasn't it?" he says quietly.

"Pretty much," I reply, just as quietly.

"Both my parents worked the whole time I was growing up," he tells me. "Both of them. Together. They own an environmental engineering firm."

"I know. That's why your sister follows me. We're all trying to save the world."

"Except me." His brows furrow for half a second. "You're trying to save the giraffes."

"They're endangered."

"But we see them in zoos all the time."

I heave an exasperated sigh. "Just because you see them in zoos doesn't mean they're not endangered in the wild. Zoos work with conservationists. Pandas were endangered for a long time. But because we knew it, people worked to save them. They're still vulnerable, but we're making progress. No one knows giraffes are endangered though. That's why it's such a big deal that Persephone, the giraffe at the Copper Valley zoo, is having a baby. It's not just about the cute baby giraffe. It's about survival of the species."

"And honeybees?" he asks.

Those are the magic words.

I can talk about honeybees for *hours*.

Mackenzie's not there. Charlie's not there. I'm just telling the underwear ape how important honeybees are for our food supply and the whole ecological chain of events that matters so much to me.

Completely and totally geeking out.

And if he's not listening, he's still making me feel like he is, nodding along, asking more questions, cracking the occasional joke that's actually *funny*.

I pause, because I realize I'm rambling, and he smiles at me.

Not a *hey, lady, want to see me in my underwear pose?* smile, but a friendly, *I get it, I'm passionate about things too* smile.

"You care," he says.

"Everybody cares about something. What do you care about?"

"My family."

He doesn't even pause, and I don't know if that's because it's the answer he's trained to give, or if he really has kept himself that grounded through the years.

He bends one long arm to scratch his neck, his grin going rueful again. "My mom chewed me out pretty bad this morning," he tells me. "Never too old to get an ass-chewing when you deserve it, you know?"

"If you need more ass-chewing, I have a friend who's really pissed at you too," I offer.

He laughs. "Yeah, I think I met her in the park this morning. She threw a yoga brick at me."

"You might've deserved it."

"I'm pretty lucky that's all she threw. That was an asshole tweet. I shouldn't have even sent it to my sister privately. She works hard. Really hard. You know we almost lost her in a car accident about eighteen months ago?"

I knew Ellie walked with a limp when I moved in next to her a year ago, but I didn't know why. I shake my head.

"She worked her tail off to walk again, to get back to work, and she just finished a project that'll save the city a buttload of money every year in energy costs. And I just model underwear and encourage people to wear comfortable stylish clothes." He shakes his head. "You keep doing you, Sarah. Save your giraffes. World needs more people like you. Give it up, Taser Lady."

He holds out a fist, and even though the last person I fist-bumped was a drunk stranger on the light-rail downtown over a year ago, I bump his fist back.

He grins at me.

And I smile at him, because it's nearly impossible not to.

"Thanks for your time," he says. "You didn't owe me anything. Really appreciate it."

"Sure," I reply. "People say stupid things all the time."

"Is that a wrap?" Mackenzie asks, and I jump.

I almost forgot she was there.

"That's a wrap," Charlie says.

Beck leans back, and I realize he was sitting here with his arm on the back of my chair practically the whole video.

And now I feel weirdly cold.

"As soon as I check my phone, we should have a draft from the lawyer for the agreement," Charlie says. "I'll send it over."

Poof.

Magic all gone.

Now we're back to work.

Which is what that video was.

Work.

Not me sharing my passion with someone who understood. Just *work*. With someone who has to pay people off enough that his team has a standard agreement that a lawyer just has to modify terms for. On a Saturday night when he should be out doing anything other than work.

"Ohmygod, the game!" Mackenzie squeals.

She darts for the living room with my phone, and a moment later, she's whooping with joy. "We won! WE WON! Two in a row! WE WON!"

"I'll look over everything and get back to you in the morning," I tell Charlie.

Okay, yes, I'm calling my parents' lawyer and swearing her to secrecy, even though I said I wasn't. I'm pretty sure they're not on social media, but their friends will be.

And I'll call them before I post the video too.

I will.

And then I'll tell Mackenzie who I really am.

I swear.

She deserves to hear it from me.

All of this is happening so suddenly though. I'm just not sure I'm ready.

Twelve more hours. Twenty-four, tops.

Beck squeezes my shoulder. "Thanks, Sarah. I really am sorry for dragging you into this."

I ignore the skitters fluttering in my belly and nod to him. "I just hope something good comes of it."

And that my life can go back to normal very, very soon.

He and Charlie reclaim their electronics from my living room and head out, but not before Beck looks back at me one more time, studying me with gravely serious eyes that make my pulse kick up and my breasts tingle before his easy grin comes back. "Thank you. Again."

He looks like he wants to say something else, but Charlie nudges him, and they depart, leaving Mackenzie and me alone again to rewind my DVR and catch up on the game. Meda spies on us from her hidey-hole in the cat tower next to my bookshelves of *Buffy the Vampire Slayer* comic books, and I act like we didn't just see an underwear model out the door while I try to figure out how to just toss out *Hey, Mackenzie, funny story about my childhood* and utterly fail.

Yep.

Life's going back to normal.

SEVEN

Sarah

THE PARKING LOT at the nature center is fuller than normal when I arrive for Sunday morning clean-up. Mackenzie and I volunteer here once a month to help pick up trash, repair trail signs, and do anything else the little preserve in the Belmont district of the city needs. I head toward the small cabin that serves as both ranger station and mini-museum for visitors to learn about the animals that live in the city, and someone calls my name.

"Sarah! Sarah, right?"

I nod at the perky woman approaching in a Belmont Nature Preserve T-shirt.

"How much did Beck Ryder pay you to do that video?" she whispers.

I open my mouth.

Then shut it.

Because *I* haven't posted the video.

I haven't even opened Twitter since yesterday morning, mostly because Mackenzie talked me out of it during my three minutes of weakness when I wanted to.

"Back up, Tricia," Mackenzie says, sidestepping the woman to link her arm through mine. "Betcha I pick up the most trash."

"How did he post the video?" I whisper. "I just sent the contract back an hour ago, and I didn't post it yet."

Her lips twitch, and she points a shaky finger at a tree, clearly trying to distract me. "Look! Do you think the baby robins have left the nest yet?"

"What. Did. You. Do?"

"You were going to edit the video," she whispers.

"Mackenzie!"

"And you didn't do it for the money," she adds as I yank her off the main trail and into a small alcove that's not nearly private enough.

"*Mackenzie.*"

My phone buzzes. I yank it out, and there's a message from Ellie.

Hey, Beck here, borrowing E's phone. Thanks for the trust. I'm retweeting the video now. Will send receipts for the donations ASAP.

My chest buzzes.

My feet go lightheaded.

Swear to god, they do.

I was supposed to have another few hours to call my parents, who probably aren't even up yet in California.

"I have to tell you—" I start, but Adriana, the center's manager, rushes from the cabin to hug me.

"Sarah! Oh, Sarah, *why didn't you tell us you were dating Beck Ryder?*"

"I—we—we're friends," I babble.

That's what the contract said to say.

Kind of.

Both parties agree to refrain from speaking negatively of the other, or from starting rumors, blah blah blah.

Okay, fine. *We're friends* is the standard Hollywood code for *we want you to wonder what we actually are.*

"So it was just a joke? That tweet about having babies but not with him?"

"Sarah! Was that *you*?"

"Sarah! @must_love_bees Sarah?"

"Oh my god! Sarah! You two are *adorable*!"

"I think your boyfriend owes you security," Mackenzie whispers.

I look at Adriana. "I have to—"

"Tell me *everything*," she says.

"—make a phone call," I finish.

There are usually a dozen volunteers, and at least half of them change every month.

But I swear there are almost fifty people here, and most of them are gathering around us.

"Great message about the honeybees," one of the regular volunteers tells me.

"I looked it up, and you were right about the giraffes being endangered," a guy says. "But not all giraffes. Just three species. The rest of the giraffes are only vulnerable. You should've—*ow*."

"Stop being an ass," the woman next to him hisses. She rolls her eyes at me. "And you shouldn't have let Ryder off that easy. He's what's wrong with the world."

"You guys. Give Sarah some breathing room." Mackenzie leaps in front of me and holds her arms wide. "Are we here to be gossips, or are we here to help make the world a better place? Go on. You. Shoo. Get to work. You too. The trash isn't going to pick itself up. And did a single one of you mention that the Fireballs *won* last night? What's wrong with you?"

The crowd breaks up, and of course, *now* I should've brought my sweatshirt, sunglasses, and hat.

But no one's talking about my parents.

So apparently no one recognized me.

I'm sagging with relief while I steal Mackenzie's hat and sunglasses, because she owes me this much. "I'm going home," I tell Adriana. "I'm so sorry, but I think I'm more of a hindrance than a help."

"Okay, but you *have* to tell me *all* the details next time." She glances around with a smile. "And thanks for bringing out all the volunteers. I didn't realize when I started getting questions about if you were coming, that it meant so many people would want to talk to you. But then someone showed me the video, and—"

"Sarah? *Sarah!*"

"Yeah. Gotta go," I say. I dart back to my car, Mackenzie on my heels.

"Are you mad?" she whispers.

"No."

"You're acting mad."

"I'm surprised. And I hate attention. And why do people think we're dating? We're not dating. And—"

"I don't know," she says with a shrug that says she *clearly* knows. "Mackenzie…"

She chews on her bottom lip and gives me the puppy dog look.

I cross my arms and glare at her, which sends someone who was halfway through calling *Sarah!* to turn around and head the other way, and which also makes me feel like slime, because I hate glaring at Mackenzie. She's my best friend. And I still owe her the truth, and I really hope she stays my best friend after I confess to her.

"Okay, look. I read gossip pages," my best friend whispers. "And it's all about chemistry. Chemistry on set, chemistry walking down Sunset Boulevard, chemistry at a secret dinner in New York City, chemistry in interviews. You and Beck have chemistry. People eat that up. And if I let you edit that video, you would've taken out all the chemistry, and like, maybe a *third* of the people who care right now would've listened. I did it for the cause. Swear on the Fireballs' winning streak, it was all for the cause. Saving the giraffes is so much more romantic when people think there's a secret relationship behind the video."

"It's not—listen, I have to tell you something."

"Sarah! Oh my gosh, Sarah," yet one more person hollers, and *dammit.*

"I have to get out of here," I tell Mackenzie. "I'll call you later, okay?"

"Please don't be mad."

I squeeze her in a hug, because she's basically family, and I might be mad, but I still love her. "Do *not* comment *at all* on *anything* related to that video. Understand? And you have to promise you won't be mad at me either."

"Sarah. Oh my god. Why would anyone be mad at you?"

I wince, because she's going to find out soon enough.

It takes a little maneuvering, but I make it out of the parking lot around the volunteers arriving for clean-up day. Half a mile down the road, I spot a strip mall with a packed parking lot. I park near the back—employee cars, I assume, so little foot traffic here—and I pull out my phone and dial a number.

The sun won't be up yet in California, but my mother might be.

An hour of yoga before the sun rises puts a beautiful day in your soul.

She answers on the first ring. "Serendipity! You called! I thought you might."

"Hi, Mom."

"So. When do we get to meet your boyfriend?"

"I don't—"

"Nonsense. Franklin already sent me the video. Sweetheart. Your hair. You're not going to keep a man like Beck Ryder happy with hair like that for long."

"He likes picking the bugs out of it."

"*Serendipity Astrid Darling*, what a horrible thing to say. I know you wash your hair too often to get *bugs*. Although—what's this about bees? I had no idea you loved bees. Have you been on beekeeper dating sites? Is that why you're on the Twitters talking about bees?"

"No, I—"

"And the giraffes! Oh, sweetheart, I had *no idea* giraffes were endangered. Do you remember the giraffe that came to your seventh birthday? You were so afraid of it. But don't worry, your father and I are making a very sizable donation to giraffe research. And I assume our dear Mr. Ryder has done the same?"

"Yes, and he has four or five thousand a year," I mutter to myself.

"Mr. Ryder is no Mr. Darcy, young lady," my mom informs me. "If I'd known you were interested in former musicians, I could have gotten in touch with my agent to see if we could arrange an introduction to Cash Rivers. Now *there's* a Mr. Darcy for you."

"Mom—"

"I know, I know, dear. It's all for publicity's sake to clear his name, and Cash Rivers *does* have that nose. Now, what can we do to help?"

"Just—just please don't say anything. To anyone. The attention will blow over. I don't want—"

"Our names involved," she finishes, and I cringe at the hurt tone in her voice.

I don't want to hurt my mom. Or my dad.

But Hollywood-level attention and I don't get along well.

Changing my name, taking a gap year in Morocco, and then enrolling in a small technical university in Copper Valley—all the way across the country from my parents and their high-profile life-style—worked perfectly to give me the anonymity I desperately needed after high school.

After my entire childhood, actually, but high school was the worst.

"It's not you," I say quietly.

"I know, Serendipity." She sighs briefly again, which adds to the guilt cockleburs sticking to my socks and making my skin itch all over. "It's just—never mind."

"What?"

"If you change your mind, you know where to find us."

I drop my head to the steering wheel. I'm the world's worst daughter. "Thanks, Mom."

"And comb your hair, sweetheart. It'll make you feel so much better."

I ignore her last bit of advice, because I don't need it. And I *did* comb my hair this morning.

This thing with Beck Ryder will blow over.

People just need a new distraction.

And I need to make sure no one ever, *ever* figures out who my parents are.

While still probably confessing to my best friend.

Probably.

I think.

I mean, if people haven't figured it out yet...will they ever?

EIGHT

Beck

LEAVING my penthouse isn't an option Sunday morning. In fact, leaving the Copper Valley area isn't an option for the foreseeable future. Every meeting I was supposed to have in New York, California, and everywhere in between has been canceled or will be covered by someone else on my team.

My invitations to public appearances have all been revoked.

All of them.

I'm on the world's shit list, waiting to see if that video Sarah posted will do anything to redeem even a fraction of the reputation I built on hard work, luck, and lots of hours hanging with kids at hospitals, schools, and in third world countries where another of my foundations helps provide clean food and water.

Of everything I do, my favorite part is helping the kids. I loved my childhood, and I've always wanted kids. Hell, I *am* a kid. But since we made that decision to sign that contract for a record deal for Bro Code, my life's been heading in a direction that convinces me more and more every year that it won't happen.

It's been five years since the second—and last—woman told me I was going to be a father. In both cases, paternity tests proved them wrong, but that was enough for me. And I haven't dated a woman since that I've been able to fully trust.

So having everything on the verge of falling apart now, when I have a bank account big enough to buy a small country, and when my businesses could operate almost on auto-pilot to keep funding more charity work like the foundation with Vaughn?

This sucks.

It's too early to call Vaughn again to grovel some more—do *not* get on a pro athlete's shit list when he's a reformed street kid who's now basketball's poster child for projects related to children, at least not if you want to form a joint foundation with him—so I'm hanging out in my small weight room, sparring with Davis.

My old neighborhood buddy and former bandmate lives an hour or so outside the city, doing some *real* job with the nuclear power plant down there at the Virginia-North Carolina border that required him to go to college after the band split up, but he came up for Ellie and Wyatt's engagement party last night.

"That tweet could've been worse," he says as he aims a right hook at my ribs. "You could've said it to an old dude."

I grunt and aim a right hook right back. "That would've actually been *funny*."

"Knock, knock, you got your clothes on?" Ellie calls from somewhere outside the weight room.

"No, we're both naked, and your brother's sucking my dick," Davis calls.

"In that case, I'm bringing a camera," she replies.

He blocks my sucker punch aimed at his gut, and he bounces back as Ellie appears in all the mirrors around the room. "Ew, put your shirts on," she says with a grin.

I use mine to wipe my face before heading toward her. "C'mere and give your favorite brother a hug."

"Touch me and die."

"Touch her and die," Wyatt agrees behind her.

Pretty sure he could take me—he's mostly a rocket scientist for the Air Force, but he takes being in the military seriously, and in addition to being brilliant, he also flies jets to test them out, which makes him badass in my book—so I settle for bending over and holding out a fist to Tucker, who's standing between them. "Hey, little man. You have fun at your party last night?"

"The grown-ups talked too much," he tells me.

"Yeah, and that never ends," I agree.

"You know your phone's blowing up on your kitchen counter?" Ellie says to me.

"What phone? I don't have a phone." Shit. If I missed a call from Vaughn, I'm probably dead.

She gives me an exasperated smile, then ruffles Tucker's hair. "Uncle Beck has a Pac-Man game here."

"No way!"

"Yep. Right through that door."

That's all the invitation Tucker needs. He's darting to my game room across the hall before I can tell him I also have Donkey Kong in there.

"Don't break it," Davis mutters with a smirk under his beard and man-bun while he pulls on a black T-shirt that matches the ink up and down his arms.

"He can't break it," I say.

He, Ellie, and Wyatt all exchange glances, and Davis is the only one looking amused.

"Dude. Shit. Did you guys break Pac-Man at my house in Ship-wreck?" They were out at my favorite little getaway in the Blue Ridge Mountains this past week for the Pirate Festival. Yes. Pirate Festival in the mountains. It's a thing.

"Relax," Wyatt says. "We didn't break Pac-Man."

"Mom sent cinnamon rolls," Ellie adds quickly, and *dammit*, they're hiding something.

But *cinnamon rolls* are the magic words.

My mother makes the best cinnamon rolls on the entire planet. I've flown home overnight from Australia before just to be there when she pulled them out of the oven. When we were kids, everyone knew when she made cinnamon rolls, because you could smell them baking all the way down to the end of the street at the Wilsons' house, and she always made enough to feed an army, because that's how many kids would show up on the doorstep looking for Saturday morning cinnamon rolls.

But when I head for the kitchen, Ellie blocks me. "Tell me you're not pulling the Hollywood fake relationship thing with my neighbor," she says in that deadly tone of voice that suggests there's one right answer and one wrong answer that will result in a titty twister to end all titty twisters.

But it still doesn't stop me from fantasizing about Sarah, which I've been trying very hard not to do all morning.

Those eyes. Those intense, wary eyes. And don't get me started on the curves hiding under her clothes.

She has me fascinated. Which is dangerous, because I know she has secrets.

"What? Fake relationship with Sarah? No. You know me better than that."

She crosses her arms and demonstrates how much she's learned about being a mom in the year since she and Wyatt started dating seriously.

Shit, she's good at that *don't give me your bullshit* glare.

"What?" I ask again.

"The apology video?" she prompts.

"She wanted to spread the word about giraffes. I wanted to apologize. Win-win." And my growing belief that it was that simple, that she's not interested in anything else, is both refreshing and frustrating, because I think I like her.

"Have you talked to your team this morning?" Ellie asks.

"Hey, nudie dude, your brains are here," Davis calls.

"Was he always this not-funny?" I ask Ellie.

"Were you always this sensitive? That was hilarious. And I take it that's a *no* to talking to your team yet."

"It's Sunday. I told them to take the day off." Not that they listened, because we're in crisis mode, but it was a nice dream.

"At this rate, I'll take a Sunday off in three years," Charlie says. She stops in the doorway too and looks me up and down, her no-bullshit meter also clearly pinging high today. "You're not answering your phone."

"You want one of my mom's cinnamon rolls? They go great with bad news. Did I miss Vaughn?"

"No, and it's not all bad news."

That means it's mostly bad news with a side of sunshine. "New plan. Cancel all my appearances for the next month, and I'll go into hiding in Shipwreck while we tell people I'm in rehab."

"Everyone who invited you to appearances for the next *four* months canceled them already. We're at a point of having to make up an event for you to have an appearance at if you're ever going to be seen in public again."

"So...we just need to spread the rehab rumors?"

"It's astonishing to me that you run a billion-dollar fashion empire with this kind of attitude," Ellie says.

I grunt. It won't be a billion-dollar fashion empire for long at this rate.

"He's a lot smarter when we're in Milan or Paris," Charlie tells her. "Being home turns him into a teenager who just wants to play video games again."

I'd argue that that's not fair, except it's true. "Home's for kicking back and relaxing. I work four hundred eighty-seven days of the year, so when I get my twenty-six to relax, I *relax*. Work hard, play hard."

"Until you fuck up hard," Charlie points out.

"Video didn't work?"

"Worked too well."

Ellie glares harder.

Charlie gives me the *you're so screwed* smile.

And I realize that whatever's going on, cinnamon rolls won't solve it.

NINE

Sarah

MACKENZIE SHOWS up shortly after noon with peace offerings in the form of caramel corn and takeout burgers. And because I would've posted the video by now myself anyway—maybe edited, maybe not—and I still haven't told her the truth about where I grew up, I let her in and hug her tight.

"Why are there two black cars with scary looking men parked across the street?" she asks me.

"Security. In case I get doxed. Charlie set it up."

"Doxed?"

"Doxed. When the crazies on the internet find someone's address and post it so weird stalker people can come by to see if Beck Ryder's really my boyfriend." I roll my eyes like it's no big deal, but the internet is a scary place with scary people sometimes.

Can't deny that I was grateful to get Charlie's message this morning that they'd put extra security in the neighborhood as a precaution.

Especially after I logged onto Twitter to see how bad it was when I got home a couple hours ago.

Currently fifty-fifty, with half the world wondering if Beck Ryder's apology was sincere enough to result in me crushing on him, and the other half of the world in total chaos arguing still over whether Beck or I are the uglier, stupider, assholier, or more desperate of the pair of us.

No one speculating about where I came from or who my parents are.

I just might've pulled this off.

"You two were really cute on the video," my best friend tells me, leaving no doubt where she falls on the scale. "I can totally see tons of people making the same mistake as everyone at the nature center this morning. Not that an underwear model could ever be another Trent Fornicus—I mean, they stuff the briefs before they shoot the pictures, right?—but it's your fifteen minutes of fame and you're using it to save the giraffes."

That's it.

That's my opening.

I suck in a deep breath to tell her, but she impulsively hugs me. "Seriously, I'm so proud of you. Where's your jersey? The game's on in ten minutes."

And the moment is gone.

I change, pop popcorn, use some of my mom's old meditation techniques to forget Mackenzie brought up Trent and to clear my mind enough to focus on how I'm going to tell her I've basically been lying to her for almost a decade, and we've just turned the TV on when she leaps to her feet and dashes to the kitchen.

"Wha—" I start, but then I hear voices at the back door.

Now familiar voices.

"Hey. Am I late?"

"No! Come in! Come in! Wait. What's that? We don't eat cotton candy during baseball games. It's bad luck. Throw it away. But is that Fletchers caramel corn? Oooh, we haven't tried that yet."

Meda's once again sitting on the top of the recliner. She gives me the *seriously, the underwear model again?* stare, and her blue eye looks a little more irritated than her amber eye, which makes me wonder if she, too, is having conflicting thoughts about him.

I shrug and ignore the little blip in my pulse.

He's not here for *me.*

He's here because it looks good.

Except…why come in the back door if that's the case? Isn't the point to get *caught* coming to see me?

Mackenzie shoves him into the living room. "Sarah! Look who wants to watch the game with us."

He smiles a self-deprecating smile that exudes sexual masculinity and the suggestion that he knows what to do with his equipment, which I also know is most likely a Hollywood lie, or if not, I can at least take comfort in that old rumor so I don't feel like I might be missing out on something.

"Gotta go with what works to keep the team winning," he tells me.

"That's your line?" I ask.

"You remember that year they went to the World Series?"

"No."

"*No?*"

"Sarah grew up in Oregon," Mackenzie says, and I wince, which she doesn't notice at all. "I converted her."

"Oregon, huh?"'

Oregon, Los Angeles, it's all the same. Except not really, but for my purposes, it counts.

Until today.

I really, really need to tell her. But not with Beck here. "Mm-hmm."

He grins, because that's apparently all he ever does. "Portland's awesome."

"Mm," I agree again. "Game's starting."

Mackenzie shoos me over so Beck can sit in the same seat he was in last night, which puts his long frame right up next to my padded hips.

He smells like bergamot and fresh cut grass today, and he's sporting thicker scruff than he had last night. If he slept as poorly as I did, you can't tell by looking at him.

He pops the lid on the popcorn tin and angles it toward me. "For luck?"

Of course he got the kind with caramel and cheese corn mixed together. That's my favorite.

"Where's Charlie?" I ask while I help myself, because it's not weird to be sitting here with an underwear model who insulted me on Twitter two nights ago, let me taser him yesterday morning and then came back for an apology video last night, and randomly showed up *for good luck* for our favorite baseball team today.

And by *it's not weird*, I definitely mean *a wormhole opened in my living room.*

I wonder if he's irritated by loud chewers, because I don't think I can chew popcorn quietly, and it's going to be crunching in his ear, and that has to be the least attractive sound in the universe.

Not that I care if I'm attractive to him.

Just like maybe he's a loud chewer and that'll be perfect because I'm not attracted to him at all.

Or curious about why he's really here.

"Charlie's on a conference call with my management team," he tells me.

"So you escaped?"

"Actually, they chased me off so I didn't fuck anything up."

"How'd Mackenzie know you were coming?"

"Psychic powers." He grins at me, and I swear that makes thirty-two panty-melting grins in four minutes, and the real dig is that I'm wearing RYDE panties, because they are *so* damn comfortable that I couldn't bring myself to burn them with the decreasing number of women posting videos on Twitter of themselves doing just that to stand with me in solidarity.

I'm betraying my biggest supporters.

But it's not like burning my panties takes any dollar bills out of his bank account. I already bought them. I won't buy more.

"Yes! That's how you start a game!" Mackenzie pumps a fist in the air. The Fireballs just led off with a single.

That's remarkably positive of them.

"You ever catch a game in person?" Beck asks.

"Every bobblehead doll game," my best friend confirms. "And Sunday afternoon games when they're at home."

"They have a home series starting tomorrow," he muses.

I stop chewing slowly—and therefore quietly—to shoot a glance at him.

Is he implying he wants to go to a Fireballs game with us?

And if so, *why*?

"You have any root beer?" he asks suddenly. "When I was growing up, we'd all crash in Cash's basement with root beer and caramel corn and watch Friday night games. Man, good times."

"Ohmygod, I love Cash Rivers," Mackenzie breathes. "He was my favorite. I even saw him as the cheetah man in that really bad first movie he made after—wait. You're not going to tell him I said that, are you?"

"Not as long as you don't tell anyone Sarah got me with a taser yesterday."

"The whole world already knows that, because it's on your video," Mackenzie reminds him.

"Huh."

Great. Now she has no leverage at all for Beck not telling Cash Rivers that she thinks her Hollywood idol's first movie sucked, which I know isn't a big deal, but she doesn't, and her face is going beet red.

"Airsh Ark ivva didge," I say around a mouthful of caramel corn that I can't chew quietly to save my life.

"Sweet," he says, and he hops up and heads for the kitchen.

"*What?*" Mackenzie hisses.

I chew fast and gulp down the popcorn. "The Barq's is in the fridge," I hiss back.

"That is *not* what you said."

"Yes, it is."

"Oh my god, it sounded like you were summoning a popcorn demon."

"It did not."

"*It did.* And popcorn demons are *not* the positive spiritual energy the Fireballs need to win today."

Okay, she has me there.

"You ladies need anything?" Beck pops his head back into the living room. "Root beer? Man, you've got shoestring fries in the freezer. I haven't had those in *years*. Fucking road diet."

This is getting weird. "Please. Make yourself at home."

"Throw some bacon in at the same time," Mackenzie tells him. "We'll melt gouda over them and toss on bacon bits and then Sarah will pretty much be yours for the taking."

"*Mackenzie,*" I hiss.

"What? I want to see you taser him again when he blatantly tries to get in your pants. Because he's still no Trent. I mean, who can ever be Trent?"

I wince and try to give myself a pep talk. *Just tell her, Sarah. Tell her why you really broke up with Trent.*

She misunderstands my wince and she also winces. "Sorry," she whispers. "But I bet he's not."

Beck, who of course has overheard everything, grins and shakes his head, then disappears back into the kitchen.

"What are you doing?" I hiss at her.

"Testing him," she hisses back. "I realized his PR people might have told him to schmooze you because of so many people shipping you."

"What-ing us?"

"*Shipping*. Sarah. They're fantasizing about you dating."

"What? No. People don't do that."

She gives me the *duh, yes they do* look, and I realize I can't actually argue that people don't do it in general, because I can't count the number of times growing up I'd hear at school that my classmates wished my parents would get divorced so one or the other of them could marry whichever movie star they happened to have just been in a movie with.

Okay, really, I just didn't know it had a name.

Because *fine*, half the Twitterverse *was* speculating that Beck and I are dating. But not *wishing*. There's a difference.

Also, a full twenty percent are still pissed at him and another thirty percent think I'm too fugly—yes, *fugly*, because ugly by itself isn't good enough—to ever actually score a hot guy like Beck, and also that women need to stay out of science.

"Okay, fine, people ship people. But not geeks like *me*," I amend.

I might look all nice and normal, watching baseball with my superstitious best friend, but I was up well past midnight last night playing *Vikings in Space* while checking in on Persephone, and I'm legitimately itching to get back to it, because my Viking captainess just made contact with a new species of aliens who can either bend time or hypnotize people with folk music, and I'm not sure which yet.

Also, the last time Mackenzie made me go to a wine and paint night, while everyone else was making spring flowers, I might've inadvertently painted a Pokémon.

"You're a geek accidentally involved with an underwear model," she whispers. "And you were *so freaking adorable* in that video. In case I haven't said it sixteen times yet."

"Whoa, you have real bacon," Beck says from the kitchen. "Not turkey bacon. What other goodies do you have hidden in here?"

Mackenzie flails her fingers wide and waves her hands in the air like every excited valley girl ever depicted on TV.

"*That's* not fake," she whispers.

"Stop it," I warn her. "Give him three weeks, and he won't even remember my name. And, as you pointed out, he's still no Trent Fornicus. Oh, look. Stafford's pitching. You think his shoulder's going to hold out for the whole season?"

"Yes. And he's not going to forget your name."

"We still have nothing in common."

"Holy shit, that's a really fucking cool *Firefly* print. Like when they were babies. Where'd you get that?" Beck calls from the kitchen.

Mackenzie smirks. "Yep. Nothing at all in common."

TEN

Beck

I HATE BEING AN ASSHOLE.

Yet here I am, falling in love with Sarah's kitchen and knowing we're doomed. I can't stay here forever with her shoestring fries and real center cut bacon and this fucking amazing artwork from my favorite space cowboy show.

And when she finds out why I'm here, I'm basically losing her forever.

Her and her kitchen.

And those big dark eyes.

It's like the taser totally glued them to the front of my memory lobes, and even knowing that I have a really bad track record with women, and that Sarah has secrets, I still can't help mourning the loss of her and her house and food and impeccable taste.

"No, no, *no!*" Mackenzie moans from the living room. "Beck! Get back here! They're losing while you're not watching!"

Sarah's cat sashays into the room, gives me a disdainful look like she knows I'm supposed to ask Sarah if she'd consider doing another video with me, or go out in public with me, or make sure to use the magic phrase *we're just friends* whenever anyone asks this week.

I want to tell my team to fuck off, that this is a terrible idea, except it's not.

Vaughn bought the video too. Hook, line, and sinker. We chatted an hour ago, and now that he's not pissed and calling me a backwoods woman-hater, he asked if I'm actually into her, or if I'm just doing it to clear my reputation.

I can't honestly tell him I *don't* like her. I do. Do I trust her enough to date her? Not so much. But I like her.

And I want this foundation to work, so when he told me to keep her happy, then you're damn right I'm going to do whatever it takes to keep her happy.

Do I feel guilty? Yeah. It's not cool to keep dragging her into this.

But it's for kids who don't have the same opportunities I had when I was growing up. Kids who need support and help to get involved with team sports and have a place to go after school, and who wouldn't have a chance to play on a team without us.

If everything falls to hell, if people quit buying RYDE clothes—and the clothes from my other lines too—I'll be okay. I have plenty of money. Plenty of options.

After what I did Friday night, I could just disappear into oblivion, but I don't want to go out like this—the most hated man in America who pulled a shithead move with a really bad joke that I thought my sister would appreciate.

Especially when if I can fix it, I can keep putting my money to good use to help the kids of the world.

So I'll be the asshole who uses Sarah, even if I don't like it.

I double-check that the oven's heating up and I head into the living room with a can of Barq's root beer to reclaim my place between the women on the couch. Score's one-nothing in the bottom of the first. No outs, no runners on base.

"Lead-off home run for Tampa?" I ask.

"Shut up and do something for good luck," Mackenzie grumbles.

I glance at Sarah, who freezes mid-chew on a mouthful of popcorn.

"She doesn't mean kiss me," she says around another mouthful of popcorn.

I'm pretty good at translating full-mouth talking, mostly because it's my first language.

Also, now that she mentions it, I wonder how much luck a kiss could really bring.

Probably not much. Especially once I finally force myself to ask her if she'll pretend go out with me.

Plus, superstitions aren't really my thing, but I'm happy to humor two lovely ladies who believe in them.

I force a grin and settle back against the couch. "Luck comes from all kinds of places," I tell her.

Probably not from doing the Hollywood cop-out of taking a girlfriend to make you look good, but definitely from other places.

Sarah slides her phone out of her pocket, and I go momentarily tense until I realize she's not planning on snapping a picture of the three of us to post on social media, which wouldn't actually be a bad thing for my image. I'm just falling very quickly out of love with the entire word *image*, and after almost having to pay a woman off to not post a sex video of me pre-second-paternity test, I still get jumpy.

But she's pulling up a YouTube feed of a giraffe eating in a concrete enclosure.

Duh. She doesn't want pictures with me. Or videos with me. She wants to be left alone.

But here I am, not leaving her alone.

"Is that the giraffe at the Copper Valley zoo?" I ask her.

"Pregnant and due anytime in the next six weeks," she confirms. "Her name's Persephone."

"Is it bad luck to watch a pregnant giraffe when you're supposed to be watching the Fireballs?" I murmur while I watch the giraffe chewing on grass out of a feeding bucket right at her head level.

"It would be worse luck for giraffes to go extinct."

"Whoa. Did you see the size of her tongue?" I lean in closer to get a better look at the screen. She has an older model phone, one of those smaller devices that Ellie's always telling me fit better in a woman-size hand and a woman-size pocket. I catch a whiff of caramel and coffee, and when my arm brushes hers, she tenses.

I pull back, because *dude*, personal space.

This growing fascination is clearly not reciprocated. "Sorry. Forgot about the bubble."

She shifts those big dark eyes at me, her brows furrowing like I'm a weirdo.

"Personal bubble," I clarify. "Ellie reminds me every time I'm in town that not everyone's comfortable with a stranger being all up in their junk."

Mackenzie coughs. "How many people are watching?" she asks Sarah, who mumbles a number in response.

"Did you just say *five million*?"

"Mm-hmm."

"Holy shit, Sarah. That's *ten times* as many people as were watching yesterday."

She doesn't answer, but her cheeks are getting a splotchy red.

"Whoa, did you see that strike?" I say.

Mackenzie glances at the TV, then back at Sarah. "*Five million*. Not bad for a little bit of public attention with a short video," she says quietly.

Sarah shovels a handful of popcorn into her mouth and shuts down the giraffe cam. She's leaning against the armrest, giving herself a lot of physical space. And she's not looking at either of us, but instead puts all her attention on the game.

And I'm suddenly insanely curious as to why she hates the limelight.

It's obvious she does.

But not obvious *why*.

I know some people are just shy. But I also know she went out and grilled the private security guards we put on the street—for her *and* Ellie and Wyatt and Tucker—and asked questions most people wouldn't know to ask.

And last night's *I speak Hollywood*—there's a story hiding under all that thick dark hair and behind those big brown eyes.

And whatever it is, if we can get past it, maybe she'll still appreciate the extra attention for the giraffes.

Maybe I'm not a total asshole for being here to ask her if we can play the accidental lovers for the world.

Tampa scores twice more, and when the first inning is finally over, Sarah rises and stretches, pulling her jersey high and exposing the barest hint of smooth olive skin at her waist.

I've done shoots with supermodels that haven't left me insanely desperate to know if their skin was as soft as it looks, and I have to shift in my seat to combat the swelling problem in my crotch.

Maybe if she tasers me again, it'll undo whatever the first shock did yesterday.

Except I'm not actually annoyed at my body's reaction to her.

More curious.

And definitely intrigued.

But still wary.

"That was fun," she says with a grimace. "I'm going to check on my bees."

I watch her hips sway under her jersey while she strolls out of the room and into the kitchen.

And I don't even realize I'm watching her ass until she disappears.

But I notice when she's gone.

ELEVEN

Sarah

HOLY HELL, he was close.

I step out into the sunshine and take my first full breath since Beck arrived. My bees are buzzing around the wildflower gardens lining the privacy fence, darting between their blocky wooden hives and the petals, and the gentle hum makes my shoulders relax even more.

I tuck myself into one of the outdoor lounge chairs under my pergola after making sure the little fairy fountains set up around my small yard have fresh water, and I pull out my phone again. I'm doing a quick search for my parents' names on Twitter—even though I'd rather google for a hint about my *Vikings in Space* game or prep more tweets about the giraffes or even just watch Persephone in her enclosure at the zoo—when my back door opens and the underwear ape sticks his head out.

"Hey. You want some of these fries? I can't tell when your friend's being serious about you selling your soul for bacon cheese fries, but I'm definitely not going to pass up a chance to prove I have culinary skills in addition to all these amazing good looks."

Is he really the kindhearted slightly egotistical goofball he's playing? Or is it an act? "If you find it in my kitchen, odds are good I enjoy eating it," I say.

Not all smart-ass.

More *teasing*. Because honestly, it's hard not to relax a little when he's being a total goofball. The self-deprecation in his *amazing good looks* line was so thick, you could smear it on toast.

And it works, because he grins that bright smile that makes his deep blue eyes crinkle at the edges. "It's not just for your cat?"

"I'm not interested in pretending to be your girlfriend," I announce.

So maybe I don't have all the teasing in me.

He ambles out, long arms loose despite being tucked into his jeans pockets.

Also, who wears jeans in this weather? It's pushing eighty-five, but here he is fancy denim that fits his slender hips like they were built for him, which they probably were because of course he'll be wearing his own line of clothes, and a mint green button-down that should make him as dangerous as a plastic Easter egg but instead is cut just right around his wide shoulders, tapering down his trim waist and hanging at mid-crotch, which is probably the length that clothing scientists determined was most likely to induce lust-comas among the general female population.

I have no idea how they determine such things, but I do know that his shirt ending mid-crotch is making me think about his crotch, which is a bad, *bad* idea.

And also the fact that I'm wearing RYDE underwear again makes this entire moment way more intimate than it should be.

He's branded my underwear.

Literally.

He stops to lean against a post in my pergola, the sun shining on his dark hair, all his model fabulousness amplified with the quaint beauty in my small backyard, blue eyes deceptively unconcerned. There's no way a guy like this isn't worried about all the boycotts being announced for his various fashion lines.

"You seeing somebody?" he asks.

"Why does not wanting to pretend to be your girlfriend have to immediately be followed by the assumption that it's because I'm seeing someone?"

"Who's Trent?"

Oh. Right. "An ex. Physics professor downtown writing computer simulations about the Big Bang. He gave me the best orgasms of my life." *Oh, shit, shut up, Sarah.*

And there it goes, right on cue. The smoldery grin and schmootzy charm. "Sarah Dempsey, are you throwing down?"

"That wasn't a challenge."

"No? Because that sounded like a challenge."

"You know what? Maybe it would be if you weren't here to ask me to play your girlfriend." There's *entirely* too much truth in that statement, because even knowing that this charming, self-deprecating, food-loving man is probably playing a role, he's still freakishly hot and funny, and I'm still a red-blooded woman.

He opens his mouth, then rubs his hand over it while he looks away.

Not at all denying that he's here to ask me to play his girlfriend.

"So you've been online today," he says.

"Sure. Let's go with that."

Those deep blue eyes swing back to study me, and yeah, I can see why this guy's looks have made him a boatload of cash.

He plays the doofus well, but he can also focus very well when he has to. Like last night. On the video. And when he left.

"You know about Ellie's accident?" he asks.

I shake my head, unsure where he's going, because yes, I know she was in an accident, but I don't know details. Not beyond the nuggets he gave me last night while we were making our video.

Wow, that didn't sound right in my head.

I really wish I hadn't grown up in Hollywood.

"Happened at Christmas," he says, clearly missing what's going on in my gray matter, thank god. "Year and a half ago. Crushed her left leg. Doctors didn't think she'd walk again."

"Oh. I—that's awful. But I wouldn't know by looking at her now."

He grins wryly. "She doesn't like to be underestimated. Clearly. Pretty sure she could fly if someone told her she couldn't."

"That's technically physically impossible," I point out.

"Dammit, Sarah, now she's gonna have to prove you wrong." His eyes twinkle, and it's not some trick of a camera. But he sobers quickly with a glance next door at Ellie's house. "I was home when we got the call, since it was the holidays. Scariest fucking days of my life. Didn't know if she'd pull through and wake up. Then if she'd walk. And how much care she'd need. How she'd be emotionally and mentally. And I realized I'm home maybe three or four weeks a year. My parents are getting older. Ellie's marrying my best friend. Making his kid officially my nephew. I don't want to be gone so much. I don't want to spend my Sundays running a PR machine when I fuck up. Family's where it's at, you know?"

I cringe, because I see my parents less than he sees his.

It's not that I don't love them.

It's more that I don't fit the ideal Hollywood image, and I never have.

Especially once I hit high school.

Add in all those little bits of my own taste of the level of scrutiny they live with and couldn't always shield me from—yes, I *was* that Hollywood child people speculated about actually being my dad's secret love child since there's no way I had my mother's beauty in me—and I haven't actually been to their house in six or seven years.

We meet in obscure locations unlikely to have reporters lurking around when our schedules line up, and we talk on the phone or video chat a couple times a month.

"You have family?" he asks.

"It's complicated," I say. Lamely.

"But you've got Mackenzie," he points out with a flirty grin.

"So you're selling off your business?" I ask him, because deflection is key.

His eyes narrow. "What?"

"It's how it works, right? You want to step back, so you have to get rid of some of your responsibilities. Unless you're quitting modeling altogether, but you're a package deal. You model your own stuff now. It's not the Beck Ryder brand if some young whipper-snapper comes in and tries to do your smolder for you. So you're selling off to someone who has an up-and-coming superstar who can step into your shoes, but not if you ruin the brand first."

"Somebody's been doing her sleuthing." He winks at me like it's adorable that I care enough to look him up.

Except I didn't look him up, because I've already seen a time or three how celebrities function in the fashion industry.

But now he thinks I'm totally into him.

If he weren't famous—and gorgeous—and I wasn't a giant geek who isn't interested in the pretty boys who are almost always a disappointment, this could go somewhere. But he's only here because he needs something. "I won't be your PR stunt."

He pushes off the post and comes to sit in the chair next to mine, legs spread wide so our knees are almost touching. I hold still, because I don't want him to see my flinch.

"You don't like public attention," he says.

"Or lies," I say, exactly like the hypocrite I am, because lying is exactly what I've been doing most of my adult life.

"Three phone calls, and I can get ten million more people watching Persephone and learning about the bees and the giraffes."

I'd call bullshit, except I know a thing or seven about Bro Code, and I know Beck's the *least* successful of the guys who stayed in the public limelight after the band broke up. It's not that I wanted to follow Levi Wilson or Cash Rivers, but living in Copper Valley, where they all grew up, it's impossible to not know about them.

Which means it's almost impossible to not know that he'd call both of them and ask them to share the video feed of Persephone and talk about giraffes being endangered.

To their gazillionty fans.

They've already publicly stood up for him on their social media platforms, while somehow also apologizing to me on his behalf.

People fuck up, and Beck's my brother from another mother who's going to make this right for the poor girl he pulled into his shit was the gist of both of their messages.

"Is this bribery or blackmail?" I ask.

"I'm not selling," he tells me, "but I *am* working on delegating what I can so I can be home more. Family *is* where it's at. This foundation Charlie told you about last night? It's something my entire family can be proud of. And it'll help so many other families, give their kids a shot at playing sports, at being healthy, at having somewhere to go after school and during the summers. I don't need more money. But making more money lets me help more families. So this isn't bribery, or blackmail. It's a guy who'd like to make a difference in the world asking for a favor that only *you* can give."

"So it's guilt."

"The attention goes away after a while. In six months, nobody will even remember this."

"Exactly. So you can wait six months and then launch your foundation."

"It's not that simple." He leans forward, hands dangling between his knees, a plea lingering deep in his eyes. "This foundation isn't just mine. I'm dragging Vaughn Crawford's name through the mud too for being associated with me, and if I think I do good for the world, I'm nothing compared to him. This is a step *up* for me. And yeah, you can say I'm doing this to save face and keep selling clothes. You could. But if my businesses tank, if I walk away and let it all die, there are hundreds of people who'll lose their jobs. Hundreds of families suffering. I don't sew the clothes. Marketing is a hell of a lot more than me smiling for a camera. Hell, I don't even design anything. I just put my mark on the things I like and would want to wear, and we buy the rights from the designers who couldn't make a fraction of what they make if I didn't put my mark on it. It's not just about launching a foundation. It's about saving hundreds of people's jobs too."

I sink back in my chair and pull my knees to my chest. "That's really not fair."

"We announce the foundation in less than two weeks. And if I don't fix my image yesterday, Vaughn's out, and the whole thing dies, because we need *both* of us in this to make it work. You're my best shot. With the reaction to the video last night, you're my *only* shot."

I'm his only shot.

I open my mouth, but instead of a rational, well-thought-out argument why this is a terrible idea, I say, "Oh, shit."

Because my back gate just opened.

And a potbellied pig in a tutu on a leash just stuck her head in.

No, we're not in an alternate dimension.

Or the circus.

Nope.

That potbellied, tutu-ed pig means one thing.

My parents have arrived.

TWELVE

Beck

SARAH BOLTS to her feet so fast my brain gets whiplash. "What—" I start, but she grabs me by the arm and shrieks, "*Inside!*" so desperately that I don't think, I just move.

Until—

"*Serendipity!* I knew it. I *knew* it! Judson, I *told* you she was keeping a big secret."

"That you did, darlin'."

The voices send chills down my back, and I turn, my jaw slipping as a couple with a tutu-ed pig on a leash shut the back gate behind them.

Sarah's still pushing me toward the house.

Toward her taser.

"Oh, shit, Sarah, *stop*." I dig my heels in, because there's no fucking way I'm letting her taser Sunny Darling and Judson Clarke.

"Nope, nope, nope, no stopping, *get out*." She's holding my arm so tight her fingernails are slicing into my bicep, but I squat lower to make my center of gravity work for me and resist.

Fuck, she's strong.

"They're not dangerous," I tell her.

I think.

I've never actually met them in person, but Cash did. Once. When he starred in that remake of *Blazing Sun* two years ago.

"Sweetheart, have no fear," Sunny says, crossing the lawn with her willowy build, lavender pants, and flowing white ruffly shirt, the miniature pig trotting happily beside her, sniffing at the flowers. "I made a few calls, and I found you the best stylist in all of Virginia. Your debut will be glorious."

"*Mom*. I'm not having a *debut*."

Mom?

I look again.

And *holy fuck*.

Sarah has Judson Clarke's eyes.

And Sunny Darling's nose.

And somebody's splotchy blush.

"We're *not* doing this," she says, and I don't know if she's talking to me or to Hollywood's not-really-retired power couple.

"Holy shit," I mutter.

"Shut up," Sarah mutters back. "Tell anyone and I'll make your life hell."

"I called my friend Giselle, and she's sure she can find you a Dr. Who dress if you want. Or one with fireflies on it. You can still be true to yourself, and you're not compromising your morals by having your hair cut every once in a while. Oh, my, are these beehives? How California of you, sweetheart. Do the bees have names?"

"Cupcake, no!" Sarah finally releases her death grip on me to shoo the pig out of the flowers. "Mom, she's going to get stung."

Judson Clarke stops in front of me and sizes me up. I have a few inches on him, but I feel about three feet tall right now.

I told Judson Clarke's daughter to *shut up and go have some babies*. But *not with me*.

On a public forum.

I'm fucking dead.

"You treating my little girl right?" he asks in a growly drawl that could go head to head with Clint Eastwood's.

"Dad, we're just acquaintances." Sarah tugs at the pig's collar, but it has motivation on its side, and I wonder if it's forty pounds of solid stubborn muscle. "Knock it off."

"You know I don't like men looking at you wrong," he growls. "Or talking to you wrong."

Yep.

I'm a dead man.

"He came to apologize, and now he's leaving," Sarah says.

"I saw that video, little darlin'. He already apologized. So what's he have to apologize for *now*?"

"I guess that depends on if he can *keep his mouth shut*," she replies. *Serendipity.*

Holy shit.

Sarah's *Serendipity Darling.*

And the—the—oh, *shit.*

No wonder she doesn't want to go on camera.

"And I'm nailing that gate shut," she adds.

"I got a guy who can booby trap it for you," I offer.

Judson Clarke narrows his eyes at me, and I swear I just heard him drawl, *try it, punk.*

Sunny Darling frowns. "You mean in a humane and environmentally friendly way, of course," she says. "The environment is *very* important to Serendipity."

Every time she says *Serendipity*, Sarah's left eyeball twitches. She grunts and pulls harder on the pig while a few bees swarm around her head.

"Do you need help?" I ask her.

"I need vodka," she grits out.

"Oh, sweetheart, it's not that bad. Cupcake, come. Come this way, baby." Sunny tugs on the leash, but the pig's still straining to eat the flowers where the bees are buzzing increasingly agitatedly.

Judson Clarke is still eviscerating me with his deadly glare, and I'm having flashbacks to every one of his cowboy movies that I watched as a kid.

And how he had deadly aim.

And always won.

Because he was always the good guy.

Always.

The back door bangs open. "*Sarah!* Bathroom! Cooper Rock is—*oh my god, Sunny Darling!*"

She looks at me.

I look at Sarah.

Sarah Dempsey.

Serendipity Darling.

Who's still struggling with a pig in a tutu in a desperate attempt to save her bees from being pork food or her pork's snout from being bee target practice.

And I thought my life was weird.

Apparently I still need to get out more.

THIRTEEN

Sarah

SO THIS IS AWKWARD.

There's an underwear model who wants me to pretend to be his girlfriend making everyone cheesy bacon fries.

My father's prowling about the house looking for bugs and taking audio notes for himself about increasing security, because *that underwear model's version of security couldn't protect a mosquito in a swamp if we could get into your backyard with a tutu-ed pig on a leash.*

My mother's doting all over Mackenzie, who's so tongue-tied she hasn't even looked at the bloodbath of a baseball game on the TV in the living room, nor has she asked me to explain *anything*, which is making me feel like utter slime.

And Cupcake is trying to hump my cat, who's just lying there under a kitchen chair and taking it like this is normal.

"Get off. *Get off.*" I tug the pig's collar again.

She looks up at me, but she doesn't stop trying to hump Meda.

Yes.

My parents' girl pig is horny.

This isn't unusual.

"You don't have to just take it," I tell Meda.

She *mrowl*s at me and stares up at me like I've betrayed her.

I pull her across the floor by the scruff to get her out from under

Cupcake, who snuffles her disappointment at being denied a new girlfriend.

"Do you like cats?" I ask Beck, because he's the only one in my kitchen actually looking at me, and I don't know if it's because he's figured out who my parents are, or if it's because he knows anything about me before I became *Sarah Dempsey*, or if it's because he was just staring at my ass.

My ass that I got from my father's stocky side of the family.

Not the slender but gracefully curved ass of my mother's side.

Actually, I think I got both of their asses. There's no shortage of booty here.

"Cats are awesome," Beck tells me as he takes Meda and holds her like a football. "Like dogs or kids, except smaller and cleaner. Who's a good kitty?"

He scratches her under the chin, and she gives me another look while she purrs audibly, her blue eye telling me *this is how to treat your queen*, her amber eye calling me a sell-out, the combination clearly broadcasting *if you loved me, you'd scratch me like this all day every day too*.

"You've been friends for *eight years*?" my mom's saying to Mackenzie. "Do you do those role-playing games too?"

"Mom, I don't do live-action RPGs anymore," I say quickly. "Mackenzie's a trash engineer. We met in school."

"Senior year," she agrees, her blue eyes still unnaturally wide. "She was the only other girl dressed up like Zoe at the Browncoat night at the campus theater."

"You went as Zoe?" Beck asks me. He glances down my body, and a slow grin spreads across his lips. "With the tight pants and everything?"

"She was smokin' hot," Mackenzie says.

"I can see it," he says with a nod.

"Stop looking at my daughter," Dad growls.

"What's a Browncoat?" Mom asks.

"It's what fans of the TV show *Firefly* call ourselves," Beck tells her. He gestures to my *Firefly Babies* print on the kitchen wall. "Still so fucking cool. Where'd you get that?"

"Internet." The internet. It's a blessing and a curse.

"Holes in the screens," my dad mutters as he passes by the kitchen windows. "Drafty. Room for a spy cam."

"He's studying up for his next role," Mom whispers to me, which

I'd already figured out, because he's using his Bat-Dad voice, which only comes out when he's prepping for a badass role. "We're not allowed to talk about it yet."

Beck's still petting Meda, who's now purring loudly enough to rattle the *drafty* windows.

And I want to climb up into my bed and go to sleep and wake up tomorrow to go to work like the last three days haven't happened.

There's not supposed to be chaos in my house.

There's supposed to be peace and calm and videogames and occasional crazy baseball superstitions and sometimes *Buffy the Vampire Slayer* or *Dr. Who* marathons, but not chaos.

And not my best friend finding out who my parents are. Not this way, anyway.

Or Beck Ryder playing the unlikely hero who distracted her with questions about the best way to make cheese fries as soon as she realized what I'd been hiding from her for the last eight years, though the distraction only lasted so long before she was back to gaping at my mom.

It's only a matter of time before she figures out I broke up with Trent last year because while the sex was amazing, I didn't want him meeting my parents.

"Where are you going, sweetheart?" Mom asks. "You're not sneaking out the window, are you?"

"Headache," I tell her.

It's not a lie.

"Oh, here. I have some herbal supplements that'll perk you up in no time."

"Don't do drugs," my dad growls at me.

Mom's shaking out her massive Prada bag all over the kitchen table.

Mackenzie's eyes are going rounder at the number of supplement bottles tumbling out.

"Let's see...not the Valerian root or the kava...oh, here. Here's some magnesium. And lavender. Lavender will help you relax."

"Mom, I don't need supplements."

"It's all natural," Dad says as he prowls to the back door. "Better than drugs. Just a deadbolt? *Just a deadbolt?*"

I need to get out of here.

"Actually, I was going to take her out for milkshakes," Beck announces.

"Yes," I agree, even though the fries are in the oven with the bacon *right now* and there's no way I'm leaving Mackenzie here alone with my parents and Cupcake, because that would be mean. "Me and Mackenzie. Because it's too hard to stay here and watch the Fireballs get creamed."

"Oh, honey, that's wonderful!" Mom claps her hands and grabs a hairbrush from amidst the piles of herbal supplement bottles. "Here, just let me do your hair quick, and I think I have the perfect shade of lipstick for you in my overnight bag."

"Need a dog," my dad growls while he stares out the window in the back door, arms folded, and studies my normally tranquil small back yard.

"Mom, I brushed my hair this morning."

"Oh, sweetie, it looks so cute when you put it in a French twist. Just two seconds—"

"I like it down," Beck says.

"Are you *trying* to embarrass her?"

"It's soft." He curls a lock of my hair around his finger, and *dammit*, the gentle tug is lighting up the nerve endings all over my scalp. "And pretty."

He's holding my purring cat and playing with my hair and standing so close that I can feel the heat off his skin, and I have to remind myself that I don't need a guy in my life to be complete.

Especially with all the other complications my life comes with.

And all the complications *his* life comes with.

Assuming he's not just playing a part here.

I mentioned *complications*, right?

"Not enough security," my dad growls.

"Fixing that right now," Beck says.

I dodge my mom and her hairbrush and trip over the pig, who squeals and rushes to Mom, who squeaks and drops the hairbrush, which crashes to the ground and splits in two. The handle spins across the linoleum and comes to a stop at Mackenzie's feet.

"I'm starting to get it," she says to me. "Screw you famous people. Me and Sarah are going to my place."

She links her arm through mine and marches me out of the kitchen, pointing a finger at the three *famous people* who try to object. "Stay. Don't burn the bacon. And hand over the cat. And if the Fireballs lose, it's all y'all's fault."

Beck hands me my cat. My mom just gapes at us, probably

because neither of us is wearing shoes. My dad tries to follow us, but Beck holds out an arm. "She has a taser. She'll be fine."

Mackenzie pulls me out the front door, where the security guys are pulling a random dude with a camera out of my gardenia bushes.

My heart stops. Just freezes in terror.

They know where I live.

They know where I live, and the next step is *they know who my parents are*, and the step after that is *my high school prom is about to be rebroadcast to the entire universe on repeat for the next twelve years*, and maybe not Tahiti.

Maybe I should find a monastery in the Himalayan mountains and take up painting and meditation.

"We got this, Miss Dempsey," the bigger of the two guys says. "You need a lift somewhere?"

"Yes," Mackenzie answers for us, and a third security guy pulls a black car to the curb. Without hesitation, we both climb in.

And I'm really, really glad I checked out all of their credentials when I got home earlier, because otherwise we'd be sticking out like sore thumbs in Mackenzie's Fireball-mobile, because I don't get in cars with security guards whose credentials I haven't checked myself.

"You have so much talking to do," Mackenzie murmurs as we pull away from the curb. "But catch your breath first." She squeezes my hand while I hug Meda tight with my other arm and she purrs like a crazy cat facing white water rapids. "You look like you need it."

"You're not mad?" I whisper.

"Not yet. You *are* going to tell me everything, right?"

"Yes."

"Then I'm definitely not mad. Also, this explains so much. I never really got the Oregon vibe off you, but I figured none of us ever really fully fit in anywhere. And for the record, I *totally* didn't get the Hollywood vibe off you. I mean, how did you even survive that?"

I'm so relieved my throat clogs, and I make a production of digging my phone out of my pocket. "I have to text my parents," I whisper.

I skip Mom and go straight for Dad, because despite the growling today, he's always understood *I need a little space to process that my cozy little life is about to be turned upside down* more than she has.

Also, I tell him to go easy on Beck.

And to make sure the pig doesn't eat my bees.
I really shouldn't have abandoned my bees.
But I'll be back to take care of them soon.
I just need a minute to figure out what I'm going to do next.

.

FOURTEEN

Beck

I'VE NEVER BEEN SO grateful for the paparazzi as I am today, because the dumbass trying to sneak through Sarah's bushes prompted the private security guards to demand we vacate the house while they secure all the surrounding blocks too.

Made for a good excuse to get away from the suspicious eyeball coming from Judson freaking Clarke that I may have aimed myself a time or seven at Ellie's former boyfriends.

I don't want to pass on *this* bit of news to Charlie and my team, but it's going to get out eventually, so I need to.

I'm still sitting on it four hours later though, even after sitting through another video conference with my manager, marketing lead, and PR team lead about the importance of getting Sarah on board with this plan of letting me woo her, because *fuck*.

Just *fuck*.

No wonder she was so gun-shy about the publicity.

And I've just made it a million times worse for her.

Now, I'm hiding from the guilt by teaching Tucker the fine art of Mario Kart back in my penthouse.

"Wyatt's household goods are arriving this week, Beck," Ellie's saying while I race through the cow pasture with Tucker and try not to think about the ultimatum I got from Vaughn when I got back to my place earlier: *I'll give you a week to prove continuing this foundation with you isn't a mistake. But to be honest, Ryder, I'm not feeling real confident right now.* "Are those photographers going to be sitting out there taking pictures of his furniture and boxes?"

Wyatt's spent the last two years at an Air Force base in Georgia, but he just got orders to the military installation north of Copper Valley, and we're all thrilled. He and Ellie will be up to their eyeballs in moving boxes this week.

"Only if they're labeled with…" I pause and glance at the eight-year-old in the gaming chair next to me, who has ears like a bat. "Really juicy suggestions," I finish.

"Have at least seven labeled *toys*," Wyatt offers.

Ellie sighs.

"I know, I know." I dodge that freaking monkey who's always getting me with banana peels. "If I had to mistweet at someone, I should've gone for Levi. Or Cooper. Or Buckingham Palace. They follow me, you know."

"For the train wreck," Wyatt says. "Use your bullet, Tucker. You'll beat Uncle Beck in two seconds flat."

I hit a bomb in the road on purpose, and Tucker zooms past me with a shriek of joy.

The elevator dings, and on cue, even though I took the pans of fries and bacon and a slab of gouda from Sarah's house—yes, I'm buying her new ones—I start salivating. "Pizza's here!"

Ellie ruffles my hair before heading over to get the grub. "You eat like such a teenager."

"Have to live on grass and pinto beans when I'm traveling. I'm eating all the shi—stuff I can cram in my belly while I'm here. Whoa, Tucker, dude, you just beat Luigi. Give it up, little man."

I fist-bump him.

He grins with his big crooked front teeth, and *shit*.

Kid's adorable.

"You like pepperoni?"

"I like anchovies."

I wrinkle my brow. "You like—oh. *Oh*. Anchovies. Yeah, that pizza joint up in Shipwreck." He has good taste. The cool little pirate-themed town out in the Blue Ridge Mountains makes some kick-ass pie in their pizza shop. I glance back at my sister, but she's not carrying in pizza.

Nope.

She's bringing in her neighbor.

Who's not wearing shoes, or carrying her cat like the last time I saw her, but what she lacks in foot apparel and added fur, she's making up for in a steely determination in her gaze. "We need to talk."

"Sure." I leap to my feet, because she basically holds my future in her hands. I wasn't exaggerating about the people who'd have to find new jobs if RYDE and all my subsidiary lines go out of business because of this. Plus she could tell me to waddle down the street bawking like a chicken, and I'd probably do it. "Come on into my office."

Wyatt chokes on a laugh.

Ellie rolls her eyes heavenward with an amused smile.

Or maybe exasperated, but I'm going with amused.

"You have an office, Uncle Beck?" Tucker asks.

"Of course," I tell him. "It's where all my serious work gets done."

Sarah's holding herself stiffly and studying all of us like we're nutjobs. Which is probably mildly accurate. But she lets me lead her around the kitchen to the short hallway to my game room.

What?

I do my best thinking here.

There's something totally Zen about chilling out with some old school Pac-Man or a foosball game.

I shut the door and prop myself on the pool table. "What's up?"

"Is that Donkey Kong? Like the real original Donkey—no, wait. Stop. Never mind. Not why I'm here."

"You like Donkey Kong?"

"Yes. I freaking—*stop it*. Stop distracting me, or I won't get this out." She pushes her brown wavy hair back from her forehead and blows out a short, heavy breath. "I'll do it."

"You'll...?"

"Pretend that I'm falling in love with you. But only under *my* conditions, and *you* have to do all the hard work. And I want it in writing, naturally. And this isn't about money. It's about controlling the story and helping the giraffes. Understand?"

I should be relieved. This is exactly what I want.

Except I'm suddenly not sure she can pull it off. And getting caught in the lie would be worse than doing nothing at this point. "Where'd you go?"

Her nose wrinkles. "To Mackenzie's house. Which I'm sure your security told you."

"After the *Hagrid* thing."

She freezes. And not just a little. She's an ice princess locked in a glacier, complete with the message of *I will bring about apocalypse by snowball if you EVER reference the Hagrid incident to me again* shooting out her pores.

Probably I should've made sure she didn't have her taser on her.

I shift against the pool table and wish I hadn't played Wyatt last, because the dude puts everything away where it's supposed to be. Every time.

So no pool sticks to defend myself or random balls to throw to distract her.

"They're going to ask," I point out. Sympathetically. With my hands over the family jewels, because I'm not always the sexy, charmingly lovable idiot I play on the runway and on shoots. Sometimes I have self-preservation skills. "You need an easy comeback to a hard question, I'm your guy. But I can't help if you don't let me."

I wait while she fights her own breath, those dark chocolate eyes boring into me like her senior prom was my fault.

After this many years in the business, the gossip rags are all easy to ignore. I'm always going broke or being abducted by aliens or partying at geriatric strip clubs and having a love child with Bigfoot's baby. You get used to it.

You accept it's part of the package.

But Sarah didn't ask for famous parents. Or to grow up under the microscope. I doubt she would've changed her name and moved all the way across the country if the *Hagrid* thing at her senior prom hadn't happened. And until I fucked up and dragged her back into the spotlight, she'd found her way out of the gossip rags and the general constancy of being torn down for being unique in the Hollywood world that values the appearance of perfection above all else.

"Control the story," I remind her. "You control the story, you take away their power."

She blinks and looks away, then marches to my Donkey Kong game.

I follow and hit the button to start a game.

Honey. That's the sweet smell she's carrying with her.

Honey.

The game starts, and she exhales a shuddery breath while she takes Donkey Kong up the first level.

"Morocco," she says quietly. "I went to Morocco after...after high school."

"Marrakech?" I ask.

"Everywhere. Rabat, Fez, Casablanca, Marrakech. I took a bus over the mountains to the Sahara. I camped. I rode camels. I read. I perfected my French. I met the most amazing people and I ate pastries every day."

Fuck, now my mouth's watering again. I've been to Morocco a few times, but always on shoots where I had to look like a fucking million bucks. No pastries or cookies for me. The crew would go to a bakery and come back with a plain black coffee for me and piles of candy crack and cookies and honey-coated goodies that I couldn't touch, because fuck if I'm gonna let them airbrush me. "Are they as good as they look?"

"I think my ass can still attest to how good they were. And the mint tea basically changed my life."

"You had it with sugar?"

"You didn't?"

"That's it. I'm going back." The next time I have a few weeks between shoots, anyway. Getting back in shape is always a pain in the ass.

I hear Tucker shriek the magic word—*pizza!*—and my stomach tries to climb out of my body to get to all the cheesy, doughy deliciousness, that I'm eating because stress burns extra calories.

And also because the mini-shoot I was supposed to do at a shelter in New York was canceled this week, which means I *do* have a couple weeks to be a little more flexible with my diet.

Sarah pauses between levels to glance at my abdomen. "You should see a doctor about that noise."

"Nah. Just a bakery. And a hamburger joint. And this guy I know who makes a strawberry malt that'll—oh, shit. Sorry." I wipe the drool and grin at her.

And her *are you for real?* eye wrinkle turns into a smile.

A wide, uninhibited, *you're a big dork* smile that makes her dark eyes sing and shows off those pearly whites and pops out a dimple in her left cheek. "You might want to rethink some of your life choices."

I don't know a single fucking man in the world who couldn't smile back at that gorgeous shining face. "Eh. Has its perks."

Her smile fades as quickly as it came, and swear on my first modeling contract, the room gets dark and chilly.

"I saw a therapist for a while when I came back for college," she tells the game. "We talked about not letting one moment in high school ruin my life forever, but it still makes me almost throw up to think about letting reporters shred my life choices all over again. Especially because it wasn't the first time. I was seven the first time I made a tabloid, and my parents made so few missteps, I was the easy target in our little family. I *like* my life now. It's quiet and I have a job I love and nobody cares who my parents are or where I grew up, and I built a following all on my own of people who care about the world the same way I do."

"You'll get it back," I promise her.

"No, I won't. My boss already texted me to ask if I want to take tomorrow off so I don't bring the circus to work. And the office gossip is asking what you smell like, and my team lead texted to find out what my favorite donuts are for our Monday morning status meeting. They forgot my name on the May office birthday cake, but now they want to know what my favorite donuts are."

"Maybe—"

"No, they don't feel guilty for forgetting my birthday, because I didn't tell them, because then they'd ask if any of my family got me anything, and I don't want to talk about my parents sending me the *Harry Potter* Hogwarts Castle Lego set *this* year because they remembered how much I begged for the sets in high school. And my mom will probably say it's because her psychic told her to, because Madame Susan knew I needed a warning that prom would come back to bite me in the ass."

"Your mom's psychic is Madame *Susan*?"

She turns after demolishing the third level to pin me with those fascinating eyes again. "*That's* what you picked up on?"

"No, I heard it all. That's just the least uncomfortable part. I'm loogry. Sorry."

"*Loogry*?"

"Yeah. I don't get mad when I'm hungry. No hanger here. I get loopy."

"Would you like to take a break to go eat?"

She's adorable when she's all logical. "Nah. I've been through worse."

Her lips part again, her brow furrowing, and she's shaking her head as she turns back to the game. "This is never going to work."

"Why not? I like you. You tolerate me. That's exactly the sort of chemistry all these people will eat up, wondering if we're for real, because this whole show's gonna go down with you ultimately releasing a statement that we're better off as the accidental friends we became after I was a public ass, but that you prefer a quiet life trying to save the bees and giraffes and educate people on solar eclipses not actually being the work of witches. Your parents will go on *Ellen* and talk about how proud they are of you and your engineering work, tell the world I'm a good guy doing good things, plug Persephone again, and in two months, none of your coworkers will care anymore who your parents are."

But I have a very strong suspicion I'll care.

And that's my burden. Not hers.

She's quiet while she runs Kong up the fourth level, and I think she's concentrating on the game, but I'm wrong.

Not unusual.

"I always wondered if I was adopted. My mom can't balance her own checkbook. My dad came home once bragging he'd gotten a role as an engineer, but he was a train driver, not a math-and-science engineer."

"Heh. Ultimate dad joke. That's funny. *Desert Heist*, right? Fun movie."

She slides an unamused grimace my way. "It was *not* a dad joke."

"You sure?"

She pauses, and a light stain of uneven color dances over her cheeks. "Well...no. I guess not. But they still didn't get it when I asked for science kits and Legos and memberships to the science center and birthday parties at planetariums. Mom would always ask if I didn't want a pedicure party instead, and Dad would offer to build me an art hut off the pool house."

I snag a stool and sit, scooting close to her. My childhood was the exact opposite—parents running their own environmental engineering firm, little sister with straight A's, and then me, the goofball who had big dreams but not enough brains to pull them off—but I never questioned if I fit in.

Had to be hard growing up in Hollywood, in the limelight, and not fitting the mold. "Your mom said they hopped a red-eye as soon as they saw the video last night. They were worried about you."

"I worry about them too," she tells me. "Mom went a few years without getting a role, and I thought she was going to fall apart. She had one director tell her she needed a facelift. Another told her she needed to lose ten pounds. One flat-out told her she was too old to ever work again. And meanwhile, Dad's actually declining roles left and right because old is *distinguished* on men but he wants to slow down. But I can't tell her to say *fuck it* and walk away, because it's what she loves. It's who she *is*. I don't understand *why*, but I guess it would be like someone telling me I was too old to care about clean energy or that I had too many gray hairs to talk about endangered species."

"Limelight sucks sometimes." I lean in and point at the screen, because Donkey Kong's about to get a barrel to the head.

"I see it," she mutters. "You know what's really stupid?"

"Soy milk?"

She barks out a surprised laugh. "Are you for real?"

"I spent six years touring the world with four of my best friends. Gets boring. Somebody had to entertain us all, and that someone was me."

"And now I understand why you're famous for your pictures instead of for your interviews."

"I'm going into personal coaching whenever I finally retire from modeling. More people should be surfing this wavelength."

She laughs again, a short, *I can't believe I'm laughing at this guy* laugh, and my day is made.

"So. Tell me what's stupid in your world."

She bites her lip while she leans into the game, battling past the last obstacle before going on to level five.

She has nice lips.

Full.

They're easy to overlook without makeup or gloss, but they're perfect.

It's like she's hiding in plain sight.

"When I was sixteen, I asked my parents if they'd help me set up a blog about pollution. I wanted to be famous for saving the world."

"That's not stupid."

"Maybe. Maybe not. But I thought I'd use their public platform to launch one of my own, when it turns out, I'm not built for life in the spotlight."

I don't answer, because I don't agree. If there's one thing I've learned in fifteen years in public life, it's that you never know what you're capable of until you try, and there's no shame in using the path you've got to get there.

I never meant to go into modeling and fashion, but it found me, and I apparently have an eye for it—or something—so I keep hiring the right people to help make me look good, and here I am.

She pauses the game and turns to look at me. "I'm only doing this for the giraffes."

"Why giraffes?"

"Because they really put their necks out there."

Now I'm choking on a surprised laugh. "Dad joke supreme, right there."

She pops another smile, and my dick sits up and takes notice. I tell it to pipe down, because dating in the spotlight is hard enough without adding real attraction to the mix.

Plus, I'm a relatively bad judge of who wants me for me, and who wants to take advantage of me.

I want to trust her—she's pretty upfront about what she wants, but she's also a daughter of Hollywood. She knows how these games work.

"Seriously," I push. "Why giraffes?"

Those big brown eyes watch me warily, and I think she's going to blow me off when she says softly, "They're awkward and weird and still beautiful just the way they are. It's inspiring."

I'm not overly familiar with that tight heat cramping my lungs, but I think it might be my heart cracking a little at the implication that she only sees herself as awkward and weird.

Yeah.

I think I have it bad, whether I like it or not.

She shakes her head. "Anyway. I want a contract."

"With a non-disclosure," I agree, letting it go. Because much as she's growing on me, I'm not the guy she needs to point out that she's beautiful in her own way too.

I come with everything she's worked so hard to get away from, and if there's one other thing I've learned the last fifteen years, it's that if something sounds too good to be true, it probably is.

"The NDA was understood," she says.

"We'll have to go out in public a few times, and my team's already working on finding any public charity event that'll sell me a ticket for some good publicity. If it happens in the next two weeks, they'll want you to go. If they can't find anything, knowing Charlie, she'll create something."

She slides me an unreadable look. "Nice. Blame your team."

"*Blame*? Nah, I'm giving them credit. It's a great idea."

"It's a terrible idea."

I cup her cheeks in my hands, because she's there, and her skin is so soft and smooth, and if we're going to pull this off, we *are* going to have to touch.

Her eyes go wide and connect with mine, and I really hope she's not packing that taser right now, because I can't protect the jewels from this angle.

"Trust me?" I say quietly.

"You're the reason we're in this mess."

I'm grinning again, because there aren't many people in the world outside my family, my lifelong friends, and my assistant who will flat-out call me on my bullshit, and I like that Sarah's not afraid to.

"This is *far* from the worst mess I've ever had to get out of."

One full eyebrow lifts.

"Ask Levi sometime about the elephant in Delhi."

"You know *elephants* are endangered too?"

"Yeah, that's why we saved its life. Cost a shit-ton to cover it up and get the elephant a new home, but he's a pretty happy guy in an animal sanctuary now."

Her eyes flare wide. "You saved an elephant?"

I could pull out pictures, but that feels like overkill. "Point is, we've got this. Okay? And if your life isn't back to normal in six months, I'll hop on Twitter and start a war with Chrissy Teigen just to distract everyone. Cross my heart."

"You saved an elephant."

Shit. She's looking at me like I'm some kind of hero. I drop my hands and stand, moving the bar stool back against the wall. I put it in here yesterday so Tucker could reach the controls. "Just the one time. And I almost got the whole band tossed in an Indian jail for it. Like the time I got caught pissing behind a bar in Berlin. But in my defense, I couldn't even walk in the men's room without getting asked for my autograph. I just wanted to take a leak in private."

"Thank you."

I shrug modestly and intentionally misunderstand her. "Always happy to set a good example when it comes to taking a piss. I'm not always a fuck-up. You want some pizza?"

She studies me for a second, then a small smile tips her lips up. "Careful, or you won't fit into your tighty-whities next week."

"That's why I'm branching out into tracksuits next."

She smiles, and once again, I smile back.

Can't help it.

Smiles are contagious.

Especially when I have to fight this hard to earn them.

FIFTEEN

Sarah

AS EXPECTED, Monday is a disaster at work.

On a normal Monday, everyone's grumpy and slow and they all pair off to talk to their normal Monday morning gossip buddies about the weekend, the Fireballs—or Thrusters in the winter—a concert or whatever they're binging on Netflix or someone's kids' activities.

This Monday, every last one of my twenty-seven coworkers stops at my desk at our small environmental engineering firm to ask me about Beck Ryder or my parents, because yes, the entire world knows now that I was born *Serendipity Astrid Darling*, geek daughter of one of Hollywood's leading but aging power couples.

Because I didn't edit out the part of the video where I showed Beck my mole. And a paparazzi caught sight of my parents out to eat last night.

And that's before Beck sends a giant bouquet of purple coneflowers and black-eyed Susans, which arrives at lunchtime.

Coneflowers. Black-eyed Susans.

Favorites of bees.

And here I am, trying to stifle the flood threatening to leak out my eyeballs, because I didn't expect this level of thoughtfulness, and I also don't want to believe it was all Beck, because that's dangerous.

And not helpful for getting my work done today.

Also, he probably really isn't as good in bed as Trent was.

Huh.

I wonder if Trent's seen the news.

Sarah, honey, I don't care who your parents are. They raised you. That's good enough for me. I just want to meet them.

He asked to see my parents, and I dumped him the next day.

And I felt horrible for it.

I really did.

But we didn't go to his apartment until *after* he got me hooked on his magic dick, and we didn't pull up his iTunes account to watch movies together until a month later, but he literally had *zero* movies in his account that my dad hadn't been in.

You like Judson Clarke? Guy's a fucking legend.

The sex got not-so-great after that.

For me, anyway.

Which was a shame, because he was super talented.

By mid-afternoon, I'm about to call it a day. I'm getting nothing done, and even my clients only want to talk about Beck and the tweet heard round the world and if I've actually forgiven him or if he's paying me off.

People are ruthless.

Oh, honey, take the day off, my mom said last night when I dropped by their hotel on my way home to apologize for abandoning them and thank them for being here and to explain the situation, because my parents have been Hollywood royalty too long for them to believe that my soon-to-be budding romance with Beck Ryder is anything more than a publicity stunt.

You didn't sign anything without my lawyer looking at it, did you? my dad said. Okay, yes, growled. He's really into whatever role this is. *And your mother's right. Take the day off. You have a trust fund for this exact reason.*

But I didn't want to take the day off.

I wanted normal.

And going out in public and doing my normal routines is good practice for going out in public *with Beck* tonight for our first official fake date.

Because I can't stop the circus.

All I can do is accept that I have to adjust to a new normal and make the most of it, and trust that this really will die down in another month or six.

The end of the day can't come fast enough, but it finally arrives, and I dart out of the building with my head down, because I don't know who's watching.

Mackenzie meets me at my house. She's got a hoodie over her blond hair, sunglasses that swallow her face, and she's wearing a scarf wrapped around her mouth and nose. Yes, around the hoodie too. She's hilarious.

"Seriously?" I say when I open the door for her.

She pulls off her gloves as soon as we're inside, then rips off her button-down track pants and strips out of the scarf and hoodie. Her fine hair stands straight up like she's touching a static electricity ball, and at least I know the weather won't be unbearably humid tonight. "I'm currently unsure as to the level of attention I want just for being your best friend, but I wanted to support you before your date."

"They'll run your license plate, and even if they didn't, you drive the Fireball mobile."

We both look back at her Smart car, painted in Fireballs colors with the mascot on her hood.

"Shit," she mutters.

"But they might think you've been burned in a horrible accident and that you had to have a face transplant," my mom says as she sails in from the kitchen to drop cheek kisses on Mackenzie. "I always cover up when I want them to think I've had a little work done. Such an ego boost, finding out they think you're less saggy and wrinkled when you've just been eating better and moisturizing regularly. Now, come come. We have canapes out in the kitchen, and I need your help convincing Serendipity to wear this lovely outfit I picked out for her this morning."

"I think Sarah looks cute just the way she is," Mackenzie says.

"She's utterly adorable," my mom agrees with a smile aimed my way. "But the paparazzi are ruthless and don't appreciate creative fashion. We need to set the tone if this relationship has any chance of surviving."

"We're just friends," I remind my mom, because that's the script for today. *We're just friends.* And I might not be built for Hollywood, but I know how to deliver a line.

I *am* Sunny Darling's daughter. And despite having to fight for roles now, she's won way more awards than Dad ever has.

Mom smiles. "Mm-hmm."

I roll my eyes. "I'm going to a baseball game, so I'm wearing a geek shirt. It's for good luck."

"It's *totally* good luck for Sarah to wear a geek shirt," Mackenzie agrees.

Mom sighs. "At least let me do something with your hair and makeup."

We compromise on a ponytail and lip gloss—though why a pony-tail needs hairspray, I have no idea—and then I distract her with the suggestion that she do Mackenzie's hair and makeup.

I haven't told my best friend all the details of what's coming with Beck, because I signed a contract promising I wouldn't, but it still makes me feel like a heel for lying to her *again*. I hope she's suspicious.

My parents know. Their lawyer did the final negotiations with his lawyer, with input from my parents.

It's for the best to have Mom and Dad involved.

They've been there, done that, and seen about everything there is to see in Hollywood. They were the smokescreen I disappeared behind when I left for Morocco after high school graduation, and even though Mom insists on calling me *Serendipity*, they helped me legally change my name to escape the shadow of their spotlight.

Beck arrives in a red Tesla Roadster an hour before the game.

"Pansy-ass car," my dad mutters as he peers through the blinds.

"That is so sexy," Mackenzie whispers to me. "Can you be friends with him long enough for me to get a ride?"

"Sure." I'm contractually obligated to stay *friends* with him for the next two weeks anyway.

"You two are so adorable together," she adds. "But if he even hints that your worth is directly tied to your uterus again, by all means, ruin his underwear modeling career."

She pauses, then lowers her voice even more. "I mean by cutting his balls off."

"Got that part," I assure her.

"I trained her to rip those balls off with her bare hands," my dad growls from my recliner.

"Oh my god," Mackenzie gasps.

"Dad, quit scaring my friends. You can practice your lines tomorrow."

"There won't be a tomorrow if we don't get our asses in the game."

Mackenzie goes from horrified to resigned in a heartbeat. "He's practicing for a movie about the Fireballs, isn't he?" she asks me.

Beck knocks before I have to answer her, and I leap to reach the door first.

My dad pulls one of those moves he learned in a kung fu movie ten years ago, though, and I end up toppling backwards over the armrest of the rocking chair, almost squashing Meda, who's been camped out on the arm since Cupcake finally passed out cold on the AC vent in the kitchen.

My legs flail, and I fling my arms out to catch myself as I start to roll sideways off the chair, ass in the air.

Dad flings the door open. "Password," he growls.

"Your daughter is a kindhearted genius who deserves better than a dumbass like me?" Beck guesses.

Mackenzie snickers.

"My, he's charming," my mom breathes.

I spin on the floor in time to catch Beck winking at my mother. She fans herself.

Dad crosses his arms over his chest. "Quit flirting with my wife."

"Sorry, sir. Natural reaction to beauty."

I get myself back to my feet just in time for Cupcake to come barreling into the room.

Meda yowls and takes off for the stairs to my bedroom. I dive for the pig before she can follow. "No, Cupcake! No stairs! Mom! Where's her harness?"

"You can't stop true love, Serendipity."

"You can't make my cat love your pig." I'm wrestling with a pig on the floor, in my best *Geeks do it in Binary* T-shirt, trying to save my cat, who loves me most when I have fresh-cooked chicken or when she's delivering a sacrifice or yesterday when I rescued her from the pig and let her hang out with Mackenzie's bobbleheads for the afternoon.

"Your cat was kneading my pig's belly five minutes before you walked in the door," Mom tells me. "She's playing you."

"So…pulled pork for dinner. Good idea or bad idea?" Beck asks.

Mom gasps.

"Bad idea. Got it. Hamburgers good, Sarah? We'll grab some at the park. Here. Let me get that pig for you." He lifts Cupcake, who flails, but despite a grunt or two of his own as he tries to finagle the pig, he gets her in a solid hold and she quits squealing. "Aww, look at the sweet piggy. You want your daddy to take you for a walk, don't you?"

I snag Cupcake's harness off the coatrack behind the door and slip it on her before Beck loses his grip. Once she's leashed and on the ground, I hand the cord pointedly to my dad. "Pretend you're auditioning for the role of a farmer and go distract all the paparazzi."

"I eat farmers for breakfast."

"Okay, Bat-Dad. Pretend you're auditioning for a role as a bodyguard for the pig that will save the world. The fate of humanity rests on your shoulders."

"This game was more fun before you were old enough to date." He's still growling in his tough guy cowboy voice, but there's a twinkle in his dark eyes when he takes the leash.

Beck slings a long arm around my shoulder, which sends a delicious shiver that I ignore down my spine. "You ready to be good luck for the Fireballs?" he asks.

"Luck hasn't exactly been on my side lately," I point out wryly.

"Then you're due." He pulls me toward the door and claps my dad on the shoulder on our way past. "Don't wait up."

Dad makes a noise between a hiss and a growl, and Beck practically pulls me over the covered porch and toward the car.

I try to ignore the four beaters that don't belong parked in the shade of the oaks along the street, because I know there are photographers inside just waiting to get a picture, and I also know they can't hurt me with the three black sedans holding bodyguards also on the street, but my pulse is still in panic attack zones when Beck opens the passenger door for me. Once I'm closed inside, having safely arrived without tripping, my clothes randomly getting sucked off by an unnatural wind, or a bird pooping on me, I suck in a deep breath.

It's just walking to a car.

They can't twist walking to a car. And even if they do, I know the truth, and they can't hurt me.

Beck climbs in the driver's seat and starts the quiet engine.

And here we are.

On a *date* that's not a date.

Alone.

With no buffer in the car to distract from the fact that we basically have nothing in common except that we both know his sister, we both know famous people, and that he pretty much turned my world sideways with a mis-aimed tweet.

He hits the radio.

The soft sounds of "America's Sweetheart," the Bro Code song that launched their career, fills the interior.

Yes, yes, fine.

I know Bro Code songs.

But only a few, and only because my first college roommate was in love with them, and also because *all* the radio stations in Copper Valley play them all the time still.

"Whoops," he says with a grin that says this wasn't a *whoops* at all. He hits a button, and the music switches to a pop song I don't recognize. "Better."

"Reliving the glory days?" I ask him.

He grins wider. "I took Tucker for a spin earlier. Introduced him to the classics. How was work?"

"*How was work?*" I repeat, because it's such a normal, mundane question while I'm sitting in a car that's probably worth more than my house, with a former boy band heartthrob who makes a killing putting his name on other people's underwear.

Again, like the pair I'm wearing today.

Seriously, him getting into women's underwear was brilliant.

Dammit.

That came out wrong.

I *meant* it's really comfortable underwear.

"My parents run an environmental engineering firm," he reminds me while we head out of the neighborhood, his fingers drumming on the white wheel, completely oblivious to the fact that I'm ruminating about our underwear. "I know a thing or two about water-saving toilets and solar panels and the energy clapback of windal speed."

"The—*what?*"

"*Energy clapback of windal speed.* Technical term," he says. "You didn't learn that one in school?"

"That's not a thing."

He grins adorably.

"You're physically incapable of being serious, aren't you?" I ask.

"Everybody loves the class clown."

"Except the teacher."

"Are you the teacher?"

"No way. I hate people. I just like information."

He coasts to a halt at a stop sign and pauses to glance at me. "I hate people too. They're so *people*-ish. All those arms and legs and noses... The noses are definitely the worst."

Once more, he's managed to surprise a laugh out of me.

"People are awesome," he informs me. "They're complicated. Everyone has something they worry about. Everyone has someone they love. Everyone's been through some kind of tragedy. But they still go out to baseball games and smile or head over to the theater and cry. The world's full of good people doing their best, and we all fuck up time to time, but nobody's really evil."

I don't actually hate people, but I do prefer to have a few tight friends to letting the entire world know my business. Also—"*Nobody?*"

"Okay, yeah, photographers who sneak through people's bushes and scum who dox people online are evil with no redeeming qualities. And don't get me started on trolls who call people fat and send dick pics. They all get anal herpes and their mothers call them ugly though, so there's that."

"You're the reason Bro Code broke up, aren't you? The other guys couldn't stand it anymore."

"Yep," he replies with yet another grin, this one totally shameless and not a bit insulted. "But really it was because they knew they'd never be this awesome. So how many frog habitats did you save today?"

I jerk my head sideways at him. "How did you know about the frogs?"

"At the windmill site? Ellie told me."

"Did she tell you which flowers bees like too?"

He smiles, but the oddest thing happens.

He *blushes* too. "Yep. Everything I learned about how to treat a smart lady, I learned from my sister."

He's fed me plenty of stories the last two days, but this is one I don't believe.

Not even a little.

Because the blush is giving him away.

I peer closer at his tan cheeks, to make sure it's not a trick of the light, and *oh my god*.

He's blushing *harder* now.

Beck Ryder.

Blushing.

Over flowers.

A warmth creeps into my belly, and my pulse amps up again. But for once, it's not a terrified race in my veins.

Nope.

It's something entirely different that I *refuse* to think about.

Because this relationship is fake. And temporary.

And only for the good of the giraffes.

And that's what I'm going to keep reminding myself.

SIXTEEN

Beck

WE MAKE it to Duggan Field a few minutes before the first pitch, and with the help of the staff, we sneak in through the players' entrance and reach our private box. Only a few people call me an asshole or ask Sarah what I'm paying her or why she doesn't have better taste or more self-respect.

The two serious personal security dudes on either side of us help.

So does Sarah plastering on a brilliant smile instead of answering a single question, despite the tightening grip she has on my hand.

We're both in sunglasses and ballcaps, and she's so tense I swear her hair and earlobes are extra stiff too by the time we get to the private box that was stupidly easy to reserve tonight.

Fan support's waning for the home team.

The Fireballs are in danger.

"Where's Mackenzie's favorite seats?" I ask as we settle into the aging cushions at the narrow table overlooking the field, where Colorado is finishing batting practice.

She points to deep left field along the third base line. "She's basically in love with Darren Greene."

So, two season tickets for Mackenzie on the left field line. First time Sarah hits the bathroom, I'm ordering them up.

"What about you?" I ask her.

She frowns and takes a slow study of the stands. We're between home plate and third base, with a clear view of the sun lingering over the hazy blue mountains to the west behind the bleachers, and an even better view of the infield and the Fireballs dugout.

"I never followed baseball until I met Mackenzie," she tells me. "So I've never given it much thought."

I drape my arm over the back of her seat and point out to the bleachers. "Ever sat there?"

"Once. The guys around us kept buying her beers, and we were both *very* happy by the time the game was over. Mackenzie caught a home run ball."

"She get it signed?"

"No, we lost fourteen-nothing that game. She threw it back. After dunking it in a beer."

"Ah. Bad luck seats then."

"Definitely," she agrees with a smile. "They have a four-and-twelve record when she gets seats near left field. Everywhere else is like one-and-six. But nowhere near as bad as the bleacher game."

"But did you have fun?"

Her smile goes wistful. "I did. I think I needed baseball in my life. It's *normal*, you know?"

"You never went to see the Dodgers or Angels play when you were growing up?"

She wrinkles her nose. "Once. The Dodgers. I was eight. All three of us went, and that was when Dad was doing the *Stone McFlint* series, and Mom had had two back-to-back blockbusters and more Emmy and Oscar nominations than she could keep track of, and we barely got into the stadium with all the paparazzi wanting pictures and shouting questions, and that was with a six-deep security detail. They both threw out a first pitch, then got invited into the announcer booth, and then into the owner's box, and then to a box where there were some basketball players hanging out, and every time we switched boxes, they got caught up in people wanting autographs and pictures. Plus, they got a picture of me that looked like I was picking my nose, and when I went back to school a few weeks later, everyone made a big fuss of me being *Booger-Eater Darling*."

"Not a great family outing, huh?"

She lifts her shoulder. "That's the life of a Hollywood kid."

I point out to center field. I don't like that people can be shit-heads, and I don't want to dwell on it, or let her dwell on it either. "My favorite seats. Right there. As soon as we were old enough to hop the buses and the light-rail, before Bro Code, me and the guys from my neighborhood would get the cheap seats and hang out with all the bleacher bums a few afternoons every summer. Levi won fifty bucks off one of them once, betting Andre Luzeman would hit a grand slam. And Wyatt would always come up with different things we could spell on our chests. Got sunburned once, except the giant B." I traced the letter over my chest and stomach. "We were *Balls* that day."

"Of course you were," she says with a laugh.

"Tried to do it again after we were all twenty-one. Got all painted up, reserved an entire row, dragged Cash's brothers into it with us, Wyatt too, of course, and we all wore hats and sunglasses and these fake beards. Got the rattiest clothes we could find. Slouched. You know. The whole deal to go incognito."

"Did it work?"

"Nah. First off, we got in the wrong order, so we were the Birefalls, and then, because we looked like really bad ZZ Top impersonators, the cameras zoomed right in on us. We'd hit the jackpot big time with the band the year before. Davis had just gotten his first tattoo, which was all over the tabloids, so between that and Cash's nose, we didn't even make it through the first inning before security was hauling our asses out of there to get us away from the fans who were getting a little rabid."

She's pensive again. "You chose that."

"We did. Had a lot of fun. Still do. We talk sometimes about buying out an entire section of the bleachers just to try it again, but it's not the same, being alone, just us. I like finding out the guy sitting in front of me collects signed baseballs and knows every player's stats by heart. Or that the grandma two rows back is at her first game to give her first grandkid the birthday present of a lifetime. The *real*ness of it. People being people."

"You really like people."

"People are fucking awesome." They are. I don't always trust them these days, but if I weren't famous, I wouldn't give it a second thought.

"What would you be if Bro Code had totally flopped?"

I open my mouth, but the words don't come right out.

Because I've thought about it. Often, matter of fact, and more recently with Ellie's accident putting a few things in perspective.

But I've never actually said it out loud.

A curious smile teases her lips. "What?" she asks again.

"It's stupid," I tell her. "I probably would've ended up working in middle management for my parents."

"That's stupid?"

"No. I mean, working for my parents wouldn't be stupid. They're rock stars. Not like, *actual* rock stars, not like Levi, but, you know, saving the world rock stars."

"So what's stupid?"

Shit, it's getting warm in here. I glance back at the two body-guards, who pretend they're not listening.

"Are you blushing again?" Sarah whispers.

I scrub a hand over my face like I can wipe the pink away. "I wanted to be a doctor."

"Why is that stupid?"

"Gotta be smart to be a doctor."

"Being mildly clueless on social media is not the same as not being smart."

"I was a B student at best."

"And now you've seen the entire planet and launched a billion-dollar empire."

"Building a fashion empire is *not* like brain surgery." And it wasn't even *me*. When the Giovanni of Giovanni & Valentino decided he wanted out, the empire crumbled, my non-compete clause evaporated, and Charlie suggested I sign on with an up-and-coming designer who needed some runway cred. I put my name on some loungewear, and it took off from there.

Not saying I didn't have an eye for what the average guy wanted in casual wear and shoes and board shorts, and that I didn't insist I'd only put my name on clothes that were actually comfortable to wear, just that it found me more than I found it, and I do a better job at hiring the right people and smiling pretty for the cameras in clothes I like than I do at being a fashion mogul.

"You wanted to be a surgeon?" Sarah asks.

"Nah, a pediatrician. More my speed, maturity-wise."

She doesn't laugh. "Can't model underwear forever."

"What? Of course I can. Got it all planned out. Underwear until I'm sixty, then I make Depends super sexy."

"You could still do it."

"Make Depends sexy?"

"No. Be a doctor."

"Huh." Right. Dr. Ryder. Not gonna happen. Even if I enrolled in college today, I'd be in my forties before I finished med school, and who wants a brand-new doctor who's half-naked on all the billboards in town? "Oh, hey—look."

I point to the scoreboard screen over right field.

Sarah glances over and does a double-take. "Is that—did you—" She whips her head around, looking at the sparsely-populated but slowly filling stands. "You got Persephone on the jumbotron."

"Who, me? No way." Of course I did. "She's famous now. *You* made her famous. Bet they're showing her all across the country."

You can do it, Persephone! flashes across the bottom of the screen under the live feed of the giraffe swishing her tail and pacing in her concrete enclosure at the zoo. The words of encouragement are followed immediately by *Save the giraffes* and an animal conservation website.

Sarah blinks quickly. She's getting splotchy in the cheeks again, and her chin quivers. But she still turns in her seat to face me.

And then takes me completely by surprise when she cups my cheeks and presses a hard smacker right to my lips.

My body lights up like a match in the desert, flaring to life under her touch, and I know I need to let her go, to not take this any farther, that it's not smart or even wise—she's probably packing that taser—but I can't help myself.

Her lips are so soft, her fingers brushing the shells of my ears, her breath sweet, her grip firm, and I haven't kissed a woman in months.

Not like this.

And I don't know why it's different. Or maybe I do, but I like being in denial.

I angle my lips to capture hers, one arm tightening around her, the other hand resting on her thigh, and—

And no go.

She leaps back like I hit her with a branding iron. "Thank you," she sputters. "For—for Persephone. And the giraffes. Have you ever thrown out the first pitch at a game? Both my parents did, that time we went. My dad made my mom go first so he could bumble his own pitch if she didn't get hers close to home plate."

I slink back in my own chair, feeling like an idiot.

Of course she doesn't want to kiss me.

I turned her life upside down. I outed her identity. And I'm sucking her back into the spotlight to clear my name.

She's not in this for anything other than the giraffes.

And I have to sit here pretending I'm totally into her for the whole game, because it's a photo opportunity for the tabloids.

That she doesn't even want to be at.

And it's not actually all pretend.

Not for me. I'm *feeling* things.

I just don't know if I can *trust* those things.

"Yeah," I say. She's squirming. I want to squirm, but I know better. "I've tossed the first pitch a few times."

I easily roll into my favorite first pitch story—the one about me missing home plate and beaning the Fireballs' dragon mascot—and I get my head back in the game.

This is about saving my reputation, my foundation, and my business.

It's not about hooking up with the woman I'm supposed to be pretending to fall in love with.

No matter how much more I'm liking her every minute.

SEVENTEEN

Sarah

IT'S JUST FOR SHOW.

This whole game and date are just for show.

Beck Ryder wasn't kissing me because he *likes* me. He thought I was playing the part, and I flinched, which probably ruined whatever look he was going for, but *I'm not an actress.*

I'm just *me.*

"Do you like funnel cake?" I ask when an awkward silence falls between us, because if I've learned anything about Beck in the last two days, it's that he's always starving.

"Oh, hells to the yeah," he replies, a full boyish grin taking ten years off his face.

Not that he looks *old*. He's...what? Thirty-two? Thirty-three?

Definitely old enough to not get excited like a puppy over funnel cake, yet here we are.

With him all but wagging his tail at the idea of fried dough and sugar.

He's adorable. And with those sexy bedroom eyes—it's a lethal combination.

He turns to the bodyguards.

"No funnel cake sold in the ballpark, Mr. Ryder," the first one says.

"Can get a really good hot dog though," the second one offers. "Or a hamburger or some pretzels."

He wrinkles his nose. "Not the same. You want a funnel cake, Sarah?"

"I can settle for a pretzel."

"But do you *want* a funnel cake?"

Twenty minutes later, ballpark security delivers a box of food.

And when I say *box*, I don't mean a little grocery store rotisserie chicken-size box.

I mean a giant box. One of those suckers that'll hold twenty reams of paper and apparently enough grease to slick a pig.

"Ah, yeah, that's what I'm talking about," Beck says.

He starts pulling out take-out cartons and bags, and the scent of fried food fills the air.

There's fried chicken. Waffle fries. Funnel cake. Okra. Peach cobbler.

"Hungry much?" I ask him.

"Starving," he replies. "You want a wing? Drumstick? We have to share the funnel cake. The cameras are watching."

The cameras.

The same cameras that were watching the night I had my first kiss, which was broadcast via all of the gossip rags when it got awkward with a strand of saliva going between his chin and my mouth because I thought he was going for a kiss and he thought we were going for a hug, and I decided to go all out, and my freshman class had a field day with making slobbery nicknames for me for weeks.

I blow out a slow breath and remind myself I'm not fourteen anymore, and that I'm in control of this story, while Beck lifts the lid on the funnel cake, holds it to his face, and sucks in a deep breath over it. "Heaven."

"You really like food."

He breathes in again, nose right up in the fried dough, and I don't know what comes over me, but I tap the carton upward, and he jerks back with powdered sugar on his nose, surprise giving way to an evil, *evil* smile.

"So that's how it's going to be," he says.

"I don't know what you're talking about," I reply, but I'm battling my facial muscles to keep from grinning back, because even if *this* picture goes all over the tabloids, I won't be the only one looking goofy. He not only has powdered sugar on his nose, but his cheeks are dusted, and his stubble and one dark eyebrow look like they just survived a concentrated attack of flurries.

And he's smiling.

He's smiling so big, so uninhibited, with those eyes dancing with utter joy, that I'm in danger of jumping on the joy train with him.

"You know how long it takes to wash powdered sugar out of your hair?" he asks as he draws his finger over the top of the funnel cake.

I'm pressing myself as far back in my seat as I can get, knowing what's coming, and unable to stop smiling back at him. "That assumes I care enough to wash my hair regularly. Ask my mom. She'll tell you. It's once a month for me."

"Come here, Sarah. We need matching makeup."

"Oh, no. It's not even until you're wearing some ranch dressing too. I'm still wearing some sriracha that I spilled last week during a game. See?" I point blindly to my gray shirt while he leans closer, threatening me with a powdered sugar finger.

"Looks clean as a daisy in springtime," he replies.

"You didn't even look."

He lunges for my cheek, and I shriek and yank his hat down his face. He knocks his elbow on the table when he tries to straighten his cap, and the food skitters precariously to the edge.

I lunge for it, he thinks I'm starting a food fight, and we end up in a tangled heap of arms and legs with the funnel cake in Beck's lap and a chicken wing down my shirt.

"Oh my god, get it out, *get it out*," I'm shrieking as I laugh and bend over as far as I can go in my seat while I try to dig it out without flashing any skin.

"You need help?" he asks, angling his head to peer at my boobs, which are squished against my leg. "I could totally be a gentleman and help."

"In your dreams, Ryder."

"You know this funnel cake's all mine now. It's a rule. If you crotch it, you...huh. What rhymes with crotch?"

"Botch?" I suggest as I finally grab the fried chicken and pull it out from beneath my hem. "Flotch? Notch?"

"Yeah. You crotch it, you notch it."

My eyes go wide. "I don't think that's about funnel cake."

He gives me the famous Beck Ryder smolder, and my body jerks to attention. *You could notch me.*

"You gonna eat that wing?" he asks. "The wings are my favorite."

I settle back in my seat and hand it over to him. "I thought the okra was your favorite."

"Favorite thing to sing about."

I bust up laughing again, because *what*? "I'm beginning to understand why Ellie doesn't talk about you."

"Too much fabulousness. She's never been able to deal."

"Uh-huh."

"Okay, okay. It's because I made her sign a contract not to. I'm a terrible diva, and I don't want anyone to know."

"You're a total goober."

His face splits into a grin, and *god*, he's gorgeous. "That's what she says too."

For once, I believe him. He snorts out a short laugh as he plucks a big piece of fried dough off his lap. "Hey, there's a ball game going on."

I glance out at the field. The scoreboard says we're actually fighting a close game in the third inning. Mackenzie's probably at the edge of her seat, biting her nails.

She gets so tense during the close games.

"Are you going to throw more food at me if I check to see if Mackenzie's texting me orders to go to the bathroom?" I ask.

He sweeps another glance down my body, and a warm flush follows everywhere his gaze touches. "Maybe."

"I know how to transport bees and hide a hive in your bed."

His laugh is rich and long, and while I know we need to look like we're getting along for the cameras—and yes, there are at least seven that I've been able to pick out, all pointed our way—it feels very, *very* real to have him laughing at one of my jokes.

"You're not allowed to hang out with Wyatt. Ever," he informs me.

"Too bad you're leaving town and he's moving in next door to me. Looks like you're screwed."

He just grins again.

Say what you want about the man, but you can't deny he's one happy guy.

Funny, that.

I ran away from the spotlight to find my happiness.

And here he is, basking in it. *Happy* about it. Even after having all manner of nasty things said about him in the last three days.

In a world revolving around looking good, he fits in well.

We couldn't be more polar opposites if we tried.

But that doesn't mean I'm not in danger of succumbing to his charms.

So it's time to remember who my parents are. Find some of that face to give the world. And tuck my heart in tight.

Because I'm not letting that world break me again.

No matter how amazing it feels to know that *I'm* a small, direct part of the reason the Fireballs are once again showing thousands of people how Persephone's doing over at the zoo.

That's what I'm doing this for.

To save the giraffes.

EIGHTEEN

Beck

WE LINGER IN the box after the game to let the stands clear out. We were supposed to leave before the seventh inning, but the game was close, and Sarah was really into it once we both got cleaned up and the Fireballs' defense stepped up.

Add in a two-run homer from my buddy Cooper Rock, and it looked like we could pull it off.

"We should've left an hour ago," she says, frowning.

"You were having fun."

She turns those dark eyes on me, and they're not full of laughter like they were when she shoved my face in the funnel cake—the guys are going to love her—but they're not mad either.

Just pensive.

"Better photo shots, I suppose," she says.

I shrug. "Maybe."

The plan is for me to take her home, then we're going our separate way for two days.

Let the pictures from tonight trickle out, let suspense build, both of us reply *we're just accidental friends*, her parents issue statements from their publicists asking for privacy, and then we'll get together again Thursday for dinner at a comedy club in the warehouse district downtown and let it slip that she's accompanying me to a Friends of the Zoo black-tie fundraiser dinner that Charlie literally pulled together for the organization *this morning* because she's magic, and because I told her if we were going to do a fundraiser, it had to be for Sarah's favorite pet project.

But this plan of taking Sarah home feels wrong. Or maybe I just don't want to let her go yet.

"When do you have to be at work tomorrow?" I ask her.

"Eight or nine. But I'll probably go in early to get work done before everyone else is there. It was…interesting today."

I swing my chair around and study her while the two body-guards check out the situation in the hall. "Lots of gossip?"

"It's human nature. But most of my coworkers were polite about it. Although I think some of them think I'm stuck-up now because I don't socialize much at the office and apparently it's because I'm *better* than everyone else since my parents are stars." She frowns, and I hate that frown.

That frown says that it's inevitable, and she doesn't like it, but it is what it is.

"I don't *like* not trusting people to not gossip about me," she says quietly. "It's the whole reason I never told anyone here who my parents are. Mackenzie's known me longest. She's been my best friend since before I knew any of my coworkers. If anyone should be offended, *she* should, but she's just rolling with it. The people at work, though…"

I nudge her. "Says you have good taste about who you let in your circle. There's a reason my best friends are all from home."

"One of my closest high school friends was the reason the owl thing happened. And I didn't know it until later, but one of my other supposed friends kept telling the paparazzi when we went to the movies or out for semi-private gaming nights, which was how pictures of me leaving the bathroom with toilet paper stuck to my heel or spilling soda all over myself or sitting with popcorn stuck in my hair always seemed to find their way to the gossip pages."

"Aw, fuck, Sarah. That sucks."

She shakes her head, eyes pensive and not looking at me, as though she's reliving it in her head. "The stories always got more out of control than they thought it would, but the owl story especially. If it had just been the pictures—well, it's not like I hadn't lived with that my whole life, you know? But when the gossip rags came call-ing…she was the one they quoted with all the rumors about what I liked to do in my spare time."

"You want me to send my mom to your office to give them all

what-for? She's got this speech that would make a saint feel guilty, and they'll be bringing you fresh chocolate chip cookies and home-made ice cream for weeks."

She turns a smile on me, and I swear the entire ballpark gets brighter, and the sun set an hour ago. "Like you said, another few months, and nobody will even remember this happened."

I will.

I will most definitely *always* remember this happened. "Gonna be late by the time I get you home. You want, I can put you up in one of my spare bedrooms. Just a few blocks over."

"Sleeping with you is not part of this agreement."

"*Spare* bedroom. Hell, you can have a whole apartment. I own the building and keep the floor below mine open for my team, because it's easier than making hotel arrangements all the time."

"You own *the whole building*?"

"Guy told me it was a smart investment once."

"A random guy. A random guy told you to buy a—how many stories tall is that thing?"

"Forty-six. And he wasn't random. He was a guy my parents did a lot of work for back in the day."

She's doing the fish, which could be a dance move if people put their arms into swimming the way they put their mouths and eyeballs into gaping.

But this is why I'm in fashion and not choreography.

A guy's gotta have *some* weaknesses.

"I was diversifying," I tell her. "And I got it for a steal, since it needed heavy renovations through the whole building."

"Which your parents did," she guesses.

"Well, yeah. Nepotism's important."

She shakes her head, clearly caught between wanting to smile and roll her eyes. "I'm trying to picture my parents helping to get me a film role, and it's not working."

"That's just because Hollywood's been lame lately with the real science movies."

Her nose wrinkles. "Yeah, that's all the geeks in Hollywood are good for, isn't it?"

"All clear, Mr. Ryder," the beefier bodyguard says, saving me from having to dig my whole leg out of my mouth once more. "Let's go."

We clap our hats and sunglasses back on, and we follow him while the second guard brings up the rear.

The walkways are mostly deserted except for staff, who are cleaning or nudging along the last of the slow-pokes. All's fine until we get almost to the valet stand at the executive parking garage.

I can see my car waiting right up front on the street, but there's a crowd of reporters between us.

"Serendipity! Serendipity!"

"Are you really dating?"

"Over here! Smile over here!"

Sarah grabs my hand while the two bodyguards hustle us through.

"Is this a publicity stunt?"

"Did you know each other before the tweet heard 'round the world?"

"Are you sleeping together?"

"How long have you been dating?"

She squeezes tighter, and holy *shit*, she could probably crush a raw egg with her bare hands.

"Ignore them," I murmur.

"Been doing this a lot longer than you, Ryder," she replies, her lips tipped up, and I grin at her.

I can't help it.

Her hand might be yelling *Save me! Save me!*, but her mouth has it covered.

"Yeah?" I murmur back in her ear. "Want to toss them a bone?"

Her lips twitch higher.

She really does have gorgeous lips. Plump and soft.

"No bones," she tells me. "But nice try on an excuse to kiss me again."

"Just because I offered you a guest room doesn't mean you wouldn't be welcome in mine. Never let it be said I'm not a gentleman first, when I'm not making an ass of myself."

We reach my car, and I pull open the passenger door for her before the valet can fight the crowd around the car. He's barely holding his own at the driver's door.

When I get around to his side, I slip him a few benjamins and climb in too.

Sarah's slouching so low in her seat, I think her ribs might have melted into her hips. "The game was fun. That, not so much."

"Should've tossed them a bone."

She pulls her sunglasses off and glances at me, and before I realize what she's up to, she hits the button to roll the window down.

"You want a real rare sight, go check out the giraffes," she calls. "Underwear models are a dime a dozen." She blows a kiss and hits the button again, sinking back into her seat once more as a loud, shuddery breath slips out of her mouth.

I squeeze her knee. "Feel better?"

"I feel like I ran a marathon between the corner and this seat. Where'd the bodyguards go?"

I check the mirror. "Right behind us."

It's hard to rev an engine in an electric car, so I hit the horn in a happy pattern—tappity-tap-tap, pause, tap-tap—and then inch the car forward until the reporters back off and give me space to go without running over anyone.

"Thank you," I tell her quietly.

I don't know what else to say.

The very fact that we got mobbed with questions about if we're dating instead of what an asshole I am suggests this is working exactly like my team and I want it to. But making Sarah face the reporters after just a couple of the stories she told me tonight makes me feel lower than dirt.

"Every time I start to think I could handle a little more attention on my blog and social media feeds, I realize I'm wrong," she says. "I don't know how you live like this."

"It's not always that bad."

"And sometimes it's worse."

True enough. Especially back in our Bro Code days.

"You like ice cream?" I ask her suddenly. Because she looks utterly defeated, and I have a desperate need to perk her up.

"Seriously?"

"Always makes me smile. Look like you could use some of that."

"I'm fine."

"I've had a sister almost my entire life. *I'm fine* doesn't work on me."

"My siblings were all ferrets or armadillos or potbellied pigs."

"So we basically had the same childhood."

No laugh.

She's getting ice cream.

I turn left when I should go right, and she sends me the suspicious eyeball of contemplation.

And by *contemplation,* I mean she might be contemplating searching my car for a taser to use on me.

"Cookies, cake, ice cream, crème brûlée, banana pudding, or dog biscuits?" I ask.

"*Dog biscuits?*"

"I would've picked the ice cream, but if that's what you want..."

"You really want dessert?" The color's coming back to her cheeks, the light to her eyes, and I want to hunt down her former best friends and slather them with honey and leave them next to an anthill for a few days for putting this much distrust into Sarah's nature.

"Hell, yeah, I want dessert. I can't take you home to your parents looking like you got attacked by feral cats in heat singing bad Broadway tunes. Dessert cures everything."

I grin at her.

She doesn't grin back.

Huh. My charms must be wearing off.

"Or I can take you home," I say sheepishly.

"You know University City?"

"Nope. Books aren't my thing."

"Whatever. You probably snuck over there when you were sixteen to sit in the library with reading glasses on to pick up the older chicks."

Huh. She didn't exactly nail it, but close enough. "That was Tripp. He always went for the more intellectual types."

"Me too. Head down Veterans Parkway toward CVU's amphitheater."

"Wait, you were trolling the college libraries for guys when you were sixteen?"

"Yes. I wanted one of those hot studs at UCLA to talk physics to me."

"Aw, look at you, catching on and schooling me. Wait. Mackenzie said you grew up in Oregon."

When she doesn't answer, I sneak a glance at her.

She's gone splotchy again. "What, you've never put on a disguise, faked an accent, and told people you were Italian?"

"Well, yeah, that's a normal Tuesday for me. But she's your best friend."

"I didn't know she was going to be my best friend when I told her I grew up in Oregon. And I like Oregon. We went to the coast there once for vacation when Mom was getting ready to shoot in Seattle, and nobody bothered us, and we hiked all over everywhere, and you could see the stars all the way out to the edge of the galaxy at night, I swear you could."

"Good wine," I say.

"I was in grade school."

"Probably still good back then."

She lapses into silence, and I realize she's staring at me.

"What?" I ask.

"Is it an act, or are you really like this all the time?"

I grin while I turn onto the ramp to Veterans Parkway. "Can't tell you all my secrets, Ms. Dempsey. That'd ruin all this beautiful magic."

"Hm."

She's quiet the rest of the drive, directing me down the dark winding streets of the campus until we stop at a strip mall about two blocks from CVU's library. An open sign glows red at a shop between a dry cleaner and a drug store.

"Kefta?" I couldn't stop a smile if my life depended on it. "Is this what I think it is?"

"You want dessert or not? I'm in the mood for chebakia."

"Oh, hell, yeah."

The parking lot isn't deserted, but it's not full either. Good sign.

The bodyguards walk us in. We lost the paps a while ago, but this is an unscheduled stop, so who knows who's waiting inside?

As soon as the glass door shuts behind us with a jingle of bells, my mouth waters. I smell cinnamon and cumin and lamb, and something sweet too. It's a typical strip mall restaurant—small entryway with a cash register on a glass counter and a dark wood hostess stand —but the lights are dim around the corner, and I follow Sarah as she peeks her head around.

Several low round tables. Rich red cushions on the matching low benches with the tables separated by shoulder-height, dark paneled walls. Paintings of high-walled medinas, the coast in Casablanca or Rabat, and the Atlas mountains hang on the deep red walls.

A woman in a hijab notices us and hustles over. "I'm sorry, we're —Sarah!"

Her accent is heavy and her smile is bright.

Sarah slips easily into French and says something so quickly that I can't catch it.

Not that I speak French.

But I've picked up a thing or two here and there. Can't travel the world and be a total dumbass, despite what I might play on Twitter.

The woman laughs and replies, also in French, and the only words I'm catching are *welcome, delicious,* and *dragonfire.*

I probably got that last one wrong.

But then, considering we just came from the ballpark, maybe not.

"No, no, you come and sit," the woman finally says. Her dark eyes dance over me. "But not him. He's fired."

Sarah cracks up. "He should be, shouldn't he?"

"Utter disgrace, to speak to you so."

"He's trying to make amends."

"Wearing that?" the woman asks with another sweeping glance over my jeans and Fireballs jersey.

"He's never had mint tea the right way."

Ah, shit, now my stomach's growling.

"Ah, fine, fine, he can come too. But no baboon business."

"Thank you, Fatima."

"Thank you," I agree.

Fatima shushes me. "You get the leftovers."

Sarah purses her lips, but she can't hide her smile. "That seems fair," she says.

I nod. "Very generous."

And when she tilts her head back with a short laugh, I feel like I won the game.

NINETEEN

Sarah

BECAUSE BECK apparently can't drive on a full stomach—and he's
very full of mint tea and chebakia and Moroccan shortbread cookies
—I get to drive his Tesla.

And, yes, it's really sweet, and I am *definitely* making him take
Mackenzie for a ride before our contract is over.

He grunts his way through climbing out of his seat when we get
back to my house. The bodyguards pull in right behind us. Three
beaters are parked across the street.

Awesome.

I let us in through the front door, and an alarm instantly erupts
and wails. My dad leaps off the couch. "Freeze, asshole," he growls.

"Dad! Shut it *off*!"

Meda darts through the living room and dives behind the TV
stand, knocking over my Captain Mal Funko Pop! figurine. Cupcake
barrels in from the kitchen, confused as hell and running into the
furniture, and oh, jeez, Mom put her unicorn eye mask on the pig.

Cupcake's flying blind.

The security guys shove Beck to the ground, then the shorter one
leaps up to grab the motion detector my dad's whacking against my
carved walnut buffet, but it keeps wailing.

"Judson?" Mom hollers. She comes sprinting down the stairs in a short pink bathrobe, her matching unicorn eye mask high on her forehead just as the noise finally stops. "Judson, are you smoking bacon in the evaporator again?"

We all stare at her.

She blinks once, twice, then turns around and goes back upstairs without another word.

"Say something about my wife talking in her sleep," Dad growls at Beck, who's slowly rolling to his feet while clutching his stomach. "Go on. Make my day."

"Those unicorn slippers are the bomb," Beck replies. "Are the flashy lights aftermarket? Or did they come like that?"

We all look at Dad's feet, and dread slithers up my spine, because Dad does *not* like to have his footwear mocked.

But Beck's enthusiasm apparently seems genuine enough to pass the Dad test. He grunts and nods. "Aftermarket."

"Nice. I had turtle slippers that sang when we were on tour. Drove Cash nuts when I'd set them off on the bus. He used to threaten to toss them to the crowd every night."

"Turtle fucker," Dad growls.

"*Dad!* Gah. What are you doing here? Why's Mom sleeping in my bed? What about the hotel?"

"Didn't trust this good-for-nothing nudist to not take advantage of you."

"I think I can handle him."

"That's my girl. Still don't trust him."

"Dad. It's bedtime."

"It's past bedtime."

"Exactly."

"Hotel's overrun with spies. The Euranians are invading downtown. Need to get to safety."

"*Dad.*"

"Sarah." Beck puts a hand to my shoulder and squeezes, and awareness floods my skin and makes my breath catch. "He's right. The Euranians are dangerous."

"Do *not* encourage him," I warn.

"Take cover," Dad growls. "The basement. Go."

"I am not—"

But Beck's scooping up Cupcake, who's still ramming into things blindly, in one arm while tugging my hand. "I've got her, sir. I won't let the Euranians get her. You better check on your wife."

"My wife is dead, you bastard."

Beck deposits Cupcake in the pig bed by the no-longer-functional radiator in the kitchen and pulls me to the basement door. Meda slinks in with us.

"He used to have fun roles," I sigh as I reluctantly let myself get shoved down the stairs. "But the *Euranians*? Really?"

"Could be worse. He could be building a ghostbusting machine in the backyard."

He's not wrong, but I don't know how he knew Dad did that for his role in that alien movie, and yes, I said build a ghostbusting machine for an alien movie. *That* never made the tabloids. And if Mom's sleep-walking, she's probably on a bad mix of herbs and supplements.

"Fuck, I'm full. You got a couch down here I could crash on for a few?"

"Uh…no."

I flip the basement lights, and Meda darts into the shadows. There are boxes piled all over, plus a shipping crate that we barely got down here, and shelves crammed with my childhood astronomy books.

"Whoa."

"Good *whoa* or bad *whoa*?" I ask him.

He slumps against the only stretch of wall open and rubs his stomach. "Is that the *Serenity*? The actual ship?"

I glance at the movie prop, still half-concealed in a wooden shipping crate amidst other boxes, and I nod. "Dad knew somebody who knew somebody on set when they were taking everything down. They'd been storing this for me for *years*, though I didn't know it. So when I told them I bought a house, they shipped it to me."

He starts to grin. "You have the fucking *Serenity*."

"You really watched *Firefly*?"

"On repeat for *hours* on the tour bus. We'd act out the scenes when we were really bored. Always made Davis play Kaylee."

"And you were Jayne."

He laughs. "Nah, I let Levi have Jayne so I could play with Wash's dinosaurs. Can I take a picture? The guys are gonna shit when they see this. Levi's been trying for *years* to find this thing."

I don't answer right away.

It's not that I don't trust him—he seems genuine enough, and I've spent enough time with him now that I'd like to think I can trust my judgment about whether he can be trusted—but I've trusted people before.

And while I'm pretty sure he *gets* it, I'm still working past old habits.

"Or maybe later," he says quickly. He shoves off the wall and grimaces.

"Still full?"

"I'd do it all over again. That tea was amazing."

He's so enthusiastic about *everything*. Not just food. But movie props. Playing a role with my dad. Unicorn slippers.

"Do you ever get tired of being happy?" I ask him.

He barks out a laugh. "No way. Why would I? Being happy's the best."

"Are you ever *unhappy*?"

He heaves a happy sigh. "Yeah. Time to time. It sucks. But the world's a pretty fucking awesome place. I mean, it would've been cool to live with the dinosaurs, but they probably would've just eaten us, and we'd be extinct now too, so I guess I'll take having the internet and being able to fly to anywhere in the world and meet new people and try all the food."

I gape at him, and that's when I realize what's going on.

He's a robot.

"Take your shirt off," I tell him.

His brows lift, but his lips spread into that slow smolder, and he does as asked, slowly undoing the buttons one at a time. "Like this?"

"Faster."

The jerk slows down. My nipples go hard. My tongue goes dry. And he slowly peels the shirt off his shoulders in a striptease that's making me both horny as hell and blotchier than my mom that time she let me put sunscreen on her when I was three.

I swallow hard and twirl a finger in the air. "Turn around. I need to find your off switch."

"My...off switch?"

"Yep. I know when I've been sent a Beck-bot. Where's the real Beck Ryder? He's in hiding in Egypt or Australia or somewhere, isn't he?"

He turns, letting me inspect his back, including that birthmark that really does look like a Teenage Mutant Ninja Turtle, but—to quote a certain underwear model—*whoa*.

Real skin.

It even pebbles into goosebumps under my fingers as I poke and prod him, looking for evidence I've been punked, even though I'm entirely too rational to fully believe he could be a robot.

"Do you really think I'm a robot, or are you just copping a feel? I'm good with either one. Just curious."

I don't know what I am, but I know that now that I'm touching the smooth skin of his back, tracing the lean planes of muscle and hard knobs of his ribs, I don't want to stop.

I haven't slept with anyone since Trent.

Kinda lost its appeal when I realized I would never be able to put my full self into the emotional component of sex.

"Sarah?" he says, his voice going gruff.

"I'm thinking," I whisper.

My fingers trail lower to the twin dimples above his waistline.

"I didn't try to kiss you for the cameras," he says quietly, something in his voice making me think the confession is just as hard for him as it would be for me. "I just wanted to kiss you."

"Our relationship is just for show," I reply, equally hoarse, because my pulse is ramping into dangerous territory and I'm getting a drunken buzz in my nether regions, which are solidly in favor of seeing if he's even half as good with his equipment as Trent was. "Not for real."

His ribs are expanding and contracting rapidly. "I had a lot of fun with you tonight."

"You'd have fun with a professional fun-killer." Why can't I stop touching him?

"I want to kiss you again."

"That's a bad idea."

"Says the woman who's stroking me."

"Your robot pheromones are hypnotizing me."

"Sarah."

Oh, crap, he's using my name against me now too.

But he's funny. And he's sweet. And there's literally not one thing about him—beyond how we met and the fact that he's a celebrity—that I can find fault with.

He's apologized profusely.

He adores his mom.

He loses video games to his nephew. On purpose.

And I just *like* him.

What's the harm in kissing?

I miss kissing.

And I've never kissed a man who knew *all* of who I was. About my parents. About the Hagrid incident. I've never even told a boyfriend about my year in Morocco.

"There's no off-button back here," I tell him.

But there is a very shapely ass clad in RYDE-brand denim that I could squeeze, if I was the bold type.

He turns, and I drop my fingers and look down, but my eye catches on the bulge in his jeans, and there's *no freaking way* Beck Ryder's turned on because of me.

Is there?

I go out of my way to *not* look sexy.

But if he's stuffing his briefs, he wasn't earlier, which suggests he's either turned on by me, or he was thinking about internet porn.

He hooks a finger under my chin and lifts my face so I'm looking up at him.

So tall. So tall, and lean, but also wrapped in a layer of sinewy muscle that I want to trace.

And lick.

I am in so much trouble.

"I like you, Sarah Dempsey," he whispers.

And those blue eyes aren't lying. They're not overflowing with confidence or ego or self-importance.

They're cautious. Searching. Like he knows he's sneaking out on a limb that might or might not hold his weight, but that apple at the end is worth the risk.

I'm his apple.

How am I his apple?

"I'm trying really hard not to like you."

His eyes crinkle when he smiles, like he knows I'm lying and that I'm not trying very hard at all, and I *do* like him, and I am *so* done for.

There aren't any cameras down here. No prying eyes. No reason for him to pretend he likes me when we have a contract that very specifically spells out that this is a bad, bad idea.

But my lips are tingling and my lady bits are stirring and his skin is so warm and soft over rigid muscle right there at his waist where my hand has accidentally fallen, and when he lowers his lips to mine, I don't fight it.

Because I want to know.

I want to know if this is all a fluke, or if it's the mint tea talking, or if it's the weird circumstances, or if he's secretly that turned on by the fact that I have a replica of the *Serenity* starship.

"You have the prettiest eyes," he murmurs against my mouth, his lips teasing mine, his breath warm and sweet.

I'm going to do this.

I'm going to kiss Beck Ryder.

Right—

"Coast is clear!" my dad bellows. The basement door hits the wall with a crash. "Go! Go now, before the Euranians come back!"

We leap apart as his footsteps thunder down the steps. Beck snags his shirt, and he's still buttoning it when Dad reaches us.

I dive into digging through a box of comic books, because it's the closest thing I have.

Dad looks between us. I don't have to look up to know he's threatening to murder Beck with his eyeballs.

"Were you compromising my daughter?" he growls.

"I was trying to figure out what the birthmark on his shoulder reminds me of," I say desperately as I lift a comic. "I'm positive I've seen it in this—erm—*Buffy the Vampire Slayer* comic."

"Whoa, holy shit, you have—ah, yeah. Birthmark. *Buffy*. Like one of the monsters or something," Beck says.

I glance at him.

He's ogling the box of *Buffy* comics I was just riffling through.

Which shouldn't be a surprise. If he likes *Firefly*, it stands to reason that he likes *Buffy* too.

"You have three minutes to get your sorry ass out of my house," Dad tells Beck.

"Dad. It's *my* house."

"I've commandeered it for the mission. And the mission is getting this nudist out of here. He has his own playbook. I don't like it. I don't like it at all."

"It was an honor to take your daughter to a ball game, sir," Beck says.

"You're damn fucking right it was," Dad growls.

Thank you, I mouth to Beck through a smile, because I don't know what else to say.

He grins back, and the wings flying my heart into my breastbone slow their flutter. "I'll call you later," he says.

Like we're teenagers who just got caught making out in the parents' basement.

"You'll call me first," Dad growls.

"Gotta go," Beck replies. "Before those Euranians get back."

He flashes me a lopsided smile that seems to be equal parts amused and frustrated, and he slips up the steps.

"Dad," I say.

He, too, grins at me, dark brown eyes twinkling merrily. "You should've dated more in high school," he growls. "This is fun."

My life, ladies and gentlemen.

This is my life.

TWENTY

Beck

TUESDAY MORNING, I'm in the middle of a virtual staff meeting on the floor below my penthouse and I'm losing my fucking mind.

"Crawford might be placated for now with all those pictures from last night and public opinion swaying back your way, but there's no telling if he'll stay that way for long," my manager, Bruce, is saying from his over-decorated office in LA. "You need to get caught buying the frumpy girl flowers. And can you get her to brush her hair?"

"Her name," I say distinctly, "is Sarah."

"Right, right. What are her parents saying? You've met them, right? Judson fucking Clarke. If we could get him to vouch for you, all of this would go away."

Charlie rolls her eyes. She and Bruce often butt heads, but it's getting worse. "You want a *man* to speak up about another man making his daughter's uterus into public fodder?"

"She's right, Bruce." Hestia, my PR team lead is also rolling her eyes. "Now, if we could get Sunny Darling to join us all on *Ellen*, that would help. Although, rumor has it she's in need of rehab."

"Sunny Darling does not need rehab." I'm going to pull my hair out. Fistfuls of it. And toss it all over the fucking floor. These people were so competent last week. What the fuck is going on? "And I'm not going on *Ellen*. We're sticking with the plan."

"You've been uninvited from the World Music Awards."

I look at Charlie, because have they been listening to a word either of us has said?

"Beck wasn't going to the World Music Awards," she tells the team. "He's on vacation that week. A real vacation. Where he's not tweeting. Or talking to people. Or doing anything else that'll require any of us to work overtime, and he's even going to do his own laundry and cooking."

I nod in vehement agreement. I didn't know I was taking a vacation that week, but I never turn down an opportunity to hang out at home and torment my sister and remind my mom how much she misses me while I'm gone.

Plus, there's the Tucker factor now, and I still have other friends I haven't caught up with in town.

"It still looks bad that you were uninvited from one more thing," Hestia says. "They'll spin it."

"You know he's going to look like a saint when we finally announce the FLY HYGH Foundation, so it won't matter," Charlie replies. "And we just threw together the mother of all black-tie dinners for Sarah's favorite giraffe on Saturday night, *and* Vaughn's tentatively on board to fly in for it too, so I don't think anyone's going to give two fucks if Beck doesn't show up at an awards show two months from now that he already declined."

"Do you really need me here?" I ask her.

"Shut up and sit down. This is still your fault."

"Fair enough," I grumble.

"You need to go play with animals at that shelter your sister likes," Hestia says.

"He needs to get Levi Wilson and Cash Rivers making more noise about him being a good guy," Bruce replies.

"He called in personal favors from over fifty celebrities and politicians and talked them all into buying thousand-dollar tickets for a fifty-dollar affair to raise money for the world's most famous endangered animal, *and* he's taking both his and Sarah's entire families," Charlie says. "You let him loose in a dog pound, he'll crack a joke about a bitch and we're done. You let the plan play out as the plan is supposed to play out, and *this will all be just fine*." She glares at me and makes a slashing motion across her throat.

Right. She's done with Bruce.

"Got a call from a movie producer who wants to know if you want a cameo in a slasher pic," Bruce tells me. "They'd make you look good when you die."

"We're not doing cameos," my marketing guru, Vicki, replies. "It's starring roles or nothing."

"Whoa, wait, we're not doing movies," I say.

My entire team shuts up and stares at me.

"What?" I ask.

"Ryder, I like you, but you're a PR nightmare," Bruce says. "We're saving your ass this time, but what happens when you call one of the royal babies ugly, or get caught sticking your dick in a goat?"

"PR nightmare? The Ryder Family Foundation gives away *millions* every year, and not two weeks ago I was all over the news when those cameras crashed my visit to the children's hospital in London."

He shakes his head. "You need to think long-term, because sooner or later, you're gonna blow it in business. So do a slasher pic. Not like you're the type to write a tell-all book. Haven't slept with enough women anyone wants the dirt on for that. And I got a guy who's interested in buying out your DRYVE and SHYNE lines. You should take him up on it. Won't get a better deal."

"*Sell my lines?*"

Charlie's not even speaking. She's just gawking. Hestia and Vicki both clear their throats and dive for coffee and cigarettes.

"Sell them," Bruce repeats. "Then you need to kiss Crawford's ass, because we all know this FLY HYGH Foundation is really just an excuse to get a partnership with him so we can branch out into footwear."

I stand and accidentally on purpose dump an entire coffee mug all over the computer.

It sizzles and fries and sparks and the screen goes blank, and Charlie slumps back in her chair with a sigh. "Took you fucking long enough."

"*Sell my lines?*" I say to her.

She rolls her eyes. "I don't care how long he's been your manager, you need to fire him. He's losing his fucking mind. And he's always been a twatwaffle. Also, I'm not replacing that computer. You can get your ass down to the Apple store yourself this time, and I don't care how many people try to run you over on the street."

She grabs her phone and types out a message—undoubtedly telling my team I fucked up and we'll talk again tomorrow at our regularly scheduled time, because that's what she does, and I probably need to give her a raise again this week—and I head for the kitchenette in the small office area. The rest of the floor is apartments.

"You like Moroccan?" I call. "Sarah showed me this place over in University City. We could order couscous. Or kefta. Or kebabs. Or all of it. With four gallons of mint tea. And cookies. Definitely cookies."

She follows me and leans into the doorway, head still down over her phone. "You can't eat this away, Beck. You still have a shoot in three weeks."

"And nothing to do in the meantime except work out and play video games." Everything's on hold. *Everything*. The designs I was supposed to look at this week are delayed. All my meetings—outside the crisis meetings with my team—are canceled. My *only* job is to not fuck up more and keep publicly wooing Sarah.

Maybe privately wooing Sarah.

I wanted to kiss her so badly last night, and I still don't know if it was a good idea or a bad idea, but it's what I wanted.

Charlie doesn't smile. "You ever seriously consider selling out and retiring?"

I told her I was going to last year, after Ellie's accident. She didn't take me seriously, but she also made sure everything on my schedule got delayed or canceled, and she's kept me booked less full so I could be home more.

"Why?" I ask her. "You want to slow down?" She sees her family less than I see mine, but she's never complained about it.

"I don't do slow, Ryder. You know that."

"Good, because even if I did sell out and retire, I'd still need you running my life, you know. Who else would make me get out of bed and remind me to brush my teeth in the morning?"

"Your mother, Ryder. Your mother."

I laugh at the image of my mom trying to get me up in the morning. She'd dump ice water on my head without hesitation, a tidbit I won't be sharing with Charlie, or she might try the same next time we're traveling.

She's smiling too, because she doesn't actually set my alarms or remind me to brush my teeth.

Usually.

"You should sign up for a dating app," I tell her, even though I think I *would* have to sell my businesses if I didn't have Charlie to keep me organized. "Meet someone. Go see the world through love's eyes."

"Rather see the world by myself, thank you very much. The pictures from the game last night are everywhere, and they're reporting both that Sarah totally denied you a kiss *and* that she started a food fight that was probably foreplay to what you did in the bedroom. The pictures are perfect. Lots of the two of you laughing. Especially her. Plus, the media likes that she's playing hard to get, and that you keep trying."

"Nice avoidance."

"You'd rather talk about why you were late after the game last night and came in looking like you just found an all-you-can-eat steak and cupcake buffet?"

"No."

She smirks. "Didn't think so. Tripp Wilson's waiting for you upstairs."

"So that's a no to Moroccan?"

"One of everything. University City. I'm on it. But you're going to have to spend an extra two hours on the treadmill."

I hate the treadmill. "I can order in."

"Nope. Can't talk and drive. Your diva ass is getting me out of a telecon with Brass and the Dinglehoppers to discuss your incompetence at attending telecons."

"Brass?"

"Bruce the Ass."

"Let's get through smoothing out my dumbass tweet, and then I'll talk to Bruce about why he's losing his mind. Two weeks. Tops. And if he's still insane, he'll be gone."

"I'm using your card to pay for lunch for everyone in the restaurant."

"Send some couscous to Sarah's office while you're at it."

"That would be filed under *duh*."

"You're an empress among assistants."

"I know. Don't eat your arm off while you're waiting for food. You need it to sign papers so we can get rid of Bruce."

She heads for the elevator while I take the stairs to the penthouse, where I find an old friend waiting for me.

And he's not alone.

"James! Hey, bud. Give it up." I hold out a fist to Tripp's three-year-old, who eyeballs me with rightful suspicion. He's in preschooler-size jeans with bright green pajama shorts over them, and at least two shirts, because I can see a yellow collar under his bright orange *Captain Beanbag* shirt.

He's also sporting a purple cape.

All of my buddies have the cutest kids.

"He's on Twitter and he knows you're a disaster," Tripp tells me.

"You're gonna have to give him something more than a fist bump to win him over."

He's holding his daughter, who's just over a year old and clearly didn't dress herself this morning, because there's no way she could've put that dress on herself.

I don't think.

Plus, if I were barely a year old and allowed to dress myself, I'd be naked. So I guess I'm assuming she's probably the same.

"Everybody screws up time to time," I say.

Tripp gives me a wry grin. "Yeah. Just time to time."

"You like playing ping-pong?" I ask James.

"You gosh to pway twuck but it fall in da fountain," he replies solemnly.

Tripp ruffles his hair. "The truck dried. We left it at home."

"I've got trucks," I tell him. "Well, cars, but they have wheels and you can make them go *vroom*."

Tripp shakes his head at me, eyes widening. "Dude, he will tear those things apart."

"What? They're just *things*. C'mon, James. Let's go check out my rides."

I get him set up playing with a couple of the model sports cars I keep on a high shelf in the game room while I play peek-a-boo with Emma, who finally decides I'm cool enough to drool on for a while. Her blond hair's on top of her head Cindy Lou Who style, and she's chewing on her fingers when she dives for me to hold her.

Tripp sags into the couch facing the TV. "Thanks. She's getting heavy."

"Need to work out more."

"You carry her for two hours and then say that again." He's sporting bags under his eyes, and he only shaved the right half his face, but he's still managing a smile.

"Holding up okay?" I don't know shit about being a single parent, or about grieving someone close to you, but I know it's work. A fuck-ton of hard work.

"I'm effing tired."

"You need a nanny."

He shakes his head. "Just overnight. It'll pass. She'll *eventually* sleep a full six hours at a time. She's just…adjusting."

They all were. Tripp losing his wife to the flu over the winter is one more reason my schedule keeps getting lighter. No place like home, especially when people need you. Though I'm frustrated as hell at basically being grounded right now, at least I'm here.

"What's the story with your new girlfriend?" he asks before I can push any harder. "Levi bet me ten grand you're falling for her, so this better be a publicity stunt."

"You guys are assholes," I tell him.

He clears his throat and looks at James.

"Ah. Right. Sorry. You're crashmoles."

He's known me too long to think I'm funny, and he stretches his legs out while he studies me. "Davis says you're quitting."

"Why the fugglenuggets would he say that?"

"C'mon, man. Ellie's accident. Your schedule. A self-sabotaging tweet, followed by a PR stunt…"

I bounce Emma on my knee and make funny faces at her. "Your daddy's talking funny."

"So Davis is right and Levi owes me some cash."

"You remember that foundation I told you we were working on? The one with Vaughn Crawford?"

"Sports programs for kids?"

"We were supposed to announce it next week."

He winces. "Ah."

"Yeah. Need to clean up my mistake so Vaughn doesn't bail, and I need to keep making money to fund all my favorite projects. It wasn't self-sabotage. I love my job. I was just a dumb-dumb head who hit the wrong button on my Twitter app and got a little too full of myself to assume mistweets couldn't happen to me. Happens when you're fabulous and haven't slept in three days."

He sucks in a grin as he shakes his head.

I get that a lot.

"Miss sleep that much, do you?" he asks. "Want to hear about a teething toddler with diarrhea?"

Emma smiles at me. Her stomach gurgles.

"She's in an industrial-size diaper, right?"

"Baby roulette, dude. You want to hold her, you take the consequences."

I eyeball the blond-haired, round-cheeked cutie.

She smiles so big that drool drips down her fingers and arms, and she pumps her chubby legs.

The elevator dings, and I rise.

Because odds are good that's my mom. She's been dropping by

once or twice a day—usually with food, because she loves me—and she's a master at baby diapers.

Another ominous sound comes from Emma's midsection. She screws up her lips and mouth, and *oh, fuck*, here we go.

I rush toward the kitchen and the penthouse entrance, and as soon as I see a body, I shove Emma toward it. "Hey. Baby?"

A single blink too late, I realize my mistake.

That's not my mom.

Or my sister.

Or even Charlie, who would probably turn around and take my credit card back to the store, because Emma does, indeed, have an intestinal disorder, and she lets it *all* go as soon as Sarah latches onto her.

It's a long, slow-drawn-out letting go, and that's *not* an industrial-strength diaper, but that is *definitely* sheer and utter horror on Sarah's face while she silently asks me what in the holy hell I've done now.

Fuck.

I just handed my fake girlfriend a baby poop bomb.

And it went off.

All.

Over.

Her.

"Oh, fungusbubbles," I croak out.

And if that look on her face is any indication, those will be the last words I ever utter.

TWENTY-ONE

Sarah

SO FAR TODAY, I've learned many, *many* things.

I've learned that it's hard to concentrate at work with people talking about me shoving Beck's face in a funnel cake and wanting to know if they can get his autograph, and also *I guess I never would've picked you as his type.*

I've learned my parents will drop by my office *just to see your desk, sweetheart* and that my father takes an obscene amount of joy in prepping for roles in public if it'll embarrass me.

And now I've learned that Beck is king when it comes to winning wars.

"Are you shi—" I start, but he clamps a hand over my mouth.

"Virgin ears," he hisses, and then his nose crinkles, and then I inhale and find out why, and—

"*Oh my god*, what is that *smell*?"

We're not alone.

Past the kitchen, there's a toddler—preschooler?—running a model car up and down the floor-to-ceiling windows overlooking the park and the mountains while watching all of us with very serious blue eyes, and there's also an adult male rolling on the ground laughing his ass off.

"I—you—here—we should—"

For once, Beck's apparently at a loss for words.

Even made-up nonsense.

"I thought you were my mom," he finally blurts.

The guy on the floor laughs harder.

"Do I *look* like your mother?"

Beck's ears go pink. "No, I just—I wasn't expecting you, and—not that you're not welcome. You're welcome. Anytime. Day or night. I—we should put her in the sink."

The guy on the floor rolls to his hands and knees and makes an effort to stand up.

"She's Tripp's," Beck adds with a head jerk at his other guest. "Really cute. Most of the time."

His hands hang in mid-air like he's afraid to take the dirty squirming toddler from me, but feels like he should, but isn't sure where to grab on her soiled yellow dress.

Because the stuff shot everywhere.

Down her legs. Up her armholes. Up her neck.

Her sweet baby smile comes with a squeal, and she pumps her legs, which sends the stuff dripping all over my shoes.

I love these shoes.

Loved.

They're my fearless shoes. Boots, really—the only thing I'll do fashionably. Low heel, leather, in theory washable, but does leather absorb smells?

Also, I can't actually work up a really good *mad* here, because the baby—toddler? I've never spent much time around kids—is freaking adorable with all those big grins.

Beck gestures awkwardly to the kitchen.

I hold the baby out while she smiles and squeals and flails her arms and legs and leaves a trail of baby goodness from the foyer to the kitchen sink, where Tripp finally meets us.

He's wiping his eyes.

"Smooth, man. Smooth," he says to Beck before taking over with the gooped-up child. "Tripp Wilson. Pleasure to meet you," he says to me.

"Likewise. Although I do try to dress up better when I'm meeting new people."

Beck winces, totally missing the joke that I don't actually dress up for anyone. "I'll, ah, call Charlie. She'll get you some…" He trails off and gestures to my clothes.

"Fashion sense?" I deadpan.

"Fu—uddlesticks, that's a custom order T-shirt, isn't it?"

We all look down at my Einstein shirt, including the baby, who blows a juicy raspberry that sprays us all with spit.

"I may not have taste, but I have consistency," I say.

"You have awesome taste," Beck assures me.

The elevator dings again. "Yoo-hoo! Anybody home?" a woman calls.

"I told you I thought you were my mother," he mutters. "Also, brace yourself. And I'm sorry."

Tripp chokes on another laugh as he strips the baby.

"Oh, good, you're all—oh *my*. Is *this* Sarah?" A brown-haired, blue-eyed woman stops on the other side of the island and utterly lights up with joy. "Oh, it's *so* good to meet you! Ellie's been telling me all about your bees and your mission to save the giraffes. And you work for Plantwell? We have so much respect for Gary and Jonathan."

She smothers me in a hug before any of us can get out a syllable.

"Um," I say, because I've never really done the *meet the parents* thing, and do his parents know, or are they totally in the dark?

"Mrs. Ryder, you might want to ease up on squishing Emma's work of art there," Tripp says.

She pulls back, looks down, and laughs.

Laughs.

"I haven't had baby poop on me in *years*. I remember the first time Beck had a blow-out."

"Mom—" he starts.

"Shush, I want to hear this," I say.

"He was eight months old, and he was so blocked up—"

"*Mom*—"

"I definitely want to hear this too," Tripp agrees.

Emma squeals as he starts hitting her with the sprayer.

I mean showering her. Not actually *hitting* her.

"—So blocked up that when he finally exploded in the car, we were finding bits of it on the ceiling weeks later."

"Adorable," I say.

"Guess you're lucky Emma got you and not Beck, because otherwise, we never would've gotten that story out of her," Tripp tells me, and I decide he's good people.

"Oh, you." Mrs. Ryder gives him a one-armed hug and boops Emma on the nose. "Is your tummy upset, noodle-poo?"

"I might have a T-shirt and sweats that'll fit you," Beck says to me while Tripp and Mrs. Ryder discuss Emma's intestinal issues.

I can't exactly go back to work in a T-shirt and sweats, but I can't drive home and change like this either. Nor do I want to go home, or back to work, which is why I'm *here*. "Great. Thanks."

"Right this way."

He takes me to a bedroom that's too bright and clean for it to be his.

I think.

I guess it *could* be his. It's bright and cheery enough. But I didn't peg him for the flowery comforter, impressionist-style paintings, pillowcases with his own mug, cardboard cutout of himself with a thumb tucked into his briefs type.

It's far more likely he has a Pac-Man comforter and at least three Game Boys at his bedside table.

Plus pictures of his family.

I'll bet he has pictures of his family *everywhere*.

"I was trying to not lose at baby roulette," he confesses, lifting that long, long arm to scratch his neck. "But I wouldn't have handed her off if I'd realized it was you."

"Just to your mother?" I ask.

He opens his mouth, then blushes.

Again.

"I'm a real shit to the women in my life, aren't I?"

"Mm."

"I would've handed her to my dad too. He just doesn't usually drop by to fuss like Mom does."

"Mm."

"Oh. Hey. I didn't even ask what was up. Everything okay?"

It takes me a half-second to remember why I thought coming over here was a good idea. And the fact that despite the baby poop, I'm feeling weirdly happy.

It's the residual Beck Ryder glow. Has to be. Like I'm soaking up his happy vibes.

"Too much gossip at work," I tell him. "And my boss was uncomfortable with the photographers staking out the building."

He winces. "Sorry."

"Not your fault. I mean, not entirely. My parents thought it was *visit your daughter at work* day. I think they're still there signing autographs."

His wince is getting wince-ier. "Will that be awkward?"

"Do you go to your parents' business and sign autographs?"

"Nah, I usually just wait for the charity auction they do for the children's hospital and then send in signed underwear."

And once more, the man's surprised a laugh out of me. "Seriously?"

"Oh, yeah. Nobody wants to bid on it, because Dad runs the auction, so usually a guy will win them for like eighteen bucks and mumble something about donating them to a bigger fundraiser at his wife's office."

He's totally shameless. But I don't think he actually has an over-inflated ego. He's too self-aware about the awkwardness of the underwear thing for that.

Plus, as noted, his underwear is really freaking comfortable.

I angle a pointed glance at the life-size cardboard cutout in the corner, and once again, he blushes. "That's…for shock value."

"You should get one of the rear view. Without the briefs. I have this weird feeling your friends would appreciate playing *pin the dart on Beck's butt cheeks.*"

He chuckles and squeezes my shoulder. "Brilliant idea. And here I was worried about what to get them all for Christmas. Glad you had a place to escape to. I promise I won't baby-bomb you next time. Bathroom's through that door. Should have soap and stuff in it. Let me go get some clothes. Be right back."

He does indeed have clothes that fit me, though the RYDE sweat pants are tight in the butt and have to be rolled to my ankles—but so, *so* soft—and the T-shirt he finds me—a Half-Cocked Heroes T-shirt he says Levi sent him as a joke—is like wearing a dress, but I also get to shower in his orgasmic shower with the wall nozzles and rain spout that are utterly scrumptious and luxurious and about the only thing I miss about life in LA.

And I've never used SHYNE shower gel before—his body care line—but holy crap, it's delicious. And smells just like Beck.

When I finally emerge from his guest room, buttloads of people have joined the crowd.

He introduces me to Levi Wilson, Tripp's brother, who's impossible to miss because he's Copper Valley's version of Justin Timberlake, and also Hank, Waylon, and June Rivers—Cash's siblings, who all have identical eyes to the boy bander who went on to be a movie star—and Davis Remington, the fifth former member of Bro Code whom I never would've identified without the introduction thanks to the tattoos, beard, and man bun.

"They're on your side first," Beck assures me. He has the little boy up on his shoulders, and I'm guessing the kid's seat of honor has something to do with the crayon marks all over the windows and removing him from further temptation.

"I always take not-Beck's side," Levi agrees. He's holding Emma, the little girl whose bowels like to make their own introductions, and appears to have no concerns whatsoever about the possibility of his white pants becoming the proud owner of doodoo stains.

And on a related note, how do men get away with things like wearing white pants?

It's mind-boggling. But I realize they're RYDE jeans, so I assume they're comfortable too.

Actually, is anyone here *not* wearing Beck's clothes?

"Not-Beck's side is usually the safer side," one of the Rivers guys agrees.

Charlie arrives with a grocery cart full of food, and I take one whiff, and my feelings for Beck Ryder might just step firmly over that line that I've been wrestling to keep them behind, which is bad, because I do *not* want to go back to a full-time life in the public eye.

Plus, who says he's even into me for real? I'm a geek who tasered him.

And all he wants is to rescue his reputation.

Still—"Did you order out Moroccan?"

"Oh, Hersheys, yeah," he replies with a grin, and I realize he's censoring himself for the kids' sake, and could he be any more real and down to earth?

His mom frowns. "Is Moroccan spicy?"

"It's *flavorful*. You're gonna love it."

He doesn't wait for Charlie to unload the cart, but instead dives right in with everyone else grabbing cartons and bags and pulling out plates and silverware. "Hey, Charlie, Sarah, you guys go first," Beck calls.

Charlie gives my clothes a once-over. "Do I want to know?"

"Emma's teething," Tripp tells her.

"She mauled you with drool?"

"Other end," Tripp corrects.

"That's a thing?"

"Yep."

"I'm never having children."

"Sometimes they throw up on you too."

"You're not helping."

"Yes, he is," Beck calls. "If you have children, you might

leave me."

"Dude, you have dependency issues," the Rivers guy that I think is Hank says.

"Job security isn't a bad thing," Charlie retorts with a glare aimed at him, and *hello*, tension.

Beck swings James down onto a stool at the island and while I fix myself a plate, he talks the boy into trying a kefta kebab. "It's like a hamburger on a stick."

"I eats ketsbup on my hambagurger," James says.

"Little man, you have *taste*. Hank, grab a ketchup bottle while you're in the fridge."

"I didn't know he was having a party," I say quietly to Charlie.

She snorts softly. "Unplanned, but once you've been around long enough, you learn to anticipate it. If it wasn't a workday, they'd be all over the game room and Ellie and Wyatt would be here too. And Davis isn't usually here on a weekday. That's odd."

"Night shift," he tells her while he grabs a spoon and dishes up some couscous. "Remotely."

She's still squinting at him like it's weird.

"He's a secret agent," June tells me.

Davis rolls his eyes.

"Double major in computer science and nuclear engineering," June adds. "Total recipe for him to be a secret agent. But we pretend we don't know and buy into his story about working for that nuclear reactor south of the city to keep the feds off our tails."

"You're insane," Hank tells her.

"You're just mad you didn't come up with the conspiracy theory first," Charlie says.

June nods. "What she said."

Hank grunts and turns his back to the women to grab a plate.

Levi and Tripp demand I sit between them in the airy dining room, which also has floor-to-ceiling windows, but these overlook the rest of the downtown skyscrapers. Mink Arena peeks through the buildings, though I can't see Duggan Field at all.

The brothers pepper me with questions about where I went to school, how long I've been in Copper Valley, where I lived in town before I bought my house, how long I've kept bees, and when I started blogging.

It's unlike any party I've ever been to with famous people, because nobody mentions movie roles, agents, managers, endorsement deals, or gossip rags. Mostly. Davis does pull up a seat at the end of the table and fist-bumps Levi for having another number one hit on the Billboard charts.

But that's it before the talk turns to last night's baseball game.

"Nice job shoving that funnel cake in Beck's face," Levi tells me. "We've all wanted to do it a time or two."

"She had to seize the moment," Tripp says. "Especially since the Fireballs probably won't last another season."

"Wait, what?" I ask.

He hands Emma a plate of mashed up chicken, vegetables, and couscous. "It's like management is trying to make them lose so Copper Valley will kick them out. They need new owners."

He slides a look at Levi, who ducks his head, but I don't miss the other looks going around the table. Between Beck and Davis. The Rivers brothers. June and Tripp.

Even Charlie's stopped clicking away at her phone, like she's supposed to be taking notes, or maybe she's mentally filing them away.

These people can talk without saying a word.

A chill slinks down my spine, because that's *tight*. Not blood tight. *Family* tight.

And I feel like I'm eavesdropping on a conversation that I'm not supposed to know exists.

"Oh, for goodness sakes, boys, get your elbows off the table," Mrs. Ryder says, breaking up the silent conversation that wasn't really a conversation, and I surreptitiously remove mine as well. But when she beams at me, I get the feeling I could leap onto the table and do the MC Hammer dance naked and she'd think I was still just utterly perfect. "Sarah, where did you say you went to college? It'll be so nice for Ellie to have someone to talk to about work. Not that Wyatt doesn't listen, of course, but it's hard for her to make girl-friends sometimes. People always want to talk to her about Beck, and they never stop to get to know *her* first."

I can't decide if I want to cry or hug her, because she clearly *gets* it. What it's like to be liked for who you're related to instead of who you *are*.

"Mom, Ellie's been in two weddings in the last year," Beck points out.

"But not for *female engineers*."

"She smells fresh blood," Levi tells me, hitching his chin toward Mrs. Ryder while I blink away the sting in my eyes. "Since Ellie's basically committing incest with marrying Wyatt—"

"Oh, stop." She points a fork at him. "They are *not* related."

"It would be like her marrying me," Davis says. "And Ellie's my sister too."

Everyone stops and looks at him, then a wave of laughter rolls through the open rooms. The amusement is so thick, it's practically lifting a level of atmospheric pressure. I *feel* ten pounds lighter, which is something of a relief after the weird tension about the baseball thing and my sudden attack of feelings about inherently realizing that I can trust every single person in this room.

It's weird. But *good*. No one here cares who my parents are. They don't care how awkward I was in high school and before. They're not angling for anything. And they have each other's backs, and they've adopted me too.

"So Wyatt's in no danger of losing Ellie to Davis?" I ask Levi.

"None of us are, and to Davis least of all. She used to babysit him."

"She did not," June says. "She was too young." She turns to me. "Don't listen to anything *any* of these guys tell you. They're complete looneys. All of them."

"Like you can talk," one of her brothers says.

"They *all* have good hearts," Mrs. Ryder insists.

Beck kisses his mom's hair. "Because we had you."

"*Awwwww,*" everyone intones, like they're making fun of him, but I don't miss the smiles coming from all of them.

Like they agree, but they have to give Beck shit as a matter of routine.

Emma joins in by squealing and throwing a handful of couscous all over the table, and later I'll contemplate why Beck has a high chair in his penthouse, but I'm already a wee bit too attached.

Especially with how weirdly *normal* this entire meal feels, despite all these people basically being strangers to me.

Until the great blow-out of this morning, anyway. I guess touching a man's kid's poop lends itself to fast friendships.

"Whoa, hey, where's the tea?" Beck asks.

"They don't make it by the gallon," Charlie tells him. "You're out of luck."

He's already eaten two plates full of food, and he's piling sesame shortbread cookies and the honey-coated chebakia onto another, but he's so crestfallen at the lack of tea that I take pity on him. "I have a teapot at home. And fresh mint. Just need some gunpowder tea."

Beck beams at me, and it feels more genuine than it should. "All that *and* she has the Serenity you've been looking for, Levi."

All eyes are suddenly on me, and another hush falls over the room, but this one's reverent.

"You have *the* Serenity?" Levi breathes.

My face is getting hot, and I know I'm going blotchy. "It's not for sale."

"Of fu—udging course it's not," he mutters. "Can I touch it? Just...just once?"

"Don't let him have it without getting something out of it for yourself," Tripp says. "He's such a spoiled brat."

Beck's grinning. "You want to touch it, you're gonna have to do something stupid while you're in town to get the paps off Sarah's street."

"Says the king of stupid distractions," Levi fires back with a grin.

"You don't get to negotiate with my ship," I inform Beck. "It's *my* ship. And he'll have to get through my father first."

"I know," Beck says with an evil grin. "I'm gonna be the one hiding in the bushes taking video when *that* happens."

"Cash says your dad's cool," June says cautiously.

"That's because he's not *Cash's* dad," I say.

"I'll put your giraffe on my video screen in my next ten concerts," Levi offers.

"Oh, fine, sure, bring out the *big* guns," Beck says. "Dude. *Any* rock star can offer her that. And you should do it anyway to save the giraffes. For the rest of the whole year. Get that baby giraffe up there too."

"I'll hijack all the national news signals and broadcast anything you want about the giraffes if I can take a picture with the Serenity," Davis says.

I laugh, but I stop when I realize I'm the only one. "Wait, you're serious?"

"It's the fucking Serenity."

"I meant about hijacking—" I start, but James interrupts me.

"The fucking Serenity!" he cries.

Tripp gives Davis the *you're going to die in your sleep* look, and this time, everyone cracks up.

They're one big, happy, crazy family.

And I have this weird feeling that if I'd grown up with them, I might like people as much as Beck does too.

TWENTY-TWO

Beck

SARAH'S ASS looks amazing in my sweatpants.

I think. The shirt's covering the pants, but the shirt's also hugging her curves right there, and *yep*, definitely amazing.

She sways side-to-side while she stares out the window at the wide expanse of Reynolds Park below. The zoo's on the far side. I could take her over there. Get her a private viewing of Persephone.

Hell, she could probably get her own private viewing.

But if I offer, she'll stop the swaying, and I'll have to stop watching her ass.

I shift uncomfortably on the couch, where I'm pretending to check my email and text messages on my phone, because my pants are getting tight.

"I should really be at work," she says.

Guilt creeps up next to me and shoves a cream pie in my face. And not the good kind with real whipped cream either. This one has fake banana flavoring in it, and I don't like it. "Can you work remotely? Ellie does that sometimes when I make the news and people talk too much to her about it."

"I can, but I don't want to." She turns away, and I manage to look away from her ass before she catches me watching.

Tripp left so the kids could nap. The Riverses all had to go back to work. So did Mom. And Levi and Davis took off for a public appearance for Levi that'll end with both of them at a bar, where I can't go, because I'm grounded. Charlie said so when she left to go work *alone* downstairs.

Leave this building and I'll quit.

So it's just me and Sarah.

"What do you want to do?" I ask. "We could sneak into the zoo. Or head out to my place in Shipwreck. Ellie beat my high score on Frogger a year ago, and I need to work on getting it back."

She bites her lower lip and stares at me.

"Or, yeah, we could make out," I agree, and it's odd how easily it comes out, and how much I mean it, because I could see letting this woman *all* the way in.

I let people in all the time. I don't care if they take my stuff. I'm usually okay with taking photos, always with signing shit. But I don't let them have *me*. Not the parts that count.

Her cheeks erupt in a splotchy flush. "I was thinking about working on my blog."

"Making out, blogging, it's all the same." I'm such a dumbass. "All of it revs my engine. You need a compu—oh. Right. Never mind."

And now I'm a dumbass who's not making any sense and who's getting a little more turned on because she's staring at me like I belong in a mental institution.

A mental institution for attractive sex gods—I swear, she's into me right now—but still a mental institution.

"I was gonna offer mine, but I spilled coffee all over it this morning," I tell her lamely.

"I have a computer downstairs in my car."

"Oh."

Her brows furrow. "Do you spill coffee on your electronics often?"

"Only when I need to get out of a video conference."

"If anyone else said that to me, I wouldn't believe them."

I grin. "Look at us, getting to know each other so well."

She crosses to sit at the other end of the couch with me and pulls her knees up to her chest, which I can't see at all under that shirt she's swimming in. She's not petite—more like average, with healthy curves to her everywhere—but I got the Ryder shoulders, which makes fitting through doorframes and buying normal shirts hard sometimes, and also makes my shirt way too huge on her.

"I'm not totally opposed to the making out idea, but you'd probably ultimately be a disappointment," she tells me, and all thoughts of clothes leap out the window and go flying to the ground forty-some stories below.

"Only one way to find out," I say, scooting to the middle of the couch and tossing my phone across the room.

She holds up a hand. "I said *not totally*. There's a large margin of error in there for how opposed I actually am."

"Okay. Hit me with the problem, and I'll fix it."

"It's you."

"Me? I'm not a problem. I'm fucking fantastic at making out."

"My mother told me once—when I was entirely too young to hear it—that the reason she and my dad worked was that he checked his Hollywood ego at the bedroom door, and knew he had to *work* for it if he wanted to see her naked frequently."

I open my mouth, then close it, because there's literally *nothing* good that *anyone* can say about someone else's parents in the bedroom.

"So," she continues in the awkward silence that's weirdly doing nothing to relieve the pressure in my cock, "here we have me, with a few *very* satisfying lovers in my past, and you, happy to claim that you're very good at making out."

And now I'm getting pissed.

And it's still doing nothing to help the swelling in my pants.

The good swelling, I mean. I don't have anything I need to see my doctor for.

Also, I'm almost positive she's baiting me on purpose, and that she's having fun watching me squirm, and that she wants me to toss her over my shoulder and carry her to my bedroom and make her scream my name.

Except I'm only at *almost*, and I've already fucked up enough in the past week where Sarah's concerned.

"*Satisfying lovers,*" I repeat.

Or possibly sneer.

"The double O is not a myth."

Fucking *fuck*. "And you think I can't give you a double O."

"I have no idea, but you have several strikes against you."

"Are you pulling the scientific experiment card here, or baseball analogies?"

She's not getting any less red, but she's also pushing through it, and there's a hint of a grin teasing her lips. "People are complex. You said it yourself. So why can't I be both?"

"I am so fucking turned on *and* pissed right now, and I don't know how that happened."

"I'm not trying to insult you," she assures me. "Merely...express my misgivings. Especially given the temporary nature of our need for contact. But since you brought up making out, I thought I'd be honest with you."

"Can you say it in that growly voice your dad uses? That might help the boner situation. If we're being honest here."

She sucks in a smile, cheeks still bright with the outline of flames. "Have you ever given a woman a double orgasm?"

"I—" I can't find the rest of the syllables for a sentence, because *fuck*. Global warming is happening right here in my penthouse. I gulp hard, then I make myself look her straight in the eye, and prepare to confess more than I've ever confessed to a living soul, which is mildly terrifying, but still not enough to alleviate the boner. "I don't have as much experience as my career might make it look like I should."

"You're a virgin?"

"No. But I don't—look, the thing about being famous is that sometimes, women want to sleep with you, but they don't care about anything other than the fact that they're sleeping with *oooh, Beck Ryder*! And I'm not—that's not—I'm more than just a dick with a lot of cash and a pretty face. So I'm picky. *Very* picky. And more often than not, that means I'm in a dry spell."

"You get lonely," she says quietly.

Like she *gets* it, despite the fact that she clearly has more experience than I do with bumping uglies.

And I never would've used that word, but— "Yeah."

"I broke up with my last boyfriend because I didn't want him to know who my parents were."

"Did he—never mind."

She smiles sadly. "Yes. But what was the point if I wouldn't let him in here?" She taps her head, then her heart. "Or here, I guess."

I reach over and squeeze her hand, because it's there, and because I know a thing or two about keeping people out. I know a thing or two about not knowing if someone likes *me*, or if they like who they *think* I am.

It's why I'm so fucking glad for everyone from home. I might not have someone warming my bed every night, but I have family. My family, who won't accuse me of fathering kids that aren't mine—and it fucking *sucks*, by the way, because I *would* love kids someday—or try to take advantage of me because they don't care about the heart under the body.

She squeezes my hand back, and with Sarah, I don't know if it means *thank you* or *let's arm wrestle and I'll kick your ass,* but I like her hand in mine.

Soft, but strong.

So comfortable.

And so easy to just sit here. Without saying anything. With a woman I never should've met, but who's quickly becoming one of my favorite people, even when she makes me squirm.

Probably because it's a rare breed of people *willing* to make me squirm, and who also understand how hard it is to trust people on an intimate level.

"You could teach me," I offer. "I'm not too humble to admit I could learn a few new tricks."

She laughs and pulls herself up off the couch. "Maybe tomorrow."

"Maybe?" That's disappointing.

I *like* her. I trust her. I *want* to make out with her.

She glances back at the windows, at the world outside. "Okay, that's not you. It's me. I have trust issues."

"I'd be worried about you if you didn't." Especially growing up under the celebrity microscope. "Want to know a secret?"

"I don't know. Do I?"

"I have trust issues too."

She studies me closely, then nods. "That's probably good for you."

"Yeah, but it's not good for getting any experience at giving a woman a double O."

She tucks a stray lock of hair behind her ear, but she can't hide a small smile and a subtle blush. Like maybe that was harder for her to say than I can comprehend, and I just scored points for my own honesty.

"I'm going to get my computer," she says. "Did Charlie say there's office space one floor down?"

Dammit. "Yeah. Let me see if your clothes are dry yet, and I'll show you."

But I'm not giving up.

Because I *like* her.

And I can't tell you the last time I liked a woman. Not like this. Is it scary? Yeah.

But worth it?

I hope so.

So slow and steady it is.

Until our contract's up.

And then I don't know what I'll do, but I have time.

I'll figure it out.

Unless I fuck something else up in the meantime.

TWENTY-THREE

Sarah

I'VE BARELY FINISHED a blog post about an upcoming meteor shower when Beck knocks on the office door.

Not that I'm surprised.

He doesn't seem like he does well when he's alone. And I don't mind, because he's remarkably easy to talk to.

About *anything*.

"Hey. You hungry?"

I push my computer back and just look at him.

Which isn't a hardship, honestly. He gets more attractive with every little twist to his personality. If I weren't biased against gorgeous men with thick dark hair and movie star blue eyes and easy grins and perfectly formed bodies—yes, including the ape arms —I'd probably call him *hot*.

Instead of a classy button-down or a polo, he's lounging in a white *Simpsons* T-shirt. His jeans still look like they cost a million bucks and they fit his slim hips and hug his long legs perfectly— again, undoubtedly from his own fashion line—but he's also bare-foot, which adds exactly the right amount of *real*ness to him.

And somehow, hearing that he hasn't had many girlfriends adds even more to the appeal. I'm not usually so forward in talking about sex—not that I have a lot of opportunities, because guys are hardly banging on my door every day—but he was the one who brought up making out.

Multiple times now.

Like maybe he doesn't care that I forget to get haircuts and I never wear makeup and I think of clothes as functional items for comfort and to prevent me from breaking indecency laws more than as fashion statements.

His lips twitch like he can't stand the silence, and sure enough, within seconds, he's talking again. Not that I mind. It's just kinda amusing.

"It takes a lot of calories to look this good," he says, as if he needs to explain why he's hungry again.

"If I ate that many calories, I'd look like a blimp."

"You work out?"

"Occasional yoga classes and tae kwon do four days a week. Except this week, because my dad went to check out the studio last night and had a fight with the grandmaster about the windows in the front of the building, and so I have to wait until my parents leave town and then send some kind of apology gift."

"Isn't martial arts above bribery?"

"Not when this particular grandmaster knows you have fresh local honey."

"Your parents should meet my parents. They'll trade baby pictures and stories for three days."

"Do your parents know? About our agreement?"

He shakes his head.

"*Beck*. You have to tell your parents."

He shakes his head harder.

"But—that's so—cruel."

"Would you tell your parents if they were normal people?"

"We wouldn't be in this mess if my parents were normal people."

"Sure we would."

"No, we wouldn't, because half the reason the world's *shipping* us, or whatever you call it, is because they want the excuse to gossip about how you feel about the world speculating that my mom should be in rehab."

He frowns. "Has your mom ever been in rehab?"

"Nope. But she disappeared to South Africa for three months one time when her career was crashing and let people think she was in rehab so that there'd be more attention and speculation when she came back. It worked, by the way. That was right before she landed that role as the single mom animal rights researcher that won her like every award under the sun."

"So you were home alone for three months? Just you and your dad?"

"Just half of it. He was wrapping a movie in LA, then we flew over to join her for a few weeks until he had to report for his next film. It was summer, so I didn't really miss school. Plus, there was the nanny when he was working. The only awkward part was when I got back to school and my teachers would randomly search my bags because they'd seen the tabloids and wanted to make sure my mom was a fit parent who wasn't getting me addicted to anything."

I go for a smile, even though it's the truth and still makes me feel uncomfortable, even all these years later.

Beck doesn't smile back for once. In fact, he's still frowning, which isn't entirely natural on him. I wish goofball Beck would come back, because there's something comforting about him tossing out nonsense and not taking any of this week seriously.

"I don't think I'd be well-adjusted at all if I grew up like you did," he says.

"I found my balance."

"When you changed your name and disappeared halfway around the world. That's extreme."

He's probably right. There's no such thing as balance for a kid from Hollywood.

"I think I would've been okay if it hadn't been for...you know," I say slowly.

"The *Hagrid* incident."

I cringe.

"Voldemort?" he says.

"What?"

"You're supposed to make that face when I say Voldemort, not when I say Hagrid."

"I didn't dress up like Voldemort and get my face plastered all over every tabloid under the sun with rumors that Sunny Darling and Judson Clarke's geeky daughter was into evil wizard role-playing sex games."

"Were you really into furry play?"

"*I was seventeen.* What the *fuck* do you think?"

"I think you need to own the story and put it out there and get over it."

If I didn't know if was physically impossible for my eyeballs to pop out of my head, I'd be trying to hold them in right now. Not to mention locking down my ribs so my heart can't crawl out of my chest. "Did you just tell me to *get over it*?"

He grins. "No, I told you to *own the story*. C'mon. Let's make another video."

"First of all, *let's make a video* isn't something to ever say to a child of celebrities. Second, we're not supposed to make another video until Friday. It's in the contract."

"Fuck the contract. This is your life. I'll interview you, you tell your side, talk about how it felt to constantly be in the spotlight you didn't ask for, and you can be a hero to all those kids growing up under a microscope *right now*. Like James and Emma. Kind of. Or any other kid who's going through hell because of *any* rumors."

"That's low."

"You want to save the giraffes, but you don't want to give hope to kids who are afraid of exactly what you went through, that you got past and recovered from?"

My heart is racing and my mouth is going dry, because he has a point.

A very solid, very powerful point. "You're evil."

"I have my moments. And yes, my mom is very proud of me."

"I don't *want* to talk about it."

He pulls a chair out from under the utilitarian table I'm sitting at and pulls it close, then sits, leaning right into my space. "Sarah. It's already out there. My team's fielding calls from all the major news networks wanting exclusive interviews with both of us, and they're asking about more than just the coverage of you and your prom. They're talking about your entire childhood. Guarantee your parents are getting them too, and I know you're ignoring your website's email inbox. So grab it. Own it. Tell your side. On your terms. Where no one profits but *you*, and only in here."

He taps my chest, high, but still at the top of my left breast, right where my heart is clawing for a ledge to hang on to so it doesn't fall off that cliff it's sitting on.

"I like dumbass Beck better than whoever you are right now," I tell him, but my voice is froggy and thick.

"Just think about it." He pulls back and stands and stretches, showing off those billion-dollar abs when his shirt lifts. "I'm thinking Mexican. Can't remember the last time I had fajitas. You like steak or chicken?"

"Both," Charlie calls from her small office across the hall. "And go buy a new computer, because I'm tired of checking your email, but then come *right back to this building*."

"You just started an hour ago," he calls back.

"And that's long enough. Why do you even subscribe to half this stuff? You need an email purge."

"Was she listening in?" I whisper.

"*She*'s the robot," he whispers back. "So probably. But she's super trustworthy. I programmed her myself."

Crap, now I'm laughing in the middle of a near panic attack. "That's terrifying."

"I dressed up like Mrs. Potts for my freshman year high school talent show and sang 'I'm a Little Teapot,'" Charlie calls, "but it came out *I'm a little pee pot*, and the football team put bags of urine in my locker every day for two solid weeks after that. If I hadn't known how to set off stink bombs in their locker room, I probably would've also changed my name and moved to Liberia."

"That's horrible," I say.

"It's on YouTube, but because some dickweed actor got caught trying to screw a hole in an oak tree while high as a kite that week, I didn't go viral."

I look at Beck.

"Beef? Chicken? Both?" he asks. "I can do tofu, but I'll have to follow it with a half-dozen churros and some fried ice cream, and that'll mean I probably do need to run, but I can't run until I know the yoga classes are all done in Reynolds Park for the day since my treadmill and I aren't on speaking terms."

"I can see now why your parents had to keep their day jobs," I say, earning a snort-laugh from Charlie and a shameless grin from Beck.

"Damn right," he says. "Both it is. But no refried beans. We learned that lesson the hard way, didn't we, Charlie?"

"Speak for yourself, Ryder. My farts smell like candy canes."

I should be at work. Dealing with a frog habitat issue on a proposed windmill site.

But this afternoon was worth the vacation time.

And it's barely started.

TWENTY-FOUR

Beck

I WAKE up Wednesday morning expecting more of the same as the last four days. Some hiding out, some badgering Sarah—it's fun, and I swear she gets prettier with every smile, plus, I had some wicked hot dreams about her and maple syrup last night, and now I'm craving waffles—some conference calls, checking in with Vaughn, some group text messages with the guys, and probably a threat or seventeen from Sarah's dad.

What I don't expect is to see a pig snout right at eye-level.

"You better not be naked under there," Sarah says, "because Cupcake likes sausage."

Been a long time since I've been grinning before I even rolled out of bed.

"Morning, honey," I say as she comes into focus in the doorway. She has the leash, which means the pig is moderately contained. "Miss me that much?"

"We're doing the video," she replies.

"You wanna shower first?"

"What?" She sniffs her pits. "I already showered."

"I meant with me. Naked. If we're doing this video, you owe me lessons in double orgasms."

"Say that to my daughter again, and I'll slice off your nipples and shove them up your asshole," her dad growls.

"Oh, fuck! Jesus! Shit! Sorry, sir. Didn't see you there."

"And I'll shove your nut sack up your nostrils," he continues, and I don't think that's him practicing for a role.

"Sorry, sir. Sorry."

Sarah's laughing as she tugs the pig away. "Leave him alone, Dad. He's probably still dreaming and thinks he's talking to a prime rib."

"And I'll slice your dick off and peel it like a banana and feed it to the monkeys at the zoo," Judson adds.

"Dad. Too far. That's gross. And monkeys are vegetarian."

I start to correct her, but realize that won't help my case.

"I don't understand why you let anyone traipse in here," Sunny Darling tells me, because apparently it's *bring your parents to your fake boyfriend's bedroom* day. "Your security is appalling."

"Mom, he gave me the code to the elevator."

"You and these seventeen people already in his apartment. Is there anyone in this city who *doesn't* know how to get in here?"

"Mom, you're going to see him naked if you stand there longer. Come on. We got him up. Now let's go find the avocados."

"Who's evil now?" I mutter to myself while I reach for my phone.

Three hundred unread emails, ninety-eight unread texts since midnight.

Time to get a new number again. And a new email address.

And this time I'm really only giving it to the guys. And Ellie and my parents. And Charlie.

And Vaughn, out of necessity.

Maybe.

But definitely Sarah.

I shower quickly and pull on my favorite RYDE jeans and an old Bro Code T-shirt, because glory days, man. Plus, this one's super soft. And it already has mustard stains on it.

My mom's in the kitchen making honey puff pancakes and bacon. I drop a kiss on Sarah's head partly to make Judson's cheek twitch but more because she smells like honey again and I'm ridiculously glad to see her. She schooled me in Donkey Kong yesterday afternoon before begging off to hang out with Mackenzie for the baseball game, and I missed her.

I also miss my mom, so I wrap her in a huge hug. "Have I ever told you you're my favorite woman in the entire universe?"

"Beckett Ryder, that is *no way to talk* in front of the best shot I have of ever getting you married off," she hisses.

"He's not wrong though," my dad tells her from the table in the dining nook, which is really like a quarter of the entire room, and is big enough to seat twenty. "You *are* the best woman in the entire universe."

She blushes and shoos me out of the kitchen.

"Sarah's a close second," I concede. "She introduced me to that Moroccan place. *And* she promised me mint tea."

I wave good morning to Charlie, Davis, Levi, Tripp, the kids, and Cooper.

Cooper Rock. Second baseman for the Fireballs. That Cooper.

Who's currently being gawked at by Mackenzie, who also apparently rode along with Sarah this morning.

"Dude. Sign a baseball," I tell him.

"I offered and she went all frozen mime on me," he replies.

"So give her your shirt instead. Women don't want balls. They want cotton."

Mom gets me with a spatula to the head. "That's enough of your mouth this morning. And you didn't tell me you were having company, so I didn't bring enough bacon for everyone."

Cupcake snorts.

"We'll pass on the bacon, dear," Sunny tells Mom.

"I like bacon," Judson growls.

"Fucking bacon!" James exclaims.

"James," Tripp growls.

Judson gets down at the kid's level. "Do you know what happens when you say *fuck*?" he growls.

Seriously. It's all growling, all the time.

James shakes his head.

"Your testicles—"

"*Dad.* Enough." Sarah shoves him out of the way and squats next to James. "Do you want to know the dirtiest word in the entire English language?" she whispers conspiratorially.

He nods, wide-eyed.

Tripp rises from the couch and glares at her. "No, he does *not*—"

"It's *snickerdoodle*," Sarah says.

James giggles.

"Right?" Sarah says. "Don't say it to the grown-ups, okay?"

"Okay, snickerdoodle," James replies. "Snickerdoodle bacon!"

"Bro, you have to marry her now," Levi announces.

My mom sniffles.

Judson peels my balls off with his eyes.

And Cupcake attacks a dust bunny that was lurking under the sofa and makes the whole piece of furniture move a foot.

"Snickerdoodle pancake!" James yells.

Emma bangs a wooden spoon on a pot my mom undoubtedly had a hand in finding for her.

"She in a wetsuit today?" I ask Tripp.

"She's naked. Baby roulette, next level."

"Snickerdoodle poop!" James yells.

Sarah rises and dusts her hands, then marches over and grabs my arm. "Now. You. Downstairs. Before I lose my nerve."

"You don't have to do this, sweetheart," Sunny says to her.

"Not with the likes of him," my dad growls. "He can't even hold off the Euranians."

Mackenzie swivels her head toward him, lips and forehead both wrinkling.

"What are Euranians?" Cooper asks, and Mackenzie snaps her gaze back to the baseball god, and swear on the pig, she swoons.

"Mackenzie. You too," Sarah says. "You're my good luck video recording charm."

"Right!" The petite blonde leaps to her feet and trips over the pig. Davis catches her, and she goes red as a cherry. "Sarah, there is too much hotness in this room. I can't cope. I just can't."

Cupcake wanders over to sniff Emma's butt, then collapses onto her side.

"You should have house parties more often," Levi tells me.

"Aren't you playing a show in Seattle this weekend?"

"Trying to get rid of me?"

"Yes."

"*Beckett.*" Mom gets me with the spatula again. "Levi's not home enough as it is. And what's this about a video? You're not making one of *those* videos, are you?"

I wrap an arm around Sarah's shoulders. "Mom. Look at this face. Is this a face you can say no to? If she wants me to make a video—"

Sarah jabs me with an elbow, and my dad chuckles.

Judson growls.

Sunny sighs.

And even though today's Wednesday—I think?—I can see every Sunday morning for the rest of my life. Right here. Hosting breakfast with the families. Bickering with my best friends. Killing pigs with baby poop.

Sneaking touches of Sarah.

It's been years since I gave up the dream of having a family of my own—since one too many opportunistic people took that slice of my soul that still believed fame wouldn't ruin my shot at finding that someone who could still see *me*—but all this?

This is nice.

It's giving me ideas again.

Ideas about a pretty friend who needs a helping hand to put some of her past behind her.

And also some really hot fantasies of her in my shower. And in my kitchen. And on my table. Covered in honey and cinnamon and whipped cream.

Maybe that's why it was *her*. She needs help moving on from her past.

Maybe I do too.

"At least promise you'll keep your underwear on," Mom says on a sigh.

"I promise, he'll keep his underwear on," Charlie assures her. "Because there are not enough hours in the day for the kind of overtime *that* video would take to recover from."

"It's for Sarah's blog, Mom."

"Oh! The science and bee blog. You have *fantastic* content. Beck, you should talk to Hank about having Sarah's website optimized and her server upgraded though. The load times are a little slow with as much traffic as she's getting."

"Already on it, Mom."

"Wait, what?" Sarah says. "Hank who? Yesterday's Hank?"

"He's a snickerdoodling genius," Levi tells her.

"SNICKERDOODLE PENIS!" James hollers.

"I'm going to snickerdoodling kill you," Tripp mutters to his brother.

And then the weirdest thing happens.

Sarah's eyes go shiny and she ducks her head and pulls on my arm. *Hard.* "Can we please just go do this?" she mutters.

My stomach growls, but I ignore it. I know how to puppy-dog-eye my way to a whole honey puff pancake for myself later. But even if I didn't, I'd still be trailing Sarah to the stairs.

"Hey," I say as I descend behind her. "What's wrong?"

She stops on the landing and glances up, but we're alone.

"You have a really awesome family," she says, clearly trying to keep in whatever's bugging her.

"Did one of them say something? I'll punch him for you. Just tell me which one."

She shakes her head. "*No.* That's exactly it. They're so...*nice.* And you all know each other so well, and it's *all* fun. All the time. Even though half of you are stalked by crazy photographers and gossips who want to say things bad about you, when you're all together, you're just...*family.*"

I'm missing something. "You have cousins you miss?"

"*No.* I have me, Mom, and Dad. That's it. Just us. And I've been freaking hiding from Hollywood for over a decade, away from all cameras and gossips and everything that defines their life, and has since before I was born, where you—you live it every day, but you're still *happy.* And all of them—and you know them well enough to let them into your place all hours of the day, and they don't think twice about dropping by, and you're *family.* A big, dysfunctional, hilarious, got-your-back, perfect *family.*"

I don't quite get exactly why she's on the verge of tears, but then, maybe I do.

Because that look on her face is exactly how I felt in those few hours when we thought we might lose Ellie. The way I felt when I got the call that Tripp had lost Jessie, and watching him go through all the arrangements once she was gone.

Like I'd finally seen how good I had it with the people I loved and who loved me, and in an instant, it could disappear.

"You've never been around big families?"

She shakes her head.

"You can have some of mine. I'll share."

That reluctant laugh bubbles out of her. "You are such a nut."

"Thank you."

"Seriously, *how*? How do you stay normal?"

I brush a lock of her hair back from her face, and *fuck*, it's so soft. I'm getting on the internet as soon as we're done with this video and googling *double orgasm how-to*. Swear to god, I am, even though I'm pretty sure I could manage on my own, because there are so many things I'd like to do to her and with her if she'd let me.

"Tell you a secret?" I murmur.

"I'm suddenly terrified," she replies with a smile that doesn't quite light those big brown eyes.

"I'm not actually normal."

"I don't think that's a secret."

"Yeah, but most people think I'm not normal because I'm fabulous. Truth is, I'm a big dork."

"Again, I don't think that's a secret."

"You wouldn't have said that a week ago."

Her lips part, but she sucks them back into her mouth with a frown.

"It's okay," I tell her. "The trick is finding the people who can look past the fabulousness to the guy under all the fame. And I had them built in. Those guys? We grew up playing ball and sneaking off to movies and fighting over whose turn it was on the PlayStation. We didn't call ourselves *Bro Code* because it was trendy. We did it because that's how we all grew up. All of us from the neighborhood. We're *all* brothers. And if you ask me my best friend in the entire universe, hands down, every time, I'm gonna tell you it's Wyatt. He's a military dude now. Makes crap pay and has to send half of it to an ex-wife. Did the most awkward interview I've ever seen for a local TV station a few months ago. He's not built for this life. But he's the first to call me out when my head's getting too big, and the first to push my buttons, and the first to show up with a shovel when we need to bury a body. He's as normal as they come. He's one of my brothers. And he doesn't give two shits what's in my bank account, because he knew me back when I tried to ask a girl to prom by spelling out her name in toilet paper on her front lawn during a rainstorm."

"Oh my god, Beck, only you," she says with a shake of her head.

"Nobody else would believe that story."

"Oh, I think they would."

"That's what my sister says too."

"So now I'm like your sister."

"No, you're definitely something more."

Her breath catches, and her eyes go wary again, and I realize I've backed her against the wall, my hands on her soft hips, and my face inches from hers.

"I'm in your bubble," I say quietly.

But I don't move.

And she doesn't push me away.

"I didn't notice," she whispers.

"I'm that forgettable?"

"That comfortable."

"I was going for magnetic and sexy, but I guess I can take *comfortable*. Better than *smelly*. Or *revolting*."

"Beck?"

"Yeah?"

"Shut up and do something about being in my bubble before I let my trust issues take over again."

It's the smile that does me in. That sweet, amused, *yes, you've talked me off my cliff* smile that has me lowering my head and rubbing my lips against hers.

So fucking soft. And plump. And I smell honey.

Her fingers curl into my shirt, and I suckle her bottom lip while her eyes slide shut and a sweet, shuddery breath slips out.

Kissing her is like discovering a new flavor of ice cream. Sweet and perfect, but *better*. With a deeper flavor, a smoother finish, fresher *everything*.

She presses her chest against mine and parts her lips, her tongue making a tentative swipe, and *fuck*, I should've googled *double orgasm* last night instead of jacking off while fantasizing about her, because if I can't live up to her expectations, I'm done.

Over.

Time to throw in the towel, accept that this is my life, exactly how it is, and I'll never have anything more.

But I *want* to be good.

I want to be *so* fucking good for her. The best she's ever had.

I shouldn't. We have a contract. She hates publicity. I can't escape it.

All of this is a bad idea.

I reluctantly pull back, even though I want to keep kissing her until I can't breathe or think. "Better?" I whisper.

She drops her head to my shoulder, hiding her eyes, still gripping my shirt. "I need one more minute."

"Take your time. I'm grounded until Saturday. And if you need more of the kissing, my lips are here all day."

Her soft laugh is everything I need to know that we're going to be okay.

And when she lets me wrap her in a hug, this doesn't feel like a favor to an accidental friend.

It feels like so much more.

TWENTY-FIVE

Sarah

I SHOULD NOT HAVE KISSED Beck.

Because now that I've kissed him, I can't stop thinking about him. And thinking about him when he's sitting right there next to me, on a very comfortable low-back red leather couch in one of the apartments under his penthouse, is making me want to kiss him again to see if it was a fluke, or if my heart would start to flutter and if my nipples would pucker and if I'd get that hard, irrepressible yearning in my lady bits.

"You're sure you don't want makeup?" Charlie asks me for the seventy-billionth time.

Beck sighs. "Charlie. Knock it off. She's gorgeous just as she is."

"*I* can see that, and *you* can see that, but the trolls of Internet-landia are assholes."

"Put too much on, and I'm a whore," I say. "Not enough, and I'm *trying too hard to make a statement*. I'm comfortable *just like this*. I don't want to be *gorgeous*. I just want to be me. Okay? Let's get it over with."

"Let's *enjoy* it," Beck corrects. "You're about to tell ten million gossips that they're doing their job wrong."

"I'm about to tell the world that I owl-bombed my high school prom to get myself labeled as a sexual deviant with a thing for deep-throating giant penises and dragon tails."

"*Ohmygod,*" Mackenzie gasps.

I gape at her. "You didn't google me when all I'd tell you was that my prom was awful and got taken wrong in the media?"

"*No.* Why would I do that? I don't want to know *Serendipity.* You're too awesome as Sarah."

And now I'm going to cry. I gulp back an emotional land mine, and it sits in my gut like a cannonball that's sprouting spikes. "You might not want to stay for this then."

She snorts. "I took the day off work to be your good luck charm. Shut up and take my help. Especially since if you don't, I'll have to go be the drooling frozen mime in front of *Cooper fucking Rock.*"

She ends with a glare at Beck, like it's his fault she's obsessed with the Fireballs.

"One phone call and I could get the whole team over, if you'd rather," he offers.

I shove him lightly when all the blood leaves her face and maybe her shoulders and arms and abdomen too. Her feet are probably swelling up like overinflated punching balloons and any second now she's going to explode toes-first and save me from doing this video.

Okay, yes, I have problems.

Beck's right.

I need to find a way to *enjoy* this.

Own the story.

"Mackenzie. They're just people. It's okay," I tell her.

"*Sarah.* They are *not just people.* They're…they're…they're *gods.*"

"Do *not* tell Cooper she said that," Beck breathes to me.

"Kinda understood," I breathe back.

"This is all fun and embarrassing for all involved," Charlie interrupts, "but are we filming a video or are we taking a walk down Cooper Rock Lane?"

"I would so walk down that lane if I could breathe when I was in the same room as him," Mackenzie sighs.

Charlie shoves a phone at her. "Let's do this."

I blow out a breath and shake my hands out.

"Hey." Beck takes them both in his hand—seriously, the man has ape hands too, with these long fingers that are genetically unlikely to be real, but I've never heard of finger extensions, so since he's not a robot, they must be real, and I suspect they can probably do some fairly marvelous things to my body—and he sets them on my lap, squeezing gently while his opposite thumb softly rubs my shoulder.

"It's just you and me talking to a weird square box that will take over the world one day, okay?"

I snort indelicately. Yes, that was kinda funny. And also possibly true.

But more because his touch is shooting strange awareness vibes all over my body. Not just between my legs and to my breasts, but also to my knees, which are tingling pleasantly, and to my ears, which are getting hot, and to my ribs, which seem to be melting into a happy matrix of cotton candy and butterflies.

"I don't know if I'm in the right headspace for this," I whisper to him. "I feel like the atomic structure of my bones is shifting from a calcium construct to powdered sugar."

"Just follow my lead, okay?"

He smiles at me—not that goofball grin, and not the smolder, but a real, friendly *I've got you, Sarah* smile—and my racing hearts starts to slow.

"Ready?"

I lick my lips and nod.

His eyes drift to my mouth, and his pupils go big and round, hiding all that beautiful deep summer sky and now I really don't care that my ribs might shatter with the barest jostle of the spun glass fibers, because *holy crap, Beck Ryder is into me.*

He's not just playing.

He's *into* me.

And if he were just a vapid, superficial underwear fashion model who only cared about his bottom line and creating a foundation to make himself look good or to get some kind of tax break, I could write him off in a heartbeat.

But this guy?

This guy loves his family, and food, and life, and he makes everything *brighter*.

I'm in so much trouble.

He shifts back on the couch and crosses one knee at the ankle, then smiles at Charlie, who's watching behind a phone on a tripod. Mackenzie points to him, and he starts talking. "Hey, there, awesome people of the world. Beck Ryder here with my friend, Sarah, because I read her blog yesterday and now I'm obsessed with stars."

"You can't see the stars from the city," I tell him like a complete and total know-it-all. "There's too much ambient light."

"You ever seen the stars in Hawaii?" he asks me.

He doesn't have gel in his hair, and it's flopping over adorably, like he just rolled out of bed, and oh, actually, *he did just roll out of bed.* But he showered, so he shouldn't have such perfect bedhead that's making me want to run my fingers through it.

"Yes," I say quickly, realizing I'm staring and not answering the question. Which requires some truth on my behalf. "That's where I saw the Milky Way for the first time. We used to go to Hawaii once or twice every winter when I was growing up."

He's watching me so closely, I can't tell if it's because he likes what he sees, or if it's because he's totally *on* in celebrity mode, waiting for a sign that we're supposed to cut the video because I've gone completely dorktastic.

"Ah, when you were growing up." There's a teasing note in his voice, and the smile that goes with it seems to both relax and speed up my heart all at the same time.

That's biologically impossible.

Clearly I'm dying.

"There are rumors flying all over the internet about who your parents are," he says.

"The ones about me being adopted by a band of cheetahs and raised by wolves are all completely true."

And now he's smiling wider. With the eye crinkle. And the smolder which might not actually be a smolder, but more of a *that's my girl*, which is even more dangerous.

"Raised *with* wolves is probably more accurate, yeah?"

"Yeah," I agree softly.

"How old were you the first time your parents got mobbed by the paparazzi?"

I frown. "I don't know. I can't ever remember a time when it wasn't just *normal* to go anywhere in LA with them and have people screaming their names and taking our pictures."

He grins and shakes his head.

"What?" I ask.

"Once, when I was…thirteen? Fourteen? Somewhere in there. Anyway, the guys and I—all the guys from the neighborhood—we all set our alarms for like two in the morning on a school night, and we climbed out our windows and met up to go move this giant dinosaur we picked up at a flea market so it was staring directly into the high school principal's bedroom window."

I gape at him. "What—but—*how*?"

"Ah, one of us was old enough to drive. Not really well with that trailer hooked to it—we used every cent any of us made mowing grass that summer, swear we did, because we had to buy the trailer too—but we did it. We got this giant—what's the dinosaur with the long neck? The giraffe of the dinosaurs?"

"You're making this all up." I'm smiling as I'm calling him on his bullshit, because there's *no freaking way*.

"I'm not," he says. "What's that dinosaur called? I can never remember it."

"Brontosaurus?" I suggest. "Or a brachiosaurus?"

"Sure. Let's go with one of those. Anyway, we did it. We got it all set up on the principal's front lawn, positioned just right, and that sucker was *heavy*, took like eight of us to move it, and then we went back home and hid the trailer in the garage of this empty house a couple blocks away. Got to school that morning and everyone's talking about the greatest prank ever pulled."

"Oh my god, *that was you!*" Mackenzie gasps. "I remember that!"

Charlie shushes her quietly, but Beck points to her and winks. "Beautiful, wasn't it?"

"It's still there."

"What? No way." He squeezes my knee. "We're taking a field trip. I'll show you."

"Why?"

"Because you don't believe me." His eyes are twinkling, and I'm still smiling back so big I'm practically laughing.

"No, I mean, of all the pranks you could pull, why *that* one? It's kinda...lame."

"You're just saying that because you're jealous you didn't think of it first."

"If I'd done that, the tabloids would've said Sunny Darling's daughter warped the space-time continuum and brought back real dinosaurs. Or that I concocted them out of DNA samples I stole out of a museum."

"Exactly. We did it, and until, well, right now, when I have a feeling a few mothers are getting ready to kick our asses, nobody knew it was us. If you'd even had the thought, you probably would've been followed by the paparazzi for weeks with them just waiting for you to screw up. That had to suck."

"It did," I concede with a sigh. "You got away with *putting a freaking dinosaur* in your principal's front yard, and the time I spritzed my hair with gel before combing all the knots out and then squirted myself in the eyeball with detangler spray when my mom's stylist was trying to help fix it, they had to pay off the paparazzi to not run the pictures of me walking into school."

"Damn, Sarah. That sucks."

Control the story. Control the story. I shrug and take a page out of his book. "Seriously, what seventeen-year-old *hasn't* had a bad hair day?"

His eyes bug out, and I let myself grin. "Kidding. I was six. But my parents still paid off the paps. And that's the only time in my life I've had really short hair. It works on my dad, but on me, I look like a confused poodle."

His eyes are going soft. "You were probably adorable."

"You could pull it off, but I scared small children and exotic pets." Okay. Yeah. I can do this, because he's right.

Letting go and being willing to poke a little fun at yourself makes it all easier.

Like it's not so *real*.

Maybe I *could* do a video series on my blog.

"You want to talk about prom?" he asks, and there I go, tensing up again.

But I'm safe here.

If I say no go to putting this video on the internet, then he won't put it up there.

But maybe I *do* need to tell my side of the story. Even knowing people will twist it and call me stupid and ugly and a whore—though I don't know how you get *whore* out of an owl story, but it's the internet, so clearly it'll come up—maybe it's time to really face it.

"I was in the geek crowd in high school, and there were probably six or eight of us who'd sit in the halls and trade *Harry Potter* cards before school and during lunch, so we thought it would be fun to go to prom like the whole cast. Who doesn't like *Harry Potter*, right?"

"He's no *Buffy*, but yeah," Beck says. "He's cool. Even if everyone knows wizards aren't real."

"Not like vampires?"

"Exactly. You went as Hermione?"

I shrug. "I had the hair for it. And my dad was able to get us a few props from one of the movie sets, which we thought was really cool, especially since most of my friends didn't have parents in the industry. And my mom had connections with a guy who raised owls for movies, so when I asked her if we could get a couple owls, she made the call for me and said it was all set, that we'd have two or three owls—and their trainer—to go with us on prom night."

"Your parents are pretty awesome," he says.

"They are." I smile and leave it at that, because I'm not dragging *them* into this too any more than they've already dragged themselves. "So we all had our costumes fitted, one of my friends found a stuffed dragon that was fairly epic—at least, until I just heard your dinosaur story—and another's parents owned a restaurant that converted itself into a whole *Harry Potter* theme for the night, so we had a delicious dinner there, and then we headed to prom, where we were supposed to meet the owl trainer."

"Supposed to?" he squeezes my knee.

"It's Hollywood. Plot twist, right? Obviously, he wasn't there. I called my mom, and she said she'd check in with him, so we went inside, and yeah, people were staring, but who wouldn't? My friend Jasmine was dressed up like Hagrid. She was on stilts even, because she had skills and she'd also found a furry beard and wig to rival mine. We found a corner of the dance floor and we were all dancing and passing around her stuffed pet dragon when the owls arrived."

I realize Mackenzie's chewing her nails like she does during ballgames. "The owls wouldn't have been so bad by themselves," I tell her, "but it was all the panic that started as soon as they started zipping through the ballroom. People were falling all over each other, tripping, and then the paparazzi showed up right as I faceplanted into Jasmine's crotch and totally took her down, stilts and all, but not before an owl up on one of the chandeliers dropped a pellet into my cleavage."

Beck swipes a hand over his mouth and shakes his head. "Jeez. And I thought getting booed off the stage at my senior homecoming dance was bad."

"You did not."

He holds up his hands and grins. "Swear on my underwear. Ask Levi and Cash. It's what prompted us to start practicing. We were gonna horrify everyone even worse at prom, except…"

"Except you went viral on YouTube and got a recording contract, and I ended up changing my name and hiding in Morocco for a year."

"Yeah." His grin slips. "That sucks rotten eggs."

"It's what I get for dabbling in black magic."

He cracks up, and now that it's all out there, I'm kinda…*free.*

Not weightless, but lighter.

"I loved Morocco," I tell him honestly. "The people were amazing. The food—"

"Delicious," he finishes. "Hey, you promised me mint tea."

"And you promised me you weren't stuffing your briefs."

He snorts with laughter and doubles over, and I go hot in the face.

"Sorry," I mutter. "It was there."

He holds out a fist, and I bump it. "Well played, black magic lady. Well played. You doing that black magic to get that meteor shower that's coming next month?"

"Do you realize we're sitting just a few thousand miles over a molten core of lava and flinging through the universe at sixty-seven thousand miles an hour? And not just around the sun. The *sun* is moving through the universe too, which means we're basically hurtling through space in a controlled spiral of awesome. I mean, how does that even *happen*? And then we get to live in this little biodome where the most important thing on the internet today is going to be that I made a joke about the size of your package?"

We officially cannot post this video.

Fabulous.

Now I have to do it again.

But Beck's still grinning. "Your blog isn't just about saving the bees and the giraffes."

"The entire planet is too fascinating to keep it to *just* endangered animals. But they're getting the priority right now."

"How's our girl doing over at the zoo?"

"She's completely and totally oblivious to all the attention, and she's taking her sweet time about going into active labor."

"You think she'll have a boy or a girl?"

"Yes." I woo-woo my fingers at him. "Unless my black magic trick to make her give birth to gorillas works."

"If you get arrested for doing black magic and making Persephone give birth to a gorilla, can I have your—"

I clap my hand over his mouth before he can finish asking for my *Serenity* ship, but I'm laughing. "No. That's *top secret*. Shush."

"Bu ees oo," he says.

"It's time to say goodnight, Beck."

He licks my hand, and I shriek and jerk it away with an astonished laugh. "You *licked* me."

"Can't sign off until we remind people to visit your blog and check out Persephone's giraffe cam," he points out. "Did my mom make you bacon again? I smell bacon."

"You always smell bacon."

He grins and looks at the camera. "Sometimes I smell hamburgers and pizza too. And that's the Must Love Bees science blog. Go check it out." He winks, and Charlie hits a button on the phone.

"And done," she announces.

I drop my head between my knees. "And now we have to do it *all over again* so I don't make a joke about your *package*."

"Oh, no, that's going up just as it is," Charlie reports. "Because that was hilarious. And it'll piss off Bruce and utterly enchant the rest of the world except for the trolls who'll call you both names."

"Bruce?" I ask.

Beck grimaces. "Not important. You worried about anything other than telling the world I have a little willy?"

"Oh my god."

Mackenzie drops to the ground laughing so hard she's crying.

"Great," Beck says. "Post away. I gotta go warn Levi and Cash to get their Dick pics ready."

"*What?*" Seriously, this time I really am putting my hands up to catch my eyeballs.

"Those guys would do *anything* for me," Beck says.

The door opens, and my mom rushes in with Cupcake, who squeals and darts right to Mackenzie, who's still wiping her eyes and bent double on the floor. She squeaks and jumps to her feet when the pig tries to hump her.

"Did we miss it? Honey, tell me you left your clothes on. And are you ready? I booked an appointment for us to go shopping at the downtown boutiques. It's not Fifth Avenue, but your father pointed out you probably didn't want to fly all the way to New York in the middle of a publicity storm."

"Shopping. For what?"

"Your dress, sweetheart." She turns a bright movie star smile on Beck. "And if this *video* embarrasses my daughter, I'll be calling my psychic on your behalf."

"Yes, ma'am," he replies.

"What dress?" I ask.

"For the black-tie fundraiser for the zoo Saturday night."

I look at my mom.

Then at Beck, who's actually looking a little sheepish. "It's just a few hours," he says. "We didn't mention it yet, did we?"

The contract.

I'm contractually obligated to go to a *fancy dinner*, which I thought I'd escape, since there wasn't actually a *fancy dinner* in the works when I signed, only the possibility if Beck was lucky enough to get an invitation.

And apparently my parents have been in on setting that *fancy dinner* up to be a fundraiser for the zoo, which I clearly can't decline.

A Black-Tie Fundraiser.

Code for *fancy gala where people with too much money talk about their self-importance.*

"You don't have to go traditional," he adds quickly. "Whatever you're comfortable in."

"Not jeans or sweatpants," Charlie says.

"But RYDE sweatpants are so comfortable," I reply.

"Fucking right they are." Beck nods emphatically. "That's why I picked them."

"You guys are ridiculous," Mackenzie declares. She points at me. "And don't even try this *I don't get fancy* crap. I saw you at your holiday Christmas party, and I *know* you had a good time. And remember the wedding Trent took you to? You can do this. And you're going to fucking *rock* it. Also, the Fireballs massacred Minnesota when you went to that wedding last year, so you basically have to wear a dress to see if it's still good luck."

My mom's lips part.

Cupcake sits back on her haunches and twists her neck to stare at Mackenzie like she has a screw loose.

But Beck grins.

That bright, *haha, she's got you now,* adorable grin. "Can't argue with that. You owe it to the team. You owe it to the whole *city*."

"Fine," I say. "But I'm not shaving my legs."

I'm totally shaving my legs.

Beck pulls me into a hug and presses a kiss to my temple. "Thank you, Sarah."

And I have issues.

Because I'm pretty sure I would've caved just for a hug from him, even though what I'd really like is to see if that kissing could go somewhere farther.

"I won't tell you you're welcome until you talk my mother out of putting me in Slimzies."

"Done."

"*Not* done," Mom replies dryly.

"We can discuss this over honey puff pancake."

"We can discuss this *never*. Our appointment's in twenty minutes. The driver's waiting, Serendipity. It's time to go."

"I got your back," Beck whispers to me. "It's not over until the former boy bander sings."

"Amateur," Mackenzie sniffs. She steps to my side and links her arm in mine. "*I've* got your back, Sarah. *He*'s staying out of it."

Mom looks Mackenzie up and down. "Do you have good taste?"

"I was raised by two drag queens. What do you think?"

Mom nods. "Excellent. Come along, Sarah. Beauty waits for no woman."

Beck grabs my hand before I can follow. "You know you're a natural?" he says. "In front of the camera, I mean. You could do regular vlogs if you wanted to. And say the word, and I'll get you a private visit with Persephone."

Mom stops and looks at him. Then blinks, and *is she going to cry*? What in the *world* is going on? "That's very sweet of you," she says.

"Wait, isn't that my line?" I ask.

"Only if you're actually going to deliver it and snag the man, sweetheart. Come along. Let's go make him rue the day he insulted your uterus by making him fall madly in love with you when we Cinderella you up."

He has this unreadable expression on his face as I let Mom and Mackenzie tug me away.

But the weird thing is, despite all my panic last weekend at being sucked into his world and then outed for who I am and who my parents are, I think I'm actually glad he pulled my uterus into it.

Because maybe I *should* do a video blog. And maybe I *should* upgrade my website.

And maybe I should stop letting my past hold me back, and grab this unexpected opportunity to figure out who I'm supposed to be in this world.

TWENTY-SIX

Beck

I DON'T HEAR from Sarah for *hours*.

Through breakfast, morning snack, second morning snack, lunch, second lunch, afternoon snack, and pre-dinner snack. Davis goes back home. Levi leaves to fly to Seattle for his weekend concert. Tripp takes his kids for some playdate at a library or something, where he'll undoubtedly have nannies throwing themselves all over him, and everyone else goes to work.

Even Charlie abandons me.

But Judson doesn't.

He and Cupcake hang with me all day, and when things get weird after I beat him in foosball and he challenges me to a gym-off —dude, don't be like me and ask what that is, or you'll regret it—I call Hank, Cash's brother, who runs a small website design company.

And by *small*, I mean he specializes in clients like me, Levi, and Cash, who have big website demands, and that he employs enough people to keep everything running twenty-four seven for his small clientele, even though he could easily expand to being one of the big dogs in Internetlandia.

But even he abandons me after getting all the info he needs from Sarah to upgrade and tweak her website.

She's texting *him*, but not me.

Still, he was enough of a distraction that now Judson's chilling on my couch, Cupcake sprawled across his lap, watching golf.

And by *watching golf*, I mean they're both sleeping.

Wyatt comes to my rescue just before I'm ready to dive into first dinner. He and Ellie have been supervising movers all day, without the paparazzi watching them, because the reporters all flocked to Shipwreck when one of my bodyguards took my car and drove out that way with the other one in the backseat covered by a blanket.

Heh.

"Barbecue at the Rivers house," Wyatt says. "C'mon. I'll drive you. Ellie's already there with Tucker, who's telling stories about the things his Beck Ryder doll did at summer camp today."

I look at Judson.

Then back at Wyatt, who rolls his eyes. "Dude. He's practically your father-in-law. You can't just leave him there sleeping."

"Ain't nobody sleeping, boy," Judson growls with his eyes closed. "This is called meditating on how I'm gonna gut your friend like a fish when he breaks my daughter's heart."

"Man, you know all the good party tricks," I say to him. "You like brisket and baked beans?"

"You got a hollow leg to fit it all in?" he replies.

"He's half-cow," Wyatt supplies. "Four stomachs. Science experiment gone wrong."

"Should've gone for four dicks," Judson says. "Might've been able to fill out your briefs. Keep it away from my daughter or die."

"You meet the best people," Wyatt tells me.

"It's a gift."

We all load up in Wyatt's SUV, including Charlie, who hasn't had a single meal with me today, but did apparently get a massage and a facial and is feeling extra helpful with suggesting different ways Judson could torture me if I hurt Sarah.

Dinner's a fucking awesome feast, because Ms. Rivers is almost as good of a cook as my mom. I say *almost* because I still remember who gave birth to me.

And it's utter perfection being back in the old neighborhood.

Old trees. Houses built in the seventies. Sidewalks. Basketball hoops on garages. That missing limb on the oak at Wyatt's grandma's old house that we accidentally took out with a bottle rocket that we may have overfueled. The weathered picnic table we used as our makeshift stage when we decided that it was stupid for Levi, Tripp, and all the Rivers kids to have been forced to take music lessons for all those years if we weren't going to somehow be famous, even though Davis, who never studied music a day in his life, had the best voice of all of us.

And ribs and cornbread and coleslaw and baked beans, and I'm really wishing I did have four stomachs by the time I'm done with the banana pudding my mom brought over.

But as perfect as it is to finally be back—I've been trying to keep the reporters from following me over here, so I haven't dropped by since getting back to town—it feels like something's missing.

And it's not because Ellie and Wyatt are all touchy-feely, or because Tripp's kids are making me mourn the family I'll probably never have—Sarah's not the only person with trust issues—or because Levi and Cash and Davis aren't here, or because I'm getting all the ribbing over the video this morning and Sarah's suggestion that my schlong is actually a *schuh*, because it's missing the *long* part.

And Charlie's report that the video has shot speculation about us sky-high isn't helping either. Nor is hearing that Vegas is taking bets on if Sarah's pregnant.

I mean, yeah, I feel bad that her life is so public again when she didn't want it to be, but it's not even guilt eating at me.

I can't put my finger on it until my phone lights up with the text I've been waiting for all day.

I might look like a girl Saturday night, but I can't promise to be happy about it.

Yep.

That's exactly what's wrong.

I wish she was here to have fun with my family and extended neighborhood family too, instead of being off shopping for a dress that she doesn't want to wear for an event that didn't have to happen if I hadn't been a dumbass.

To see her dad making Cupcake do tricks in her tutu and challenging Wyatt to an arm wrestling contest. To watch Hank and Waylon making bets over if June's new boyfriend will stick around after this. To listen to the mothers all chattering about wedding plans and Ellie insisting her wedding will be a *small* affair, thank you very much.

As if she has a choice in it.

I'm still grinning at my phone, debating what to reply, and I decide to send her a quick video of my view from the backyard instead.

"Hey, dinglehoppers, say hi to Sarah," I call.

"You can do better than this guy," Hank says.

"He makes terrible jokes," Waylon agrees.

"Awful poker player," Wyatt says.

"I'll serve his eyeballs on a platter for breakfast next to his spleen if he hurts you," her dad growls.

"Beck is a *wonderful* young man, and we're so glad you tolerate him," Ms. Rivers says.

"Mom, that wasn't nice," June hisses.

"But, honey, it's accurate."

"Love you, Beck." Ellie blows me a kiss. "Sarah, if you taser him again, I want it on video."

"Snickerdoodle vagina!" James yells.

"I want to see the tasering," Tripp agrees.

"Be nice," his mom chides.

Emma farts. Loudly. Cupcake pretends to fall over dead. And I kill the video and send it to Sarah.

"Aw, honey, you know we love you, right?" Mom says.

"Almost as much as we love Ellie," Dad agrees with a twinkle in his eye.

Judson's studying me through slit eyes. "You might be okay with this crew to keep you humble," he growls. "But I still don't trust you around the Euranians."

"Rightfully so, sir," I agree.

My phone buzzes again with another text from Sarah.

I see where you get your sense of humor. Definitely from the pig.

She has her own sense of humor. And it's fun to see it coming out. Because the woman I met Saturday morning who freaked out and tasered me isn't the same woman who's charming the world on a video we posted from my social media accounts this morning.

Mom used to talk about the year Ellie bloomed.

I didn't get it.

But I feel like I'm watching Sarah bloom.

And it's the greatest fucking thing *ever*.

TWENTY-SEVEN

Sarah

NO MATTER how many times I try to tell myself this isn't a real date, I can't stop my heart from pounding and my knees from knocking and basically everything from going into panic mode while I wait for Beck to arrive Thursday night.

After Trent last year, I realized I'd never be relationship material. That I hold too much of myself back, and I was okay with that, because—well, probably because I was being really stupid. And afraid that no one could ever love me for all of me despite the complications of my life.

And now, here I am, about to go on a fake-real date with the guy who pulled me back into the limelight, who I'm getting more and more attached to by the day, who has a lot on the line if the media decides he's actually the asshole his tweet made him out to be, and who I still trust anyway.

Despite my very nervous heart's warnings that we take it slow.

Physical relationships never used to make me squirrely. Not until Trent asked if he could meet my parents. But getting attached to Beck and his goofball personality and that irresistible smile and his easy acceptance of who I am makes me quake, because I don't have an easy out if I let myself fall all the way over the cliff and he really is just that good at acting.

This isn't all physical.

Not even close.

I'm in a Mom-approved T-shirt—classic Rolling Stones gets her every time—and hip-hugging jeans that loudly proclaim to the world that I love dessert more than I love to exercise, but I'm not muffin-topping, so Mom doesn't object to them either. I let her French braid my hair and agree to some Burt's Bees lip gloss, but otherwise, I'm all me.

Right down to the plain cotton bra and RYDE underwear.

He's right on time, and when he knocks, my dad doesn't growl or threaten to feed his testicles to the pig.

I think they bonded over a one-armed push-up contest that my dad won yesterday. And the world will never know if Beck let him or if my dad is that much of a badass, because I'll never get a straight answer out of Beck.

Who's now smiling at me from my front porch like I'm the person who set the sun and moon and stars into their dynamic, beautiful dance through space. "Hey," he says.

I smile back, and it's not because I know there are photographers capturing my every move, but because it's impossible not to smile back at him. He's this unexpected combination of complete goofball and absolutely zero self-doubt, and he's rubbing off on me.

"Have her home by ten," Dad says in a less growly voice. "And call before you walk in so I can turn off the alarm."

"Judson, honey, Serendipity knows the code now. And she's an adult. Almost *thirty* even. She can stay out all night with a man if she wants to."

"He's not a *man*. He's a beast hell-bent on taking my daughter's innocence and flushing it down a sewage-filled vat of toxic sludge."

"I hope your genitals are insured," I murmur to Beck, because clearly that's what Dad's going to threaten next. Again.

Beck coughs, his eyes dancing. Mom grips Dad by the arm and tugs hard enough to uproot him and make him trip over Cupcake, who's looking for Meda, who's hiding from Cupcake.

Dad points two fingers to his own eyeballs, then to Beck. "I'm watching you."

"I'm watching me too, sir." Beck gives him a salute, and then tugs my hand. "Ready, Sarah? Don't want to miss the show."

"We don't?"

"Oh, yeah. It's gonna be awesome."

I wave to my parents, equal parts curious about just how funny a comedy show can be and eager to put Dad's death glare behind us.

And also grateful that I don't have to dress up for *this* one like I will Saturday night, when there will be hundreds more eyeballs on me. "Don't wait up."

"I'll wait up," Dad growls.

"No, you won't, Judson. One more night on that couch will throw your back out. Serendipity, sweetheart, we're going back to our hotel. Are you sure Meda's okay here by herself? Cupcake misses her terribly."

"Cupcake terrorizes her."

"Nonsense. They were cuddling while you were at work today. I have pictures."

"Let them go, Sunny," Dad growls. "The sooner they leave, the sooner I can disembowel this filthy piece of rat dung trying to compromise my daughter."

"Looking forward to it, sir," Beck says, and we're finally off.

"You do know he's sixty percent serious, right?" I ask as we dash to his car.

"Nah. He's just making up for all those boyfriends he didn't get to threaten since you left home. And I'm an easy target."

We get strapped in and we head out of the neighborhood, security behind us, paparazzi behind them. My neighbor at the end of the street, out watering her flowers, does a double-take at the car, squints to see in, and then flips us off.

"I don't know what virus is going around town, but it's giving people a horrible case of rigid digits," he says. "Better wash your hands good. Often."

"Is that your real story?" I ask, a smile creeping up at his ridiculously optimistic version of what's going on. Mackenzie's been filtering what I see, and by *filtering what I see*, I mean she stole my phone and removed my social media apps and installed a filter on my computer that won't let me access the sites either, and she's sending me regular screenshots of nice things people say.

"It helps." He cuts a glance at me at a stop sign. "I've learned my lesson. Promise. And I'm still sorry I dragged you into it. Mostly. But only for the painful parts. You're pretty awesome. I like hanging out with you."

"You're not half-bad yourself, despite your questionable judgment in fashion advice."

He grins. "I've been saying that for *years*, but people keep being all, *No, Beck, you're brilliant, take our money*."

"Obviously they feel bad that you have to carry around those ape arms all the time and are trying to make you feel better about yourself."

He grins wider.

I twist to face him. "Do you *ever* get offended? Because that was really mean of me."

"Sit back and let your seat belt do its job, and yes. I get offended. I get offended when people are assholes to my family. Or when that jackoff on Twitter said Persephone was an ugly twat."

"*What?*"

"Yeah. Said Jagger—her baby daddy—probably threw up after he fucked her. Charlie had to throw my phone in the toilet to keep me from replying, because she's gorgeous. Persephone, I mean. Were you watching today? She licked the camera. It was gross and adorable at the same time. Do you know giraffe tongues are like eight feet long?"

One day.

I want *one day* of being as happy about life as Beck Ryder is.

"What?" he asks as I stare at him.

Oh my god. I'm falling for Beck Ryder.

Hard.

"Is it working?" I ask, because informing him that giraffe tongues are *not* eight feet long will make me feel even more of a frumpy stick in the mud than I am on a normal day, and I don't want to just be a frumpy fact-spouting geek.

Not that I'm about to be much better.

"Is what working?"

"This. Us. To keep your foundation on track."

I might be staying off the internet and letting Mackenzie only give me the good news while on temporary social media hiatus, but I did go to work today.

And I heard the whispers.

She's probably just doing it so she can say she bagged Beck Ryder.

Do you think she's planning on jumping ship and going to work for Ryder Consulting when this is all over?

How much did she have to pay those impersonators to pretend to be Judson Clarke and Sunny Darling?

Can you imagine how much he's paying her?

Holy shit, look at that picture. She's eating giant dick. CLEARLY eating giant dick.

The weird part was that they rolled right off. Mom used to say you learn real quick who your friends are.

I'm having gut instincts confirmed.

And it makes me wonder if this fake blooming relationship is actually doing what it's supposed to.

He stares at the cars in front of us at a stoplight as he slowly nods. "Yeah. It's working. Vaughn's a good guy, and he's about ready to stick up for me. Looks like we'll still be on for launching the foundation on schedule. And that should clear up the rest of my reputation."

"That's…great."

His brow twitches like maybe it's not so great. "I guess. Sucks that so much of the world has to be wrapped up in labeling you all good or all bad based on one night of your life or one little tweet. I mean the generic you. Not *you* you. But…all of us."

Did I say *falling* for Beck?

More like plummeting through the atmosphere with a rocket strapped to my back without a parachute.

I stop myself when I realize I'm reaching for his thigh just to touch him, because despite that *oh my god* kiss in the stairwell yesterday—that he *stopped*—I don't actually know what our boundaries are. "So your life will go back to normal soon."

"Sounds like it."

"And you'll have to quit eating so much?"

His shoulders relax, and his grin comes back. "Maybe I'll take another few weeks off before normal. I'm getting an itch to spend some time out in Shipwreck. You ever been?"

I shake my head.

"Best town on the entire planet. After Copper Valley, I mean. And maybe the island of Capri off the Italian coast, but that's not a fair comparison, since the Blue Grotto is magic."

One-tenth of his enthusiasm would be utter magic. "What's special about Shipwreck?"

"Cooper Rock's from there, but don't tell him I said that makes it special. What's really awesome is that it's a pirate town in the mountains."

"I've been in Copper Valley for over a decade, and I still don't get how that works."

"Like eight hundred years ago, this pirate dude, Thorny Rock, was getting ambushed by the Norwegian army off the coast of South Carolina, so he snuck all his Chinese galleons onto a covered wagon and let unicorns pull it inland until they lost their horns, and that's where he buried his treasure and founded a town, and now his descendants keep the pirate tradition alive every year out there. Ellie and Wyatt hooked up at the Pirate Festival last year, then went back this year to get engaged. It's fucking magic. And one day, I'm gonna take a metal detector over the whole town and find that treasure. You watch. Don't laugh. I'm serious."

"*Eight hundred years ago?*" I'm not touching the unicorns, but I *am* laughing. "Norwegian army? Chinese galleons?"

"I'm really bad at geography."

"History."

"That too." He shoots me another grin. "I'm really glad you like to laugh, because that's basically all we're doing tonight."

"You're making up stories?"

"Nope. We're hitting amateur hour at the comedy club. No, no, don't make that face. It's *awesome*. There's this ventriloquist—"

"No. Way. Hard stop."

"Don't get freaked. She's funny. *And* she's super smart. Like smarter than you and Ellie and Davis and Cupcake all rolled together."

"*Cupcake?*"

"Dude. Pigs are smart. Science says so."

"She freaked over a piece of green onion on the floor when Mom was making omelets this morning and ran head-first into the table leg and almost gave herself a concussion."

"Understandable. Green onions are terrifying."

I throw my hands up, laughing. "Okay. You win. You are officially the funniest man on the planet, and I will never win an argument with you, *ever*."

"You maybe could. I mean, it might cost you lessons in double orgasms, but I'd let you win an argument."

Zing! And there go my panties. "You're not going to let that go, are you?"

"Not until I'm sure I don't have a chance." He slides to a stop again, and this time, when he looks at me, his goofball side has retreated and that very manly mannish side is front and center. "And right now, I know I have a chance."

I suck in a shuddery breath, because *whoa*, yes, he really does.

And it's not just because he's using the smolder.

It's because I can still remember the feel of his lips on mine. It's because every time he touches me—hand, leg, back, face—my skin buzzes to life like a neon sign. It's because I should hate him for his ignorant tweet last week, but he's still managed to sneak past my defenses with his apology, because I honestly believe there's a vulnerable human being capable of true regret and determination to do better and a whole hell of a lot of love for everyone around him hiding under that gorgeous surface.

I can pass on the smolder. I grew up around schmootzy smolders.

But the man underneath is getting to me.

"We're temporary," I remind him. "And this isn't real."

"This is very real. And it doesn't have to be temporary."

I don't have a solid argument for him, so I just sit there and stare at him dumbly with heat spreading over my skin and my heart pumping a fist in the air and shouting *Yeah, baby!*

He doesn't smirk. Or grin. Or fluff his feathers.

Nope.

The man squeezes my knee and turns his attention back to the road.

"Why did you stop kissing me yesterday?" I whisper.

For once, he doesn't answer quickly, and when he does, he's still just as quiet and serious. "I've been…taken advantage of before. And it sucks. And your parents aren't the only people who've ever had to pay someone off to protect someone they love."

I choke on a breath, because that's *not* what I expected him to say.

"I get it, Sarah. You didn't sign up for this. You didn't ask to be shoved back in the public eye. So no rushing. I like you. I *want* you. But I don't want you to think I'm kissing you just because we have a contract, because I'm *not*."

My heart squeezes and my lungs tighten and my breath gets short.

He knows the right things to say. And I trust the raw honesty in his eyes and in his voice, which is scary.

Because Beck isn't just *Beck*.

He's everything I ran away from when I left high school. Famous. Followed by paparazzi. Navigating celebrity politics.

How can someone so deep in the game of putting on a face for the world feel so *real*?

"When I kiss you, I want you to know I'm kissing *you* because I *want* to," he continues, his voice dropping into husky territory. "Not because it looks good. Not because you just happen to be the woman saving my ass in a business deal. But because I *like you*."

My hesitant hand goes to his thigh, and I squeeze the tight muscle. "I like you too."

"Scary as hell, isn't it?"

"Scarier."

He grins, and I sink back into my seat with an embarrassed laugh. "I'm sorry you've been taken advantage of," I say softly.

"I chose this life. I knew the risks." He covers my hand with his and squeezes.

"It shouldn't have to be a risk to do what you love."

His lips curl up in a smile, and I want to kiss him, because *gah*, that smile.

"Oh, I don't know," he says. "I'm starting to think the things most worth having are worth working for."

And there go more bubbles fizzing in my chest, because he makes it sound like he's talking about *me*. "Like being a pediatrician?"

"Ah, the lady's aiming for the heart." He clutches his chest in mock injury while he grins at me. "Dangling impossible dreams out there for me to never hit."

"Would you have? If this wasn't working, if your fashion empire tanked, would you go back to school?"

"Trying to talk me into staying?"

"Who we could've been is always a part of who we are. If I hadn't been an environmental engineer, I would've wanted to be a travel writer."

His smile's going affectionate, which is just as dangerous. "I can see it."

"So? Would you have gone back to school? What else would you do if you weren't the famous Beck Ryder?"

"Become very, very good at giving double orgasms."

TWENTY-EIGHT

Beck

WE HAVE a back door pass to get us into The Laugh Track, the comedy club downtown, which is just as effective at getting attention as buying a ticket at the front door since the paps were tipped off that we'd be coming, except we don't have to wade through everyone else buying tickets, which is really just an excuse by my team to save my ego from the people who'll tell me to suck dick and die.

I agreed to the back door because I didn't want Sarah hearing any of the bullshit that people are spouting on Twitter about her looks that the occasional dumbass is brave enough to utter in person, and also because Charlie flat-out warned me that she'd quit for real if I punched anyone.

That would be like Ellie refusing to buy me any more Christmas presents for the rest of my life, and Ellie gives the best Christmas presents.

Like the Justin Bieber electric toothbrush she got me two years ago.

Epic. Prank level infinity right there. How's a guy supposed to live without that in his life?

"Spoiled asshole," one of the bouncers mutters as we pass through the back door.

"I'm working on it," Sarah replies cheerfully. "Seriously, I asked my parents to donate my usual birthday Ferrari to a B-lister this year. That's not being an asshole, is it?"

I suck in a surprised grin and tug her in the door while the bouncers choke on their own spit and my bodyguards shuffle her faster too.

"What?" she mutters. "Like they've never stuck their feet in their mouths."

"That was awesome. Did you practice sassing the paps when you were growing up?"

"No, I always thought of the perfect comeback five minutes too late, and Mom always said it wasn't worth baiting them anyway."

"She's right," one of the bodyguards grunts.

"I know," Sarah sighs. "But that felt really fucking fantastic. For like two seconds there, I was the girl with the comeback. It'll never happen again, and honestly, my heart's about to pound out of my chest, but it was worth it."

I am *definitely* practicing double orgasms with her when this contract is over. Triple. Quadruple. Can a woman go for a quintuple, or would that kill her? Because I'm pretty sure a quintuple would kill me.

I'll have to ask a doctor.

We're steered around the back of the stage to a round two-person table off to the left in the open seating area, bodyguards at the table beside us. We're both angled with a good view of the black curtain blocking the stage, and our server rushes right over, only giving me a small lip curl before turning her attention to Sarah. "Hi, hon. What can I get you? We have a strawberry cosmo that's delicious. Makes the company more bearable. By the way, I can*not* stop watching Persephone. Do you think she'll have the baby this week?"

"I—she could go another couple weeks, but it's really exciting, isn't it?"

"She is *so* pretty."

"I love her tongue," I say.

"We have the best cheese fries in Copper Valley," the lady tells Sarah, completely ignoring me. "Bacon, scallions, and we don't just use goopy orange cheese, though that's totally delicious at the ballpark. We melt gouda, swiss, and cheddar together."

My stomach grumbles.

"I'm *really* hungry tonight," Sarah says. "Do you have hamburgers? Like half-pounders?"

"I can totally get you a half-pound burger. Bacon? Barbecue sauce? Fried egg?"

Sarah orders the mother of all burgers, with everything from avocado to bacon to provolone to fried onions on it, and I have to surreptitiously wipe the drool off the corner of my mouth.

What? I worked out today. On a fucking treadmill instead of out in the glorious summer day, but hey, I live in a time when I can run in a three-foot-by-two-foot space so I don't have little old ladies spitting on me or other little old ladies asking me to kiss their dogs since those other old ladies actually believe I'm honestly sorry for the tweet heard 'round the world last week.

Not that I snuck out of my apartment this morning for a stroll to the Apple store and had any of that happen.

Really.

Don't tell my team, okay?

Sarah finishes her order by asking for a large Cobb salad with extra bacon, sweet potato fries, onion rings, steamed broccoli, a sweet tea—*just bring a jug, please, because I'm extra thirsty*—and a Nutella almond malt.

I've never fallen in real love before—I mean, with a human, because I've fallen in love plenty with fried cheese sticks and a solid steak—but I'm growing more and more convinced that feeling after the taser incident wasn't just residual voltage.

When the server finally dashes away, I angle closer to her, draping my arm around the back of her chair so I can whisper in her ear. "Can I kiss you? Right now? Because that was the sexiest fucking thing I've ever heard in my life, and I'm having a really hard time keeping my hands to myself."

She pretends to be puzzled, which makes her eyes sparkle and shine and yeah, definitely not residual voltage. "That sweet girl insulting your interpersonal skills and asking about Persephone?"

"You, ordering mounds and mounds of food. I'm having these fantasies about spreading it all over your body and feasting for hours."

"If you're not careful with all that dirty talk, we're both going to regret what those photographers post to the world in about two minutes," she breathes, her eyes going dark like *yes*, she wants me eating all over her.

And now I'm wondering what color her nipples are and if she's the silk, lace, or cotton panties type, or if she's in a thong, or boy shorts, and *fuck*, is it possible to be aroused in your stomach at the same time as you're sporting a redwood, because everything's pretty much revving engines right now.

"I don't care about the photographers," I tell her. "I'm so turned on right now."

"Oh, because you think I'm going to share?"

Her lips are smiling and teasing, but her eyes are dark. *So* dark. Not just normal Sarah dark, but intense and deep and shadowed by her lowering lids, but still sparkling. The room's dimly lit, but it's glowing just for having her sitting in here.

"Name your price. Anything. You want my Frogger game? My car? A house in the mountains? A willing student with an eager tongue who really really wants to learn that double orgasm trick?"

"I think you're cheating," she whispers.

"I think you're the world's most perfect woman and I'm in serious trouble here."

"It was really *that* sexy?"

"If I was lying, I'd say you were the alien queen of a distant planet come here to hypnotize all the men and steal pieces of our spleens to start a master race of sex slaves on your own planet."

She cracks up even as she leans closer to me, her fingers coming to rest on my cheek. "*How* did you *ever* become a fashion mogul? That's more cutthroat than Hollywood, and I swear you're a thirteen-year-old boy in a man's body. Which I'm completely okay with, by the way. I like you this happy and goofy."

"How has no one ever noticed before how gorgeous your eyes are? They're like pied piper eyes. You should have men following you like puppies everywhere you go just for opening those beautiful eyes every morning."

"Looks aren't everything."

"But your eyes are. Your eyes are *everything*."

Inches. *Inches*. I could be kissing her in mere inches. And I'm completely dead serious about everything I'm telling her.

She *is* hot and sexy. And her eyes—yeah, I could drown in those eyes. Happily.

"Lavoie. Lavoie, look. It's the underwear guy."

Sarah jerks back and looks up.

Two solid-looking familiar dudes are sizing me up. I know these guys.

"Ohmygod, Nick Murphy and Duncan Lavoie," Sarah gasps.

Right.

Hockey players. The Thrusters.

They steal two chairs from the table on the other side of us and shove me out of the way to box her in. Murphy smiles at her and I want to punch his smarmy goalie face. Lavoie takes her hand and presses a kiss to the back of it, and I want to dunk his entire upper body in a toilet.

"This guy bothering you?" Lavoie asks.

"No," she assures him with a smile. "He's very good company. And harmless."

"I am *not* harmless," I object. "I can kick your ass in Pac-Man."

Murphy looks at me again with his dark green gaze. "You learn your lesson about talking to women yet, or do we need to step outside?"

"Stop," Sarah says. "He's definitely learned his lesson. He even just offered to let me have his car. He's very, very sorry. And his mother chewed him out and apologized on his behalf too. Sorry, bud, but you can't touch that."

Nick's brow furrows. "Yeah, I got a mom like that. Except I never fuck up."

"Dude," Lavoie mutters. "Are you fucking serious?"

"Hey, *I* wouldn't tweet that shit to my sister or any other woman."

"Just to your sister's exes," Lavoie supplies.

"I'm avenging the fucking world." He points at me. "And that's my sister about to go up on stage, so you better laugh your ass off. But only at the right spots. And don't even think of tweeting anything about her. *Anything*. Even anything *good*. I'll be watching you."

My bodyguards are useless.

Or possibly they're enjoying this.

Hard to tell. But I'd be enjoying this if I were them.

"Can I get a picture?" Sarah asks. "My friend Mackenzie loves the Fireballs first and foremost, but the Thrusters are her second favorite."

"*Distantly*," I add. Helpfully.

Sarah grins, and these two hockey players have clearly taken one too many pucks to the head, because neither of them falls at her feet and worships her just for that gorgeous sight.

"Well, yeah, but they're still second," Sarah agrees.

"You haven't asked for a picture with me," I point out.

"Oh, I think I have a *lot* more than a picture with you." She tosses me another smile that hits me so hard in the chest that I almost fall out of my chair.

Or maybe that was a server tripping over the chair leg.

Possibly on purpose while trying to hit me in the head with a serving tray.

But still.

I *feel* that smile all the way to my bones.

And not just the boner growing harder with every passing second behind my fly.

The server delivers Sarah's drink and milkshake and a complimentary basket of fried pickles while they're taking pictures. After Sarah texts Mackenzie, Murphy gives me the same double-fingered *I'm watching you* point that Judson got me with before we left Sarah's house.

"Laughing. You. In the right spots. Off Twitter. Got it?"

"I giggle when I'm nervous," I tell him, which makes Sarah snort sweet tea out her nose. "Oh, shit. Sorry. Here." I lunge for napkins and dab at her nose and mouth, which are *fuck*, so pretty.

How in the world has she hidden this long?

"I'm okay," she sputters around a laugh. "Thank you."

After making sure I'm not going to accidentally kill her, Murphy and Lavoie leave us alone.

But they sit close all through open mic night.

Which is so-so, except for the ventriloquist, who's fucking hilarious, and not just because Nick Murphy will kick my ass if I don't think so and laugh in all the right places. That goat puppet she's using reminds me of Wyatt. Totally straight-laced.

Which I think makes me the cat puppet named Lucy, which is a little awkward, but I can deal with feeling a kinship with a cat puppet.

Sarah shares all of her food with me, our chairs pressed tight together so I can loop one arm around her the whole night, because I'm having fingergasms just from touching her, and by the time the show's over and every last amateur comedian and comedienne have had their turns, the photographers lurking across the room have gotten an endless supply of good shots of Sarah and me enjoying the show.

And I'm pissed.

Because she should be able to go out and enjoy a comedy club without knowing that her every move is being watched and scrutinized by the world.

"We need to call this off," I tell her when we're back in my car, headed for my building. Security can sneak her out in an unmarked car from there.

"What? Why?"

"Because I don't like those assholes taking pictures of you."

She watches me as we pull into my parking garage and I take the hard left to head into my private underground garage behind the lift door that most people assume is for deliveries.

"Maybe it's not so bad," she finally says as I'm parking. "I did some selective googling at work today. Donations to animal conservation projects are up twenty percent this week."

I want to be fucking *up twenty percent*. With her.

But I'm also the moron who just told her we needed to call this off, and *fuck*, she probably thinks I mean *all* of us.

"I could make two phone calls and get that tripled and you wouldn't have to smile for another camera in your entire life."

"I *like* making a difference." Her cheeks start to go splotchy, and I can't help tracing the uneven edges of red in her cheeks. "I care," she whispers. "People can see it. And that means more than Levi Wilson or Cash Rivers giving it lip service."

"I was going to blackmail one of the British princes and remind someone whose name I'm legally not allowed to mention that he owes me a favor, but I can call Levi and Cash too."

She lights up so fucking bright when she smiles.

But I wasn't actually joking.

"My mom's been asking me for years to go on vacation with her and Dad," she tells me. "I've always had an excuse, but we all knew I just didn't want to have my picture taken with them. Maybe now…we could try it. I'm not so afraid anymore." She smiles hesitantly, like she feels silly for putting her parents off for so long. "Maybe you did me a favor by being an internet jackoff. And I'd never actually gotten to taser anyone before, so there's that too."

Instead of answering, I release my seat belt and lunge across the seat to kiss her. I stroke her thick, silky hair and wish it wasn't tied back, and she latches onto my wrists, but instead of pushing me away, she clings tight and angles her lips against mine and leans all the way in.

This.

This is what I've been searching for my entire life without even knowing I wanted it.

This desperate hot need to not just kiss a woman, but to *be* kissed by her.

To be everything *she* wants.

To step up my game. Try harder. Be smarter. More gallant.

More gallant?

Shit. I'm turning into some kind of medieval knight for her.

And I'm totally balls-to-the-wall on board with going all knightly on her ass if that's what it takes.

Especially when she parts her lips and lets me all the way in.

Fucking. Heaven.

Her hands trail down my forearms, she deepens the kiss, and I'm two seconds from blowing my load just because a woman's gliding her tongue over mine.

I might not be the world's most experienced lover, but I don't do premature anything.

And I don't think she'd kiss a guy just to kiss a guy.

Especially not *this* guy.

So I have a chance.

A real chance.

My hand is drifting down her shoulder toward her breast when my car horn blasts out of nowhere.

And not just the horn.

The whole damn alarm

Sarah flings herself backward, her fingers going to her lips, eyes wide, and she fumbles for the door handle.

I drop my phone between the seats trying to grab it to pull up my car app and deactivate the alarm, but as soon as Sarah leaps out of the car, I realize what's going on.

Charlie.

Charlie's phone is hooked to my car, and she just activated the alarm.

And I'm positive it's her, because she's standing right there, in front of my car, phone in hand, and the alarm stops as soon as Sarah shuts her door.

I glare at my assistant.

Not in the contract, she mouths.

I flip her off.

She smirks.

It's a smirky, know-it-all, serves-you-right smirk. Possibly with a side of *if you're going to woo the woman, do it right, after you're not contractually obligated to just act like you like her anymore, when she knows you're really just into HER and not what she can do for your career.*

I drop my head to the steering wheel, because *fuck.*

She's right. Even with telling Sarah this isn't about the contract, she has no guarantee. Which means she's going on faith.

Faith in me.

I should probably be grateful there's no emergency airbag deploy button on the app.

I'm also revoking Charlie's privileges to run my car app.

"Ready to go home?" She's asking Sarah as I finally pull myself out of the car.

Sarah nods, face splotchy red, without looking at me.

"You want to come over tomorrow and watch movies?" I hear myself ask.

She glances at me and holds eye contact, but gets redder with each passing second. *Shit.*

"I have plans, but thanks for the offer," she says.

Dammit dammit *dammit.* "Anytime. You're fun." *You're fun?* What am I, *twelve?* I had all the right words earlier, and now I'm completely fucking this up.

Charlie's sucking her lips in. I know she's stifling a smile, and I'm getting hot in the face too.

One kiss.

One single goodnight kiss.

And my assistant goes and ruins it.

I should fire her.

Except she's probably right.

I shouldn't be kissing women when it's not clear if it's for me or the stupid contract, because if I were Sarah, I'd be doubting every word I said about liking her for her.

"I meant going out in public," I say to her. "We should call off going out in public."

"Not gonna happen, Romeo," Charlie says. "Or I'll fire *you.*"

Sarah flashes me a brief smile that doesn't reach her eyes, and I think I've just fucked up again, but I don't know *how,* or *why,* or how to fix it. I just know I don't want her to leave.

And not because I don't want to be alone.

But because I want to be with *her.*

"Can I call you?" I ask as Charlie ushers her toward the back door of the garage.

This time, she stops and looks at me. She's still blushing, but she finally lifts those gorgeous eyes to meet mine, and *wham*.

"Yes," she says with a shy smile.

"Window's closing to get you out before you're going to be followed," Charlie says, and Sarah and I both sigh.

I'm about to tell her she can just stay when she ducks her head again and lets Charlie hustle her out the door.

I slouch against my car.

That was the best date I've ever had in my entire *life*.

It was just a comedy club. With good food. Some photographers watching us. A near-miss with having a beer or seventeen spilled down my crotch.

But I haven't split a burger on a date since I was seventeen and couldn't afford to get my date more. I haven't let my fingers linger in the fry basket in the hopes that we'd accidentally touch in even longer. I haven't wished the show would be over so we could be alone again, or been so simultaneously sad when we left because it meant I was that much closer to having to let her go home.

And listening to her snort-laugh at some of the really bad jokes tonight—I don't get why the internet as a whole isn't tripping all over itself to talk about how gorgeous and funny and smart and kind she is.

My phone dings. Text from Charlie.

Go to bed, Beck. Business meetings all day tomorrow.

I sigh and head for the elevator, where there's ever-present security watching over my garage hidey-hole. "Not your usual type, Mr. Ryder," the guy says.

I scowl at him. "Damn fucking better."

His smirk slides off and he goes pink in the cheeks. "Yes, sir."

This world.

I thought I was the fuck-up last weekend.

But maybe the whole damn world has lost its mind.

TWENTY-NINE

Sarah

CHARLIE DOESN'T MENTION the kiss as she accompanies me in a black Audi driven by a bodyguard on the drive home. Nor does she ask how the date went. Or even tell me stories about Beck or his family or his business.

Nope.

We chat about my bees. She's thinking of getting a hive someday, whenever she's finally ready to slow down and *find* home, since she's seen enough of the world to know she can go anywhere she wants but she's still narrowing down exactly where that is.

And I pretend my lips aren't still tingling from kissing Beck, and that I can stop myself from continuously reaching up to touch them to make sure they're still the same lips they were pre-kiss.

It's not like it's the first time he's kissed me.

But this one was *more*.

And if we hadn't been interrupted, I don't think we would've stopped at kissing.

When we pull up to my house, the lights are all on.

My parents must still be here.

And when the bodyguard walks me to my door and sees me inside, I realize they aren't alone.

Nope.

Mackenzie's here.

And the Fireballs are tied at two in the bottom of the twelfth inning.

"Sarah! Sarah, sit. Eat popcorn. You have to try the popcorn, because we *cannot* lose this game after we've fought *this long* to get here, and the popcorn is good luck. Wait. What's that look? Why are you making that face? Did he try something? Do I need to go kick his ass?"

My dad goes on alert instantly, his dark eyes raking over me like he has an internal mind reader app in his brain while he shoots to his feet. My mom, though, claps her hands. "Oh, sweetheart, I knew he was more than just a pretty face."

"Whatever. He's just doing this to *save* his face," Mackenzie says. "I mean, he seems like a nice enough guy, and if there wasn't that whole fame factor, I'd be into letting him date you, provided he's actually as nice as he seems, but you know Hollywood. No offense, Sunny and Judson. Did he touch your boobs? Do I need to call my friend Bubba-Shark to take care of things?"

"*Bubba-Shark?*"

"He's this guy my dads know. I don't like to talk about him because *reasons*, but desperate times, desperate measures. Did he show you his peepee?"

"Strike out!" my mom cries.

"What? He got the strike-out? Go, bullpen! I didn't see that coming."

With Mackenzie distracted, Mom winks at me.

Dad makes the Bat-Dad growl.

And I realize I'm touching my lips again.

I sink into the recliner, then bolt up again when Cupcake squeals indignantly beneath me. "Who put the pig in my chair?"

"Ssh!" Mackenzie says. "She's good luck. And I'm totally getting the rest of this story out of you as soon as we get this last out."

"Anybody else want ice cream?" I ask them all.

"Right! Ice cream is good luck. Crap. Beck was good luck. Was it so bad that you can't text him and ask him if he'll do that butt wiggle he did last time we got a final out in an inning?"

I don't bother telling her that he won't text back, because he has seven million and growing unread text messages, but instead, I step into the kitchen and do as she asks because I hope he does reply.

And when he replies right away, I smile so big that I know my heart's in serious danger.

With or without my pants on? And do you need video?

My brain whispers *without*, but my mom steps into the kitchen behind me and heads for the cabinets, making the bowls rattle loudly while she whispers, "Was it a good kiss?"

"Yes," I whisper back.

She beams. "I had our PI look into him and his family, and your father and I officially approve."

"Mom. He's doing this for the contract." He's not doing this for the contract, but I can't stop the old habits from rearing their ugly heads. *You like HER? You know she's adopted, right? There's no way that geek came from Sunny Darling's loins. And she saves her ear wax to make statues with it.*

Apparently my issues run a little deeper than just that moment that the owls invaded prom.

"Mm-hmm," Mom murmurs. "You know that's how your father and I met."

"*What?*"

"Yes, his agent approached mine because he'd been caught in a compromising position with a rather scantily-clad woman who needed a ride in a certain part of LA, and they wanted my name attached to him to clean up his image."

"You said you met when you were an extra on the set of his first movie."

"Oh, no, dear, he had a trailer on the right side of *that* movie set, and I was barely allowed to even say my one line. By the time rumors were flying that he hired escorts, I'd started to make a name for myself, and Hollywood ate up the story that we'd been secretly dating for months. And now, we've been happily married ever since. Also, the poor girl he gave a ride to was an undercover detective who was so charmed by his manners and his ability to resist her come-on lines and offers of paid sex that she came to our wedding. Who do you think I called to look into our dear Mr. Ryder?"

I plop the vanilla ice cream on the counter and go digging in my cabinets for sprinkles.

Tonight definitely calls for sprinkles.

"I like him," I whisper, because I can't make myself say it any louder.

"The biggest rewards require the biggest risks."

"Isn't that a line from one of your movies?"

"Yes, but it's still true."

And the exact *opposite* of me wishing that the things we love were the easiest things in the world.

Maybe she's right. Maybe I *do* need to fight for him. And stand up for him more when people call him an asshole, and quit hiding from social media and get out there and take a stand.

Dad lumbers into the room, studying both of us through narrowed eyes. "Did that motherfucking asshole flash you?"

My phone dings, and a text pops up with a video attached.

A video of Beck's ass, in black RYDE briefs, as he shakes and wiggles and flexes it in a very, *very* fine booty dance. I'm hypnotized by his back though. All that lean muscle, that long length, the dimples at the base of his spine, the birthmark, the width of his shoulders.

How the hell does he eat like he does and still have a back made for back porn?

"OH MY GOD, DID YOU SEE THAT PLAY?" Mackenzie yells. "Third out! Third out! Third out!"

We all stare at my phone.

Then the living room.

"Shit," Dad mutters.

"Play that again, sweetheart," Mom urges.

Mackenzie leaps into the kitchen, startling Meda, who shoots off into the living room from her hiding spot under the table and who will probably hide under my bed for the next week. "Did he do it? Did he do it?"

Mom grabs my phone and shows her the video before I can stop her.

"*Yes!* Tell him to stand by. Cooper's up first at the top of the inning after the commercial break."

"Go on," Dad growls at me. "Tell him we need our team to win."

Our team. My dad's a tried and true Dodgers fan, but he's adopted the Fireballs. "I'm making ice cream," I inform him with a smile.

Dad bumps me out of the way and grabs my spoon to take over ice cream duties. Mom shoves my phone back at me. I start to text Beck, but Mackenzie squeals again. "No! Don't text him! You need to call him. This only works when you two are in the bathroom *together*, and since you're not together, you have to be on the phone. It's the next best thing."

"I—" I start, but she sneaks in and hits the *call* button at the top of my text message with him.

And now I'm committed.

Because it's not like I can hang up and expect he won't call me back.

Not after that kiss.

Holy shit, that kiss.

And his *I'll call you*.

"Don't you have to work tomorrow?" I ask her.

"Sarah. The Fireballs might win their third game in eight days. Nobody's gonna care if I fall asleep at my desk."

Beck answers before the first ring has even finished. "Hey. It worked, didn't it? Tell Mackenzie I'll do that every night if she'll convert fully to Team Beck."

'Team Beck? What's *Team Beck*?"

"I'm *totally* on Team Beck so long as him dancing in his under-wear results in the Fireballs winning," Mackenzie says, like she's on this phone call and not me.

I take a heaping bowl of ice cream topped with uneven whipped cream and chocolate syrup and half a container of flower sprinkles from my dad, and I head for the bathroom. "The Fireballs are up," I tell Beck.

"I know. I'm watching on my tablet in the bathroom. Are you in the bathroom?"

"Esh," I answer around a mouthful of ice cream.

"Ah, man, you're eating something. Not popcorn. Popcorn's too loud. I really didn't want to stop kissing you. You're just so—so—"

I cringe, waiting for him to say *different*. Because that's what I am.

I don't wholly fit into the geek community, but I don't fully fit into my parents'—and also *his*—lifestyle either.

"Special," he finishes quietly.

Warmth spreads through my chest, out to my fingertips, and I put my ice cream down so it doesn't melt, even though I'm familiar enough with thermodynamics to know that it's impossible for my skin to heat enough to instantly melt an entire bowl of ice cream through the ceramic.

"Everyone's special," I say quietly.

"But you're *Sarah* special. That's specialer."

I laugh softly. "*Specialer?*"

"It's my word. I like it. I'm keeping it. Can I see you after our two weeks are up? I meant it. I hate the contract. I just want to date *you*."

"Why?" I catch sight of my goofball grin in the mirror, and instead of blushing, I grin bigger.

"Because I like you. *Like* you like you.

"*Why*?" I press.

Not because I don't *like* him like him too, but because the lifestyle he comes with isn't one that's ever appreciated my brand of *specialness* before, and I had eighteen years of living it before I finally escaped to find where I thought I fit.

"Because you have excellent taste in movies and TV shows, your friends love you enough to threaten me with things that'll send me to therapy for years, and you didn't have to ask to know that fried onions are the best extra topping ever invented for a hamburger. You know how to use a taser, you keep bees to try to save the world, and the only thing you want from me is for me to step up to the plate and do my duty as a citizen of the Earth to help save it. Also, you haven't asked me for free underwear, or if I'll sign your boobs—though I totally would for you, because I'm shameless and I'll take any excuse to touch you—or if I'll get you hooked up with free tickets to Levi's concerts or Cash's movie premieres. And also because you have high enough standards to demand that I deliver a double orgasm in the bedroom. Nobody ever wants me to be *better*. They just want me to be *naked*. You're...real. And unimpressed. And it makes me want to impress you."

"What happens when that novelty wears off?"

"You're too fascinating to ever not be fascinating. Aaaaannnd I'm the dumbass who just said that really lame sentence. Sorry."

I smile at my melting ice cream. "No, you're actually really sweet and adorable."

"And sexy and hot and you want to strip me out of my teddy bear robe."

"You are *not* wearing a teddy bear robe."

My phone gives me a text alert, and I pull it away from my ear to glance at it.

Sure enough, that's a picture of Beck. In a fluffy white robe with brown teddy bears all over it.

I bust out laughing. "Is that your normal evening wear?"

"I wasn't watching what I grabbed when I saw you were calling. Tripp's kids gave it to me for Christmas. James was on a bear kick. And now we know it's good luck for the Fireballs, so I'll have to wear it every time they play a game."

"Do you have any idea how attractive it is that you love your family as much as you do?"

"Not a clue. You're going to have to spell it out for me. Use lots of complimentary words. My ego needs a boost."

"HOME RUN! OH MY GOD, SARAH, HE HIT A HOME RUN!"

"Hold on," I tell Beck, and I put him on hold while I play my toilet flushing app. "That's great," I call back to Mackenzie.

"Stay! Stay in the bathroom!" she shrieks back. "And whatever you're doing, keep doing it!"

Beck's chuckling when I lift the phone back to my ear. "We have to keep talking, don't we?"

"Yep."

"Awesome. What's her email address? I'm sending her season tickets tomorrow."

I blink.

Then blink again, because my eyes are getting hot. "You know most guys would say *flowers*, right?"

"I know I sent you some earlier, but the truth is, I hate sending flowers. You grow them, they're happy and all connected to their roots and eating and drinking and basking in the sunshine—or a grow lamp, I guess—but then you cut them, send them to someone, and they die well before their time. Season tickets are the gift that keeps on giving. Until October, anyway. Or until she decides going in person is bad luck. Shit. What if she decides going in person is bad luck? Then I'll have ruined baseball for her."

"She won't decide it's bad luck to be there in person," I tell him. "She's more likely to decide her seats are wrong, but she won't say that, because she's more polite than she is superstitious. But you do know you don't have to do this, right?"

"Sarah?"

"Hmm?"

"I'd really like to be kissing you right now."

"AAAHHH!!! A DOUBLE!" Mackenzie yells. "DARREN GREENE JUST HIT A DOUBLE!"

I swallow hard. "Did you see that?" I whisper.

"Yep." His voice is softer, but also deeper. "Sounds like we need to keep talking about kissing."

"My best friend is totally setting us up."

"She clearly has awesome taste in men. And since it means I get to keep talking to you about how delicious your lips are, I'll take this little gift from the universe and go with it. And your lips *are* delicious."

"It was the onion rings."

He chuckles softly. "No, Sarah. It's *you*."

"You weren't half-bad," I tell him, even though the truth is that he was *amazing*. I know what actually *dating* dating Beck would mean for my future—and my relative privacy—but that part of me terrified of having my life torn apart is doing the talking for me again. I clear my throat and try again. "I mean, you were at least seventy percent of the way to giving me an orgasm just from kissing me."

"If we were alone, I'd kiss you from head to toe, and I'd learn all your favorite spots, and I'd pretend like I didn't know what you meant when you told me to go lower, or harder, or faster, just so I could build all the anticipation until I finally hit all your magic buttons," he says, his voice low and husky and making my skin tingle all over.

I toe the bathroom door shut and sink to the floor with my back to it so no one can walk in. "What else?" I whisper, even though the doors are paper thin and my parents and best friend are still on the other side.

"I'd strip you out of your socks and blow on your toes," he whispers, and it shouldn't be a turn-on, but my toes squirm and I get a straight jolt of lust between my thighs.

"And then I'd caress your ankles and lick a trail up your calf and test to see if your knees are ticklish before spreading your legs and having dessert."

Holy honeybees. My knees drop open, and I reach under my shirt to rub at one aching nipple. "You think you're any good with dessert?"

"I'm terrible. I'm going to need *hours* and *hours* of practice."

I'm going to need some serious private time with my fingers in a minute here. I pinch my nipple, and a hot arrow of pleasure rockets from my breast to my lady bits. "Hours?"

"Hours. With my face between your legs."

I whimper.

Because what are words again?

"Dammit, I'm doing this wrong. I was supposed to talk about how much I want to kiss that mouth again first."

"Not...wrong," I manage.

I can *hear* him smiling. "Sarah Dempsey, are you turned on?"

My head drops back, my eyes squeeze shut, and my hand drifts lower. "Just...little."

"Oh. Only a little? I'm hard as a cast iron frying pan."

And now I'm picturing him with an erection straining his black boxers, and there's an overexcited buzz happening in my pussy. My pussy is the yapping chihuahua of pussies right now, wagging its tail and calculating a plan to ride across town with my head hanging out the window so I can attack his boner.

I whimper.

"I'm doing this wrong," he says. "You want me to stop?"

"*No.*"

"Ah. So you *would* want me to kiss those lips again. And strip you down to your bare skin. And suck on your earlobes."

I hate having my earlobes touched, but offering them as tribute if that's what Beck wants to suck on sounds utterly divine. Especially if I got to hang on to his broad shoulders and bury my face in his hot skin and taste the very essence of him. "What…about…you?"

"There's not a single inch of my entire body that wouldn't be completely turned on if you were touching me."

I smile. It's a breathy smile, and I want to rub my clit so bad.

"I really want to kiss you again," he whispers. "And I want to peel you out of your clothes and worship your body and learn what you like and taste you and stroke you and love you until you can't remember a time when you were unhappy about *anything.*"

I suck in a shuddery breath, my skin alternating between flaming hot and icy cold. "I don't think you actually need lessons in anything."

"Don't rob me of my fantasies here. Any of them. Not the ones in my bedroom. Or my hot tub. Or on my patio. On a picnic blanket surrounded by fried chicken and biscuits and peach cobbler."

I laugh softly while I rub my jeans over my clit. "Strawberry shortcake."

"Donuts." He groans softly. "Banana pudding donuts."

I picture him using a donut as a cock ring, and I'm suddenly so turned on that my panties are dripping, but I'm also laughing.

It's a weird mix, but I like it. "Cream cheese Danish," I say.

"Fuck, Sarah, warn a man." He blows out an audible breath, and I wonder if he's honestly as turned on as I am. His ragged breath suggests he might be.

"Okay. Control. Okay," he rasps. "Pepperoni pizza."

"Mint tea and gazelle cookies."

"If I were next to you, I'd be slamming into you so hard right now, neither one of us would be able to walk tomorrow."

It's not his words.

It's the way his voice has gone completely hoarse and shaky, like he's a man on the verge of losing control.

"Are you touching yourself?" I whisper.

"Do you want me to?" Gritted. Harsh. Like he's not in control.

"Yes."

"I wish you were touching me."

"I wish you were touching me too."

"Where?"

"My nipples are very sensitive."

"Sarah," he groans.

The bathroom door suddenly jolts against my back. "Sarah! SARAH! The booty dance! TELL BECK WE NEED THE BOOTY DANCE!"

The game.

Shit. Dammit. Hell.

I leap up, my legs wobbly, my nipples pebbled so hard they've probably turned inside out, my head light, my heart pounding. "No! No booty dance!" I shriek.

"Sarah?" Beck's voice is pained, half-moan, half despair.

And then there's silence. For half a second before Mackenzie pops the door and peers in at me with one eyeball.

One very wide blue eyeball.

"Oh my god," she whispers.

I make some motions with my hands that I hope mean *go away and do not tell my parents and I might hate you right now but I'll still love you tomorrow.*

"I mean, if that's what it takes for them to win, I guess you're going to be really fucking satisfied by October. Good for you, girl-friend. But can you text me that video?"

"*No!*"

"Okay, okay. Sheesh. Just asking." She pulls the door shut again. "No, Judson, she's taking a bath. Leave her alone. She gets all shrieky when people see her naked."

"Did you use the bath salts we sent for Valentine's Day?" my mom calls.

I drop my head to the bathroom door, suddenly missing orgasms more than I have at any time in the past year.

"I owe you something better than chocolates for this, don't I?" Beck says in my ear, making me jump.

"You totally got off, didn't you?"

"You like waffles? Or omelets? I make a killer waffle-omelet sand-wich. I could come make you breakfast in the morning. Or right now."

"It's fine. I have a vibrator."

"Fucking hell, I'm going to be thinking about that all night."

I wince. "Sorry."

"Don't be. I'm going to enjoy the hell out of these fantasies."

"You're adding funnel cakes and barbecue to them, aren't you?"

"Sarah Dempsey, I'm going to talk you into marrying me one day."

I laugh.

He doesn't.

Probably because he's salivating over the idea of me masturbating while surrounded by food.

"You sure you have plans tomorrow night? We could head out to my place in Shipwreck. I've got a telescope out there."

My heart squeezes behind my still tingling nipples. "Maybe next weekend?"

"Done. You're on my calendar. No backing out now."

"Did you just text Charlie?"

"Nope. I put it on my calendar all by myself. Right next to *eat at that Indian place down the street*. But I can move that."

"Wait. Which Indian place? The one with the garlic naan that you can smell baking halfway through Reynolds Park?"

"Is there any other Indian place in this city?"

"Technically, yes."

"It's a date. Indian, then Shipwreck. And banana pudding donuts."

"OH MY GOD, WE WON! WE WON IN EXTRA INNINGS! WE WON WE WON WE WON!"

I smile at the white wooden door and Mackenzie's shrieks in the living room. "Thanks for being the Fireballs' good luck charm again," I say softly.

"Anytime. Especially if it gives me an excuse to talk to you."

The belly flutters join the warmth in my heart and the frustration in my lady bits.

This feels *real*.

And fun.

And easy.

I just hope it can last.

THIRTY

Beck

I'M SO HYPED up Friday morning, I can't even concentrate on Donkey Kong. I keep hearing Sarah's ragged breath and soft gasps, that *need* in her voice, and I don't even want second breakfast.

I want to go find her.

But I'm stuck in meetings with my team that I can't get out of by frying another motherboard, especially since my coffee this morning is from a local shop down the street that uses cinnamon sticks as stir sticks and it's delicious and I'd have to go get a different cup of coffee to dump on my computer if I don't want to cry while I'm doing it.

Plus, Bruce has decided that Operation: Fix Beck's Reputation has gone so well that we need to jump on getting Vaughn signed up for doing a business partnership around socks.

Yes, *socks*.

"It's an easy market," he insists. "Who else is doing designer socks? And we could pull the girl into it. Those shots of you looking at her while she's making that donkey face with the penis shoulder are exactly the sort of thing that would sell if you were sitting on a couch together, showing off your socks."

"Donkey face with the penis shoulder?"

Charlie slides me her phone, and I look down to see Sarah laughing so hard her mouth's open and her eyes are squeezed shut, and somehow her braid's hanging over her shoulder but looks fuzzy enough that okay, yeah, if you have a dirty mind, it could possibly look like a penis, but *Christ*, you really have to twist it.

"She looks like she's having fun," I say.

"Whatever."

"*Not* whatever," I growl, and I don't give two shits that I'm currently contemplating asking Judson if we can hire some of those Euranians to go toss flaming poop bombs on Bruce's front step, because *I'm not doing a business partnership over socks.* "Her name is *Sarah*—"

"Serendipity, technically," Hestia says.

"Her name is Sarah," Charlie says. "And I'm violently opposed to the idea of trying to bring profit into this partnership with Vaughn. It's for kids, not for growing already overinflated bank accounts."

"Vehemently," Hestia corrects.

"No, *violently*."

"Honey, you're just the assistant," Bruce says.

"She's a fucking genius, and you're getting on my nerves," I growl.

Huh.

I get why Judson's doing it.

It feels really *fucking* good to growl when you're pissed.

Everyone goes silent. It's four talking heads on my video screen, all gaping at me.

Except Charlie.

She's glaring at my computer screen like she's squishing Bruce's head with her mind.

"We're not asking Vaughn to go into socks with me," I tell Bruce. "Next."

There's another hour of mind-numbing business discussions about some small-time partnerships that I have with a rising celebrity chef, an Instagrammer, and a tea company—my team was pissed about that one, but dude, sometimes a guy on the road needs a solid cup of chamomile, and Snore-Tea fucking rocks—and by the time we hang up, I don't want food, or to go take a run, or to go hang out at my parents' house and see who's around from the neighborhood.

I want to see Sarah.

Her phone goes to voicemail.

I send a text, but that doesn't even show as read.

"No," Charlie says when I grab my keys.

"I'm going out to get a burger."

"You're going out to drive past Sarah's house and her office."

"*And* to get a burger." Two burgers. Or five. I don't actually know what her favorite toppings are, because I'm pretty fucking certain she ordered that burger last night for me, and while she ate it, that doesn't mean it was her favorite.

I need to figure out what her favorite burger is.

And what she likes on her pizza.

And if she eats whipped cream straight out of the can.

Fuck, I'm getting a boner again.

"She's visiting a client site today," Charlie informs me. "Doing her actual *job*. And I might not make it another week before Bruce drives me to quit, but you can be damn certain I'll be suing you for hostile work conditions if I quit."

I scrub a hand over my face. "I'll call him. Don't quit. I'll give you my firstborn *and* a peanut butter factory."

"You're not having children, and the beauty of peanut butter is that I'm not stuck with one kind for eternity. Tell. Bruce. To. Knock. It. Off."

She looks pointedly at my phone.

"Okay, okay. Right now. I'll call him *right now*."

It's easier to chew his ass out about respecting everyone on the team—including Sarah—when I realize this guy could actually have reason to talk to her, or my mom, or my sister one day. He reminds me he's done a shit-ton of work to help me launch and keep not just the RYDE line going strong, but also my loungewear and body care lines, and I remind him that that's exactly what I pay him to do, and if he fucks up this foundation with Vaughn by trying to weasel more business out of him when I've specifically told him not to, I also have a crackpot legal team and I know he's been cheating on his wife.

I don't *actually* know that until he blusters that I'm full of shit and trips over his tongue daring me to prove it.

Call it a gut feeling.

When I hang up, I feel like shit, because I hate chewing people out.

I find Charlie in a small office across the hall. "Why didn't you tell me a year ago he was this much of an ass?"

"He wasn't until his last mistress dumped him. Now he's seeing some twenty-three-year-old who thinks he's richer than you, and the stress of going broke pretending is getting to him."

I gape at her.

"But I've had Hank monitoring your bank accounts and any attempts to make unauthorized transactions, plus your legal team has combed through his employment agreement, so you're fine."

And now my eyes are going to fall out of my head.

"Beck. When we're on the road, you're going twenty hours a day. You don't play the diva, you don't tell the photographers to wrap it up, you don't complain about living on watercress and four black beans a day, you make us stop so you can play soccer with random kids in public parks, and you give me raises every single month. My last boss slapped my ass regularly, would pitch a fit if his coffee wasn't exactly 183 degrees, and ultimately quit paying my salary because he ran out of money after one of his mistresses discovered he was cheating on her and hacked his bank accounts. It's in my best interest to make sure you can still pay me."

I've been in this business a long time. Her story doesn't surprise me, and that pisses me off. I hold out a fist. "You're a total badass, and I hope you punched him in the nuts when you quit."

She bumps me. "I got to quit. That was good enough. Plus, I don't actually like to punch men when they're down, and his second mistress put him in the hospital with a bleeding kidney. Don't piss off a woman wearing stilettos. Also, you have a phone call with Vaughn at eleven—don't piss him off either, because he's letting his people keep working with our people to keep this going—and Tripp's upstairs waiting for you. Apparently you're his best chance for adult conversation. Poor man. Telecon with your Ryder Family Foundation manager in thirty. Don't be late."

He's not Sarah, but I'm still smiling when I head up to my apartment. James is flying an airplane around my living room and Emma's gnawing on a stuffed giraffe. "Hey, watch it, kid. Those things are endangered." I boop her nose and dive out of the way of James's airplane. "Aahh! Out of control airplane's gonna get me!"

He chases me around the living room and kitchen, giggling and shrieking, until we collapse on the floor in front of the couches and he flops onto my belly to *vroom* the airplane into my nose.

"And up you go," Tripp says, pulling him off me and turning him to stare at some cartoon on the TV. "Uncle Beck needs his pretty nose to stay pretty if he's going to stay employed."

"Are you kidding? Being injured while saving bunnies and children from runaway evil airplanes will only add to my mystique and improve my reputation."

He shakes his head and runs a hand through his brown hair. "It's like having a third kid," he mutters.

I grin. "Just like being on the road, except now your actual kids are smaller."

"And growing."

"Do I need to wrap Emma in a plastic tarp, or is her butt better?"

"There's nothing left in her until we feed her again. Your floors are safe for now."

She glances at us, tosses her giraffe to the side, and then goes down on all fours to dart over to James's abandoned plastic airplane, which also goes straight in her mouth.

"Huh. I should've thought of that," I say. "That looks like it's delicious."

Tripp shakes his head. "You selling out?"

He's lounging on my couch, and he's pulling off relaxed—helps that he's in a RYDE cotton shirt, because dude, those things are so soft they'd melt on hot toast—but I've known him since I could talk, and there's something gnawing at him.

Also, why does he keep asking me that?

"You going stir-crazy?" I ask with a head tilt at the kids.

He props his elbows on his knees and steeples his hands. "Yes. No. I—yes."

"No guilt, dude. Remember when our moms used to dump us all on the men and disappear for whole weekends away?"

His smile goes sad. "Yeah. Mine always felt guilty."

"What? Why?"

"Because she had to dump us on somebody else's dad."

"Nobody cared."

He opens his mouth, then shakes his head again. "Heard a reliable rumor the Fireballs are for sale."

"Aw, snickerdoodles," I mutter. Not that I'm surprised. "Mackenzie's gonna die."

"Sarah's friend?"

"Yeah, she's—" I stop myself, because thinking of Mackenzie's superstitions makes me think about last night, and thinking about last night makes me think of Sarah, and thinking of Sarah is making me think of Sarah whispering about food porn, and thinking of Sarah and food porn makes me think of Sarah naked, with me, alone, and I'm reaching for my phone to text her again before I realize Tripp's sitting there staring at me like I've lost my mind.

"Got it bad, Beck," he mutters. "Just...be careful."

From a man who married a Hollywood darling.

Not that Sarah's a Hollywood darling, but her parents are.

And now he knows what it's like to lose the woman he loves. So his warnings are coming with layers.

James glances at his sister and an unholy shriek fills the entire penthouse floor. "STOP EATEE MY AYAPWANE!"

Emma bursts into tears and throws the toy to the ground.

And Tripp sighs and rubs his forehead.

"I have ice cream," I tell him.

"Feed them sugar, and they're yours for the next six hours."

Wouldn't be so bad.

I'm out of other playmates and it would be a great excuse to get out of some meetings, at least until Sarah's home.

"You think the Fireballs can find new owners?" I ask Tripp while I hold out a magazine for Emma to chew on.

He gives me the *don't play the dumbass, dumbass* look.

And now I get it.

He *wants* me to sell out.

Holy fuck.

He's not looking for someone to hang with.

He's looking for a business partner.

"Bro," I mutter. "Seriously?"

He shakes his head, but I don't think he's telling me *no*. "You remember how many days we'd spend there before the band? Even before we could drive ourselves?" He tilts his head at his kids. "You know how many games I want to take them to? You ever think of taking your own kids someday?"

I swallow hard. I don't know what a baseball team costs, but despite the millions we made in the band, and the tens of millions Cash, Levi, and I individually bring in every year—my empire is worth over a billion dollars, but that's not hard cash, it's assets and equity—I doubt any of us have enough money to outright buy a team.

Even the losingest team in baseball.

Which means my buddy's asking me if I can liquidate something.

Go into business *with* him. Probably all the guys. Reunite for a new cause.

And buy our hometown baseball team.

I gulp again, but in the midst of gulping, I can't help a smile. "That would be so snickerdoodling *awesome*," I mutter. My brain's spinning in a way I don't often make it spin, but *shit*. Owning our own baseball team?

Bringing the Fireballs back to glory?

He doesn't smile back. "Snickerdoodling complicated and hard and risky."

"You got numbers?"

He nods once while James darts over to shove the plane in my face. "Unka Beck! See it fwy?"

"Fly, little airplane," I tell it. "Gaaahhh! Fly away from the meteorites!" I crinkle a page out of the magazine and toss it in the air, and James darts off, giggling.

Then I shoot a look at Tripp. "Email me."

He snorts. "You mean email Charlie?"

I shake my head and toss James another meteorite to dodge. "Email *me*."

"It's a snickerdoodle-ton," he says, so dead serious I have to wonder if he's talking about even more than we're all worth together.

"Yeah, and we're five guys from a middle-class neighborhood in Virginia who ruled the snickerdoodling world for five or six years. Levi in?"

"I'm starting with the easy targets."

That gets a laugh out of me, but it's true.

I'm the easy target.

Davis might technically be the youngest of all of us, but I'm the kid. "This is nuts. Even I know that."

But I'm not thinking about *nuts*.

I'm thinking about excuses to be home even more.

And the look on Sarah's face if I told her I saved her best friend's baseball team.

If I told her we'd be in the limelight less. Because who, outside of Copper Valley, really cares about the Fireballs?

And now I'm smiling again, adrenaline kicking in just like it did the night we all climbed onto a tour bus for the first leg of our very first tour.

"You have a crazy bone," I say to Tripp, who was always the one watching our backs on tour, because yeah, he's the dad of the group.

He thrusts his hands through his hair. "Sometimes, a guy needs a change."

He just might be right.

THIRTY-ONE

Sarah

ONCE IN A BLUE MOON, Mackenzie and I do paint night at a cute little art shop a few blocks from my house. When they announced one of their new painting options is a night scene of Duggan Field, she signed us up.

Pre-Beck, of course. Because we had to sync a paint night with a day game, because it wouldn't do to be painting Duggan Field while missing a game.

But now it's the two of us, plus my mom, Ellie, and Mrs. Ryder.

When the staff realized it was *me* coming, they asked Mackenzie if she'd rather reschedule or bring enough people to fill the shop ourselves, since they didn't want me to be uncomfortable with being fawned over.

"I'm not a freaking celebrity," I mutter to her while we start on our wine. I have two glasses—one red, one white—and a newly cleaned seat and brand-new brushes because apparently I'm still going to be the person of the hour tonight, which is ridiculous.

I'm just *me.*

"Yes, you are," she mutters back. "And one day, when you take Beck up on his offer to let his video team help you set up a few vlogs about your favorite subjects, you'll realize there are all kinds of stars, and you're the kind you're supposed to be."

Ellie takes the seat on my other side with her wine and her paint tray. "If my mom asks how many babies you want, just tell her three, and she'll be so overjoyed that she won't ask you anything else the rest of the night," she whispers.

"I heard that," Mrs. Ryder says. "And I'd rather talk about your wedding, sweetheart."

"I adore weddings," Mom announces. "I've had seventeen of them."

"*Seventeen*?" Mackenzie gasps.

"Sixteen were for roles," I tell her.

"Oh. Right. Yeah. That makes sense."

While Mackenzie asks Mom which was her favorite, I sneak a peek at my phone.

Beck texted, which gives me more of a thrill than I'm willing to admit out loud. Because I know what his unread text messages look like.

I just spun James so fast that he puked macaroni and cheese, and now Tripp says I've lost my babysitting privileges. This sucks. Flash me a picture of a cheeseburger to make me feel better? No, wait. Send me a picture of you EATING a cheeseburger to make me feel better.

I cast a quick glance around to make sure nobody's paying attention, then snap a selfie of me lifting the glass of red wine to my lips.

Because my mother attacked me with eyeliner and that *perfect shade of lipstick*, I look a little like a surprised raccoon with purple lips, but if he's still honestly attracted to me after this picture, then I'm definitely posting that blog I drafted this morning.

And I'm getting back on social media and diving in head first.

Once I send the text, his reply is almost instantaneous.

That's not a burger, but I do love seeing those pretty eyes. Where are you? Do you need me to order fried cheese sticks for delivery? Or I could send naan. I sucked up bigtime at that place down the street between meetings this afternoon.

Alicia, the lady leading paint night, taps a brush on her easel to call us all to attention. "Good evening, ladies. We're *so* thrilled to have you here. Who's ready to get started?"

"Are you texting with him?" Mackenzie hisses. "Should've been doing that when the Fireballs were playing this afternoon."

"I was at work this afternoon," I hiss back.

She grins. "Okay, yeah, I wouldn't have wanted you to get fired for being indecent."

"Ew," Ellie whispers on my other side.

"So, ladies, let's begin with your big brush. This one here." Alicia holds up a brush with thick bristles. "And dip it in your blue paint to get started on the background."

We dutifully begin painting the deep purple-blue background above the penciled-out shape of the ballpark on our canvases.

I squint at my canvas.

Mackenzie sighs. "Just once, Sarah?"

"But it's a Pikachu when you squint and look at it sideways." I gesture to the rounded edges of the bleachers. "Or maybe a Pac-Man ghost, if you add some more legs. Or whatever those swishy things are that count as their legs."

Ellie looks at me.

Mrs. Ryder looks at me.

Mackenzie sighs deeply again as she goes back to painting her background, and my mom raises her hand. "What I if I want to paint this as Dodger Stadium?"

"Oh, of course, Ms. Darling," Alicia gushes. "We encourage freedom of expression here."

"See?" I murmur to Mackenzie. "Freedom of expression."

I grab a pencil and modify the shape on my canvas.

Ellie and Mrs. Ryder share a look.

Mackenzie reaches for her wine.

And when they're all distracted, I pull my phone out, because it's buzzed with at least three more messages from Beck.

I miss those pretty eyes.

How much longer are you going to be? Do you like pool? Or air hockey? I can whip up a trophy sundae and we can play for rights to lick it off each other's bodies.

Sarah? Shit. We don't have to lick anything if you don't want to. And your dad is giving me a death glare again like he knows I'm trying to sext you, so if you could just ignore that last text until you can get here and save me from him and his rabid pig, that would be awesome. And then we can... you know. In person. If you're free after you're busy. I'll be here all night.

"That's a massive text," Mackenzie says, and I jump and drop my phone, then spill my rinse water when I dive for it before Ellie can see what all her brother's text says.

Everyone leaps up to help me, but they're all grinning.

Even my mom, who prefers to smile benevolently and graciously rather than *grin*, which isn't at all what Hollywood producers are looking for in matronly roles these days.

"If you can handle how much Beck talks, then we're never letting you go," Ellie says.

"He is rather verbose for a male of the species, but charmingly so," his mom concedes, as if I haven't already decided I love her. "He just loves people."

"Was that all a set-up?" Alicia asks. "That tweet to you? I mean, that apology video was utterly adorable. You had to have been planning it for weeks, right? This is just a Hollywood play because he's about to announce a new fashion line or something, right?"

"Alicia," Mrs. Ryder says, very calmly and with a smile that rivals some that my mom's used while eviscerating a reporter or two over the years, "are you going to teach us to paint Duggan Field, or do we need to find another instructor?"

"Oh. Yes, ma'am. Although I'm still a proud card-carrying member of the Bro Code Sweethearts, and I was *really* glad when he apologized because I didn't want to have to hate him. Let's continue painting the background on our baseball park..."

"I haven't been to a Fireballs game in ages," Ellie says as I finish mopping up my mess with another of the staff's help and everyone else gets back to the painting.

"We should go!" Mackenzie's bouncing and in danger of spilling her rinse water and her wine now. "I have two season tickets," she adds in a loud whisper, like if she doesn't intentionally contain herself, the people four blocks over will hear too, because I know she's been waiting for the right moment to shout it from the rooftops. "I mean, Sarah, you're okay with me taking other people on occasion, right? Even if the Fireballs win while I'm taking someone else, that won't mean you're not good luck."

I wave my brush. "By all means, spread the love."

"You knew he was going to do that, didn't you?" she whispers.

"He may have mentioned it."

"That's bribery. And it's working."

Ellie snicker-snorts into her wine glass, and Mrs. Ryder looks back at us with an indulgent smile.

"I love this shade of midnight," my mom announces. "It reminds me of a few producers' black hearts. Alicia, what *is* that painting? I can't decide if it's a duck or a Ferris wheel."

"This one?" Alicia points to one of the samples high on the wall that Mom's gesturing to with her paintbrush. "It's the fountain in Reynolds Park, Ms. Darling."

"Mom, where are your reading glasses?" I ask.

"They're for reading, dear, not painting."

They're not actually reading glasses, but we call them that

because she refuses to acknowledge that she's been blind as a bat for years. She also refuses laser eye surgery and must've forgotten her contacts tonight. Probably thought a few extra beta carotene supplements would cover it.

No wonder I like Beck so much.

I actually come from a family of goofballs.

Huh.

While everyone stares at the fountain and probably also silently contemplates if my mother's on drugs, I sneak another glance at my phone.

Did you know your dad loves Scooby Doo? For the record, I don't have any desire to try a Scooby Snack. A guy's gotta have some boundaries. But I did eat fufu in West Africa. Pretty decent.

Mom's waving her Perrier bottle and telling a story about the time she had an argument over artistic vision with a director who refused to see the symbolism in the shade of curtains in a certain scene, so I text Beck back.

Dad loves Road Runner even more. And if you scratch Cupcake behind the ears, she'll be your best friend for life.

"I see you," Mackenzie whispers, so I tuck my phone away.

But I keep finding opportunities to slip it back out and check the running commentary of Beck's guys night at his place.

And the invitations to come over and join him for anything from weeding the potted plants on his patio to helping scrub behind his ears after an apparently well-aimed cupcake bomb thrown by James.

And by the time paint night is over, there's nowhere I'd rather go than back to Beck's place.

Which might be a sign that I have a serious problem.

I don't think he's just acting the part. But I also know there's been at least one photographer lounging at the outdoor café seating across the street all night, and the longer we're together, either because of a contract—or more, if all of this is *real*—the more I'll be back in the public spotlight.

Mom links her hand in mine and tugs me toward the back door, since we have a driver waiting for us out of sight of the street. "Come come," she says brightly. "Tomorrow's the big night. And someone needs her beauty rest."

The mention of *the big night* sends a chill down my back, because formal events and I don't get along well when cameras are involved. Beauty rest won't solve my paranoia or my legitimate fears.

But I still want to see Beck.

The very reason that I'm in the spotlight and have to get dressed up fancy and make a grand entrance and pretend to be someone I'm not.

Out in the alley behind the building, Ellie and Mrs. Ryder slip into one waiting car and Mackenzie hugs me before getting into a second. We're being chauffeured around like celebrities, with bodyguards in each car.

It's making me itchy, which I'm actively ignoring, because *I can do this*.

I can do this for Beck.

Mom shuffles me into the last car. "Anticipation makes the heart grow fonder, sweetheart," she whispers. "If he's *honestly* interested, let him stew for a while."

I don't want to let him stew.

I want to go see him. Despite all of the complications with photographers and gossip rags and having to have freaking *bodyguards* to go about my business in the city, I want to see him.

"Plenty of time after your contract is over," she adds, and a momentary chill washes over me.

She's right, of course.

When it comes to fame and tabloids, she usually is.

"Dad likes him," I say slowly while our car pulls out of the alley.

"Your father's a pushover, and we both know it," she replies.

And she's not wrong about that either.

"I like him too, Serendipity. But take your time. And make sure he's worth it. He *has* to earn your affections for his career right now. Let's see if he tries so hard when *you're* the only thing at stake."

"Thanks, Mom."

"Don't use that tone with me, young lady. You know full well you're a gem worth seventeen of his careers. But I want to know that *he* knows it."

I sigh and drop my head onto her shoulder, and then I feel like a total heel because it's been *years* since I've leaned on my mom, and she's leaving town sometime next week, while Beck will be here long after.

"Thank you for being here," I whisper.

She squeezes my knee and presses a kiss to my forehead. "There's nowhere else I'd rather be."

THIRTY-TWO

Beck

I CAN'T SIT STILL.

It's two hours before the gala starts.

Two hours until I see Sarah again.

Even more hours until I'm alone with her again.

I thought I'd talked her into coming over last night, but she texted a picture of her bedroom around midnight and said that she and Meda were crawling into bed after her mother's night-before-an-event routine, but don't worry, she was pretty sure her skin survived.

It's not weird to have memorized everything about her bedroom, is it? Pale yellow walls, a lavender comforter on what's probably a king-size bed, flowery throw pillows, with the cat curled up on the right side.

She has a bookshelf next to her bed with an eclectic mix of science fiction and romance novels, all with well-worn spines, but not so worn that I couldn't read the titles when I zoomed in on the picture. And the reading lamp suggests the books aren't just for decoration.

There's a painting—impressionist era—of a child in a straw field, and another of Monet's waterlilies. Very similar to the painting I have in my guest room, which feels like serendipity.

Serendipity.

Sarah.

It's impossible to think of her names without smiling.

Also, those fuckers who posted her picture from paint night in the gossip pages this morning speculating that she sleeps in a custom rocket ship bed with posters of David Bowie in *Neverending Story* and blueprints for how to get through the toughest Pac-Man levels can rot in hell.

Not that there would be anything wrong with her bedroom *however* she wanted to put it together, but because they're trying to box her in with one part of her personality.

They keep trying to tear her down.

While my popularity rating keeps skyrocketing like I'm not the reason she's in this mess in the first place.

If she'll let me, I'm taking her to Shipwreck and away from all this once tonight's gala is over.

Except she posted another blog this morning.

This one's about the science of gossip, public shamings, and trolls.

My girl is *hitting back*. She ignored every last troll comment, but she started tweeting back to people who were talking about actual science stuff.

She's fucking *blooming*.

And I haven't seen her in too many hours.

Not even Tripp's proposition about the Fireballs yesterday can distract me from thinking about her.

I have it bad. But in the best way.

"You never done one of these before?" Dad asks me while he's flipping through the channels. Mom and Ellie are having their hair and makeup done in the guest room by one of my people, but Dad, Wyatt, and I don't have to get ready just yet. Tucker's hanging with Tripp and his kids and mom tonight, which sounds better than what we're about to do, if you ask me.

Except for the part where Sarah's not there.

"One of what?" I ask Dad.

He looks at my bouncing knee. "One of these benefit dinner things."

I force myself to quit fidgeting. "Oh. Yeah. Tons. Remember, I took Mom to an awards gala two years ago in Milan?"

He smiles. "Said she couldn't understand a damn word anybody said, but the eye candy was spectacular."

"Pretty sure the problem's that he's never had a real date before," Wyatt offers.

"Ah. That makes sense."

I don't argue with them, because they're not wrong.

Not entirely, anyway. I've been on dates.

Tons of dates, especially if you count the ones that didn't end with a woman in my bed.

But none where I felt like the fate of my heart rested on it going well.

And none in the last five or so years where I was willing to risk my heart for the woman who will be on my arm.

I trust her.

I trust her.

That's kinda...huge.

"Your mother said her dress is beautiful," Dad tells me.

"She'd be beautiful in a paper bag," I reply.

Or preferably without anything at all.

And there I go getting stiff as a marble rolling pin again.

After a while, we pull our tuxes on, and Mom and Ellie emerge from the guest bedroom looking like dark-haired angels of mischief. Mom's in a soft blue long-sleeve gown that I should probably be able to tell you all the technical terms for, but women's evening wear, shoes, and purses are three places I refuse to go with my fashion lines.

Both of them have their hair curled and pinned with jewels, and Mom looks twenty years younger.

All of us stare at Ellie expectantly until she lifts the hem of her burgundy gown to reveal she's in flats, because even though she barely has a limp anymore after recovering from her accident, we all know heels aren't her wisest choice.

"Good girl," Wyatt says.

She rolls her eyes, but she also smiles and presses a kiss to his cheek, then wipes the lipstick off. "I thought you were wearing your fancy uniform."

"Didn't want to show up your brother when he needs to look good."

"Oh, or drag the Air Force into it if he makes an ass of himself again. Right. Got it."

"Hush," Mom tells her, though I probably deserved that, and it's delivered with a teasing grin that softens the blow. "Everyone makes mistakes. Like you hating Wyatt for twenty years."

"Totally different," she replies with a happy smile.

"Completely," Wyatt agrees, though he'd agree with anything she said if he thought it would get him laid.

Fucker. That's still my sister.

"Are you all ready?" Charlie breezes into my kitchen in a slinky black dress and fancy 'do, phone clutched in her fist. "Our ride's here. Time for Sarah and dinner."

My stomach growls.

My cock might too at the mention of Sarah's name, but thankfully, it's really quiet about it. And I tell it to simmer down, because I'm *not* getting pictures taken of me sporting a boner on the night I'm supposed to be making the ultimate *I'm sorry* to Sarah and the world.

My knee's hopping the entire ride. Mom's beaming. Dad's shaking his head and smiling ruefully. Ellie's rambling about how much Tucker would've loved this car, especially with all the buttons next to the seat.

And I'm feeling like a dumbass for using a stretch Hummer to haul around three environmental engineers on our way to meet a fourth.

But it's not like we could take the light-rail.

Okay, technically, we could've. But not without causing a scene.

Made enough scenes this week, and I'd like to put off the air of competent fashion mogul tonight instead of complete and total dumbass.

"Work mode, Ryder," Charlie reminds me quietly when we pull up to the planetarium where she set up this last-minute fundraiser. There's a red carpet rolled out and photographers and video cameras lining the ropes giving us a path inside the glass-and-steel domed building.

"Holy shit," Wyatt mutters. He reaches for his bow tie, but Ellie grabs his hand before he can mess it up.

"Smile for the cameras," she tells him. "They'll love you."

"A few more than there were in Milan, aren't there?" Mom says. She's also shrinking back some.

"It'll be quieter once we're inside," I tell her. "Ellie's right. Just smile. They'll love you."

"Of course they will," Dad agrees.

Charlie climbs down first and steps aside. Wyatt's next, and he waits just outside the door to help Ellie. Cameras flash, and shouts of *It's the Ryders!* go up in the crowd.

"Are you this popular, or are they all hoping you'll fall on your face?" Dad asks me with a wink and a grin.

"Both," I reply.

I hope I'm not wrong about the reporters inside.

Charlie vetted the media and my team hired extra security for the night. Once we're in the main space for the semi-private dinner, there are exactly four reporters authorized to join us in the building, and since we personally vetted every one of the seventy-five guests—mostly Copper Valley businesspeople, some athletes and musicians, and local politicians, and I bought most of their tickets and just asked them to be here without doing anything other than dressing up for a show and dinner—I know everything will be fine.

I think.

I hope.

This week hasn't exactly been an exercise in smooth sailing, and I know Vaughn's waiting on the final reports out of tonight to decide if the foundation is still on. We invited him, of course, but he couldn't make it.

Or possibly didn't want to be here if I blow it again.

But it feels like the stakes are so much higher than getting to help some kids and reclaim my image.

Because of Sarah.

I hope like hell tonight's not torture for her.

Dad climbs out of the Hummer and helps Mom down, and I can see her blushing all the way down her neck as she smiles at the waiting press.

I follow them all, tug my cuffs down, and flash the smile that landed me my first modeling contract before stepping to Mom's other side and offering her my arm. "Two escorts for the belle of the ball?"

She laughs and tucks her arm into my elbow. "You are such a charmer."

"I learned from the best."

She smiles up at Dad. "I know."

He winks at her, and the six of us head inside past shouted questions about if I've learned my lesson, if Sarah's here, if her parents arranged all this to revive Sunny's career, if I'm paying off the picketers at my factory in Hoboken, how much I'm paying Sarah to date me, how much she's paying me to talk about Persephone, and is it true that I'm selling out to finance a rocket ship to Mars so I can offend all the little green men too?

"Is it always like this?" Mom mutters.

"Usually they're asking him to flash his underwear," Charlie tells her. "So this could be considered an improvement."

"They're just looking for reactions," I assure her as the glass doors part and let us into the cool lobby.

And I do mean *cool*.

Not only is it ten degrees cooler than the summer evening outside, but it's also just wicked awesome.

The rounded walls are black velvet with stars sprinkled like glitter, and the recessed lights of the ceiling three stories above illuminate an artist's rendition of the solar system in brilliant colors and textured paint that makes you think you could reach up and feel the flames in the glowing sun.

There's a compass designed into the marble floor, and the ladies' shoes *click-click-click* subtly amidst the murmur of the distinguished guests who could make it on such short notice.

Wouldn't be here at all if there hadn't been a wedding cancelation. The bride's a former Sweetheart though—that's what the Bro Code fan club was called back in the day—and she agreed to let us take over the venue on the stipulation that she get to attend.

Easy enough.

I greet the other last-minute stragglers, then cast my eyes upward again, scanning the cantina lofted on the second floor at the top of a staircase that hugs the curve of the wall.

My daughter will accompany you, but only if she's allowed to make an entrance in style, Sunny said during negotiations for how tonight would go down.

Fuck.

Not even a week ago.

Charlie needs another raise for pulling this off.

Ah, there's Sunny at the top of the metal stairs now, in a butter-colored gown that hugs her trim figure. Judson's at her side, his head twisted to say something to the woman standing behind him.

I can make out a trail of golden fabric, but I can't see Sarah.

That has to be Sarah.

Unless she's backing out.

But because she doesn't want the attention?

Or because I was the dumbass who shouldn't have told her how much I want to kiss her the other night?

I do want to kiss her. And strip her. And make love to her.

And I wanted to be there in her bedroom with her last night, or to have her in mine.

But if she's not ready, I can wait.

I'll wait a fucking century if I have to, because she orders food for me and posts blogs that tell off trolls who don't realize they're being told off, and she sasses bouncers who call me an asshole even when I deserve it, and she has no idea she's gorgeous and strong and a fucking inspiration for just being *her*.

Judson steps aside, and every thought, every breath, every heartbeat stops.

Complete, full, no question *stops*.

Swear on my underwear, even the earth stops breathing.

I lock eyes with those gorgeous brown orbs, hidden behind layers of mascara, but still *there*, looking for reassurance, and fuck me with a hand beater, when her rosy lips tip up in a tentative smile, I'd sell off every last one of my lines and homes and buildings and buy her a first-class ticket to Mars if that's where she wanted to go.

Or Saturn.

Or to the scoop in the Big Dipper, so she could try drinking out of the well of Space.

I swallow hard when Wyatt nudges me. "Think you're supposed to go get her, not gawk at her, dumbass," he mutters with a grin, and my feet start working again.

Mom gives me a little shake from the other side, and I realize I forgot I'm still holding her hand in my elbow. I let her go, and I head toward the stairs to meet my date.

"Hurt her and you'll only wish you were dead," Judson growls as he and Sunny greet me at the bottom of the stairs.

"I'm really falling in love with this growly thing," Sunny murmurs to him. "Will you talk to me like that in bed tonight?"

I try to focus on them, because I'm supposed to smile ruefully and shake their hands and thank them for being here with us tonight, but Sarah's still waiting, and I can't take my eyes off her.

Her thick dark hair is pulled high in a fancy twist, with a few expertly curled ringlets hanging loose. Her gown—she's wrapped in golden lace, all of her curves on display, with two thin straps over her shoulders. Sunny's clearly gotten to her with the makeup, and the dudes up in the International Space Station can probably see her lashes from there. And the rose on her lips—of course it's perfect.

But it's her eyes that have me completely captivated.

Big, dark orbs of apprehension mixed with anticipation.

They're even more uncertain up close.

"Hi," I breathe when I reach her.

"I really hate that your underwear is so comfortable but you refuse to do that kind of magic to the monstrosities known as women's shoes," she says through a fake smile, and even though I know she's probably already in need of some TLC on those poor feet of hers, I can't help smiling even bigger.

"I'll put research and development on it first thing Monday morning." I brush a kiss to her cheek, close to her ear, and whisper, "I missed you."

"I miss me a little bit right now too, but I missed you more. Let's let all these people take your picture so we can go eat. *Someone* I know has me obsessed with food now."

"I don't think they want my picture," I tell her honestly, which earns me a pursed-lip, straight-laced, *don't be ridiculous* eyebrow arch that I've watched photographers spend hours coaxing out of female models. "If your feet hurt that bad, I could carry you."

"Don't you dare. This dress is so tight it'd probably split and flash my Slimzies at every last reporter down there."

I tuck her arm into my elbow and lead her down the curved steps. "Why so tight?"

She sighs, eyes on me. "Because I loved it," she confesses. "Apparently I have some of my mother in me after all."

"I have a tailor—"

"Beck. My mother is *Sunny Darling*. This dress has been through six tailors. Even my Slimzies has been altered."

I can't stop smiling. "I mentioned I missed you, right?"

"I missed you too," she whispers again with a soft smile, and *boom.*

My heart implodes with happiness, then builds itself back up again to fist-bump my stomach. "I'm going to ask you out on another date," I inform her, "but this time, I'm not going to start it with a really bad post on social media."

She finally laughs, then grimaces. "Did you hear that? Or was that my imagination?"

"What?"

"I swear I just popped a seam."

"Where?"

"My back."

"You know if I lean back and check it out, there will be a million pictures of me checking out your ass all over the tabloids tomorrow. Not that I don't want to check out your ass—I totally do—but my PR team would kill me, my mother would disown me, and Ellie would die laughing, at which point Wyatt would find my cold lifeless body and bring it back to life to kill me again for killing my sister."

Her nose wrinkles while she laughs again. "You are utterly insane and I really, really missed you."

"You had important work to do. Like that blog post. Which was excellent, by the way. I had Ellie translate the big words for me."

"Beck."

"Okay, okay, I read it and understood every word. Don't tell anyone. I have a reputation to uphold."

"I like you more than I like your reputation."

We get to the bottom of the stairs, and I catch Charlie's eye and manage to communicate a request that she check Sarah's back seams while my parents hug her and Judson gives me the *we're heading out to the pasture for me to put a bullet in the back of your brain and bury your body amidst the tumbleweeds* glare, which has to be for the cameras, because we're at least two thousand miles from the nearest tumbleweeds.

Though definitely not that far from the nearest pastures.

Huh.

"You certainly clean up nice," Sunny tells me with a bright smile. "And what are your intentions for my daughter after this evening's over?"

"Ice cream," I reply without hesitation. "We're going out for ice cream."

We're among the last to arrive—as planned—so I'm not surprised when Charlie gives me the *keep moving, slowpoke* head jerk. Along with a thumbs-up indicating Sarah's dress is fine.

We pair up and head through the exhibits toward the tilted dome theater. Sarah pauses as we make our way through the winding hallways, sometimes pointing out a particular moon on Jupiter painted on the walls, and sometimes, I'm pretty certain, just to catch her breath, and I have to wonder just how tight that dress actually is, and if she's going to be able to sit in it.

Copper Valley's mayor, who's straggling behind enjoying the artwork, does a double-take and gawks at Sarah.

So do two pro soccer players and the quarterback for Copper Valley's football team when we finally enter the theater.

"They're waiting for me to fall on my face, aren't they?" she whispers as she accepts a flute of champagne from a server.

"Not a chance." I squeeze her hand. "They're wondering how a dumbass like me got the most gorgeous woman in the room."

She snorts softly. "Uh-huh."

"Too bad for them, they don't know I got the smartest, biggest-hearted one with the worst taste in dates too."

That gets a smile, and also causes a guy in a tux to trip over his date's chair as he tries to get to an open seat.

Sarah stops and glances at him. "You okay?"

"Ergalaaargh," he replies as he stares into her eyes.

"You need a paramedic?"

"*Sit down*, Jeremy," his date hisses. "And stop staring at her boobs." She mutters something about implants as I nudge Sarah along our path toward the front of the room.

Her brow furrows. "Did I miss something?"

"You are so fucking adorable," Ellie declares with a grin.

Which doesn't help Sarah's confused expression.

But my whole family is clearly falling in love.

As they should be.

I gesture her into the front row, greeting familiar faces behind us because that's what I'm supposed to do, before I take my spot beside her. When she glances at the dark curved walls around us, I decide I'm putting a planetarium theater exactly like this one in my place if it'll make her smile again.

Shit.

I don't have it bad. I have it *baddest*.

And that's before she slips her hand in mine and squeezes when the planetarium show starts with the livestream of Persephone pacing in her enclosure at the zoo. "I forgive you for making me wear Slimzies," she whispers.

"Next time *my* tailor's in charge of your dress," I whisper back.

"I don't think so," Sunny murmurs on my other side.

Before I can ask if she means there won't be a next time, or she's fighting me over the rights to dress Sarah, the zoo curator steps to the front of the room to welcome us all, to thank the Friends of the Zoo for putting together tonight's event, and to give a special welcome to one very dedicated blogger for bringing Persephone to the attention of so many people around the world.

The lighting in the theater is low so that we can all see the video of Persephone pacing in her habitat, but I can easily make out Sarah's cheeks light up with that unique blush.

She gets a round of applause so long that she starts shifting and mutters something about her damn dress.

The curator doesn't mention her parents. Or me. Or Charlie, who basically ran the Friends of the Zoo this week to pull this all together.

Which is how it's supposed to be, because tonight's not about *me*, or Charlie—who clearly never sleeps—or about anything other than Persephone, and Sarah.

When the applause dies down—seriously, it reminds me of back in the day when the guys and I would finish a concert and there were demands for an encore—the curator smiles at Sarah once more. "And we hope we'll be seeing many, many more of your very enlightening videos. Solo, I mean. Without the aid of a camera hog."

Everyone chuckles, Sarah smiles and blushes harder and hides it behind a sip of champagne.

We're treated to a twenty-minute show about the big bang theory —sung to rock music, because *dude*, that's way more awesome than somebody talking—and then we're led into a conference space that's set up for a formal sit-down dinner.

We take our time getting to our seats, mostly because everyone in the room wants to talk to Sarah.

About Persephone. Or something on her blog. Or about how gorgeous she looks tonight, which is the only thing she wrinkles her nose at.

Like she doesn't believe it.

I'm starting to get pissed.

Not because she doesn't believe she's pretty, but because nobody ever noticed before she slathered on the makeup and shimmied into Slimzies.

We finally make it to our table and I pull out her chair for her.

"No," she says suddenly, turning to me with a spark of mischief in her eyes that once again robs me of the ability to breathe.

It takes me a minute to find my voice. "No, what?"

"No, I don't care how tight this dress is, you may *not* have my single chocolate truffle for dessert."

"Arm-wrestle you for it," I reply instinctively.

"*Beckett*," my mom hisses from across the table.

I snap straight and turn to her, because I could be seventy-eight and that tone would still scare the shit out of me. "Ma'am?"

"How many of these fancy dinners have you been to and you still put your elbows on the table and offer to arm-wrestle ladies for their desserts?"

"To be fair, Michelle, we raised him," Dad says.

While leaning his elbows on the table.

And eyeing Mom's—what the *fuck*?

He's eyeing Mom's dessert.

"Why's there only a single truffle for dessert?" I ask.

"I'll scalp your truffles if you don't quit staring at my daughter's chest," Judson growls.

"Excuse you, he was looking at her *eyes*," my mom snaps.

Judson blinks once, then twice, then slinks back in his chair. "Begging pardon, ma'am."

"We should come to these things more often," Ellie says to Wyatt, who chokes on his water and vehemently shakes his head *no*.

Sarah slides me a grin.

I grin back.

And slide my hand under the table to squeeze her thigh, which I can't do very well, because *holy shit* that dress is really fucking tight.

"Hands to yourself, Beckett," my mother says.

I point to Wyatt, who's undoubtedly touching Ellie under the table.

"They're engaged," Mom replies primly.

"Don't even think about proposing just to touch me," Sarah says under her breath.

My mind instantly snaps to the reminder that I need to prove myself in the bedroom, and suddenly, I wish I'd planned this whole week better.

Sarah pats me on the thigh under the table. "But you *can* think about that," she adds softly.

My mom beams at her.

Even though, yes, Sarah's touching me under the table.

And I'm certain my mom knows it.

Actually, I'm certain that's *why* my mom is beaming at her.

Gotta love moms and their double standards. Especially since it means I get to hold Sarah's hand while she inches it up my thigh.

"Serendipity," Sunny says sweetly to Sarah, "while he cleans up nicely, you don't know where his leg has been."

"The lady has a point," my dad agrees.

"*Christopher*," my mom hisses.

Ellie and Wyatt snicker some more, and as the servers roll into the room with domed dinner plates, I just grin.

Because *this* is as normal as normal gets. And when I need these people to have my back, they're right there.

And Sarah's drawing circles on my leg with her thumb, and yeah.

This moment?

With my family and the woman I'm going to spend the rest of my life with, no matter what I need to do to win her over?

This moment is fucking perfect.

THIRTY-THREE

Sarah

I AM A TWO-FACED ASSHOLE, but you can't tell, because there's so much makeup glooped on my face that I could actually be Cupcake's twin and nobody would know there was a pig snout hiding under all these layers of construction-grade plaster.

Here I am, in a dress I kinda love more than I'm willing to confess to Beck, even if I can only use about forty percent of my lung capacity right now, and I'm torn between wanting to just stare at him in his tuxedo all night long and rip it off him with my teeth.

No amount of telling myself it's because the man under the tux is a kind, sweet, sexy gentleman will convince me that I'm not two-faced for drooling over his utter physical perfection.

Nor will any amount of reminding myself that he's just as attractive in jeans and a Fireballs jersey, or in a teddy bear robe, or while letting himself be chastised by his mother.

Although I'm definitely bothered that he's not devouring every last bite of his steak.

"Are you sick?" I whisper.

"Hungry," he whispers back, "but I'm officially on duty, which means I can't make a pig of myself."

"You really can have my truffle if you want it."

"No way. If I eat your truffle in public, my reputation is officially shot and I'll have to turn to modeling socks if I ever want to make enough to help my parents retire."

I get a jolt of lusty need straight between my thighs when he says *eat your truffle*, but when I try to suck in a breath, my Slimzies and my dress squeeze me so tight that all the circulation is cut off to my nipples and I end up simultaneously trying to suck air back in and choking on my own lack of air.

Beck's eyes go wide, and he pats my back. "You okay?"

"Woman problems," I blurt.

And then I go so hot that half my makeup is probably going to melt off.

My mom, Beck's mom, and Ellie all lunge for their clutches. Most likely to grab tampons.

"*Dress* problems," I correct quickly. Dammit, I swear the people at the two tables behind me heard that.

"Just breathe shallow, honey, it'll be okay," my mom advises.

"My Slimzies are killing me too," Ellie says.

"I told you not to wear that shit," Wyatt mutters.

I like him. He's very practical.

"I'm okay," I tell Beck, who's still watching me so closely that I'm starting to wonder if I have an errant nose hair or something. I nod to his plate. "Are you sure you don't need more food?"

"We'll grab takeout somewhere later. *After* we get you out of that dress. *Ow!* Mom! It's *physically hurting her*."

He still grins at me though, and my heart takes up a new rhythm at the implication that I'll be with him for takeout.

And out of my dress while we're eating it.

"I gave birth to you. I'm aware of what's going through your head," his mother says.

Nope.

Not killing the buzz at all.

Maybe there's something wrong with me after all.

"Serendipity's staying with us tonight," my dad growls.

"Um, no, we're having a girls pajama party," Ellie corrects.

"We are?" Wyatt asks. And then he, too, mutters *ouch* and rubs his leg under the table. "Oh. Right. I guess you are. Without warning me. *Ouch!* Okay, okay, I'm shutting up."

The curator of the zoo suddenly rushes to the front of the room, where staff are hastily pulling up a projector screen. "Ladies and gentlemen, if I could have your attention for one moment," he calls, "I've just received word that Persephone is in active labor."

I straighten. Beck shoots a look at Charlie two tables over, like she arranged this and he's going to need to give her a raise. She rolls her eyes and mouths back *only you.*

I snort.

Because I think she's right.

Only Beck could have this kind of luck.

"He's just saying that to get a few more donations, right?" he murmurs to me.

A projector flickers to life, and a woman three tables back screams.

"Ah, nope," I tell him while I look at the very pregnant, very squatting, very *delivering* giraffe on the screen.

"Oh my," my mother murmurs.

The Ryders all put their forks down.

My dad goes pale.

Persephone gives a mighty push, expelling baby giraffe legs and amniotic fluid, and my dad wipes his brow.

The mayor's still eating at the next table.

Murmurs are going through the crowd.

"I can't eat through this," someone whispers.

"It's nature, Felicia. You can too," someone else whispers back.

"Oh, god, she's so beautiful, I might cry." The curator shakes out a white handkerchief and wipes his forehead.

Persephone snorts and shakes her head atop her long neck.

Beck's enraptured. "She's so fucking strong."

"Most women are, dear," his mom says.

Persephone pushes again, and I poke my mom and point to my dad.

"Oh, here we go again." She scoots her chair back and wraps an arm around his shoulders. "Head between your knees, Judson. Just breathe. Breathe the love in, and breathe the pain out. Love in, pain out."

Nearly all sounds of silverware clanking on plates have stopped. Beck's still watching the screen, but he drapes his arm over my chair and leans in close, smelling like cinnamon and cloves tonight. "You ever seen anything like this before?"

"I saw a documentary about elephants giving birth once, but not *live.* And I watched that eagle cam, but birds hatching isn't quite the same."

"She's just—wow," he breathes.

He's not at all grossed out, or horrified, and his stomach gives a rumble that he doesn't seem to notice.

I squeeze his leg and press a kiss to his clean-shaven cheek, because I can't help myself. He turns a smile to me, not a smolder, not a face for the cameras, but a soft, honest smile that sets the bees buzzing through my belly.

He scoots closer and instead of keeping his arm casually draped around the back of my chair, he wraps an arm around me, and I lean into him, breathing in his scent, my hand resting on his long, lean, solid thigh while we watch Persephone give birth to a brand-new baby giraffe.

A gasp goes up through the room when the baby plops to the ground, but within minutes, Persephone has helped the little one to its feet, and I'm not crying, but I'm definitely choked up.

The curator is weeping.

And Beck just breathes, "Wow."

"One more giraffe in the world," I whisper.

"Is it a boy or a girl?" someone calls.

The curator blows his nose and holds up a finger.

"They won't know until they can examine it," I tell her.

The curator points at me, then at his nose.

My dad's still doing the breathing exercises with my mom, his head under the tablecloth.

Beck seems to remember we're not alone, and he straightens suddenly with a broad grin. "That was epic."

"You have the craziest luck," Ellie tells him.

"Right? What are the odds that tweet would've brought us Sarah?"

And there goes more mushy warmth in my chest, because she clearly meant luck with the timing of Persephone giving birth, but instead, he wants to talk about *me*.

Dad recovers, and the gradual noises of people eating returns to the banquet hall. People start milling, all while the live video of Persephone tending her newborn calf plays on the projector.

No owls swoop in.

My dress doesn't split.

Beck keeps a hand on me at all times. On my back. Brushing my hair out of my face. Touching my elbow to turn me to meet someone new.

No one asks about the tweet, but several people stop at our table and want to talk about Persephone or my blog or one of the projects the Ryders have worked on or how Ellie's doing after her accident or what Wyatt's plans are for after the military or how honored they are to have my parents here in Copper Valley.

They tease Beck about his underwear.

At least, until I point out it's the most comfortable underwear on the planet and challenge them to prove they're not wearing it.

All with a Mom-approved smile, of course. I *am* still Sunny Darling's daughter.

The live feed on Persephone times out before any of us get a really good look at her calf, and the zoo's curator tells us updates will be posted online as soon as the zookeepers are able to check over both mama and baby giraffe.

As the crowd begins to clear out and Charlie gives us the *time to go* signal, I pause and dig my phone out of my purse and hit the camera function. "How's the light?" I ask Beck.

His brows knit together. "The light?"

"The light. We need to post another video. Since Persephone gave birth."

His intense scrutiny slowly turns to a wide smile that makes my heart go skipping over itself. "Yeah?"

"Yes. And hurry up before Charlie marches us out of here and I lose my nerve."

He takes my phone from me and holds it out, his long arms working to our advantage. "Ready?"

I nod, and he hits the button to record us.

"Hey, Must Love Bees followers, this is Sarah Dempsey. And this guy I picked up at some fancy dinner tonight. And I'm too excited to wait to get home and change before asking if you all saw that Persephone the giraffe gave birth tonight. If you were watching along with the rest of us, wasn't she amazing? Such a beautiful creature. And if you haven't seen it yet, well, don't do what my dad did and pass out under a table. Maybe just wait for the pictures if you're squeamish, okay? Hit the comments and tell me what you were doing when Persephone gave birth! I'm heading home for a nice long bubble bath and to wait for news about whether we have a girl or a boy."

"She had a girl," Beck says.

"You think?" I ask him.

"Definitely. Did you see how strong she was and how fast she stood up? Totally a girl."

"Boy giraffes can *also* stand up soon after birth."

"I guess, but I still think our baby's a girl."

My belly flutters. "Then I guess by default, I'll have to guess he's a boy."

He grins at me. "Want to put money on it?"

"Nope, but I'd bet an ice cream sundae."

"You're on, taser lady."

I wave at the camera. "Congrats to Persephone and the Copper Valley Zoo on their new addition."

Beck shuts the video off, and before I can lose my nerve, I post it to my feed.

"You're such a natural, sweetheart," my mom says with a sniffle.

"I'm going to throw up."

"No, you're not." Beck pulls me in for a hug and presses a kiss to my giant hair. "You're the bravest fucking badass I've ever met," he whispers.

"You've obviously lived a very sheltered celebrity existence."

He laughs.

"Time to *go*, folks," Charlie says.

We filter back out of the planetarium, thanking the staff as we go, and the bride whose wedding was canceled, which I didn't know until Beck introduced me to her and she thanked us for saving her reception.

I hug her extra tight on the way out, because I know a thing or a million about *awkward*.

When we reach the three limos waiting at the door, Beck grips my hand. "You really going to girls' night?" he murmurs.

"Depends. If I go home with you, will I need my clothes?"

"Nope. I got this amazing teddy bear robe you can borrow."

The laugh sneaks out of me, and the next thing I know, I'm waving bye to everyone while we dive into the back of the first limo, and then his lips are capturing mine, his arms wrapping around me, and suddenly the only thing in the entire world that matters is kissing him back.

Because this isn't what I've been waiting for from the moment he came back to my house to apologize after I tasered him.

This is what I've been waiting for my entire life.

THIRTY-FOUR

Beck

I CAN'T KEEP my hands to myself.

Or my mouth, for that matter.

And since Sarah's kissing me back, her hands clutching my shirt, I decide that I'm just going to live right here, in the back of this car, and kiss her—and more—for the rest of my life.

Thank fuck I live in a time when we can order food to be delivered to the back seat of a car.

And when I can meet a total stranger who just might be the love of my life thanks to invisible waves floating through the air to computers in our pockets.

What an awesome world.

The car jerks to a stop, and I realize we're back at my building.

Huh.

"Do you want to stay here or go upstairs?" I ask her. On a pant. I don't want to quit kissing her.

Her nose wrinkles, and I realize she probably wasn't thinking about living in a car just to make out, but now I want to know what she *was* thinking about.

I can't read her through all that makeup.

"Upstairs," I say, and I get distracted by her collarbone, because it's undoubtedly the shapeliest collarbone in the history of bones. And collars. And it's right there on display in this dress that I hate despite how pretty it is as far as dresses go, and how much of her collarbones it shows, because she's not comfortable in it.

Dammit.

I have to get her upstairs and out of this ridiculous getup.

I move so fast she's gaping at me as I reach across her and fling the car door open. "C'mon. Upstairs. Go."

"Bossy."

"I'll make out with you in the elevator."

She laughs, then she winces when there's a distinct ripping noise.

But she's climbing out. I strip out of my coat and fling it around her shoulders so that wherever she's ripping, nobody has to see, and we're not exactly alone here, because we're being dropped at the front of the building, not the back, or in the garage. I hustle her inside and to my private elevator and hit the button for the penthouse, and then I have my hands on her again.

Her hips. Her ass.

"Oh, no, here." She swipes her thumb over my mouth.

I must be wearing her lipstick. Not that I mind.

Especially if it means she's touching me.

"I hate this stuff," she mutters, and yeah, I hate it too. Not because I'm wearing it, but because all that mascara is obstructing my view of her eyes.

"I want to kiss you until I can't remember how to breathe."

Those gorgeous chocolate pools lift to meet my gaze, and I feel like I've taken another ten thousand volts to the chest.

So fucking gorgeous.

So fucking perfect.

"It's the dress," she says.

"Sarah." I blow out an impatient breath. "I don't care what you're wearing. It's *you.*"

Her brows furrow, but she's wearing a smile as she continues to wipe at my lips. I capture her hand and press kisses to her fingers.

"You make me feel pretty all the time," she whispers.

"You're so much more than just pretty."

We get to the top floor, and I lock the elevator, because hell if I'm letting anyone else in right now. And then I pull Sarah to the kitchen.

"What—" she starts.

Her eyes go round when I pull a pair of scissors out of the island drawer.

"How much do you like this dress?" I ask.

"Zipper!" she shrieks, and there's one more distinct sound of a seam ripping.

"Hold on, baby, I'll have you breathing free again in just a minute." Sure enough, there's a zipper on the back of her dress. I yank the tab down, and she sucks in a giant breath as the fabric opens.

"Oh my god, that feels so good."

Her legs are still shrink-wrapped in the dress. "You honestly like this thing?"

"Don't start, fashion police. *I like gold lace*, okay? It brings out my eyes."

"I love your eyes. Especially when they're not surrounded by insect legs. I'd like your dress better if it wasn't strangling you."

She's laughing as she turns, giving me another look at those shoulder blades, and fuck if I'm not hard in an instant.

Her shoulder blades are just as sexy as her collarbones.

Maybe more so.

So shouldery. And bladey. And covered in soft Sarah skin. And leading down to the curviest ass that I want to stroke and knead all fucking night long.

"The zipper goes lower," she tells me over her shoulder. "If you can get it…down…"

I stop her before she spins in a circle trying to reach it herself, and I stand behind her and tug her zipper lower, below her mid-back, to her waist, and lower, over the curve of her ass, my hand shaky, my dick aching.

I can't see her skin lower than her shoulder blades, because it's all still held in by a nude bodysuit. She casts a furtive glance at the solid wall of windows looking out over the twinkling city lights.

"Mabel, dim the windows," I say.

"Dimming windows," my digital assistant says, and the blinds automatically lower from their case in the ceiling.

"Oh my god, that was so hot," she whispers. "But Mabel's not spying on us, is she?"

"Mabel, go to sleep."

"Behave yourself and use a condom," she replies in her electronic voice. "Night-EE. Night."

"Fucking Hank," I mutter.

But Sarah's laughing, and then wheezing. "Oh my god, get me out of this thing."

Who am I to deny a lady in need?

I try to wedge a finger under the undergarment, and my digit starts to go numb in seconds. "I forbid you to ever wear a piece of shit like this ever again," I inform her.

"You forbid me?"

"Don't use that *don't go all macho man* voice on me. This is your circulation we're talking about. I can't give you a double orgasm if you can't feel your pussy."

She stops talking.

She also sucks in a deep breath, which makes the industrial-strength rubber band she's wrapped in pinch my finger tighter, and fuck, I hope I don't cut either one of us, but it's not like I'm calling in reinforcements to get her naked.

And I don't even care about getting her naked.

I mean, I *do*, but I'm really more concerned about making sure she can breathe.

"If I cut my finger off, I want you to carry on without me," I tell her while I angle my finger deeper beneath the death Lycra. "You need to breathe more than I need the tip of my finger."

She laughs again, but I manage to use my superhuman strength to stretch the mutant rubber band away from her skin far enough to snip the edge of it, and then I drop the scissors and pull.

And grunt.

And yank.

Shit.

And then I have to pick the scissors up again and snip-snip-snip my way down the bodysuit.

While she shakes with silent laughter.

I'd make a fool of myself all night long to hear her laugh.

When I have it split down to the base of her spine, I put the scissors down—again—and this time, I wrap my arms around her belly and press a kiss to her shoulder. "The entertainment part of the evening is now complete," I tell her.

She shivers, and goosebumps erupt all over her smooth skin.

"You want some sweatpants?" I ask, my lips still on her delicious skin.

Honey.

She always tastes like honey.

"No," she whispers.

"Dammit, don't tell me you want more rubber bands. We'll have to go down to the office. If you're into bondage, we can do it in ways where you'll still be able to breathe. I think. I'll have to google that too."

"Beck."

"You have the sexiest voice."

She twists in my arms so she's facing me, and her fingers go to my bow tie. "I have a confession," she whispers.

"I'm a vault of silence. Please don't ever stop touching me."

God, that smile.

But it's wrong. It's not the right color.

"I have a thing for guys who wear real bow ties." She expertly unties me and leaves it hanging loose around my neck, then starts on my buttons.

"I have a thing for ladies who have things for guys who wear real bow ties."

Her fingers still while she studies me. "Then why the frown? You never frown."

Because I can't see her eyes clearly through all the goop on her lashes, and her lips are the wrong color, and this isn't *Sarah*.

It's the Hollywood Fake Sarah.

I don't like it.

She squeals when I swing her up in my arms. "Beck? What—"

"I miss *you*," I tell her.

And I'm fucking going to find her.

THIRTY-FIVE

Sarah

MY DRESS IS DANGLING on my top half and still clinging to my lower half when Beck carries me down the hallway and turns into a bedroom.

A large, airy, silver-and-black bedroom with a marble fireplace and two huge armchairs, a bookshelf full of comic books, and a king-size bed with rumpled sheets and a black comforter tossed half-off. The room opens onto a patio that I can't see well through the glass, but there are definitely fairy lights out there, among other lights. He turns another corner, and then we're in a bathroom the size of my bedroom with a massive soaking tub and a glass-walled shower with a rainspout and wall nozzles. He sets me gently on the marble counter, riffles through a drawer in the vanity beneath the sink, and comes up with a makeup remover cloth and two clean black washcloths.

I suck in a breath.

Of *course* he has makeup remover.

"Close your eyes," he says gruffly, and because he's so very serious, I do as asked.

He warms the water, and a moment later, he's wiping a warm washcloth over my face, removing the makeup, then rubbing soft, slow circles over my skin, massaging my face.

And not talking.

Beck.

Not talking.

I start to pry open one eyelid, but he whispers, "Closed, Sarah."

And then he's softly wiping my eyes too.

So gentle.

So *very* gentle.

Like I'm delicate and he doesn't want to break me.

I suck in a shuddery breath while my heart swells, because in my entire life, no one has *ever* treated me as though I'm delicate.

My feelings, yes—my parents walked on eggshells for a few years after prom. Before it too, if I'm being honest, because my teen years were ugly for *all* the reasons.

But physically—not like this.

He uses the warm washcloth to massage my forehead. My cheeks. Around my eyes. My jaw and chin. So very gently over my lips. Down my neck.

All with one hand holding the back of my head, his fingers carefully massaging the base of my skull, his scent filling my senses, mingling with the scent of my arousal, his touch setting my skin on fire.

"There you are," he says softly, and I blink open my eyes to find him studying my face with a mixture of awe and reverence. My cheeks tingle with relief at being in fresh air again, and there's an awkward lump clogging my throat, because I swear, he's thinking I'm gorgeous without any makeup at all.

I've never wanted to be gorgeous.

It's superficial and unnecessary.

But having the most gorgeous man on earth gazing at me with utter adoration for just being *me* makes me feel beautiful.

And strong.

And so very, very sexy.

I'm half-naked, with my dress gaping in front, my split Slimzies curling down, and my legs still stuck in a dress, with hair that's probably sticking up, and no makeup to hide my blush or my birthmark.

And he makes me feel like an irresistible goddess.

He touches my cheek with a light finger, and then he's kissing me.

But it's not a normal kiss, just lips and tongues and teeth.

No, this is like our souls are saying *hello*.

I unbutton his shirt slowly. He shifts my body as he peels my dress down over my hips, kissing me and plucking hairpins out. I reach his pants and unhook them too.

He groans into my mouth as I push them over his hips and they slide to the floor. My hands curve around to cup his ass, and my already wet panties get positively soaked.

My dress hits the floor, and he grips the edges of my Slimzies and yanks, and they split in two.

I shudder in relief as my body's finally fully free, and then I realize I'm completely naked.

Except for a small pair of RYDE panties.

"You are so fucking gorgeous," he whispers as he cups my breasts, then bends to press a gentle kiss to each nipple before suckling one into his mouth. I gasp at the intense shot of pleasure that radiates from my breast, through my ribs, and down to my center. I clutch his head in place, my fingers in his thick hair, and I spread my legs, because I need him to—

Yes.

To touch me.

He strokes his thumb over the fabric covering my clit, and I gasp again and arch into him.

"You like?" he whispers against my breast, which makes my skin pebble everywhere his breath touches.

"Yes," I manage.

He still has his shirt hanging open, tie dangling low on one side, with a white undershirt and black boxers.

I'm still in my strappy heels.

He straightens and guides my legs around his hips, and then he's carrying me into his bedroom, hands kneading my ass, kissing me again, lowering me to his bed, where his hands roam over my body. "Tell me to stop and I will," he whispers.

"Take your shirts off."

He smiles as he does as asked, the dress shirt flying one way, the tight white T-shirt beneath going the other. "Better?"

I crook a finger at him, and he lowers himself onto his arms above me. I cup his cheeks, then move my hands down his neck, around his shoulders, over his chest, and I smile back at him. "Much better."

His stomach growls, and we both look down at it.

"You didn't get enough dinner," I whisper.

"I'm about to fix that," he replies, and then he's kissing his way down my body, from my neck, between my breasts, over my belly, beneath my belly button, until he stops short at the top of my panties. "Sarah Dempsey, you're wearing my underwear," he breathes against the elastic band.

"Yes," I manage, because it's all I can say. He's teasing the edges of the panties with his thumbs, taking his time, his mouth drifting lower to press kisses to the top of my mound over the fabric.

"I like you in my underwear. But I think I might like you more out of them."

"*Yes*," I gasp again.

He breathes in my scent, and I strain to open my legs wider.

I'm so wet already, and the anticipation of Beck's mouth on me is making my heart throb in my clit. "Want—you," I manage.

"How mad will you be if I tear these off?" he asks my pussy.

"*Beck.*"

"What? I can get you a new pair." He blows on the fabric, and my hips lift off the bed. Everything's buzzing and shimmering in anticipation.

He guides my legs so he can tug the panties off—"Too awesome to waste," he says, which makes me laugh despite myself—and then pauses at my feet. "Fucking hell. Don't these hurt?"

"Nothing hurts right now."

"Sarah. They're *cutting into your feet*." He mutters to himself while he undoes the small buckles and pulls them off, then lifts my feet for inspection.

My toes glitter in the low light, and he lifts a grin to me that goes dark and hooded when his gaze locks on my bare pussy.

"You painted the universe on your toes." He releases my foot, but glides his hands up my legs as he stretches back out to center himself with his mouth over my hips. "Beautiful."

I don't know if he's talking about my toes or the rest of my body, but it suddenly doesn't matter, because his tongue is teasing my clit and his thumbs are drawing lazy circles on my inner thigh, and *oh my god*, why did I ever doubt this man?

My hips lift, my toes curl, my shoulders arch, a pin in my hair digs into my skull, and I'm chanting incoherently while his mouth explores my pussy until I'm beyond capable of breathing.

And just when I can't take it anymore, he sucks my clit between his teeth, and everything clenches hard, and I come apart in a starburst of blues and purples and reds, sparks shimmering behind my eyes, Beck's mouth coaxing me higher and longer while my body shudders out transcendent sensations that rock me from my roots to my toenails, with pleasure radiating so thick and heavy from my clit that I will most definitely never be able to walk again.

I sag against the rumpled sheets as the waves gradually subside, and he peppers kisses to my inner thighs that tickle enough to make aftershocks jolt through my ovaries.

"So fucking gorgeous," he murmurs, and when he lifts his gaze again, there's so much heat in his eyes that I almost come a second time just from that giddy feeling of knowing, without a doubt, that he really does think I'm beautiful. And irresistible. And sexy.

Until he suddenly frowns. "Does your hair hurt?"

"Wha...?" Huh. Now that he mentions it. "Oh. Yash. Yesh. Mm."

He shoves up to sitting, and guides me to do the same. I get an eyeful of the strain in his boxers—holy *yes*, please—but then he's behind me, plucking more hairpins out, his erection pressing into my lower back, his lips dropping to my neck between untangling the unholy mess. "Did they put an entire pin factory in here?" he murmurs as half my hair finally falls down my back.

"Mom—massages—buttered me up—no will power," I murmur.

"I'll give you massages. And I'll get you a spa pass. And your own personal massage therapist. Just—fuck, Sarah. Don't let them do this to you."

"Beck?"

"Mm?"

"When you talk like that, I want to jump you."

His hands still in my hair. "Like the good kind of jump, or the taser kind of jump?"

"Mm-hmm," I murmur, my fingers lifting to rub my nipples.

He laughs into my hair, and then his fingers join mine.

Just one hand.

The other's still searching out random hairpins.

But he's quite talented at teasing my body one-handed.

Especially when his hand trails down my belly to tease the curls just over my clit. "Still sensitive?" he murmurs into my neck while he plucks one more hairpin out.

"Touch me," I reply.

His cock swells harder against my back, and I'm instantly aroused again.

There's something so powerful about being *wanted*. And even more so for being wanted for *me*.

All of me. The good and the bad.

His fingers drift lower, and I groan and let my legs fall open while I drop my head back against him.

"Sarah," he whispers, so reverently he might as well have whispered *I love you*.

I twist in his arms and go up on my knees, then grab his cheeks and kiss him.

Hard.

Deep.

Desperate.

I didn't expect him.

I didn't *ask* for him.

But I can't imagine ever letting him go.

I'll have to—his life is out there, globetrotting around the world with photographers chasing him, while mine is rooted here—but not tonight.

Tonight, he's mine.

I straddle him there, with his back against his headboard, and I free his cock from his briefs.

He groans into my mouth as I stroke his hard length, and then he's fumbling for a condom in the nightstand.

"I want you," I whisper while I help him roll it on.

His breath is ragged, his eyes dark midnight under heavy lids, his lips parted, and when I sink down on him, taking him deep inside me, we both shudder in relief.

"So fucking perfect," he grits out.

I clamp my mouth shut, because otherwise, I'll start chanting *I love you*, and it's not something I can take back, and love scares the hell out of me.

But Beck?

Beck doesn't.

He thrusts up into me, neck straining, his eyes locked on me while he fills me and stretches me and pumps into me and I ride him hard, taking him so deep that he's hitting that special spot over and over, building that tension, my walls tightening in anticipation, until I'm so, *so* close.

"Sarah," he gasps. "I'm—can't—need—come, Sarah. Come for me."

He flicks his thumbs over my nipples and, groaning, lets his head fall back. I feel the pulse of his release, and it carries me over the edge too, clenching hard around his spasming cock while he wraps those long, strong arms around me and holds me so tight, buried so deep, connecting so thoroughly that I can't imagine a time we'll ever be disconnected.

No matter the miles.

No matter the mountains or oceans between us.

I didn't even know I wanted him, and now I can't imagine ever letting him go.

"Sarah," he gasps again into my shoulder as his body begins to relax, and I wrap my arms around him and hold tight too.

Beck doesn't just have a piece of me.

He has all of me.

And it's the scariest and most thrilling feeling I've ever known.

THIRTY-SIX

Beck

SHE'S MINE.

I called her. You can't have her. You snooze, you lose. I licked her. She's mine now.

Okay, okay.

It's more like I'm basically going to spend the rest of my life as putty in her hands, because *holy fuck*, she's everything.

"Oh my god, I think I'm drooling on your shoulder," she murmurs as we sit—lay? Slump?—in my bed.

"Mm, drool." My arms are jelly. So are my legs

My cock's awful damn proud of itself, and still buried deep inside her, and why did I think I wanted to live in a car with her when we can just stay in bed like this forever?

She's laughing a breathy laugh, and it makes her walls squeeze my dick again.

He grins proudly and sits up straighter.

I'll high-five him later.

"You want a grilled cheese?" I ask. "I can go for giving you four orgasms, but I need a grilled cheese first."

"Four might kill me."

"You're getting three whether you like it or not, because I don't tie. I come in first."

"You're already in first."

"Nuh-uh. Don't stroke my ego. I'm earning this one."

"Beck."

"Sarah."

She lifts her head, and *god*, her hair. It's crazy, sticking out every which way, still full of hairspray and probably some kind of animal sacrifice, and I fucking love her like this. Real and sleepy and fucking gorgeous.

"You...*know* me," she says quietly. "I've never slept with anyone who...*knew* me."

I stroke her wild hair. "Their loss."

She sighs and snuggles in closer again. "Thank you for showing me what I'm capable of."

"We haven't hit three yet," I remind her.

"I meant with facing the world and not hiding from it."

"You would've figured that out in your own time if I hadn't been a dumbass."

She shakes her head, but doesn't reply.

And then my stomach rumbles, and we both crack up.

"Okay, fine. Food," she says.

I get her a robe and dispose of the condom, and we spend the next hour eating gourmet grilled cheese sandwiches with brie and bacon and pears, and she tells me about her favorite projects that she's worked on, and I tell her about the biggest mishaps we've ever had on various shoots.

We check in on Persephone, and Sarah squeals with glee at the sight of the baby nursing. "Look! Look at that spot on the baby. Doesn't it look like George Washington's head?"

I squint closer, and she's not wrong.

"It's a sign," I tell her. "This baby will save the giraffe population of the world."

She laughs and kisses me, and we both have orgasms over my culinary creations, which, no, doesn't count as her third.

I take care of that in the shower afterwards.

And then I carry her to bed and rub her back until she falls asleep, and I drift off too, with my arms wrapped around her, because *this*.

Sarah's what my life has been missing.

The piece I never thought I'd find.

That I never even thought existed.

Life is pretty fucking awesome. And it just keeps getting better.

THIRTY-SEVEN

Sarah

WE'RE HAVING mint tea and waffle-omelet sandwiches on Beck's patio Sunday morning, lounging side-by-side on the wicker couch and debating names for Persephone's baby girl, when both our phones blow up.

To be fair, his is always blowing up, which is why he keeps it on silent, but the screen has been lighting up all morning.

Mine, however, just had three text messages waiting for me when I woke up—one from my parents just checking in, one from Mackenzie checking in, and one from Charlie asking if I wanted new clothes delivered this morning, or if I preferred that she dash over to my house to pick something I already owned.

Yep. Just those three messages. Until the end of breakfast.

I slide a look at mine and start to ignore it, because seventeen text messages in a minute spells doom, and I don't want doom.

I want to feed Beck the last half of my waffle-omelet sandwich and accidentally have to lick the crumbs off his bare stomach.

Considering he feasted on me again this morning for first breakfast, it's only fair that I eat him for dessert.

But when my phone doesn't stop, he picks it up.

His brows furrow, and then he grabs his own phone.

"Are you texting someone back?"

He shakes his head.

And he's doing that silent thing again, which is always a little worrisome, especially when coupled with the frown and the subtle growl coming out of his lips.

"Beck?"

"Not bad," he assures me.

"Then why do you look like you want to tear someone's arms off?"

He hands me the phone, open to a news article with a huge headline. *Meet America's Geekheart.*

I half-smile. "Cute name," I say, but when I scroll down— "Oh my god."

It's me.

There's a picture from last night, at the top of the stairs in the planetarium, and I almost don't recognize myself.

I look like Sunny Darling and Judson Clarke's daughter.

And Beck's in it too, and *oh*, the picture of Beck.

He's watching me as he climbs the stairs, and that look on his face —my breath catches.

The man thinks I hung the moon.

I glance up at him.

He's scowling.

Beck Ryder.

The man who didn't even scowl when I *tasered* him, or when my father threatened to do unmentionable things to his manhood, or when his own mother chastised him in public last night, is scowling.

"You…don't like the nickname?"

"I don't like that as soon as you put on a dress and makeup and some fucking Hollywood-approved hairdo, suddenly you're socially acceptable. This?" He tucks a strand of hair behind my ears, then brushes his thumb over my cheek. "*This* is you being gorgeous. *That*'s you putting on a show. And I *hate* the assholes who think the show is all that matters. Because *this* is what matters most."

His hand comes to rest on my heart, and if there was any doubt left how I feel about him, it evaporates like the morning dew. "I love you," I whisper.

And then I clamp a hand over my mouth, because I've never said it before, and if he doesn't—

He pulls my hand away and crushes my mouth with his, holding me tight against him until I crawl into his lap and straddle him. His hard cock presses against my clit, and I moan into his mouth and pump my hips to rub my aching nub against him.

"Sarah," he gasps.

"I love you." I can't stop. I want to shout it to the world. And I'm on a rooftop. I could. I could shout it from this rooftop right here, and all of downtown Copper Valley will hear me, and they'll know that I have fallen head over heels in love with Beck Ryder and I'm not taking it back, because he's the kindest, biggest-hearted, funniest, sexiest, strongest man I know, and I don't know how we'll work out his travel schedule with my day job needing me here, but we will, because— "I love you."

I fumble with his pants, freeing his cock again.

"Sarah, I don't—"

I ignore him and slide down his body, taking his erection into my mouth, and when his breath hitches and his hands tighten in my hair, I suck his hard length harder, rubbing the flat of my tongue along him, taking him deep and then pulling almost off him, then taking him in deep again, curling my tongue around him, over and over until he tries to pull back.

"Sarah, I'm gonna—"

I ignore him again and take him as deep as I can until he comes down my throat, his cock pulsing against my tongue while I swallow him down.

When he's spent, I release him, press a kiss to his tip, and tuck him back into his sweatpants, and then climb back up to snuggle him. Just as I get up to his shoulder-level, he explodes in a huge sneeze.

My eyes flare wide. "You okay?"

He winces. "Hypno—therapist—shit."

I burst out laughing, even though I shouldn't, because I've heard of this. "You sneeze when you orgasm?" I whisper.

"Cured—mostly," he pants. He pulls me into his arms. "If I—say —you know—it's not—because—of that."

"I know," I whisper.

"You—so—fucking—amazing."

I'm in a bear robe with crazy hair and no panties, and he's clinging to me like I'm his lifeline.

Me.

The crazy geek with famous parents who's never quite fit in anywhere and is obsessed with endangered animals and who tasered him for trying to apologize.

But he makes me feel like I fit here.

"I love you," I tell him again.

"I'm quitting," he announces. "Selling it all. Moving home. I want *you*. And family. All the time. Forever. Except we have to see the world. Together. You and me. We'll start in Morocco, and we'll spend a month there, and then I'll take you to France, because cheese and bread, and have you ever been to Iceland? We have to go to Iceland. Summer *and* winter. It's two different countries."

I'm smiling so big my cheeks hurt. "Your enthusiasm is very contagious, but I know you're not just quitting. It's okay."

"You can still work if you want to, but you'll have to work for my parents, because I know normal people won't let you take off six months out of the year to travel with me."

And now I'm laughing. I know he's not being serious—not entirely, because of course he's not giving up his fashion empire—but I can imagine jetting off to Paris or Morocco or India with him, just to see more of the world. "I can still work under *your* terms, can I?"

"Or I'll bring the world to you." He grins. "YouTube is almost the same as seeing Machu Picchu in person."

"Oh, that's low."

He pulls my fingers to his lips and kisses my knuckles. My nail polish from yesterday is already chipping, which will probably make my mom sigh, but she'll also help me get it all off, because that's what she does.

"Come to Shipwreck with me this week," he says. "Just…get away from all of this until we announce the foundation. I mean, if you can take vacation. I know your job's important to you."

"You know I have a trust fund, don't you?"

"So? Having a trust fund won't save your frogs."

"I mentioned I love you?"

He smiles.

And it's not a camera smile, or a goofball smile, or a smolder smile.

It's a raw, honest, wide, happy smile. "I loved you first," he announces.

I burst out laughing. "Are you kidding me?"

"Swear to god, when you hit me with that taser, I was like, *she's the one*. Those eyes are deadly enough when there's only two of them, but man, you juiced me, and then you had four, and I was a goner."

I'm still laughing when he angles in for a kiss.

"I love you, Sarah Dempsey," he says against my smiling lips. "And I'm going to make you laugh every single day for the rest of my life."

THIRTY-EIGHT

Sarah

LIFE IS PRETTY DAMN AWESOME.

After a huge family dinner last night with my parents and Cupcake, Charlie, Mackenzie, Beck's family, and his adopted neighborhood family—I completely understand why they called the band *Bro Code* when I watch him with all of his adopted brothers, not just the guys who were in the band—I stayed with him again, and now I'm on my way to work with plans to ask for the rest of the week off.

Nobody from the office texted about the media coverage of Saturday night. My video about Persephone giving birth has more views than any other video about the giraffe except for the zoo's official feeds, and I'm weirdly happy about my new nickname.

America's Geekheart.

I don't really care about being famous, and I know somebody will twist this and make it ugly before long, but they can't take away my self-worth.

They *won't* take me away from the people I love.

Not again.

I'm getting a ride from one of Beck's bodyguards, so I spend the trip texting with Mom, who's been taking care of Meda and making sure my bees and flowers have water since the dinner Saturday night.

She wants me to quit work and be a full-time science video blog-ger, because *it's your passion, sweetheart, and you share it so eloquently.*

Dad pops in with the occasional text asking if it's possible for a girl pig and a girl cat to have babies together, because he thinks Cupcake is in heat.

I think he's trying to see how far he can push me.

Either that, or he hit his head the other night while Persephone was giving birth.

Or possibly he's practicing for his role, which he has to report back to California for on Friday.

We reach the office early, and I slip in unnoticed around the other early arrivals. I'm sorting my projects to figure out what I need to get done this week and what I can push off, so I know how much time I can take off to go hang out with Beck in Shipwreck, when someone in the cube behind me gasps.

Thirty seconds later, another gasp goes up in the cubicle farm.

Followed a minute later by four in rapid succession.

And then there are footsteps.

Lots. And lots. And lots. Of footsteps.

"Unplug your computer," my boss orders.

Someone else dives under my desk and does it for me.

I look at the sea of white faces around me. "Did we get a virus?"

"Yeah, it's called *the scourge of humanity*," one of them mutters.

"Your blog is really awesome. I didn't realize that was you until after...you know. But I've been following it for months."

"Those fuckers shouldn't—sorry, Gary. Those *inbred shitheads* who troll people shouldn't be allowed on the internet."

My phone buzzes, and Mackenzie's face lights the screen.

I gesture to it and look at my boss. "May I?"

His frown deepens. "Is it a friend?"

"My best friend."

"Then yes."

I swipe to answer. No one leaves my cubicle, and someone else bursts into the building shouting, "Did you see what those asswipes said? And what a total *dick*. I can't believe he—"

"Shut up!" someone else yells.

"Hey," I say to Mackenzie. "Are you at work?"

"Yeah, but Sarah—listen, don't get on the internet today, okay?"

"Um, that's not exactly a problem right now."

"Can you get me in touch with that guy who was helping with your website?"

"Mackenzie?"

"No, that's me. I mean the guy who kinda looks like Cash Rivers. The one Beck set up to upgrade your servers? That guy."

"What's going on?"

"Assholes are going on. Just…stay off the internet. And can I have Beck's number too? Because…*because*… We'll handle this, okay?"

"Handle what?" I eyeball my coworkers. Some won't meet my eye.

One rubs my back. "We never knew you were so reserved because you'd been exposed to that before, but it all makes sense now. I just can't believe he's dumping you like *this*."

My entire body freezes.

Just ices over.

Heart and all.

"The internet's being the internet." Mackenzie sighs audibly. "Will you please just send me his name and number? And maybe don't go to work today."

"I'm already here."

"Oh, shit… Just text me his name and number. And Beck's number. And promise you'll stay off the internet. *Promise me*. Like pinky swear on the Fireballs' winning streak."

"I can't hear you. We're going through a tunnel. Shh-wusshhh-sshhusshh."

"You just told me you're at work."

"I mean we just had a power surge. Ssshh-wussshhh-sshhussshhh."

Yes, I feel bad for hanging up on Mackenzie, but I'm tired of being treated with kid gloves.

I need to face this.

And know that it doesn't matter what random internet trolls are saying. That my worth isn't tied up in what gossips say.

It's tied up in how I feel about myself and in having people who love me unconditionally despite my quirks and fears and poor choices.

I pull up my site on my phone.

Or try to.

It won't actually load.

"Uh-oh," I mutter.

"Are you checking the internet? No! Stay off the internet!"

Someone lunges for my phone, but I twist and keep hold of my phone only because my normal tae kwon do classes have kept my reflexes relatively quick.

"Will someone *please* tell me what's going on?"

Gary scratches his bald head. "Did you want to maybe take some time off? You have lots of sick days you never use."

"Gary…"

"I don't understand it. They loved you yesterday. America's Geekheart. Really cute name. But then Beck…" He trails off, and the ice threatens to grab my heart again, but I know Hollywood.

I know the game.

"I knew he was playing her," someone mutters, and I ignore her, because I have to.

"Shut up," someone else hisses.

I sigh and pull up Twitter.

And—yep.

Here we go.

And my parents are probably seeing this.

Dammit.

I swallow hard to keep the panic at bay, because panic is exactly what's rising like bile in my throat.

America's Geekheart back when she was just a geek, reads one post, complete with a picture of me with ketchup smeared across my cheek when I was probably not quite in high school.

Geekheart? More like FREAKheart, reads another with a picture of me, this one from late high school, contorted sideways and looking at the gum on my own ass, my hair tilted at an odd angle that makes me look like an octopus is growing out of my head, and a list of cities in the *Binary Babes* rock band's tour on the back of my T-shirt.

Finally, the truth: Underwear model's new girlfriend FAKE. Sunny Darling blackmail scheme EXPOSED.

Beck Ryder PR rep confirms: Model and daughter of Hollywood power couple part as "good friends;" ask for privacy.

It's the last one that sends a quake through my bones.

Because that one was issued by Beck's official Twitter feed.

The same feed that not ten days ago drew me back into the public spotlight.

That's the line. It's what we're supposed to say.

But not until Friday.

"Yeah," I say to Gary. "Sick time. *Aaacchoooo.* I might need a—a week. Thank you."

"We're not answering any calls from the press," he tells me while he walks me out to the parking lot, my knees threatening to give way while more camera crews are pulling in and Beck's bodyguard is waiting by the front door in a standard black Audi. "And that's a really gutsy thing you're doing, going public when so many people are being fu—ah, I mean, inhumane."

I won't cry. I won't give them the satisfaction of seeing me cry. "I'll email you what I'm having to put on hold."

"Thanks, Sarah. Sarah, right? You don't want to be—"

"Sarah," I confirm, and I climb into the car.

"All okay, Ms. Dempsey?" the bodyguard asks.

"Yeah." No.

"Home or to Mr. Ryder's place?"

"Home, please." I want to see my cat. And check on my bees for myself and see if I need to harvest any honey. It's still early, but my hives have been pretty active this summer.

I slink low in the seat and pull up Twitter again, even though I know better.

It's rolling.

It's rolling up a freaking *storm*.

That picture of @must_love_bees makes her look like a monkey squished in a suit that's about to burst.

Only whores get off on watching animals give birth. Get a life, @must_love_bees.

I know @must_love_bees in person, and I can promise you this thing with @Beckett_Ryder is all a hoax. She's gross.

I breathe slowly to calm my racing heart, because this doesn't matter.

It doesn't.

I can't believe @must_love_bees hacked Beck Ryder's account to get her fifteen minutes of fame. #sweetheartforever

Can't wait to hear @Beckett_Ryder's announcement Friday! I hope he's auctioning off a date. Come to mama! I got the $$!

I don't care if his heart isn't really broken, I'll comfort @Beckett_Ryder any day.

I shake my head, because I know this is just the public version of events. It doesn't mean anything.

One call to Beck will clear this all up.

So why am I not calling him?

Why is he not calling YOU? an insidious little voice whispers in the back of my head,

I glance down at Twitter again.

I dated @must_love_bees a year ago. Coldest fish EVER. Ryder can have her, the lying bitch. But I guess he figured her out, didn't he?

My jaw drops.

Because that's not some random internet troll making up a story about dating me.

That's *Trent*.

And he added a picture of me from when we were dating. Out for seafood. I have butter smeared on my cheek, my hair's falling in a gravity-defying flippy-do thing, one eye is half-closed, and my teeth are doing some weird thing that makes me look like a braying donkey as I open wide for a bite of crab.

"People are so shitty," I mutter.

"Only the shitty ones, ma'am," the bodyguard says. He glances at me in the rearview mirror. "Sure you wanna go home?"

I nod.

My parents should be there. They've been here. They've done that. They'll know all the right things to say.

And it doesn't matter what an ex-boyfriend says, or even what ugly pictures he wants to post.

Especially since he's not wrong.

I *was* cold.

I wouldn't even tell him who my parents are.

I probably deserve that.

But I'm better now. I'm stronger. I'm *owning* it.

A dark whisper of *because you had to* flits through my mind.

Along with another whisper of *and you're still that dork that gets butter all over your face and can't take a good picture to save your life.*

If Beck hadn't shown up to apologize for that tweet, I'd be the same old boring Sarah, hiding from the world, lying to my best friend, dating guys who snap ugly pictures of me, quietly working at making a small difference instead of contemplating how to make a *big* difference.

So does that really make me better?

Or just opportunistic?

Either way, I'm starting to wish I hadn't eaten breakfast.

THIRTY-NINE

Beck

I'M GAPING at the video screen and wishing Charlie hadn't taken away my coffee before we started this video conference. Bruce stares back, belligerent. The rest of the team looks just as shocked as I am.

Except Charlie.

She looks like she's been taking notes on some of those things Judson threatened me with, and she's fixing to fly out to California and practice them on Bruce as soon as this call is over.

"Start over, and use small words," I tell Bruce, "because it sounds like you just said *you canceled the contract with Sarah early.*"

"It was time." Bruce nods, his bald spot shimmering in the light off his desk lamp. "Public opinion of you has never been higher, and we get to paint her as the one taking advantage of you. We bumped up announcing the foundation to Wednesday. Full buy-in from Crawford, especially when I told him you really liked her and were disappointed she called it off, though I don't know why he believed that."

"Who the *fuck* gave you the authority to do that?"

"Ryder. My email's exploding with notes from buyers at all the major retail chains and online outlets. Everyone wants to feature not just RYDE, but your other lines too. We can't take the chance of the girl fucking this up."

"Her *name* is *Sarah.*"

"Her name is *trouble*. You're in too deep and you need to get your head back on straight and quit thinking with your dick, though I'm a little worried about it if that's what you honestly go for in a woman."

My head's spinning, because *what the ever-loving fuck*? "Take. It. Back."

"Too late, Buttercup. And you're welcome."

I thought being pissed was bad enough. But now legit fear is gripping my chest, because that sounds very ominous. "What. Did. You. Do?" I growl.

Vicki's eyes go wide. Hestia chokes on the green juice she's drinking.

And Charlie smiles.

It's one of those ugly smiles.

"What do you mean, *what did I do*? I'm sitting here running your fucking empire for you while you piddle around with the horse girl."

"Horse girl," I repeat, and I see red.

I don't like seeing red.

It makes the world an ugly fucking cesspool of rotten olives, and olives are one food I actually can't stand.

I push my chair back from the desk and gesture Charlie to step up front and center. "Hestia, Vicki, I'll call you later. Hang up now. Charlie, have the honors."

I'm dialing the head of my legal team before Charlie's done telling Bruce he's fired. Actually, before she's even gotten started.

She's getting a promotion.

And I—

Fuck.

I need to find out what Bruce did, and stop it before whatever he did gets to Sarah, because I have *zero* doubt that whatever he did, it involves her.

I give my legal team a run-down on Bruce's firing and ask them to prepare for a fight, and also to investigate if I can threaten to sue him for breaching a contract on my behalf, if that's actually what he did, which I need to figure out *pronto*.

Maybe firing him was too hasty.

Then again, maybe not. I'm hanging up with my legal team when Hank turns the corner, laptop in one hand, the largest vat of coffee I've ever seen in the other.

He jerks his head to the office across the hall. "Sarah's got problems, and *what the fuck is wrong with you*? I liked her. Tripp liked her. My sister liked her."

My heart leaps into my throat.

Fuck the fashion world.

Sarah.

Sarah's what I'm passionate about. "What? Where is she? How big? What's wrong? Can you fix it?"

He squints at me for half a second before the squint turns to a smirk. "To answer your questions, one, you're a dumbass if you let her go. Two, I'm IT, not psychic, so I don't know where she is. Three, it depends on what you call *big* and if she had the poor taste to actually like you back, which is actually two separate problems at the moment"—he smirks at me again—"and finally, Ryder. Come on. Can I fix it? Whoa. Is Charlie *yelling* at someone?"

"She's firing Bruce."

He shoves the laptop at me. "Here. You get started. I gotta listen to this."

"*Hank.*"

"Ah, fuck. Fine. But you owe me big. I've been wanting to listen to her blow for *months.*"

He picks the office across the hall from where Charlie's still listing Bruce's flaws—she's gotten to the *you're a sexist asshole* part, which either means she's just getting started or wrapping up soon—and he opens his laptop. "Get your phone out and figure out what to do about Twitter, but do *not* type anything yourself, okay? I gotta get her website back up. You really break up with her?"

My veins frost over. "Fuck, no. Why—" I can't finish the sentence, because I can't make those words come out of my mouth together.

He looks at me.

Then points to my phone. "Twitter, dude. Your job. Computer? My job."

I open Twitter.

And *fuck.*

Just *fuck.*

Tweet after tweet saying she didn't deserve me anyway. That she's ugly. That after all I did for her and her giraffe lover, she should be grateful, not a bitch who dumps me on a Monday morning.

Charlie stomps in, looks over my shoulder, and gasps. "What the *fuck*? They loved her yesterday. Did Bruce do this? He's dead. He's deader than dead."

I switch over to my profile, and there it is.

The canned statement announcing we're done.

"Can you get rid of this?" I ask Hank, pointing to the tweet.

Because I can't just take it down. You can never just *take it down*. People get screenshots and share that shit for eternity. He'll be playing whack-a-mole.

Fuck.

"One thing at a time," Hank says. "Her website crashed again from all the hits."

"Don't make me call Davis."

"Already calling him," Charlie says.

"I can fucking handle this on my own," Hank growls at her.

"Shove your ego in a dirty gym bag. It's for *Sarah*." She pauses, then mutters, "And Davis is faster."

"I'm gonna pretend you didn't say that."

"I can say it louder."

I leave them to their bickering and head for the elevator, already dialing Sarah's number.

When she doesn't answer, I call Judson.

"Where's Sarah?" I ask.

Fuck.

Fuck.

This is so fucking stupid. It's none of anyone's damn business who I date or how I feel. And now they're dragging her through the mud without knowing a damn real thing about either one of us.

And they're hurting her.

They're fucking *hurting* her.

I put Judson on speaker and text Hank and Davis both with orders to hack Twitter and take the whole fucking site down.

"She's with her mother in the garden. What the fuck did you do *now*?" Judson growls.

"Is she okay?" I hit the button for the garage level, knowing full well I might lose signal, but there's no way I'm wasting another second getting to her. "She hasn't seen anything, right? She's okay? She doesn't believe it, does she? I fired the dumbass. I mean, I let Charlie do it, but I'm cleaning house with my team and if they don't like Sarah, they're *gone*. Is she okay? Tell me she's okay."

"Depends on your definition of *okay*," he growls, and that's the last thing I hear before the signal drops.

"Be okay, be okay, be okay," I whisper to myself.

She's not darting off on a jet to Morocco and changing her name. She's in her backyard with her mom.

She's not digging a bunker. Judson would've said she was digging a bunker if she was digging a bunker.

She's not packing up her bees to move to some small town in Kansas without internet. Plus, all of Kansas has internet. I think. I've been in a small town or two in Kansas, and they always had internet, even though everyone in LA and New York thinks they don't.

"Be okay, be okay, be okay," I mutter.

I point the bodyguard in the basement to my car. "Drive. Sarah's house."

My hands are shaking.

I can't drive myself.

If she's not okay, I'm going to be so pissed at myself for dragging her into this.

I'm already pissed at myself for dragging her into this.

But when I finally get to her house, when I push past Judson and the pig and the cat and out into the backyard, I discover it's not bad.

It's worse.

Way. Way. Way. Fucking. Worse.

FORTY

Sarah

I'M LEANING over an open tackle box of eyeshadow colors when Beck bursts through the back door, sweeps his hot blue eyes over all of us, and then erupts in a rage.

"What the *fuck* are you doing?" he howls.

He crosses the patio—my yard is full, but not large, so it only takes him four steps, and he bends down and gets right in my mom's face. "She. Is. Beautiful. Just. As. She. Is."

I leap up in alarm and grab his arm. "Beck—"

"No. *No*. You don't have to prove any single fucking *thing* to those losers who are jealous that they're not as smart and dedicated and passionate and naturally gorgeous as you are." He flips the whole makeup case over and glares at my mom again, then growls at my dad, who's leaning out the back door and watching with narrowed eyes. "And you two. Didn't you ever tell Sarah she's perfect just the way she is? What the fuck's wrong with you?"

I gape at him, because Angry Beck is like the Incredible Hulk, if Hulk wore sky blue so well that it brought out his eyes perfectly and highlighted all that anger simmering on his cheekbones and had a week's worth of binge-eating delicious food to fuel his rage.

And also if he were hell-bent on being my hero.

"I forbid you to wear that shit," Beck declares.

I choke on my own spit. "You forbid me."

My dad gapes.

My mom leans back in her lounge chair and gapes.

And Beck thrusts his fingers into his hair and attempts to pull it out. "Okay, look, I know I can't *forbid* you to do anything, because I'm not a total moron, and I just fired an asshole for that tweet, which was a total lie, and also for being a dick to my assistant and so many other things I should've fired him for years ago, but *damn* it, Sarah, you don't need that shit, and I'm going to hunt down every last fucking troll on Twitter and dunk their heads in dirty toilet water until they cry uncle and realize that there's no fucking thing as one definition of beauty and that their souls make them the ugliest assholes in the history of assholes. I. Love. You. Just. The. Way. You. Are. Not with all that goop all over your face and in shoes that hurt you and wrapped in Lycra torture devices. And I'm not letting you go without a fight if you really did try to dump me this morning, even though I know that was my asshole manager being a dick, and I can't think of more creative things to call him because I'm that pissed. But the point is, fuck anyone else who tries to make your self-worth tie to how you look."

I wait while he paces over my short patio, because odds are good he's not done.

But he doesn't say anything else.

Nope.

He stops suddenly, and he looks at me.

Just looks at me.

At first with his nostrils flaring and the blue flame in his eyes threatening to singe his eyelashes off, but the tight lines around his mouth loosen, and his brows untangle, and he drops into the seat I just vacated and wraps his arms around my waist. "Please tell me they didn't hurt your feelings, and please tell me you didn't see that tweet, or if you did, that you didn't believe it, because I swear, I will never forgive myself if they hurt you, and I'd really rather just be here with you than out avenging your honor all over the world for the next six years."

"I know a good asylum for the insane," my dad growls.

"Judson, hush, and come give poor Beckett a hug. He's had a rough four minutes."

"Can I talk?" I whisper to Beck.

"I love when you talk," he says against my belly.

"Have you eaten today?"

"Four times."

I stifle a smile and stroke his hair. "I think I've been around celebrities enough to know not to listen to anything I don't hear out of the horse's mouth," I whisper to him.

His arms tighten around me. "I'm a very good horse," he says into my stomach.

"A very good stallion," I correct.

He huffs a laugh, and I keep stroking his hair, because it's so thick and perfect and so easy to touch, and *I missed him*.

I might also be a little wobbly in the knees with relief, because while I *did* know that tweet was all PR baloney, I needed to hear it from him.

And I might've been hiding from the fear that he *wouldn't* want me anymore when pulling me into his circle will always mean that we both have to deal with me being such an easy target on social media.

Except I don't feel nearly as worthless and small right now as I did in high school when I'd make the tabloids. Because in the midst of the storm, there are still people talking about Persephone and her new baby. And about going to watch a meteor shower for the first time.

And about an old, old news article I shared about sand.

Yes, *sand*.

Because when sand is magnified, it's not just little grains of nothing. It's an entire universe of miniature shells that we all walk all over to get to the beach without realizing the beauty right under our feet.

Maybe we're all tiny universes of miniature shells. And maybe I should be more like the sand and be fabulous just as I am, even if very few people will ever stop to look closely enough.

Like Beck has.

"I'm quitting, Sarah," he says hoarsely. "I swear, I'll sell it all. I'll retire and come home and talk you into taking vacation every other week to go see the world and I'll stay home and cook you dinner and second dinner and dessert and breakfast and show up at your office with second breakfast and morning snack and lunch and second lunch."

My heart is so full, it's warming my entire body and making words hard. "Beck. You don't have to do that for me."

"I don't want those shitheads saying nasty things about you. I don't want *anyone* saying nasty things about you."

"It doesn't matter."

"It *does*. You're sitting here looking at makeup and you're not wearing a geeky T-shirt."

"Are you sure you've eaten?" I ask lightly.

"I'm getting hungry again, but that's not the point. I can push through it."

"Beck. Compromising isn't always a bad thing."

"I should've eaten three or five times?"

"No, I'm saying if I'm going to do more video blogs, I can wear *very light* makeup to make up for the fact that I'll be under harsh lights."

His neck goes tense under my fingers. "You're making more videos?"

"I can concentrate on how many people are saying ugly things, or I can realize that I have a unique opportunity to share some of my passions with the people who want to listen despite the circus. If I quit, if I disappear again, then it doesn't matter who wins. It matters that I lose. I don't want to lose. Especially when I'm basically losing to myself."

He looks up at me finally, studying me with eyes so serious, they almost don't look like his.

But they are.

And they're full of worry and concern and—

My breath catches, because that's utter adoration.

For me.

Still.

"You are such a fucking badass," he says reverently.

I laugh and bend down to kiss him. "Not always."

"I'm still going to hunt them down and hook their nipples up to a car battery while I give them flushies."

"Serendipity, it's time," my dad growls with a thicker growl than normal. "He's proven himself. He can join the fight against the Euranians."

I laugh again and stroke Beck's tense shoulders. "Thanks, Dad. But I don't know if I want to lose him to the war."

"Sacrifices have to be made in the name of justice."

"Judson, dear, at least let them get married and have babies first. It makes for such a better gut-wrenching story when he dies as she's giving birth."

"*Mom.*"

"What? It does. In fiction, naturally. Not in your life, dear."

A yowl erupts from inside the house, and I jerk my head to the back door. "Oh, no. Cupcake's alone with Meda."

Beck releases me and follows me as I dart into the house, where I find Cupcake sprawled on her back in the middle of the kitchen floor, with Meda grooming her little pig snout.

"What—" I start.

"I told you they loved each other," Mom says.

Beck slips his arms around my waist and rests his head on mine. "Huh."

While we watch, Cupcake starts to get up, but Meda yowls again and bops the pig on the ear, and Cupcake meekly goes back to lounging so Meda can knead her pork shoulders and clean her face.

I just gape at both of them.

"Love always wins," Dad growls.

Beck's arms tighten around me, and I lean back into him. "Can we still go check out this Shipwreck place you love so much?" I ask.

He grips me tighter and nods into my hair. "Yep. Leave your clothes here. You won't need them. *Ow!* Dammit. Sorry, sir. Forgot you were standing there. Meant I had some that'll fit her. Promise."

"Shipwreck?" Mom asks. "What's Shipwreck?"

"Dirty little town. Terrible. No vegan food. They all swill ale out of community pots. *Ow!* Hey, I needed that rib."

"You're lying to my mother. Very badly," I whisper.

"I know, but it's the easiest way to get you all to myself without having to share."

"You'll always have to share," Dad growls.

"Can it wait a week?"

"Wait, back up." Mom frowns at him. "Are you serious about retiring from fashion?"

"Yes. No. I don't know." He sighs into my hair. "And I have to be back to announce my new foundation on Wednesday. But I want to be home more. Here. And I don't want Sarah to deal with all the shit that comes with public life."

"Beck—"

"I know. *I know.* You're strong. You can handle it. But you shouldn't have to."

My mom smiles brightly. "Excellent."

Dad and I both eyeball her, because we both know that look. "What?" I ask her.

"I need a new job. Train me to run your fashion empire, and I won't have Judson gut you for touching our daughter."

"*Mom*."

"I love clothes. And these underwear are ridiculously comfortable. I've been meaning to retire, but I don't do boredom well. I might as well help run an empire. Plus, that way we can really stick it to him if he's ever stupid enough to leave you."

My jaw is totally unhinged.

And my mother's smile is growing. Growing, and taking on an evil, evil glow. "Plus, it will be *so* refreshing to be the one telling men that they're too old or not pretty enough for a job. The best revenge is to succeed when everyone around you is trying to keep you down."

"That's my girl," Dad growls.

Beck's speechless.

No, seriously. He looks like Mackenzie when faced with Cooper Rock the other day. I tap his cheek. "Hey. You okay? You don't have to hire my mother to get me. You know that, right?"

He looks down at me. Then back at my mom.

He shakes his head, tosses his phone into the sink, and then sweeps me up into his arms and marches through the house.

"Beck?"

"I'm completely useless," he declares.

I grip him tighter. "You are not."

"Completely, totally useless. I can't even solve my own calendar and life to be with the woman I love. The *only* thing I'm good for is kidnapping you and taking you to Shipwreck and trying for a fiver."

And there go my panties.

Again.

"Beck."

"And I don't even know why I deserve *you*, when you're clearly smart enough to know what you're getting into with *me*, so I am. I'm kidnapping you. Don't try to stop me."

"Mackenzie went through my email and found an invitation from the zoo for us to stop by and see Persephone and her baby girl."

He stops in the front doorway and looks at me. "So I can't even kidnap you properly."

"We could stop and grab burgers before we go to the zoo."

"I love you."

I didn't know it was possible to smile this big. "Are you sure that's not just your stomach talking?"

"We both love you. Sunny, Charlie will call you to talk details in five minutes because she's psychic, and I'm promoting her to being my new chief of operations, which she also probably knows since she's psychic." He backs out of my front door and doesn't hesitate as he carries me to his car. There are two beaters parked along the street, and I don't care.

Let them take all the pictures they want.

I can't stop running my fingers through Beck's hair, and I add a kiss to his cheek before he sets me back on my feet so I can climb into his car. "Have I told you yet that it was really sexy when you yelled at my mom over makeup?"

His bright blue eyes connect with mine, and a slow grin follows. "Yeah?"

"Very. Because I think my dad really could kick your ass, and he's excellent with surprise attacks, so you were literally taking your life into your own hands to defend my honor."

"Is that a warning?"

"Let's just say I suspect life for both of us is about to be far more entertaining than I ever thought I'd enjoy."

He seems to realize we're once again the subject of camera lenses, and instead of helping me into the car, he pins me against the side of it. "Want to start it with a bang?"

I loop my arms over his shoulders. "You want me to taser you again?"

He's laughing as he lowers his mouth to mine. "No. I want you to love me."

"Done."

And I pull him tighter as our lips touch, and I don't care who's watching.

Because this man?

He's worth it.

EPILOGUE

Beck

A MONTH after Sarah tasered me, I finally get to take her to one of my favorite spots in the entire world.

Shipwreck, Virginia.

The quirky little pirate town nestled in the mountains outside Copper Valley always makes me happy. Probably because they have amazing banana pudding, and friendly people who treat me like one of their own and tons of hiking trails through the mountains, and also, my house out here is where I keep my Frogger arcade game.

The one that Ellie and Wyatt *beat my high score on* a year ago.

I'm still pissed, but I'm dealing. And plotting to get it back, because Sarah's kick-ass at video games and between the two of us, I know we can do it. Eventually. When we get tired of kissing. And touching. And making love.

Huh.

Maybe we won't ever get my high score back, and I think I'm okay with that.

I slide a glance at her in the darkness, watch her features in the dancing firelight, and wonder how much it would take to talk her into handing off the sleeping baby. She's so natural with Emma cuddled up to her, and it's making me want *everything*.

"You making that one for me, Ryder?" Cash calls, and I jerk my attention back to the second most important thing in my life. Okay, third.

The marshmallow I'm roasting comes after the people who come after Sarah, who are all out here with us this weekend.

My parents, Ellie and Wyatt and Tucker, the guys from the neighborhood, Charlie—yeah, she's family.

Sarah brought Mackenzie, who's adjusting pretty well to the level of celebrity surrounding her. It helps that Tripp's feeling her out on her baseball opinions, because she can talk baseball for hours.

So long as she doesn't realize Cooper showed up a few minutes ago and brought Darren Greene and Jose Ramirez with him, since they're on their All-Star break. Though she's flipping out a little at Vaughn Crawford also sitting across the fire, shooting the shit with Levi and Davis and my mom about something.

It's late, and we're all gathered around the firepit in my backyard, celebrating *everything*.

Ellie and Wyatt being happy. Sarah and I burning that contract we signed. The foundation launching solidly.

Sarah being Emma's favorite human being in the entire world right now, since apparently baby poop bonds people.

Levi's latest album going double platinum.

Cash's latest movie topping the box office.

Charlie's promotion to Chief Operations Officer for all of RYDE and my subsidiary lines.

Sunny—who's not here, though Sarah video called her earlier—taking like a duck to water at RYDE and running like mad with new ideas, new models, and new opportunities.

Like going into *cougar fashion*.

She calls it *mature fashion*, but those marketing ideas she's blowing Vicki and Hestia away with are way more *cougar* than *mature*.

Sarah's mortified, of course, but I've assured her I'll only let the most respectful younger men be in commercials with her mom. Charlie's encouraging it all. Judson, naturally, wants to slice my balls off, but he's wrapping his apocalyptic cowboy baseball player movie, and apparently he's lined up for a romantic comedy role next, so my manhood might be in less danger soon.

"S'more?" I ask Sarah, pulling a perfectly toasted marshmallow off the fire and sliding it onto a waiting graham cracker before it falls off the stick.

"You should—" she starts, but before she can finish, Cash dives across her and Emma and snatches it from me.

"Aaaah, yeah. Dude. I haven't had a Beck Ryder s'more in *years*."

"That's for *my girlfriend*, asshole. Give it back."

He shoves the whole thing in his mouth and moans. "Ee oos ee oos," he says, which I easily translate to *she snoozes, she loses*.

"She's *holding a baby*."

"That's not right, man," Cooper says.

"We need to take care of him for you, Miss Sarah?" Darren asks.

"Beck can make another s'more," she replies with that amused smile that I love so much. "The first three would've been for him anyway."

"The first one is *always* for you."

She leans over and kisses me on the cheek, and I get a whiff of sleepy baby, and yeah.

We're totally doing that.

We're gonna make babies someday. And I'll quit everything to stay home and rock the fuck out of being a dad while Sarah saves the world. Whenever she's ready.

"I love you," I whisper.

She smiles again, this time like she knows what I'm thinking, and I get another kiss that's interrupted by a squeal of terror. "*Oh my god, it's...it's...AAAAAHHHH!*"

"You should've warned her," Sarah whispers against my lips.

"You don't taste like s'mores yet. I need to fix this," I reply.

"Is that the catatonic one?" Darren mutters to Cooper behind us.

"Yep. And this dude still needs to be taken care of for stealing Sarah's s'more."

Cash leaps up and races around behind everyone sitting at the fire, crashing between Charlie and Hank, who are giving each other the silent treatment, which is pretty hilarious if you ask me.

"Y'all are the best kind of nuts," Vaughn tells us all.

And somewhere off in the distance behind the house, someone sneezes a very loud, very feminine sneeze.

"Mother*fucker*," I mutter while most everyone around us groans.

"Get a room," Davis yells.

"We didn't need to hear that," Tripp agrees.

"Bless you," my mom calls. Awkwardly. While sharing a look with my dad.

Oh, *fuck*.

I gape at them. "*Seriously?*"

Sarah snort-laughs so hard she's in danger of waking Emma.

She did a week-long series on weird side effects of sex last week, and yeah, she included the not-so-mythical sneezegasm. And Ellie and Wyatt have disappeared. And *everyone* reads Sarah's blog.

Also, yes, I *did* go back to my hypnotherapist, and I'm just fine now.

Most of the time.

But more to the point, most of the guys know about the sneezegasm problem. So we all know what's going on back there in the woods.

Which I'm choosing to ignore, since I have my own plans for lots of orgasm time this weekend.

"I love your laugh," I tell Sarah, because I do, and I don't even care that she's laughing at me, so long as she's laughing.

"I love *you*," she replies.

"You really hanging up your underwear, Ryder?" Vaughn calls across the fire.

"If it keeps me home with this brilliant, beautiful lady more," I reply. And I am. I'm slowly handing over control to everyone else, because I *do* want to be home more.

And I don't know everything the future holds, but I know that between Tripp's plans for all of us to pool our resources to save the Fireballs, and my own itch that I've been getting since talking to Sarah more about science and the world, that itch to maybe try college, and who knows, maybe med school after that—well, one way or another, I'll be more than *that retired underwear model who plays video games all day.*

His teeth flash in a grin. "Good on you, man. Just don't propose by tweet. Who knows who you'd actually pop the question to."

Everybody gets a good laugh—yeah, it's funny—and I spear another marshmallow to make Sarah the best s'more in the history of s'mores.

"I could live like this every day," I murmur softly to her.

She leans into me with another one of those smiles I love so much. "Me too."

"They're not too much?"

"They're *family*. And they're yours. And they're perfect. And we're still locking the bedroom door tonight."

"You're utterly perfect, you know that?"

She laughs softly. "Far, far from it."

"But you're perfect for *me*."

"Who knew one little tweet could change our entire lives?" she murmurs.

"Clearly, I did."

She laughs again, and Emma startles awake with a cry. I wave Tripp off when he starts to get up, because he's helping Mackenzie breathe. Also, Sarah and I have conquered worse than a fussy baby.

"Trade me?" I hand her the marshmallow stick, and she shifts to let me take Emma.

And then we sit there together, me calming a baby back to sleep, Sarah proving her marshmallow roasting skills surpass mine, our friends and family chattering happily all around us, and yep.

Life is pretty fucking perfect.

ABOUT THE AUTHOR

Pippa Grant is a stay-at-home mom and housewife who loves to escape into sexy, funny stories way more than she likes perpetually cleaning toothpaste out of sinks and off toilet handles. When she's not reading, writing, sleeping, or trying to prepare her adorable demon spawn to be productive members of society, she's fantasizing about chocolate chip cookies.

Find Pippa at...
www.pippagrant.com
pippa@pippagrant.com

Keep in touch with Pippa Grant!
Join the Pipsquad
Get the Pipster Report
Friend Pippa
Like Pippa
Hang with Pippa on Goodreads
Follow Pippa on BookBub
Follow Pippa on Amazon
Follow Pippa on Instagram
Join Pippa on Book+Main

COPYRIGHT

CPSIA information can be obtained
at www.ICGtesting.com
Printed in the USA
BVHW041515310523
665083BV00002B/101